FEVER OF PASSION

"Come here, Maleaha," Kane said in a soft voice.

She stood on shaky legs, calling on all her courage, and stepped out of the darkened corner.

Kane Drew in his breath as his eyes took in the perfection of her body. Before him stood the most beautiful woman he'd ever seen. He was silent for so long that Maleaha raised her head and looked into his eyes. Seeing the adoration there, she froze.

Kane walked slowly toward her and reached out to draw her body into his arms. Maleaha's senses reeled as she felt his torso press against hers. Then his lips moved over her face—and his hands over her flesh. He could feel her trembling.

"Don't be frightened," he coaxed. "I will not harm you."

Kane searched her eyes and saw their fever-bright glow as he aroused a need in her. That was the look he'd hoped for. . . .

MORE TEMPESTUOUS ROMANCES!

SAVAGE DESIRE (1120, $3.50)
by Constance O'Banyon
Mara knew it was fate that brought her and virile Tajarez together. But destiny would not allow them to savor the joys of love. They would only be bound by SAVAGE DESIRE.

GOLDEN TORMENT (1323, $3.75)
by Janelle Taylor
Kathryn had travelled the Alaskan wilderness in search of her father. But after one night of sensual pleasure with the fierce, aggressive lumberjack, Landis Jurrell—she knew she'd never again travel alone!

LOVE ME WITH FURY (1248, $3.75)
by Janelle Taylor
When Alexandria discovered the dark-haired stranger who watched her swim, she was outraged by his intrusion. But when she felt his tingling caresses and tasted his intoxicating kisses, she could no longer resist drowning in the waves of sweet sensuality.

BELOVED SCOUNDREL (1259, $3.75)
by Penelope Neri
Denying what her body admitted, Christianne vowed to take revenge against the arrogant seaman who'd tormented her with his passionate caresses. Even if it meant never again savoring his exquisite kisses, she vowed to get even with her one and only BELOVED SCOUNDREL!

Available wherever paperbacks are sold, or order direct from the Publisher. Send cover price plus 50¢ per copy for mailing and handling to Zebra Books, 475 Park Avenue South, New York, N.Y. 10016. DO NOT SEND CASH.

ENCHANTED ECSTASY

BY CONSTANCE O'BANYON

ZEBRA BOOKS
KENSINGTON PUBLISHING CORP.

ZEBRA BOOKS

are published by

Kensington Publishing Corp.
475 Park Avenue South
New York, N.Y. 10016

First printing: June, 1984

Printed in the United States of America

This book is dedicated to my lovely daughter Kimberly, who was born in the land of enchantment and reflects its beauty and mystery in the blue of her eyes.

LAND OF ENCHANTMENT

Oh, this land, this enchanted land—with your mountains,
   your valleys, your soft shifting sands.
As I stand beneath the canopy of your warm blue sky,
I am bewitched by your loveliness, as I watch an eagle
   fly.
Once proud Indians walked your lovely lands.
Time has erased their footprints, in your golden shifting
   sands.
It seems I hear a voice from when time first began.
It whispers to me softly, carried gently on the wind,
As I watch from atop your mountain, surveying the beauty
   where I stand
I will never wish to leave you, oh, fair enchanted land.

CHAPTER ONE

New Mexico Territory, 1867—Major Kanen Benedict shifted his weight. The straight-back chair he was sitting on was uncomfortable, and patience had never been his strong point. He stood up, revealing the fact that he was a very tall man.

His silver-gray eyes moved over the room with bored indifference. He noted the cluttered appearance of Colonel Johnson's office. The clock on the mantel showed the lateness of the hour. Sighing inwardly at his commanding officer's tardiness, Kane pushed an unruly lock of ebony hair off his forehead.

The room was stifling hot, and Kane wished he could remove the blue jacket of his uniform. His increasing impatience took him across the room to the open window where he looked out on the compound, hoping to catch a glimpse of Colonel Johnson.

A slight breeze filtered in through the window, but it brought no relief from the awful heat. If anything it made it worse. The wind was like a blast of hot air from hell, he thought.

New Mexico Territory. What was he doing here, he wondered for at least the hundredth time.

His silver eyes narrowed against the glare of the noonday sun. The fort was silent for the moment, since most of the soldiers were either eating lunch or out on patrol. His eyes scanned the ramp that ran the length of the stockade wall. Kane felt momentary pity for the lone sentry who paced the wall in full-dress uniform. He could imagine how uncomfortable the man must feel in the grueling heat.

His eyes wandered past the fort to the gate, which stood partially open. His gaze fastened on the distant Sangre de Cristo mountains, which were dubbed the foothills to the Rockies. Whoever had called them foothills could not have been more mistaken. The mountains were tall and majestic, rising high into the heavens. Kane knew if he were in those mountains now it would be cool and green. What a relief it would be from this heat, he thought.

What a paradox this land was—the lush green mountains with their dense pine forest were surrounded on the outside by a desert of cactus and scrub bush. This was a harsh land, a land of contrasts, ready to prey on the weak, testing a man's strength and endurance. New Mexico Territory—aptly named the Badlands.

When Kane had first received his orders to come to New Mexico, he had been told to expect a desert populated with tumbleweeds and Indians. He had certainly not been misinformed. The fort stood as the only defense against Indian attacks in this part of New Mexico.

To Kane's surprise, he had found the social life of

Santa Fe acceptable. The town itself was a quaint little village built mostly of adobe. The populace consisted of Spaniards, Mexicans, Indians, and, of course, the badly outnumbered white race. But among these he had found many prominent families. Of course, since he was an officer, he was invited to the more important functions, often rubbing shoulders with Santa Fe's elite. And most of the time he enjoyed these social events, where the men outnumbered the women, two to one.

So far Kane had been seen in the company of many beautiful women. Some of them had been respectable, most of them were not. Lord, he thought, he was becoming bored with his life.

He watched as a dust devil whipped up the loose sand and swirled it around in a miniature tornado. He closed his eyes. It was a long way to his home in Boston. No, Boston was not his home. It never had been.

Kane's father owned one of the largest shipping firms in the country, a fleet of fifteen ships that sailed all over the world. Kane was an only child, and his father had groomed him from childhood to one day head Benedict Shipping.

Kane remembered how angry his father had become when the War Between The States had ended and his son had reenlisted instead of returning to Boston as had been expected of him. Kane knew he had only reenlisted to thwart Eli. He had called his father by his first name for as long as he could remember. If he had ever called him Father, he was not aware of it. Kane smiled bitterly, remembering his father's face the day he had told him he had reenlisted.

Eli had been livid as he raged at Kane. "You are doing this just to spite me, Kane. You know I have been waiting for the day you could come into the business as an equal partner," Eli had shouted at him.

Kane still became angry when he remembered his father's using his influence to get him a desk job in Washington after the Battle of Gettysburg. He thought of the argument that had ensued when he found out that his father had gone to a family friend, a senator, and asked him to make sure his son did not see any fighting.

Kane drew in a deep breath. That was the past. He stared out the window and watched the changing of the guard with disinterest. Checking the clock on the mantel, he ground his teeth. Colonel Johnson was never on time. One thing Eli had instilled in his son was the importance of being punctual. Kane was never late for an appointment, and he had very little patience with anyone who was.

Since Kane was bored, he allowed his mind to wander once more to the past. Eli would find great satisfaction if he knew that his son now regretted reenlisting. Kane thought back again to the day he had told Eli about his decision to stay in the army. His father's face had flushed with anger.

"I offer you a position that any young man would give his eyeteeth for, but you, in your arrogance, throw it back in my face!"

Kane had stood his ground that day, refusing to be intimidated. "I want nothing from you, Eli. You want me under your thumb so you can run my life. Nothing matters to you except money and power. You killed my mother, and you want to destroy me as well. I warn you, Eli. I am not weak like my mother was. I am like you more than I would care to admit, but with one exception . . . I am motivated neither by power nor greed.''

Once more Kane had seen his father's face redden with anger.

''You still blame me for your mother's death. That's what this is all about, isn't it?''

''Hell, yes, I blame you. You killed her just as surely as if you had drawn a gun and shot her. And you thought you could run my life. Do you have any idea how I felt when I found out you had arranged for me to spend most of the war at a desk in Washington?''

''There was nothing wrong with my using my influence to keep you out of the fighting. You should be grateful to me. You might well be dead right this moment, had I not used my influence to help you.''

''You will excuse me if I don't show my appreciation for what you did, Eli.''

Eli Benedict had not gotten where he was without being able to manipulate people, so he tried another approach with his son. ''Kanen, son, I am an old man. Who knows how much longer I have to live. I built this business out of nothing, hoping one day to pass it on to you. With a suitable wife at your side . . . say someone like Lucinda Blake, all I have would someday belong to you.''

Kane had studied his father's face. ''You didn't have me in mind when you accumulated your fortune. What you did, you did for yourself and no one else. You would like it if you could dangle me on a string before your friends as your creation, your puppet. As far as Lucinda Blake is concerned, I will never marry her. I can see where you might think she would be the ideal wife for me. You think just because she is from one of the best families in Boston, she is perfect.'' Kane laughed bitterly. ''You couldn't be more mistaken, Eli. I have had her in my bed and . . . she leaves me cold.'' Kane did not know why he had spoken so freely of his past relationship with Lucinda. It had never been his habit to tarnish a lady's reputation. He supposed he had wanted to show his father that his perfect choice was no lady.

His father had practically choked on his anger that day. ''You dare to seduce a girl of one of Boston's most prominent families, and then make sport of her? If you had any decency about you, you would do the right thing by marrying her.''

Kane had only laughed. ''Would you believe me, Eli, if I told you that the lady seduced me? I might also add that I was not the first to be with her.''

''You are no son of mine. I am well aware of your reputation with the ladies. In the past I have overlooked your little affairs, thinking one day you would settle down and be a son to be proud of. Apparently I was wrong.''

''A rotten apple won't fall too far from the tree,'' Kane told him. ''I am also aware of your little affairs. That is the reason my mother is dead—she just didn't want to live anymore. You should have been more discrete, Eli.''

His father's face had drained of all its color. ''Who told you that? I suppose it was your mother.''

''What does it matter now? The deed is done, but don't go pointing a guilty finger at me. If I ever did decide to

12

get married, I would not cause my wife's death by being unfaithful to her. If I couldn't be satisfied with just one woman, I would never marry, and I doubt I ever will. No woman holds my interest for very long.''

Eli had struck Kane that day, and Kane had stormed out of the house vowing never to return.

Kane was now feeling very dissatisfied with his life. He had drunk too much, gone to too many parties, had too many women, and still his life was empty. What did he want? What was he searching for? He didn't know, but whatever it was had always eluded him. Here he was in New Mexico, jumping-off place of the world, and he was at a standstill. There had been a parade of beautiful women tripping through his life, but none of them had meant anything to him. He supposed he was more like his father than he cared to admit. He used women for his own needs, never caring about their feelings. That thought was very distasteful to him. He didn't want to think he was anything like Eli.

Glancing at the clock once more, Kane frowned. Most probably Mrs. Johnson had the colonel hanging curtains, or some such nonsense. The colonel had been stationed in New Mexico for over fifteen years. His command had become lax, and Kane liked things neat and orderly. As second-in-command he had tried to whip the men into shape, but it had thus far been a thankless task. Lately there had been trouble with the Indians, and Kane knew that was what his commander wanted to see him about.

Kane stared down at the toe of his shiny black boot. Lord, the boredom was about to get to him. He crossed the room and sat down once more in the straight-back chair and crossed his long legs. Hell, he didn't have any answers, and he had pretty well burned his bridges behind him. Unbuttoning the top button of his blue jacket, he leaned back in the chair. Was he a user? Did he only take from others, never giving of himself? He had learned at an early age that women were susceptible to his charms. He had been with so many different women that he couldn't even remember their faces. Of course he had always avoided the marriageable ones. With his parents' marriage as an example, he wanted nothing to do with matrimony. He would leave marriage to young fools and old men. He didn't need a woman cluttering up his life. Last night he had visited Rosita's Cantina. The singer there was a fiery redhead who usually inspired passion in him, but last night she had left him feeling unmoved. He knew he would not seek her out again. It was always the same now, as soon as he came to know a woman he would become bored with her. He knitted his brow thoughtfully. Had there ever been a woman he had wanted that had not come to him willingly? No, he could not remember a one who had not been his for the asking. Perhaps that was where the trouble lay.

Sighing heavily, he stood up and ran his hands through his ebony hair. His shoulders were broad and his waist was narrow. His face was handsomely arrogant. His silver-gray eyes were what was usually noticed about him first. They were almost transparent in color, and more often than not were piercing and unsettling. One smile from his sensuous lips and many ladies had fallen prey to his charms. His manner of speech was clipped, and it was obvious he was well educated. Those silver eyes could hold a woman spellbound, but no woman had ever caused them to soften with love, though many had tried.

Kane heard the sound of a rider entering the fort. Walking over to the window he watched the stranger as he dismounted and made his way toward the colonel's office. Kane thought the man would be somewhere in his fifties. He had a sturdy build of medium size, and iron-gray hair. The man's face was handsome, and he walked purposefully, proudly. His manner of dress proclaimed him to be a rancher and not just some drifter. The look on the man's face was unsmiling, and Kane thought he would be a dangerous man to cross.

Before Kane had time to wonder who the stranger was, he saw Colonel Johnson, hurrying across the compound to greet him, and their voices reached Kane through the open window.

"Well, Johnson," the man drawled, "you had better have a good reason for asking me here today."

"I do, Jonas. Come into my office where we can talk in private."

Kane quickly rebuttoned his top button and stood at attention as the two men entered the room.

Colonel Johnson eyed his young major, then looked back at the man beside him. "Jonas, I would like you to meet my second-in-command, Major Kanen Benedict. Kane, this is Jonas Deveraux."

Jonas nodded at Kane but ignored his outstretched hand, as if he dismissed him as unimportant.

"Jonas here owns the biggest cattle ranch in New Mexico, major. He is Santa Fe's leading citizen," the colonel elaborated.

Kane recognized the name at once. He had heard a lot about Jonas Deveraux since coming to New Mexico. It seemed everyone held him in high esteem. He watched as Jonas's eyes narrowed and he gave Colonel Johnson a look of contempt.

"Spare me your attempt to elevate me in society, Johnson, and get down to the reason you sent for me today."

Kane frowned at Jonas's pointed dislike for his commander. Colonel Johnson looked flustered for the moment, overpowered by Jonas Deveraux.

"Jonas, we have been friends for a long time."

"Correction, Johnson," Jonas interrupted, "you and I have known each other for a long time. We have never been friends."

The colonel squared his shoulders. "Sit down, Jonas, I have something important to talk to you about."

"It must be of great consequence for you to send for me."

"I wasn't sure you would come."

"I damned near didn't, until my curiosity got the better of me." Jonas sat down on the edge of the desk, and nodded at the colonel. "Have a seat, Johnson," he said, and Kane was surprised when the colonel readily complied.

Jonas turned and favored Kane with a glance, and Kane was aware of his piercing green eyes. Never had he seen eyes such a deep green color before. Kane smiled slightly, and thought he detected a hint of a smile on the rancher's face. Jonas Deveraux was enjoying himself, he thought.

"All right, Johnson, I didn't ride all the way out here

to pass the time of day with you," he said turning to the colonel. "What do you want?"

The colonel cleared his throat nervously. "I am sure you have heard about the raids on the outlying ranches. We have evidence that points to the Jojoba tribe."

"What kind of evidence?"

Colonel Johnson opened his desk drawer and removed a knife and handed it to Jonas. Jonas examined the knife and handed it back to him.

"Yep, that's a knife belonging to someone of the Jojoba tribe, all right. It's silver and turquoise, with the design of the sun and the moon. What does that prove, Johnson?"

"This knife was found at the scene of the last raid. The Jojoba are wreaking havoc across the territory, and it is my job to stop them."

Jonas smiled. "Maybe it was the Jojoba, maybe it wasn't. If it was, it is merely Mangas's way of leaving his calling card. There was no harm done, a few barns burned, a few horses and cattle stolen."

"It could have been worse, Jonas. What if some of the ranchers and their families had been killed? It's my job to protect the people of this territory. These raids are widespread. My men can't be everywhere at once."

"If it was Mangas, as you suspect, and if he had wanted to kill someone, they would now be dead, and not you, me, or anyone else could have stopped him."

"Suppose your ranch is next, Mr. Deveraux?" Kane could not help asking. "Would you treat the matter so lightly then?"

Jonas fixed his green eyes on Kane and frowned. Then

his mouth eased into a grin. "You must be new around here, soldier."

"I have been stationed here for the last six months, Mr. Deveraux."

"Well, seeing as how you *are* new here, I will forgive you for your stupidity, Major Benedict." Jonas said.

Kane's eyes narrowed. "Explain, Mr. Deveraux," he said angrily.

Jonas looked at Colonel Johnson. "You tell him. He is your fetch-and-carry boy," he said insultingly.

Kane's eyes blazed angrily at the insult. He was about to make his anger known when he saw Colonel Johnson shake his head and send him a warning glance.

"Major, Jonas here was married to a Jojoba sq . . . woman."

Jonas clenched and unclenched his fists. "What you meant to say was my wife was a Jojoba princess, wasn't it, Johnson?"

"Yes . . . of course, Jonas," The colonel amended quickly.

Jonas waved his hand impatiently. "It's very nice reminiscing with you this way, but I am becoming bored. Why have you sent for me?" There was steel laced through the man's words and Kane thought once again that he would be a dangerous man to cross.

"I was hoping to convince you to ride along with a patrol to Mangas's camp. No one knows where his camp is but you, and you speak the language. Your daughter is . . ."

Jonas's eyes narrowed to green pinpoints. "Let's leave my daughter out of this."

18

"Will you help me, Jonas?"

"Hell, no, I wouldn't give you a drink of water if you were dying of thirst."

"The past is the past, Jonas. We are talking about the lives of your friends and neighbors."

"My neighbors know me, and my friends would never expect me to put myself between the army and Mangas."

"You are saying you refuse to help the army because of what a few misguided soldiers did a few years ago?"

"Damn right," Jonas said, rising to his full height. "If that's all you have to say, I am leaving."

Colonel Johnson stood up eye to eye with Jonas. "You cannot straddle the fence forever, Jonas. One day you will have to choose sides."

"My choice was made long ago. I still remember vividly how you and your kind treated my wife. In the end, it caused her death. Don't ever send for me again."

He walked to the door, then turned to Kane. "Major, you are new here so I am going to give you some advice, and it won't cost you a cent. If you stay in this land, and if you have any prejudices, get rid of them. You will be much happier, and you might live longer." With that as his parting shot, he walked out the door, closing it softly behind him.

"What a strange man, colonel," Kane said, feeling at a loss as to how else to describe Jonas Deveraux.

The colonel walked over to the window, and, looking out, watched as the rancher mounted his horse and rode out the gate of the fort.

"I would rather have that man's respect and friendship than anyone I know," he said softly, as though talking to

19

himself.

"I spoke the truth when I said he has the biggest ranch in the territory. Deveraux Ranch is as legendary as its owner. Jonas took this Indian princess, married her, if you will. They were married in an Indian ceremony, their marriage was never sanctioned by the church. Some people accepted her, many did not. My wife was one who did not." He turned to face Kane. "She was beautiful, had the darkest hair, it was almost blue-black, and her dark eyes were soft and gentle-like. Jonas was devoted to her. Her name was Cimeron. They had a child, a daughter. Cimeron was out riding one day, when she was brutally attacked and killed. Seven soldiers were suspected of the offense, but nothing was ever proven against them."

Kane frowned. "They went unpunished?"

"They never came to trial, if that is what you are asking, but they were punished all the same. Punished to death."

"Who, how?"

"The how was . . . have you ever thought how it would feel to be rendered manless with a knife? I am sure it was a very painful way to die." The colonel shrugged his shoulders. "The who, I'll leave you to guess. It could have been Cimeron's father, who was then chief of the Jojoba, or it could have been Jonas. No one knows for sure."

"Why is it that I have never seen any Indians from the Jojoba tribe, colonel?"

"That's because the Jojoba keep very much to themselves. You will never find them hanging around the fort, asking for a free handout. No one except a chosen few knows where their village is located. I am told that when an offense is committed against them, retribution is swift and sure. For years they have lived in seclusion. I wonder why they have suddenly tried to stir up trouble?''

"I can understand why Jonas Deveraux didn't want to help us, colonel. One can hardly fault him for his bitterness.''

"Yes. I knew his answer would be no before I asked for his help, but it was worth a try. If we don't locate Mangas soon, there could be a lot of needless bloodshed. Tomorrow I want you to take a patrol and try to find his camp. I don't have a clue as to where you should start looking. I don't have to tell you how dangerous it will be. Had Jonas consented to take you to the Jojoba village, Mangas would not have attempted to harm you. The Jojoba are very loyal to Jonas. At one time it was because of his wife, and now it is because of his daughter, who is a Jojoba princess.''

leaned his head to rest against the chair back, his eyes going to the painting that hung over the huge fireplace. His eyes softened and he raised his glass in a silent salute to the woman and child in the painting. His daughter, Maleaha, had been only four when a local artist had come to the ranch to paint the portrait. His eyes caressed the image of his wife, Cimeron, lovingly. She had been dead nine years now, and there had not been a day that Jonas had not missed her. The pain was every bit as acute as it had been that awful day she had been killed. Jonas knew if it hadn't been for his daughter, Maleaha, he would have lost his mind. He had to go on for her sake; he knew Cimeron would have wanted him to look after their daughter.

Maleah was seventeen now. She had been only eight when her mother had been killed. Jonas had bitterly decided that his daughter would never be exposed to the prejudices her mother had been forced to endure. Maleaha had been only fifteen when he had forced her to attend the fancy boarding school for young ladies in Boston. She had loudly protested leaving her home, but Jonas, who usually gave in to her slightest whim, stood firm in his decision to send her away to school. Some of the edge had been taken off Maleaha's protest when her best friend, Betsy, had accompanied her.

Jonas always bought Maleaha the best of everything. Her gowns were straight from Paris. He had all the money a man could want, and he spent it lavishly on his daughter, determined that she would never have to suffer as her mother had. He smiled. Maleaha often liked to dress in buckskin gowns, as her mother had, and he thought he liked it better when she was dressed that way.

Maleaha was accepted into every home in Santa Fe. Welcomed by all the best families, she was treated with a respect that had never been offered to her mother. She had returned from Boston two weeks ago, and Jonas was glad she was home to stay. Maleaha should have been spoiled by her father's indulgence, but instead she was of a kind and loving nature, as her mother had been. Of course there were times when her temper would flare like her father's, and her green eyes would blaze defiantly.

The two years Maleaha had been away at school had been long years for Jonas. Many times he wanted to go to Boston and bring her home. The first summer he had taken her and Betsy to England and France. It was during that trip that Jonas realized his daughter had blossomed into a beautiful young lady. More than once he had noticed the admiring glances directed at her. The gentlemen would stare at her in open admiration, but Maleaha seemed completely unaware of her beauty.

"Father, I did not realize you had returned from the fort." The lovely, musical voice of his daughter broke into his thoughts.

Jonas favored her with a smile. "I didn't even hear you enter the room. You move as silently as the mountain lion."

"It's my Indian blood," she told him, laughing as she kissed him on the forehead. Sitting down beside her father, Maleaha rested her head on his shoulder. "It's good to be home. I never want to go away again. This is where I belong."

He took her dainty hand and squeezed it. "I never want

you to leave me again. Two years is a long time."

"It wasn't my idea to leave, Father. You forced me to leave, remember?"

He chucked her on the chin. "Yes, but look at you now. That fancy school carved off all your rough edges and gave you a certain class. You are now a proper lady."

"Margaretta says ladies are born, and not created," Maleaha said, smiling at the housekeeper's words. "I never did understand why you wanted me to go away to school, but while I was there, I worked very hard so you would be proud of me."

His eyes went to the portrait once more. "I wanted you to be able to hold your head up and be proud of who you are."

"I always have been. There has never been any shame in me for the father who sired me, nor the mother who bore me. Why should there be, when I have known only love from both of you."

"Never be ashamed of your mother, Maleaha. She was one of a kind. She would be so proud of you today."

"I loved my mother, and I am proud of the Indian blood that flows in my veins."

"Did you meet any special young man while you were back East?" Jonas asked, changing the subject.

Maleaha smiled. "No one I couldn't live without. I suppose the men in Boston are too civilized for my taste."

Her father laughed. "What you mean is they aren't as good at riding and shooting as you are. You are too used to the old cowhands on the ranch. I am glad that you didn't bring back one of those dandies, though."

Maleaha stood up, "Have you had lunch?"

"No. I missed it altogether, but I will wait until dinner."

Maleaha walked over to the portrait and studied it silently.

Jonas looked at her. Her movements were so graceful. She wore a simple white cotton blouse and a green cotton skirt that fit snugly about her tiny waist and flared out around her. Her hair, which was as black as ebony, hung down below her waist. Her skin was smooth—not white, what most white women treasured—nor was it bronze as her mother's had been, but a soft golden hue that caused the startling green eyes she had inherited from her father to appear more prominent. Delicately arched eyebrows and long silky lashes enhanced the emerald-green color of her eyes.

Jonas could not help but feel pride that someone so lovely could have come from him. She appeared to be delicate, but Jonas knew she could outride and outshoot any woman and most men of her acquaintance.

Turning to face her father, she smiled. "Would you like me to bring you a light snack, Father? It is at least two hours until dinner."

"No. Come and sit with me," he told her, patting the cushion beside him.

Maleaha sat on the arm of the sofa and slipped her arm about her father's powerful shoulder. "Why did Colonel Johnson want you to come to the fort?" she asked curiously.

"He wanted me to take a patrol of soldiers to find

27

Mangas.''

"Are you serious?" Maleaha asked in surprise. "I know Colonel Johnson is a bit misguided at times, but I never considered him to be a foolish man."

Jonas's eyes narrowed. "He has no conception of how Mangas thinks. Mangas would never allow soldiers to ride into his camp. That man is going to send out a patrol in search of the Jojobas, and not a one of them will come back alive, if they do manage to find them, which I doubt!"

"Why does the colonel wish to talk to Mangas?"

Jonas looked at the ceiling for a moment, then he glanced at her. "There have been several raids lately on the outlying ranches, nothing serious, a few barns burned, some livestock stolen. The evidence seems to point to the Jojoba tribe."

"I can understand your refusing to go with a patrol, but could you not have gone with one man—say, the colonel?"

"You think I should have?"

"Yes, if it would help avoid bloodshed." Maleaha knew her father to be a kind and generous man, but he could also be ruthless if he was crossed. His dislike for the soldiers at the fort was all too apparent. "Father, please reconsider. Mangas will listen to you, he respects you."

"That's exactly why I am not going, I have never thought the army dealt fairly with the Indians. You know my views on that subject and I will not lend my support to the army, for any reason!"

"Do you think Mangas is responsible for the raids?"

28

Jonas shrugged. "Who can say? It's possible."

Maleaha had not seen Mangas since she was thirteen. She remembered him as being highly intelligent and very compassionate. She let her mind reach back to the time four years ago when her father had allowed her to spend the summer with her mother's sister in the Jojoba village.

Maleaha had been watching as many of the Jojoba maidens splashed and played in the river that ran through their camp. The maidens had taunted and teased her because she would not go into the water. Maleaha, who did not know how to swim, had not wanted them to know of her fear of the water. She had set her chin stubbornly, and gathered up her courage while wading into the water. The current had been swift and she soon felt her feet being swept out from under her. She felt the water closing over her head. Gasping for breath, she had tried to keep her head above water. She remembered thinking at the time that she was drowning and what grief her father would feel at her death, when she felt strong arms go around her waist. Relief washed over her as she looked into the handsome face of Mangas. He had saved her life! Her heart had raced as he smiled down at her just before he lifted her in his arms and carried her to the riverbank.

Maleaha had always thought Mangas was handsome, as did all the young maidens of the tribe, but he had never paid the slightest attention to any of them. He had been in his twenty-second summer that year. Her grandfather was grooming Mangas to take over as chief after his death, since he had no sons or grandsons to succeed him.

Maleaha could still remember how it had felt to be carried in Mangas's strong arms. When he had reached the riverbank, he had not set her down immediately but had held her in his arms, speaking to her while the other maidens looked on enviously. He pushed a strand of wet hair gently from her face.

"Poor, brave Little Flower. You do not know how to swim and still you went into the water." His black hair hung down to his shoulders and was encircled with a leather band. His eyes, which were as black as his hair, looked at her with such compassion, and his handsome face was creased into a worried frown. Maleaha could feel the powerful muscles in his shoulders since her hands had been clasped about his neck.

"I shall teach you to swim, Little Flower, and soon you will outswim all the other maidens who mocked you today."

Maleaha remembered how her young heart had raced at his soft-spoken words. She had thought he never noticed her, and had felt happy that he would want to teach her to swim.

Mangas had kept his word. The next morning he had come to her aunt's teepee and taken Maleaha to the river for her swimming lesson. He was gentle and patient with her, and, wanting to please him, Maleaha had tried her best.

That summer the days and weeks seemed to fly by, and all too soon her father had come to take her back home. She remembered the last time she had seen Mangas. He had stood tall and proud beside her grandfather, with his arms crossed over his powerful chest. His dark eyes had been unreadable as he watched her.

Her grandfather had hugged her tightly. "I shall miss

you, little Maleaha." He then spoke to her father. "I thank you, Jonas, for allowing Maleaha to stay the summer with us. In her I see her mother. She is as sweet as she is lovely."

"Cimeron would have wanted our daughter to get to know her people, Catana, and I want her to respect the Jojoba, as I do."

That summer was the last time she had seen her grandfather. He had placed his hand on her head. "When you leave here, little Maleaha, know that you take with you your grandfather's heart. It is a difficult road you walk, with one foot in the Indian world, and the other in the white world. Have courage, and always feel pride in the Jojoba blood that runs in your body." Maleaha had grown very close to her grandfather that year, and it saddened her that he had died while she was away at school.

She remembered being surprised when Mangas had touched her cheek. He then slipped a silver chain with a huge turquoise stone attached to it over her head.

"A reward for learning to swim so well, Little Flower."

She had been moved by his kind words, and was unable to speak.

"I like a maiden who does not talk much. Go to your home and blossom, Little Flower. We shall meet again one day."

Her father seemed to read her thoughts, bringing her back to the present. "Mangas is not the young buck you remember. He is now chief; he is dangerous as well as ruthless."

"I find that hard to believe, Father. He was always kind to me."

"Yes, I remember being troubled by the attention he showed you the last time you were in the Jojoba village."

"Do you know if Mangas has taken a wife?"

Jonas shrugged. "I have had little contact with him in the last two years. The last time I saw him was when your grandfather died and I went to the village to pay my respects. I didn't think to ask Mangas if he had taken a maiden to wife, and he didn't volunteer the information. He did ask about you, though."

Maleaha smiled, feeling pleased that Mangas should remember her. She pushed her memories aside and returned to more important matters.

"I wish you would take Colonel Johnson to the Jojoba village, Father. Please reconsider."

Jonas stood up abruptly. "No, and that's my final word on the subject. I have some important business in Albuquerque. I am leaving in the morning and will be gone for two weeks. If, by the time I return, there have been more incidents, I will ride to the Jojoba village and talk to Mangas, but I go alone."

Maleaha knew better than to argue with her father, but she feared that anything could happen in two weeks. She shuddered when she thought about a war between her mother's people and her father's race. Either way it turned out she would lose. She stared at the brightly patterned rug, while a plan formed in her mind.

The patrol was mounted and waiting as Kanen Benedict strolled toward Colonel Johnson's office. He nodded to the soldier who was holding the reins of his horse.

"Prepare to move out as soon as I report to the colonel," he said, working his fingers into his leather gloves.

He saw the men staring at something and turned to see what had attracted their attention. He swore under his breath as he saw an Indian girl walking in the direction of the colonel's office. He would find out later who had allowed her access to the fort, but right now, he would personally escort her to the gate. There were two old Indian men walking on either side of her. Stepping up his pace, Kane tried to intercept her before she reached the colonel's office.

She was dressed in soft buckskin that came to just below her knees and high-topped moccasins that disappeared beneath the fringe at the bottom of her dress. Black hair hung down her back to her waist and was encircled with a turquoise and silver-beaded headband. She was slender and moved with a grace that surprised Kane. He could not see her face, but instinct told him that she would be no different from the many other Indian maidens he had seen, with their dark eyes and high cheekbones. His eyes traveled over her hips, which seemed to be moving enticingly, and Kane felt a flicker of desire. He had never been drawn to an Indian before, and he thought one look at her face would discourage him. He had never been partial to midnight-black eyes.

Kane knew he would never overtake her before she reached the colonel. He watched her climb the steps, while the two old Indian men stationed themselves on either side of the door. Who in the hell did she think she was, going into the colonel's office uninvited?

As Kane reached the steps, the two Indians eyed him

for an instant, then dismissed him as unimportant. Kane suspected one of them would be the girl's father.

"My dear, what a pleasant surprise. You are looking very lovely. I had heard you were back home. What brings you to the fort?" Colonel Johnson said, smiling brightly. Kane heard the friendly greeting to the Indian girl, so he did not show her the door as he had intended. He didn't have time to fool with her anyway; his men were waiting in the heat for him to join them.

"Excuse the interruption, sir, but I am ready to leave," Kane said, snapping to attention.

"Proceed carefully, major. Mangas is not to be underestimated," the colonel said.

"Wait!" the Indian girl said, turning to face Kane.

His eyes widened and he was speechless as he saw her beautiful face. He stared openly at her lovely green eyes, trying to remember where he had seen eyes that color before.

The moment Maleaha turned to face Kane she was struck by his handsome good looks. She was startled by the color of his eyes. Never before had she seen silver-colored eyes. She noticed he was assessing her, and for some reason she took an immediate dislike to him, though she could not have said why. She knew he was the kind of man that most women were drawn to, but she did not trust him. His eyes were insolent as they moved from her face to the swell of her breasts and then down her body. She could tell he expected her to join the other women who worshiped him on first sight. It seemed to be something he expected, and she doubted he had ever failed but for this time. She found to her dismay that she was trembling.

Kane flashed a smile that showed his white teeth. How was it possible to find such beauty in such an unexpected place? He realized he was staring, and he knew he was making her feel uncomfortable. Who was she, and what was she doing here?

"My dear, I would like to introduce you to Major Kanen Benedict. Major, Miss Deveraux. You met her father yesterday," the colonel said, breaking the spell that seemed to hold both Kane and Maleaha.

So this was Jonas Deveraux's daughter. A half-breed, Kane thought. That explained her green eyes.

Maleaha studied the handsome man. His eyes seemed to probe to the very depths of her soul. She held her breath, thinking that their meeting was predestined, that it was fated to happen, and wondered why she should feel that way.

Kane had never been introduced to an Indian maiden before, and he did not know how to acknowledge her. Would she be insulted if he took her hand as he would if he had just been introduced to a white girl?

Seeing indecision in his face, Maleaha nodded her beautiful head slightly and turned back to Colonel Johnson.

"My father told me of the talk you had yesterday."

Kane noted that her voice was lovely, deep and throaty, and her command of English was perfect. She seemed well educated.

"Did Jonas tell you he refused to lead us to the Jojoba village?" The colonel asked her.

"Yes, but if you will allow me to, I shall go in his

stead.''

The colonel looked at her in surprise. ''You would be willing to help us find Mangas?''

Maleaha laughed. ''Mangas is not lost, colonel. I know where he is.''

''Of course, you would know where Mangas is!'' He looked at her thoughtfully. ''If you go along, it may work out better than if Jonas had agreed to go.''

Kane circled around the desk so he could have a better view of the Indian girl. His eyes swept over her beautiful face, taking in her delicate features.

Maleaha looked briefly at the major, then spoke to the colonel. ''I have known Mangas for most of my life, so I will ask you to trust me to know the best way to approach him. It would be reckless and very foolish to ride into his camp with a group of soldiers. I will take you to Mangas, but you must come alone. Otherwise, I must refuse to go with you, as did my father.''

Colonel Johnson nodded in quick agreement. He knew her well enough to tell she meant just what she said.

''Does your father know you are here?'' The colonel asked, knowing the answer before he asked. Jonas would never allow Maleaha to go to the Jojoba village without him.

Her eyes flashed mischievously, ''No. He will be in Albuquerque for the next two weeks. By the time he returns it will be too late for him to prevent me from going.''

''He will be angry, you know,'' the colonel said softly. ''Why are you doing this, my dear?''

She took a deep breath. ''I know Mangas, and I cannot

believe he is the one responsible for the raids, and I do not want to see needless bloodshed. Tell me, colonel, do you accept my terms and agree to come alone?''

''Yes, I gladly accept your terms, but it will be Major Benedict who will accompany you, and not me.''

Maleaha's eyes flew to the major, who was staring at her boldly. She felt instant anger at the way his eyes were moving over her body. She had never felt so disturbed by a man's attention before.

''I would prefer that you go, colonel. Mangas is a chief; he may feel insulted if you send a mere major to talk to him,'' she said, giving Kane her haughtiest look. She saw anger flash in his silver eyes and smiled smugly to herself, knowing she had struck a nerve.

''I am sorry, my dear. I cannot get away at the moment. I am afraid Major Benedict will have to be my representative.''

Maleaha placed her hands palms down on the desk and leaned forward. ''Colonel, if you are playing me false, I shall not be responsible for the consequences. Mangas is not a man to trifle with.''

''I would not try and trick you, my dear. Tell me,'' he said, changing the subject abruptly, ''what is Mangas like? As far as I know, very few white men have ever seen him. With the exception of your father, I know of no one who has talked to him.''

''My assessment of Mangas might surprise you. I know him to be a gentle, kind man. As to no white men ever having seen him, chances are you have seen him many times without even knowing it. He often comes into Santa Fe dressed inconspicuously. You may have been as close to him as you are to me right now and never suspected who he was.''

The colonel laughed. ''Maybe you are going to be more useful to us than I thought, if you think Mangas is a gentle man. Perhaps you have seen a side of him which has not been revealed to others.''

Maleaha stood up proudly and faced Major Benedict. ''I will be waiting outside the gates. Good-bye, colonel. I do not know how long it will take, but give us two weeks.''

Kane stared at Maleaha and then turned to the colonel. ''You do not expect me to ride out with a . . .'' His voice trailed off.

''A squaw, major?'' Maleaha finished for him. ''I will wait for you for ten minutes! If by that time you have not come, I will ride for home.'' She spoke softly, but there was anger in her voice.

After she had left Colonel Johnson turned to Kane. ''You will treat Jonas Deveraux's daughter with the utmost respect, major. Do I make myself clear? She is the only thing that stands between you and hell. If she were so inclined, she could ride home this minute and where would that leave us? You have less than ten minutes, I suggest you get a move on.'' The colonel's voice was angry and Kane knew there was no use telling him he had not intended to call the Indian girl a squaw, he had merely meant to call attention to the fact that she was female.

CHAPTER THREE

When Kane mounted his horse and rode through the gates, he found the Indian girl and her two companions waiting for him. He wondered what his father would think of him if he could see him now, riding to meet a potentially dangerous enemy, with a beautiful Indian girl and two white-haired Indian men as his guides.

As he rode to the side of the girl, she did not look at him but nudged her horse in the flanks and moved forward.

Maleaha had resisted the urge to ride away and leave the man who apparently had no respect for her. He thought her little better than a savage. Her Indian blood had been offended. She had no wish to tell him she was probably as "civilized" as he was. Let him think what he would, it didn't matter to her. If only this mission were not so important, she would leave him in the desert somewhere, she thought angrily.

Lamas and Salador rode just behind her, and Maleaha felt comforted by their presence. The two brothers were from the Jojoba tribe. The had lived at the Deveraux ranch since her mother had come there as a bride. They usually worked with the cowhands, but Maleaha knew they were also there to look after her. Whenever she rode away from the ranch, one or both of them would mysteriously appear at her side. Long ago they had both been accepted by the people of Santa Fe as her protectors. Maleaha knew they were always watchful for trouble of any kind. She suspected they had been ordered by her grandfather to look after her after what had happened to her mother. Maleaha never felt like she needed guarding. She had never been treated with anything but the greatest respect. Until today. Major Benedict had treated her as if she were a lowly piece of humanity. For the first time in her life, Maleaha could feel some of the pain her mother had experienced.

Kane could sense the Indian girl's anger as he rode along beside her. Every once in awhile he glanced at her, but she kept her eyes straight ahead, never acknowledging his presence. No woman had ever ignored him as she was doing. She was rude and infuriating, he thought.

They skirted the town of Sante Fe and rode to the south into open country. The two old men did not attempt to draw even with Kane and Maleaha, but rode just behind them.

After they had ridden hard for about two hours, Maleaha pulled up her mount. "We walk now, major. The horses need to rest," she said, dismounting.

Kane clamped his teeth tightly together in anger, knowing it should have been he who gave the order to dismount. Who did she think she was, telling him what to do? He was in charge. He bit back his angry words and

40

dismounted. He had never liked aggressive women, and he liked this one less than most.

He removed his canteen from his saddle horn and offered the Indian girl a drink. She shook her head, then continued to ignore him. Kane took a long drink, wiped his mouth on his sleeve, and squinted at the sun, which seem to be beating down on him unmercifully. Glancing at the Indian girl, he saw she was watching him.

"How long have you been in New Mexico, major?"

"Six months."

"The sun burns hot here. It is not wise to drink too much when you have been out in the heat for any length of time."

His eyes glinted. Did she think he was a complete fool? He started to reply, when the girl turned to one of the old Indian men and spoke to him in words Kane did not understand. The man nodded and mounted his horse, riding back the way they had just traveled.

Kane looked at the Indian girl questioningly.

"We are being followed, major. Whoever it is is keeping well behind us, but I have known about them for the last hour. I warn you, if it turns out to be your soldiers who are following us, I will not take you to Mangas."

"I gave no order for my men to follow us. Whoever it is, it's not soldiers."

Maleaha looked at him doubtfully, but said nothing. Lamas would find out who was trailing them.

Lamas soon rejoined them, and spoke rapidly to Maleaha. She gave Kane a scorching look and bounded onto the back of her horse with fluid grace. Kane quickly remounted his horse and rode hard to try and catch up with her. Just as he drew even with her she swerved her mount off to the side and pulled up behind some bushes. As she slid from the back of her horse, she motioned for Kane to follow her.

"What's this all about?" he demanded as he dismounted.

"Hush, major. I told you we were being followed. You played me false. Did you really think I would not detect your men? I have no intentions of allowing your soldiers to find out where Mangas's village is located."

"If we are being followed, it's not by the cavalry," he ground out between clenched teeth.

She placed her hands on her hips and leveled a green gaze at him. "Lamas may be old, but his eyesight is impeccable. He tells me no less then six of your men are following at a discreet distance, major. This is where you and I part company!"

In one graceful motion she mounted her horse, but she was prevented from leaving by Kane's hand on her reins.

"Wait! I know nothing about this. I swear to you this is not my doing."

Maleaha hesitated for a moment. He seemed so sincere, she could almost believe him. It was imperative that the army talk with Mangas to avoid bloodshed. If he was telling the truth . . . ? "Show your good faith then, major. We ride hard to lose your men." She jerked her reins free from his grasp, and kicked her horse in the flanks, leaving Kane no choice but to remount and ride after her. They rode in the direction of the distant mountains. Riding through mesas and winding through gullies, they finally reached the foothills. There they dismounted and led their horses up the steep incline. When they reached the other side, one of the old men gathered up the reins and led the horses away to hide them.

Lying on her stomach, Maleaha looked toward the north. Kane lay down beside her and watched for riders. He hoped she had been mistaken. He didn't want to think that the colonel had gone behind his back and sent men to follow him.

"Major, I am constantly amazed by the white man's stupidity."

Kane felt the sting of her words, but said nothing. What could he say if she proved to be correct?

"Your men go blundering around, thinking they could go undetected. If I knew they were behind us, what chance do you think they would have had when we neared the Jojoba village? Mangas would have known about them before they were within twenty miles of his camp."

"How did you know we were being followed? I was unaware of it."

"Don't feel too bad, major. I am an Indian, remember?" She turned back to her vigil, then smiled as six blue-clad soldiers emerged over the distant mesa. They were riding about in confusion, trying to pick up the trail that had been lost on the rocky ground.

Kane expected the Indian girl to feel smug because she had been right. He waited for her to give him that I-told-you-so look, but she didn't. Turning over on her back she rested her head on her arms and closed her eyes.

"We will give them an hour or so, major, to discover they have lost our trail. By then they will have no other option but to return to the fort.''

Turning over to his side, Kane propped his head on his hand and studied her beautiful features one by one. Her eyes were closed and she seemed completely relaxed. ''Do you believe that I had nothing to do with those men following us?''

She smiled slightly without opening her eyes. ''It doesn't much matter if you are telling the truth or not. Your men will be unable to trail us, thus you will have to go alone with me to Mangas's camp.''

''For what it's worth, I was telling the truth.''

''For what it's worth, I believe you. I know Colonel Johnson, and I expected him to have me followed.''

She seemed to drift off to sleep. Kane noticed the rise and fall of her chest. She had to be the most beautiful girl he had ever seen. She was mysterious and provocative. He found himself wanting to know more about her. Her command of the English language was perfect. Did she live with her father, or with her mother's people? Where had she received her education? She seemed highly intelligent, and her manner of speech was very refined. He watched as a strand of black hair blew across her face, and he had the strongest urge to reach out and touch it to see if it was as soft as it appeared.

Maleaha was very much aware of the man who lay beside her. He was extremely handsome, and she could feel the raw strength that was confined behind his tall frame. He had a magnetism that seemed to draw her to him. She loved the way his silver eyes flamed when he was angry. She could feel his eyes on her now, and she felt a tightening in her throat. She knew if she opened her eyes at that moment she would gaze into those fiery silver eyes. She wondered why she had not ridden away and left him when she discovered they were being followed. Something about his sincerity had made her believe him when he said he said he knew nothing about it.

A short time later Maleaha opened her eyes and noticed that the major had closed his. Her eyes fell on his hands, which were brown from the sun. What would it feel like to be touched by those hands, she wondered, blushing at her daring thoughts. She closed her eyes, trying to think of something else, but soon her eyes opened to once again rest on his face. How many women had fallen in love with the handsome Kanen Benedict, she wondered? She noticed the way his dark sideburns framed his face. Her eyes flickered over his sensitive mouth, and she felt an ache deep inside as she wondered what it would feel like to be kissed by him. She sat up quickly, feeling guilty for the way her mind was beginning to work. She had never had these thoughts about a man before. She had never even been kissed, other than on the cheek. She had been well protected all her life. First by her father, and later at the finishing school in Boston. There had been any number of young men in Santa Fe who had paid marked attention to Maleaha, but she had never been drawn to any of them as she was to the man who now lay beside her. Maleaha was very disturbed by her feelings for this man. She stood up and dusted off her dress, then went in search of Lamas and Salador.

Kane sensed rather than heard someone standing over him. Opening his eyes, he saw one of the old Indians holding the reins of his horse. Kane stood up and stretched, trying to relieve his cramped muscles. Mounting his horse, he followed the Indian to the bottom of the hill. Kane had no idea if the man spoke English, and there was no time for him to ask the question that was plaguing him. Had the Indian girl ridden off and left him? Had she decided that he had been the one that had ordered the men to follow them?

As they topped a hill, he saw her waiting for him and was overcome with relief. As he drew even with her, she urged her horse forward.

After they had ridden for about an hour, Kane began to feel hunger pangs. He had eaten nothing since before sunrise, and he could tell from the position of the sun that it was now late afternoon.

Maleaha slowed her horse to a walk and Kane slowed his mount to keep pace with her. His jaw tightened in anger. The Indian girl was still in command, and there was nothing he could say to her for fear she would refuse to lead him to Mangas.

Maleaha reached into the leather bag that was strapped across the back of her saddle, removed something, and offered it to Kane.

"We ate while you were asleep, major. We did not disturb you, thinking you needed the rest more than the food." It was said without accusation, but Kane still felt the sting of her words. She as much as implied he could not keep pace with her. Kane took the food she offered him, looking at it suspiciously, wondering what it was. He was hungry, but still he hesitated, having heard all kind of stories about what the Indians ate. It appeared to be some kind of meat between two slices of bread, but what kind of meat?

"What is this?" he asked. He noticed the way she smiled at him as if she had read his thoughts and was amused by them.

"In the language of my mother's people it is called *macha haja*."

He raised the food to his mouth but again hesitated to bite into it. "What does that translate to?" he asked.

Her laughter bubbled out as she enjoyed his discomfort. "It translates to roast beef and homemade bread, major," she told him as she kicked her horse in the flanks and shot forward, leaving him feeling foolish once more.

Kane stared after her angrily. Ever since he had met her this morning, she had been making him appear a blundering fool, and he was beginning to resent her for it. He had half decided to throw the food away, but his good sense won over his anger. He had no doubt that if he did not eat the food it would only serve to amuse her further.

They stopped just before sundown and made camp beside a small stream. Once again the Indian girl had taken charge by deciding where they would camp for the night. Apparently she was not going to consult him about anything, he thought angrily. As he unsaddled his horse he noticed she was taking care of her own horse. His first instinct was to help her. After all, even if she was an Indian, she was still a female, and females were supposed to be pampered, or so he had always been taught. He observed how easily she lifted the saddle and placed it on the ground. No, he would not help her. She did not deserve any consideration from him. If she wanted any help from him she could ask for it, or better still, let the two

Indians help her.

He unfastened his cinch as he spoke to her. "Apparently an Indian girl can take care of herself, not needing the help of a man, while the women of my acquaintance bring out the protective instincts in a man." His words sounded harsh, and Maleaha blinked, knowing he was trying to insult her. Why was he deliberately trying to hurt her?

"How nice for you, major. It is always nice to feel useful, even if it is only unsaddling a lady's horse for her. How fortunate for the ladies of your acquaintance to have you to perform that menial task for them."

As she turned her back to him, once again Kane felt he had come out the loser. She had made him feel petty and vindictive. Inside, his anger smoldered. One day he vowed, he would show that high and mighty little Indian baggage just how he felt about her. She was arrogant, smug, and the most irritating female he had ever encountered. Never had he met anyone who could cause him to lose his temper so quickly. All the women he had ever known had been only too willing to please him, and yet this mere girl seemed not to be aware of him as a man at all, and she definitely did not try to please him. She was beautiful all right, there was no denying that, but he would never be drawn to her. She was too headstrong, too obstinate for his taste. Kane hobbled his horse and went down to the stream to wash his face. The water was cool and sweet, and he cupped his hands and took a deep drink.

They were camped at the edge of a pine forest and Kane could smell the pungent odor of the pine trees.

Looking about him, he thought what a beautiful spot this was. He had not heard the Indian girl come up beside him until she bent over and filled what appeared to be a coffee pot with water from the stream.

"Do Indians drink coffee? he asked, tongue in cheek.

Green eyes spit fire as she quickly stood up, sloshing water over the tip of the coffee pot. "Oh, for certain, major, but usually we prefer firewater, whenever we can obtain it from some unscrupulous white man."

Kane cursed under his breath as he watched her walk away from him. Damn, he was always saying the wrong thing to her. He could see himself as she must see him, self-appointed bigot. There didn't seem to be anything he could do to correct that impression.

He stood up and walked farther upstream, with the intention of bathing. It was almost dark when he returned to camp. He could smell the aroma of bacon cooking and was reminded how hungry he was. The roast beef the Indian girl had given him earlier had been very good, but that had been a long time ago. His stomach was telling him it was time to eat again.

The Indian girl looked up at him as she removed several slices of bacon from an iron skillet.

"Major, you are welcome to eat with us if you would like. I am aware of the kind of food the army provides for its men when they are on patrol. It is none too appetizing, is it?"

He sat down and crossed his long legs. "I would appreciate it if you would share your food with me. You were right when you said army chow is not too good."

Maleaha handed him a tin plate and he ate with relish.

Then he enjoyed two cups of coffee before he leaned back against his saddle to rest.

"How is it that you know about army food?" he asked.

"I am acquainted with several soldiers from the fort, major. At least I was two years ago."

He stared at her for a moment, wondering just how close she had been with some of those soldiers. He was aware that many of the soldiers were on very intimate terms with some of the Indian women who came to the fort looking to trade their favors for food and blankets.

"Just how well did you know the soldiers? You should not have needed either food or blankets, being the daughter of Jonas Deveraux. I can only assume you sought the soldiers out for your own pleasure," he said, wondering why the thought was so distasteful to him.

He heard her gasp and looked quickly into her face.

Maleaha tried to speak, but no words would come from her mouth. Anger and hurt battled inside of her, each wanting to be the dominating emotion.

Lamas looked at her, seeing her expression, and, knowing the insult she had just received from the white man, spoke angrily. "Say the word, Maleaha, and I will carve the heart from the white dog. No one speaks to Jonas Deveraux's daughter so insultingly and lives," he said as his hand went to the knife at his waist. He had spoken to her in Jojoba and she answered him in kind.

"No, it is not important. When this mission is completed, then I will deal with this man in my own way." Maleaha could never remember a time when she had been so angry and hurt. She felt the sting of tears in her eyes. No, she would not cry, she told herself. She was too proud to let this hateful man see her in tears.

Kane saw the different emotions that played across her beautiful face. He heard the Indian man's soft voice and saw him reach for the hilt of his knife. God, he thought, what was it about the Indian girl that brought out the worst in him? He knew he had made a grave mistake, but saw no way to make amends.

"Major," she said in a deadly calm voice. "Today you are a fortunate man, because you are still alive. No one has ever dared to speak to me in such a manner before. I have taken into consideration that you are a foolish and pompous man. You and I have an important mission to fulfill, but once the mission is completed, you are never to approach me or speak to me, for if you do, you shall surely die."

Her words had been delivered quietly and without emotion, but the threat was obvious. He had not meant to insult her. Many of the soldiers at the fort traded pretty trinkets, blankets, and food, to the Indian women for their favors, and everyone knew it. Perhaps he had been wrong to call attention to it. The Indians didn't seem to live by the same moral code as the white man did. He watched as she cleaned the pan she had used to fry the bacon in. He was sorry if he had insulted her. It could be that she had been taught differently from the other Indians. Yes, that must be it. Since her father was a white man, maybe she had been brought up more as a white girl. He decided it would be best to let the matter drop.

"How do I address you? You never did tell me your name," he asked, thinking to change the subject.

She stood up and gave him a cold glare. "You were introduced to me, have you forgotten? You may call me Miss Deveraux.''

He smiled, ''But surely you have a first name.''

She was thoughtful while she added more wood to the fire, then, standing up straight, she turned to face him, and Kane could see the reflection of the campfire in her green eyes. It looked for a moment as if her eyes were on fire.

''I have a name, like everyone else, but only my friends are allowed to use it. You, major, are not my friend,'' she said icily.

Kane shifted uncomfortably. ''Miss Deveraux, I would like to apologize to you for my bad manners. The only defense I have is that I have never talked to an Indian girl before. I don't really know how to treat you.''

''Oh, are there separate rules, major? Should you treat an Indian girl any differently from the way you would treat a white girl? The more I come to know you, the less I like you.''

Kane folded his arms behind him and lay back on his bedroll. ''I doubt that I shall lose much sleep over not being in your good graces, Miss Deveraux. From the moment I met you I have made one blunder after another. If you are an example of what an Indian girl is like, I can well live without them,'' he said lazily.

Maleaha clenched her hands tightly together, seething on the inside. ''I doubt that any of my race would ever live with you, major,'' she said turning her back on him and walking away.

Kane closed his eyes, and listened to the sounds coming from the forest. The wind made such a lonesome sound as it blew through the tall pine trees. He heard the call of some kind of bird he was unfamiliar with, and far off in the distance a coyote howled. There was a cool breeze blowing, and Kane felt himself beginning to relax.

Opening his eyes lazily, he saw that Miss Deveraux had bedded down on the other side of the campfire. What a strange girl she was. She could ride like the wind. She had a kind of quiet beauty about her. She was soft-spoken. Even when she was angry she never raised her voice. He had yet to see her smile, but he imagined her smile would light up her green eyes. He watched as the two old Indian men lay down on a blanket on either side of her. They must think they needed to protect her from him, he supposed. He smiled to himself. She was safe enough from him. He had to admit grudgingly, that he admired her spirit, but his taste in women ran to the more feminine kind. He liked women dressed in silks and satins, though she was rather appealing in her soft buck-skins. Kane liked his women to be docile; he liked to feel superior to them in some ways. But she was intelligent, and nothing about her was docile. He had always had a fascination for creamy white skin. Her skin was a golden color. He wondered if her whole body would be that same beautiful golden color, or just the parts that were exposed to the sun. He thought of how her hips moved gracefully as she walked. Her lips, so sensuous and inviting. Good Lord, he thought, turning over on his side. Obviously he had been out in the sun too long today. Closing his eyes, he tried to fall asleep so he could block out the Indian girl, whom he did not even like very well.

Maleaha lay on her back, gazing at the moon that was

barely visible through the tall pine trees. She felt crushed. How was it possible for that man to have the power to hurt her so deeply? He seemed to think she was some kind of wild savage with no morals and no feelings. If the major had a sister Maleaha doubted that she had been brought up much differently from herself. She had attended Mass every Sunday, gone on picnics, danced at balls, and had been well educated. The only difference might be that she was half-Indian, and had spent some time with her mother's people. True, she rode astride like a man, but that was more because of her father's indulgence than the fact that she was half-Indian. New Mexico was very different from the United States; most of her friends also rode astride, and here no one thought the less of them for it.

For some reason it seemed to displease the major that she could unsaddle her own horse. It would never occur to her to have a man peform that duty for her. Her father had taught her to care for her horse, and she never expected anyone else to help her. She had always curried and groomed her own horse. She was not, nor would she ever be, a helpless female, a fact that her father took great pride in.

Maleaha tried to shut her mind off and go to sleep, but found it impossible. Was the major bothered by the fact that she was half-Indian? She had never come up against anyone who resented her because her mother was Indian. It was a new and devastating experience. Today was the first time she had run into prejudice in any form, and she found that it wounded her deeply. Today she realized for the first time what her mother had been forced to live with. She didn't know why it should matter to her what the major thought of her, but it did matter. It mattered a great deal.

Perhaps if she had acted like some mindless, helpless female, he would have treated her quite differently. Or would he? No, it was the fact that she was part Indian that he resented. Well, she could not change who she was, and even if she could, she would not want to. She had always been taught to be proud of who she was. Perhaps it was her pride that the major resented. Did he expect her to lower her head and act as if she were inferior to him?

She closed her eyes tightly. Oh, Mother, she thought, what you must have suffered for loving my father. I have suffered only one day of prejudice, and you had to live with it every day as my father's wife.

With a troubled frown on her face, Maleaha finally fell asleep.

CHAPTER FOUR

The next morning Kane awoke to the smell of coffee brewing and bacon frying. He was a light sleeper, and yet he had not heard the Indians moving about, watering the horses and cooking breakfast over the open campfire. He felt the hard ground beneath him, and as he stood up and looked around he saw no sign of the girl. One of the Indian men was tending to the bacon that was sizzling in the skillet. His dark eyes moved over Kane with a look that plainly dismissed him.

Kane removed his shaving kit from his saddlebag and made his way downstream. By the time he returned, the girl was dishing up the bacon onto a tin plate. Her black hair was wet, giving evidence that she had bathed in the stream as he had. She handed him the plate without a word, then made her way to the stream to clean the pan. Kane poured himself some coffee from the pot, and the Indian man emptied the grounds onto the fire and followed the girl to the stream with the empty pot.

Kane ate the food hungrily, and when he finished he downed the last of his coffee. Making his way to the stream, he bent down by the girl to wash his tin plate and coffee cup. The girl did not acknowledge his presence, and Kane felt irritated.

"When do we reach Mangas's camp?" he asked gruffly, unable to hide his irritation.

"We will be there in three days' time, major. If I were to take you directly to his village, we could make it in two days."

"What do you mean by that?"

"What I mean is, I shall take you the long way around, so you cannot later lead the army to the Jojoba village."

Anger stirred within Kane once more. Miss Deveraux seemed to provoke him beyond endurance.

Maleaha smiled to herself. She knew she had made him angry, and for some reason it gave her pleasure.

Kane stood up, and with his great height he seemed to tower over her. "I am surprised you have not blindfolded me, Miss Deveraux. That way you could be certain I would not see where we are going," he said acidly.

"Oh, that comes later, major. Never fear. I would not take you into the Jojoba village without first blindfolding you." Her eyes seem to gleam mischievously, and Kane watched her, too dumbfounded to reply. He watched silently as she walked away from him, noticing the gentle sway of her hips and the way her hair gleamed in the morning sunlight.

They rode silently all morning. Around noon, Kane called for a halt. He would have some say in this mission, he decided. He expected the Indian girl to question his authority, but she said nothing as she dismounted and walked beside her horse.

Late in the afternoon, Kane decided where they would set up camp for the night and was again surprised when the girl voiced no objections. They had been riding hard all day and by now were deep within the mountains.

Kane had hardly spoken to Miss Deveraux all day. He unsaddled his mount and removed his saddlebags and bedroll. By the time he tethered his horse, the girl had disappeared. The two men had gathered wood and built a campfire.

A short time later, he made his way down to the stream to wash his face. He was just returning to camp, when he heard the sound of gunfire coming from somewhere in the forest. The Indian men did not seem to be concerned. Apparently they thought the girl could take care of herself.

Kane sat down on a fallen log and watched the last dying embers of the sun. It was peaceful here, he thought. Nature had done her best here in these mountains. Somehow Kane felt attuned to this land, and he thought it would be a shame to see it taken over by the white man. The tall pine trees swayed gracefully in the evening breeze, and the musical sound of the nearby stream seemed to soothe him. He saw the girl coming out of the woods with a rifle resting on her shoulder and a dead rabbit dangling from her hand, and he thought that she was a part of this land. He was the intruder.

Kane rested his back against a huge boulder and watched as the girl skillfully gutted and cleaned the rabbit, then handed it to one of the men, who put it on a spit, to roast over the fire. Yes, he thought, she was a part of this country, as proud and as graceful as the tall pines that dominated the land. He watched quietly as she sat down not far from where he was and began cleaning her rifle.

Kane watched as her eyes traveled to the top of the boulder he was leaning against. At that moment he heard the horses acting up, as if they had been spooked by something, or someone.

"I better check that out," he said, starting to rise.

"No! Don't move, major. Just talk to me calmly," she told him as she slipped a bullet into the chamber of her rifle. "Don't move, there is a cougar right over your head," she said calmly, as she cocked her rifle and raised the barrel above him to aim at the top of the boulder.

Kane felt the taste of fear as the shot rang out. He jumped to his feet and looked above him just in time to see the cougar leap into the air and run into the woods. Then he turned back to face the girl.

"You missed," he said feeling as if his stomach was made of butterflies.

"I didn't miss, major. Had I intended to kill the cat, it would now be dead. An Indian will only kill for food, unless he is forced to kill to defend himself."

"What would have happened had your shot not frightened the cougar away?"

She shrugged her shoulders and smiled. "A cougar, like an Indian, will only kill for food."

Kane moved away from the boulder and sat down on his bedroll, trying to relax. He owed his life to Miss Deveraux, but he could think of no way to express his thanks. For the most part, she ignored him. Looking across the camp to where his three companions were talking together, he realized he was experiencing the chance of a lifetime. How many white men had had the chance to travel with three Indians? And he would soon meet Mangas, whom very few white men had ever seen.

One of the Indian men was talking softly to the girl, and Kane heard her laughter. Suddenly he wished he could join in their conversation. He wanted to get to know them; he would like to have their friendship. He knew what the girl must think of him, but he was not really as bad as she thought.

Standing up, he walked across the camp to where the girl was sitting on a rock. She was listening intently to one of the old men and was smiling at whatever he was saying to her.

"The white man is not so bad, Maleaha. It is my belief that he speaks out of inexperience, rather than out of malice," Lamas said to her.

"You may be right, but I do not like him very much," Maleaha said.

Lamas laughed. "I think you like him well enough. Wait and see."

Maleaha shook her head. "When we return home, I never want to see him again."

Kane sat down on the rock beside Maleaha, and she slid him a sideways glance.

"Tell me about Mangas, Miss Deveraux," he said coolly. "I would like to know what kind of man I will be dealing with."

The two Indian men seemed to fade away as she turned her full attention on the major. Why did he have to be so handsome? She noticed the way his blue uniform fit snugly across his broad shoulders, and the way his pant hugged his long, powerful legs. Her heart skipped a bea as she looked into his beautiful silver eyes, eyes that she was sure could see into the very depths of her soul.

"I have not seen Mangas since I was thirteen. That was four years ago."

So she was only seventeen, a mere child, and yet she was bright and intelligent. He supposed Indian womer matured faster than white women did. She would not be so sure of herself if she were put up against a womar dressed in silk, moving among the polite society that he was used to, he thought sadly.

"Mangas was very kind to me when I was a child," she continued. "Even then he was strong and power-ful, and my grandfather was grooming him to be chie after his death. I found Mangas to be very kind and gentle."

Kane heard the reverence in her voice, and he felt an-ger. "It was not a kind and gentle man who raided the ranches and stole their livestock, Miss Deveraux."

Maleaha looked at him with returned anger. "Major, had it been a white man who raided the ranches, he would have received a trial before you condemned him, and yet you judge Mangas guilty without benefit of a trial."

"It has to be Mangas, Miss Deveraux, the evidence points to him."

Maleaha stood up and put her hands on her hips. "If you accuse Mangas of these deeds to his face major, you will die. I doubt even I could stay his hand should you speak so rashly to him."

"Why have you not seen him in four years, Miss Deveraux?'' Kane said, ignoring her warning.

"I have been away, major," she told him as she walked over to the campfire and began removing the rabbit from the spit. They all ate in silence, and afterwards Kane lay down on his bedroll, thinking he would never win the girl's approval.

The next two days they rode hard and took so many twists and turns that Kane knew he would never be able to find Mangas's camp on his own. No words passed between him and Maleaha until the afternoon of the fourth day, when she halted her horse.

"From here on you shall be blindfolded, major."

"And if I refuse?"

"I shall ride away and leave you. I do not have the patience to indulge you in this."

Kane nodded his head in grim acceptance, knowing she would do just what she threatened if he did not consent to the blindfold.

"Does Mangas know we are here, Miss Deveraux?"

"We have been observed since we broke camp this morning. We are being followed even now," she told him.

Kane felt a prickle of fear, but soon pushed it aside. He was no coward, but somehow the elusive Mangas spelled danger to anyone with white skin. The only one who stood between him and disaster was the beautiful Indian girl, and he knew she did not feel too charitable toward him at the moment. "I am completely at your mercy, Miss Deveraux," he told her.

"Yes, major. You are at my mercy." She gathered up the reins of his horse and led him forward.

It seemed to Kane that they had been riding for over an hour, but in truth it had been only a few short minutes.

Suddenly, he could hear the sound of many horses, and he knew they had been joined by other riders. He could tell when they entered the village by the sound of children's laughter and the barking of a dog.

Maleaha reached across and removed his blindfold from his eyes. He blinked at the bright sunlight and saw that he had been surrounded by many fierce-looking warriors. Some of them wore long leather breeches, and others wore only a breechcloth. The many dark eyes were hostile, and Kane could feel the tension in the very air he breathed.

"Do not dismount, major," Maleaha warned, as she slid gracefully fron her horse. Kane watched as she spoke rapidly to one of the Indians, who quickly disappeared into one of the teepees. Kane and Maleaha both watched the teepee, and the camp became silent.

Suddenly the tent flap was thrown open and a tall Indian emerged. Kane needed no one to tell him the man was Mangas, chief of the mighty Jojoba tribe.

Maleaha stood silently, hardly daring to breathe. Would Mangas remember her? He had changed but little, she thought. His bronze chest rippled with muscles, his whole body seemed to speak of undeniable strength. As she looked into his handsome face, his black eyes fastened on her. Moments passed and the silence lay heavy across the camp. At last Mangas gave Maleaha just the slightest smile as he walked toward her with wild animal grace. His black hair was encircled by a plain leather band and glistened in the afternoon sunlight. He wore long buckskin trousers, but his chest was bare. He stopped inches from Maleaha and his smile broadened.

"So, Little Flower, you have blossomed into womanhood."

She returned his smile. "I was not sure you would remember me, my chief," she answered him in the Indian language in which he had spoken to her.

He reached out and picked up the turquoise stone that hung about her neck, the stone he had given her that day so long ago. "I would recognize you always, Little Flower," he said softly. His eyes switched to the white man in the soldier's uniform, and Kane saw the distrust, or was it hate that was registered there?

"Why have you brought this soldier to my village, Maleaha? I am not pleased with you for doing this."

Maleaha swallowed hard, then she looked into Mangas's eyes. "This is Major Kanen Benedict, my chief. I beg you to grant him an audience. He has something of great importance to say to you."

"Who asks this of me, the white side of you, Maleaha, or the Indian side?"

"Both, Mangas," she replied. She refused to lower her eyes, but stared bravely back at him, knowing that to show weakness would only gain his contempt.

"I will speak to this white man, but you shall act as an interpreter."

"But you speak English very well," she said, puzzled by his request.

He smiled slightly. "I can observe him and assess his sincerity better if he does not know that I understand him. Bring him to my teepee."

Maleaha watched as Mangas strolled back to the tent, then she turned to the major, who had remained silent while she was speaking with Mangas.

"Dismount, major. Mangas says he will speak with you."

Kane obeyed and followed her across the camp to the big teepee that Mangas had entered only moments before.

Inside, Kane saw the huge buffalo robes that covered the floor, and he was immediately impressed with the cleaniness of the teepee. He had also observed earlier how neat and clean the women and children appeared. It did not fit what he had been told about Indians.

Mangas was seated with his legs folded. He motioned for Maleaha to sit beside him and indicated that he wanted Kane to sit across from him.

"Tell the lying white eyes to speak," Mangas told Maleaha.

Kane saw the black eyes boring into him, and he felt the man's contempt.

"Mangas asks you to speak, major."

Mangas laughed. "Why did you not translate exactly what I said, Little Flower?"

She smiled in response. "It is the white side of me that will be your translator, my chief."

He looked at her with an amused smile. "This should prove interesting."

66

Kane took a deep breath, "Tell Mangas I come to him on behalf of the American Government, and in the name of peace." Kane paused and looked straight at the chief. "Tell Mangas I am honored to meet the mighty chief of the Jojoba."

Maleaha spoke to Mangas, not bothering to translate since he understood every word spoken by the major. "I believe this man to be honest and sincere, Mangas."

"I have found no white man who speaks the truth, but your father, Little Flower."

Maleaha turned to Kane. "Mangas says you are welcome in the Jojoba village, major," she said daringly.

Mangas laughed deeply. "See, Little Flower, you prove my point. The white side of you lies to the major."

"Not so, Mangas, I merely anticipated what your next words would be," she said, giving him a mischievous smile.

"You have grown into a beautiful woman, Maleaha, as I always knew you would."

Maleaha looked at Kane. "Mangas asked if you had a pleasant trip, major."

Kane saw the way Mangas was looking at Miss Deveraux, and in any language the look would have been the same. He was admiring her, his black eyes were almost caressing as he stared at her.

"Tell him the trip took one day longer than it should have, due to the roundabout way you escorted me to his camp," he said bitingly.

"Mangas, I was very careful to bring the major a way that he would never be able to trace."

"I have always been fascinated by the color of your eyes, Maleaha. Never have I looked into eyes that were so lovely, so open, so desirable," said Mangas.

"Major, Mangas wonders if you would like something to drink?"

Kane was becoming angry. It seemed that Miss Deveraux was playing some kind of game. He was not a fool, he knew the chief was speaking passionate words to her.

"Tell him I want nothing but to talk," he replied angrily.

"Please hear him out, Mangas," Maleaha said, hoping Mangas would not continue his bold conversation, for he was making her feel very uneasy.

Mangas frowned. "Have him state the reason he is here. I confess I am curious."

"Mangas asks that you tell him the reason you are here," she said to Kane. Mangas no longer probed her face with his dark eyes, but looked at the major instead.

"Tell him that the raids on the ranchers must stop or there will be bloodshed, and many people, both white and Indian will die."

"Mangas, did the Jojobas raid the ranchers? I cannot believe you would be a party to such mischief."

He frowned. "I would not consider it wrong had I raided the white man. They are the intruder, they take our lands and treat us with contempt, but in this I am not guilty. I do not know what he speaks of, believe me, Little Flower."

"Yes, I believe you. The Mangas I know would never sneak around under the cover of night to wreak mischief and steal a few horses. He would meet his enemy face to face, giving them even odds. I remember your kindness one summer to a half-white girl.'' She had spoken with such conviction that he stared for a long time into her eyes.

''I am pleased that you should believe this of me. I have often thought of you these past years. I have waited patiently for you to grow up, Little Flower.''

Maleaha turned to the major. ''Mangas says he is not responsible for the raids on those ranches.''

Kane looked at her doubtfully. ''Do you believe this man?''

''Yes, Mangas does not lie. What would be the purpose? He is safe from retribution; the army could never find him here. He is innocent, major. As are the people of the Jojoba tribe. You will need to look elsewhere for the guilty ones.''

Kane considered her words. She seemed sincere in her beliefs. Was it possible that Mangas spoke the truth, he wondered?

''Ask Mangas if he knows who is responsible for the raids.''

''Do you have any idea who is responsible, Mangas?''

''Yes, it is the Arapaho. They sweep down out of the Colorados to spread mischief, hoping the Jojoba will be blamed. As you know, they are our sworn enemies, and I believe the time will come when they will go on a bloody raid, hoping to place the blame on us. But I doubt you can convince this white man, or any of his kind that I speak the truth.''

Maleaha sighed deeply as she turned to the major,

fearing Mangas might be right. The white man was always suspicious of that which he did not understand. The Jojoba tribe had never conformed to what was expected of them. They were a nomadic tribe that followed the game trail, never bothering to put down roots, nor to plant corn, and they refused to live off the charity of the United States government, but only wanted to be left in peace.

"Major, Mangas says it is the Arapaho who are responsible for the raids. The Jojoba and Arapaho are enemies, and the Arapaho seek to implicate the Jojoba."

"There was overwhelming evidence that it was the Jojoba. I did not tell you this before, but there was an armband with the sun and the moon engraved on it, the Jojoba symbol, found at one of the burned-out barns. I assume your father told you about the knife that was found."

"You do not believe that Mangas is telling the truth, that the Arapaho deliberately implicated the Jojoba?"

Kane looked directly into the eyes of the chief, and in that moment he did believe that this man spoke the truth.

"Tell him that if he can convince me that he is innocent, I will do all in my power to see that the Jojoba tribe is exonerated of all suspicion, and will strive to see that the guilty party is punished."

Maleaha turned to Mangas. "I believe this man, my chief. Have you any proof?"

"Why should I prove that I am innocent in this? I have done nothing wrong. This white dog will pay for his insult!" Mangas's eyes were blazing dangerously and Maleaha saw the danger to the major.

She placed her hand on Mangas's arm and spoke softly. "It is not the fault of Major Benedict. He is merely the instrument of the United States Government, and while I, like you, do not think the army deals fairly with the Indian, there is nothing much we can do to stop it."

Mangas looked down at the delicate hand that rested on his bare arm, then into her beautiful green eyes.

"My heart often overrides my good judgment, Little Flower. Were it within my power to drive the white man from this land I would do so, but your grandfather, in his wisdom, convinced me that soon the white man would have all this land. Where then will the Jojoba tribe go? Where will my people live? What will I feed the women and children? I will never go begging to the white man for his handouts."

Maleaha was moved by his words and his sadness. "I do not know, Mangas. I wish I had the answers for you, but I do not."

Mangas stood up. "Tell him I will deal with the Arapaho in my own way."

Maleaha stood up, and Kane also rose to his feet. "Major, Mangas says he will deal with the Arapaho himself."

"No! Tell him that is exactly what he must not do. The army will not stand by and watch two Indian tribes wage war among themselves. Tell him it would lead to serious consequences."

Maleaha turned to Mangas, who did not wait for her to speak. His voice was quiet, his tone menacing, "Tell the white eyes I do not answer to the army. *I* will decide what I do. I am the chief of the Jojoba. It is my people who have been falsely accused."

"Major, Mangas will not allow the army to dictate to him. He will handle the Arapaho."

"Try to convince him otherwise, Miss Deveraux. It would be foolhardy and dangerous to start an Indian war where many people would die."

Maleaha did not speak to Mangas, but answered on her own, her anger very apparent. "The Jojoba people do not need the army to tell them what to do. How do you suppose they survived all those hundreds of years before the white man came to this land? We are a proud people and we shall do as we must, and not you or anyone else can tell us any different!"

Maleaha had not been aware that she had spoken as if she herself was a member of the Jojoba, but Kane noticed, and Mangas did too.

Mangas was smiling as he watched her green eyes spark angrily. He felt pride in this small girl who was beautiful as well as loyal. He had thought of her so often, and he knew at that moment why he had never taken a bride. Lamas had kept him informed on Maleaha's life. He had known that summer when he taught her to swim that he wanted her for his wife, and now he was more sure of it than ever.

"Ask Mangas if that is his final word?" Kane said, ignoring her outburst.

Maleaha looked at Mangas and then lowered her head in shame. "I am sorry, my chief. I spoke without thinking."

His dark eyes caressed her face gently. "Tell him I have nothing more to say to him. Tell him since the hour is so late he may stay the night, but I shall expect him to leave in the morning.''

''Major, Mangas will talk to you no more, but if you will go with Lamas he will find you a place to sleep for tonight. We must leave early tomorrow morning.''

''But nothing has been settled.''

''Mangas will speak no more to you,'' she repeated.

Kane looked as if he would like to object but had thought better of it. He had noticed the way Mangas looked at Maleaha and felt anger because of it. He turned to leave the teepee and Maleaha followed him until Mangas put a restraining hand on her arm. ''Stay a while and talk with me, Little Flower,'' he said.

Kane heard the tone of his voice and looked angrily at Maleaha. ''It is not hard to see where you will be spending the night, Miss Deveraux.''

Maleaha opened her mouth to protest, but the major had already left.

Mangas's eyes narrowed as he stared after the white man. ''What is that white man to you, Maleaha?''

''He is nothing, I only met him three days ago.''

''He wants you,'' Mangas said.

''No! You are mistaken. He does not even like me, and I do not care for him at all.''

''You are mistaken, Little Flower. He would like to be with you, but he does not want to show his feelings. I wonder why?''

''No! You are mistaken.'' Maleaha said, feeling very upset by Mangas's observation.

He looked down at her and smiled, ''I do not wish to speak of the white man. I would rather speak of you. Sit beside me, Maleaha,'' he said as he lowered himself to the buffalo rug and held out his hand to her.

Maleaha sat down hesitantly. She had been aware of the deep undertones in Mangas's voice. He had said some rather personal things to her this afternoon, which she had tried to ignore.

"Tell me, are you glad to be home, Maleaha?"

"Yes, I never want to go away again."

"And is there no man in your life, Little Flower?"

"No, I am still too young to be thinking about marriage."

"Not for an Indian maiden, Maleaha. I was proud of you today when you stood up to the white man. Tell me, do you think of yourself as Indian or white?"

"It is hard to separate the two. I feel pride in my Indian blood, but I am also proud to be my father's daughter."

"That is as it should be. Do you think you could be happy living here with me, Little Flower?"

Maleaha tried to avoid his eyes. Was he suggesting that she become his wife? Fear and uncertainty nagged at her. She did not know how she felt at the moment. Maleaha only knew she wished she were safely home at Deveraux Ranch.

"I do not know, Mangas. I have not thought about living anywhere but with my father," she said, hoping he would not pursue the matter.

"One day you will have to leave your father's house, Maleaha. A maiden has to look to the future. I would like for you to be the mother of my sons. We could have strong sons, Maleaha. You have the blood of a Jojoba chief in your veins."

She stood up slowly, "I . . . I do not wish to be married at this time; I am not ready." Maleaha knew that if the chief of the Jojobas wanted a woman of the tribe for his bride he could take her whether she was willing or not. Fear gripped her as she raised her eyes to his, wondering if it was his intention to force her to be his wife.

Mangas read the fear in her eyes and touched her face softly. "Do not fear, Little Flower, I will not force you to be my wife just now. I would much rather you come to me willingly. I believe we would be happy together. You are a beautiful woman and I desire you."

"Why have you not married?" She could not refrain from asking.

His bronzed hand moved softly over her ebony hair. "Someday I shall tell you, but not now. Go to your aunt, Little Flower. I know she is waiting to see you."

Maleaha rushed to the tent opening on shaky legs.

"Maleaha, I will not wait too long," Mangas said. It was not only a statement but a promise.

Kane paced up and down in the teepee that he was sharing with one of the Indians who had accompanied Miss Deveraux. His mind was in a quandary. He wanted to ask the Indian man if Miss Deveraux was spending the night with Mangas. He was angered by that prospect. Hell, she was half-white. She had no right to give herself to that Indian. For all Kane knew, the man might have a wife, or several wives for that matter. But why should he care? It was his responsibility to look after her, he reasoned. After all, she had made this journey with him. She was Jonas Deveraux's daughter, and Jonas would not approve of his daughter staying with the Jojoba chief. Kane knew that the chief had been speaking very intimately to the girl today, but he could not tell what her reaction had been.

The old Indian looked at Kane with an unreadable expression on his face. Kane saw the man reach for the bowl of food that had been brought to him earlier by an Indian woman. Kane had no intention of eating the food even though he was hungry; there was no telling what it contained.

Lying down on the robe, he focused his eyes on the opening at the top of the teepee. The night was dark, with only a few stars twinkling overhead. He thought of the Indian girl. She was so beautiful. Kane was honest enough with himself to admit that he wanted her. It did not matter that she was half-Indian. It did not matter that she was obstinate and made him appear to be a fool at every turn. It did not matter that probably at this very moment she lay in Mangas's arms. He wanted her as he had never wanted a woman in all his life, and he despised himself for it.

For so long now Kane had been bored by the women in his life, but since he had met Miss Deveraux he had experienced excitement again. And he was certainly never bored with her. He wondered what it would feel like to have her lying in his arms at this very moment.

He wanted to see those green eyes heavy with passion, passion that he had evoked. He wanted to taste those lips that could tease him with a smile or scorch him with angry words.

"Damn," he said aloud, and was aware that the old Indian had raised up on his elbow to look at him.

Kane turned over on his side and closed his eyes, trying to put the girl out of his mind. He tried to think of his mission, which might or might not be considered a failure, depending on how the colonel viewed it. "Sleep, I need sleep," he said, to no one in particular.

When Maleaha left Mangas's teepee she found her Aunt Kosha waiting for her. It had been three years since Maleaha had seen her aunt, and she was glad to see that she had not changed. Kosha had no children of her own. In her youth she had borne one daughter who had died the same day.

Maleaha knew her Aunt Kosha loved her. She had spent many happy days with her as a child. There was happiness reflected on Kosha's face as she enfolded her dead sister's daughter in her arms and led her to her own dwelling.

That night many friends of her childhood came to her aunt's teepee and they talked long into the night. It was good to be with her mother's people, she thought, and she felt the love and respect they communicated to her. After all, her aunt told her, she was a princess of the Jojoba, and the people had also loved her mother a great deal.

It was almost dawn when Maleaha fell asleep. It seemed she had only closed her eyes when her aunt shook her gently. "You must eat, Maleaha, you have a long journey ahead of you, and you do not want to get a late start.''

Maleaha was having her breakfast with her aunt and uncle when Lamas entered the teepee to inform her that Mangas wished to speak to her before she left. Kissing her aunt and uncle good-bye and promising to visit them again soon, she made her way to Mangas's dwelling.

Mangas was waiting for her, and he led her inside.

''I wanted to wish you a safe journey, Little Flower, and to tell you to be on the lookout for the Arapaho. I would not want anything to happen to you.''

''I will be quite safe; you need not be concerned for me.''

''Come, I shall walk you to your horse. Lamas will not be going with you at this time, so stay close beside Salador. He is sworn to protect you with his life.''

They were outside the teepee now, and the sun was just coming up over the distant mountains.

''Why does Lamas stay behind, Mangas?''

''I wish to send a spy into the Arapaho country. He is familiar with the land and he also speaks their language. Do not worry, he will return to you in a very short time.''

Maleaha nodded. ''I will say good-bye then, Mangas. I hope you can settle the problem of the Arapaho.''

He touched her cheek softly, ''It is not good-bye, Little Flower. We shall meet again soon.''

Maleaha was not aware that Major Kanen Benedict watched her as he prepared to mount his horse. He had seen her coming out of Mangas's teepee, and it was not hard for him to draw the conclusion that she had spent the night with the chief of the Jojoba. He did not miss the loving way Mangas touched her face. Mounting his horse, he stared straight ahead. His eyes blazed angrily, thinking what a little slut she was.

Maleaha walked gracefully across the camp and mounted her horse. Noticing the major's foul mood, she did not wish him a good morning as she had intended to.

Mangas raised his hand in a silent salute, and she raised her hand to him. She looked about for her aunt and saw her standing beside her husband, so she raised her hand to them as well.

Angrily spinning his horse around, Kane nudged it in the flanks and rode away, leaving Maleaha and Salador to follow.

CHAPTER FIVE

All morning they rode in silence, and late in the afternoon Kane pulled up his horse. He had not eaten since the day before at breakfast, and he felt almost weak with hunger.

Maleaha offered him some of the corncakes her aunt had given her, but he refused, deciding he would eat a can of beans he had brought along instead. Maleaha wondered why he was behaving so strangely, but he did not choose to enlighten her, and she would not ask.

They rode until almost sundown before Kane halted and announced they would camp beside a stream. Maleaha dismounted, unsaddled her horse and led him to the stream to drink. By the time she returned she saw that the major had opened his can of beans and they were warming over the campfire he had built. Salador had disappeared earlier, but he soon joined them with two good-sized rabbits which he gutted and cleaned, then placed over the fire to roast. The aroma of the sizzling meat was almost more than Kane could bear. He spooned some of his beans onto a tin plate and offered it to Maleaha, but she refused it, saying she much preferred the roasted rabbit.

Kane took a bite of the beans and frowned.

"Major, I would suggest you wait until the rabbit is done. I am aware that you have eaten nothing since yesterday. I do not relish the thought of nursing you, should you become ill."

His silver eyes sent out sparks. "I will tolerate no more of your insults, Miss Deveraux." He grabbed her arm and propelled her against him. "I have had to endure your bad temper and your sharp tongue for days now." His grip tightened on her wrist, and Maleaha could feel herself being drawn tightly against his body. She looked around for Salador, but he was nowhere in sight.

"Release me," she said as fear prickled her spine.

Kane brought her captured hands up to rest on his chest, and Maleaha's eyes widened as she felt the strength in him. Raising her head, her green eyes collided with his silver eyes, and at that moment she was swept away into the depths of a silver river. Emotions such as she had never experienced came crashing to the surface. She wanted to look away but found she could not. She was aware that he had released her hands, but still she did not move. Swallowing past the lump in her throat, Maleaha felt his hands move caressingly over her back. Tiny shivers danced on her skin where his hands blazed a trail.

"You little devil, you get inside a man's mind and torment him," Kane said harshly.

Maleaha's eyes moved down to his lips, and she heard his deep intake of breath. "Please release me," she pleaded. Fear such as she had never known crept into her body. She felt weak and her stomach seemed to be tied up in knots. His hands stopped at her waist, and she felt him apply pressure, bringing her body even tighter against his. Something akin to pain, and yet not pain, wracked her body, and she melted against his hard masculine form. She tried to speak, but no words passed her lips. His handsome face seemed to loom over her and she tried to struggle, but she found she was no match for his superior strength.

"You are half-child, half-enchantress," he whispered against her ear. Maleaha felt his warm breath as it stirred her hair. Suddenly, she did not want to be free. She did not know what was happening to her, but she felt that it was something she had waited all her life for. It was as if this moment was destined to happen.

Maleaha laid her head on his shoulder and closed her eyes. This was what it felt like to love a man. She had often wondered what the love between a man and woman would be like and now she knew. It was beautiful, it was painful, but it felt so right. She seemed to fit perfectly in his arms; it was as if God had created them for each other.

"Did Mangas hold you in his arms like this?" Kane asked harshly.

It took a few seconds for his words to penetrate Maleaha's mind, and when they did, she raised her head to look into his eyes. "I do not understand," she said in total confusion.

His grip tightened as he crushed her in his arms. "It does not matter. All that matters is that you are now in *my* arms. Why should I care who has shared your favors before me. I have never demanded innocence in the women

83

I make love to.''

Maleaha pushed against his arms and stepped back. ''I am not sure I understand what you are saying to me,'' she said, hoping she had not read his meaning correctly.

''Do not play innocent with me. It does not matter that you are not a virgin. I would not be interested in you if you were.'' His voice was deep and insulting, and Maleaha felt hurt to the very depths of her being.

''I . . . I . . .''

''God,'' he cut in as he pulled her back into his arms. ''You act so pure and innocent. If I did not know better, I could almost believe you. I have never wanted a woman as much as I want you.'' He was raining kisses over her upturned face, and Maleaha fought the battle that raged inside her. His lips were making her body want to surrender, but her anger held that desire at bay.

He thought she and Mangas had spent the night together!

Maleaha pushed against him and whirled out of his arms. ''How dare you insult me! I would not let you kiss me if you were the last man on earth.''

Kane gave her a mocking smile. ''Your eyes say otherwise, as did your desirable body when I held you in my arms. What game do you play, Miss Deveraux? Do you want me to beg for your favors before you bestow them on me? I can assure you that will not happen. I could easily have a more willing partner with much less effort.''

Maleaha did not doubt his words. There must be many women who had succumbed to his charms, as she almost had a moment ago. Raising her head proudly, she gave him a scorching glare.

"You must think more of your power over women than I do, major. I believe I can just manage to save my virtue," she said insultingly.

His deep laughter made her nerve ends stand on edge. "I doubt that you have any virtue left, Miss Deveraux. How many men from the fort have sampled your charms, and how many from the Jojoba tribe, notwithstanding the chief, have you had? Do not misunderstand me, I am not condemning you, I am merely asking what difference one more would make? I can promise you pleasure," he whispered in a deep voice.

Maleaha tried to cover up her confusion. Hurt and anger once more battled for supremacy. He thought she had not only been with Mangas last night, but with many others as well. She could feel the sting of his accusations in the very depths of her heart, and the unfamiliar sting of tears just behind her eyes. She would not let him see the weakness of tears, nor would she allow him to see how much he had wounded her. Her pride came to her rescue.

"Major, you do think a great deal of your power over women! Perhaps in the past you have had many successes, but let me set you straight on one point. I will never be one of the women you love!" Her anger carried her one step farther. "You seem to think you are a gift put on this earth to please women, but I do not find you in the least to my liking."

His eyes narrowed, and the muscle in his jaw twitched. "Let me set you straight on a few points, too, Miss Deveraux. I have never loved the women I have been with, and none of them seemed to prize themselves as highly as you do. As for liking me, it is not a requirement. I only want

85

to bed you, not win your affection!''

Maleaha was at a loss for words. She had no idea what Major Benedict was talking about. She had been raised on a ranch and was not ignorant of the way baby animals were conceived, but in her wildest imaginations she could not fathom what love between a husband and wife would be like, nor had she ever given it much thought. She had always thought that one day she would fall in love and marry, but what the major was suggesting was degrading and insulting! Did he think that because she was half-Indian she was promiscuous? She was ready to set him straight when she heard Salador returning. The major, however, had not heard the quiet moccasin footsteps.

"Everything we have said to one another does not amount to anything," Kane said. "I felt you yielding in my arms a few moments ago. I have been with enough women to know when one is ripe for making love, and you, Miss Deveraux, are overripe."

Salador stepped in front of Maleaha, his hand resting lightly on the hilt of his knife. "Shall I carve this man's heart out, Maleaha? I heard the words he spoke to you. Your father would kill him if he knew of this."

Maleaha answered him in the language of the Jojoba as he had spoken to her. "Leave him alone, Salador. I will find an effective way to satisfy my honor, never doubt it. One day I will bring the proud and arrogant Major Kanen Benedict to his knees." She turned and walked to the other side of the campfire. Salador looked at the white man and then he also turned his back. Maleaha would do as she had threatened, he had no doubt. He could almost find it in him to pity the white man. Almost, but not quite.

The next morning the silence between the three weary travelers was ominous. Maleaha wanted nothing better than to reach home. She felt miserable; the last night she had hardly slept. She had been affected more deeply than she would like to admit by the cruel words Major Benedict had said to her, and this morning he had hardly acknowledged her presence. Maleaha knew that had she been white he would never have treated her in such a disrespectful manner, and her Indian blood cried out for revenge.

It was well past noon, and the heat from the sun that beat down on them was becoming unbearable. Kane unbuttoned his blue jacket, but still felt no relief. The distant mountains seemed to beckon to him with their promise of cool breezes and the shade of the pine forest.

They were riding through a canyon with small rocky hills on both sides, and Kane scanned the rocky incline. That would be a bad place to be ambushed, he thought, becoming alert. It was just at that moment that he heard a blood-curdling war whoop and realized that that was just what was about to occur.

He observed that not less than twelve Indians were bearing down on them. It flashed through Kane's mind that it would be useless to try and outride the Indians, since their horses had been ridden hard all day and would never outdistance the Indian ponies.

Kane reached for the reins of Maleaha's mount, but she whirled away from him and rode toward the hills. "Miss Deveraux!" He yelled, as a bullet whizzed past his head.

Maleaha bent low over her horse and kicked the animal

in the flanks, trying to gain more speed. She supposed that the major and Salador rode close behind her. When she reached the base of the steep hill she seemed to freeze. She knew what would happen to her if she were taken alive by the Indians, and that fear held her captive, unable to move.

Kane jumped from his saddle and lifted her to the ground. He already had his rifle in his hand, and he quickly withdrew her rifle from her saddle holster. Then he half pulled, half carried her up the hill, and when he reached the top, amid flying bullets, he pushed her down behind a huge rock and lay down on his stomach, raising his rifle to his shoulder.

Maleaha crawled over to his side, and both of them saw Salador, as he turned his horse and rode back toward the enemy.

"No!" Maleaha cried as she raised her hand in a silent plea. "No! Salador!" She would have risen but Kane pushed her roughly to the ground.

"Lie down, you little fool, do you want to be killed?"

Maleaha watched helplessly as Salador raised his rifle and fired at the oncoming Indians. Two of the Indians fell from their horses, then another, as Kane fired his rifle. Salador was now surrounded. Maleaha screamed as she saw him raise his gun to fire one last time. Another enemy fell to the ground, but Salador was mortally wounded, and Maleaha watched helplessly as he fell from his horse and the Indians trampled his body beneath their horses' hooves.

Raising her rifle, she fired, not taking aim, but firing out of grief and anger. "He sacrificed himself for me!"

she cried, blinded by tears. Suddenly her anger pushed her grief aside. She would kill the men who had taken Salador's life.

Kane aimed his rifle, and once more one of the enemy fell.

Maleaha stood up, raised her rifle to her shoulder, and took aim. The bullets were whizzing all around her, but she did not seem to take notice. Taking careful aim, she fired and was rewarded as an Indian fell from his horse.

Kane grabbed her and pulled her down beside him. ''You crazy little fool. You may not care what happens to you, but I do,'' he said angrily.

He reloaded his rifle, thinking to himself that they were fortunate—they had the advantage of the higher ground. The Indians would have to show themselves if they tried to climb the hill. Taking careful aim, Kane fired and watched as an Indian rolled to the bottom of the hill. Now there were only a few of the enemy left, and Kane began to feel they might have a chance. Whatever happened he would not let the Indians take Miss Deveraux, he thought, as he aimed and fired but missed his target. Maleaha, however, fired and hit the Indian she had been aiming for. One less to worry about, Kane thought grimly.

He checked his supply belt and cursed himself for not bringing his ammunition pouch with him. He only had two shots left and Maleaha could not have much more. Surprise and relief washed over Kane as he saw the remaining Indians mount their horses and ride away in a cloud of dust. He had not been aware that Maleaha had stood up and aimed her rifle. She fired twice in succession and two more Indians fell. Throwing her now empty gun aside, she reached for Kane's gun, but he stood up and shook his head.

"They are leaving, let it be."

"No! They killed Salador. I will kill them all," she cried.

Kane held her in his arms as she sobbed out her grief. "Hush, hush, it is all over," he said soothingly.

"I loved him and they killed him," she sobbed.

"I know, but he would not want you to cry."

"You do not understand! Salador and Lamas have lived at Deveraux Ranch since before I was born. They always looked after me and protected me. Salador is . . . was . . . I loved him."

"It would seem his last thoughts were for your safety. He knew what he was doing when he rode toward those Indians."

Maleaha wiped tears on the back of her hand and moved away from him. "You are right. Salador would not want me to cry," she said, squaring her shoulders and raising her head proudly. Kane saw her battle with the tears that were shining in her eyes.

"Those Indians were Arapaho, major. If you want proof to take back to the colonel, I suggest you look for it among their dead bodies."

Kane followed her down the hill. When he reached the bottom he began to examine the dead Indians, while Maleaha found Salador's body. It was hard to recognize Salador, he had been so badly mutilated. Maleaha picked up his knife and began digging frantically in the soft sand. She would not leave him until he had a proper burial. She felt rather than heard the major kneel down beside her. With the butt of his rifle he helped her dig the grave that would be the brave Salador's final resting place. When the hole was deep enough, Kane lifted the dead Indian in his arms and laid him in the shallow grave. Then once more working with his rifle butt, he covered the grave over with sand.

He watched as the Indian girl raised her hands to the sky and chanted some words he could not understand. Then she knelt down and clasped her hands as if she were praying. As she stood up she looked at Kane.

"What were you saying just now?" he asked softly.

"I asked the Great Spirit to accept the soul of a brave warrior."

"You believe in the Indian god?"

"I respect the Indians' belief, major, although I myself was raised as a Christian. You might find, if you took the trouble to look, that the Indian God and the one you worship are one and the same."

"I was not condemning, Miss Deveraux, merely curious."

"Did you find anything to prove it was the Arapaho who raided the ranches?" she asked, changing the subject.

"I found this silver armband with the sun and the moon carved on it. I believe it is like the one found at one of the ranches."

Maleaha took the armband from him and studied it, turning it over in her hand. "Yes, this is the symbol of the Jojoba. Very clever of the Arapaho to try and implicate the Jojoba tribe by leaving this behind as evidence. Do you believe Mangas now, major?"

"With this, and my report on what happened here today, it should not take long to place the blame where it belongs, Miss Deveraux."

"We have one problem, major. First we must find our way home. And it seems we shall have to walk, since the Arapaho have cleverly taken our horses, believing we are as good as dead without transportation and water."

Kane shoved the armband into his pocket and picked up his rifle. Looking at the grueling sun, he removed his jacket and unbuttoned his white shirt. "Shall we go, Miss Deveraux?"

CHAPTER SIX

Kane had not taken many steps when he realized the Indian girl was limping. Taking her arm, he stared down at her. "Why did you not tell me you had hurt your foot?"

"It is nothing, I can manage."

He shifted his rifle to his other shoulder and took her arm. "Lean on me for support, Miss Deveraux. Try not to put too much weight on your injured foot." Kane put his arm around her waist, lending her his support.

They were making slow progress as Maleaha tried to keep up with Kane's long strides. She did not want him to know just how painful her ankle was, knowing they must put as much distance between themselves and the Arapaho as they could before nightfall. She did not really expect them to return, but it never paid to underestimate one's enemy.

Maleaha stumbled and would have fallen if Kane's strong arms had not been supporting her. Kane was beginning to suspect that her injury was much worse than she would have him believe, so he swung her up into his arms, over her loud protest, and carried her as easily as if she weighed nothing.

"I will do the walking for both of us," he told her.

Maleaha put her arms around his neck and rested her head against his shoulder. She could hear the steady drumming of his heart as she closed her eyes. How right it felt to be in his arms. She loved the feel of his soft white shirt against her cheek.

She had felt pride in him today. He had been fearless as he took charge against the Arapaho, and she herself had felt little fear because he had given her courage as they faced death together. Maleaha knew that if it had not been for his quick thinking and bravery she would, at this very moment, be just as dead as Salador.

Together they had faced overwhelming odds, and together they had won. Of course Maleaha knew they would not have stood a chance had it not been for Salador's sacrifice. He had bought them enough time to get to safety, and by doing so he had lost his life. Maleaha felt a great emptiness inside her knowing how much she would miss Salador. She had always accepted his presence as a fact of life, but until today she had not known how much he loved her.

Maleaha felt the major's eyes on her face and she looked up at him. "You were very brave today, Miss Deveraux. I do not know of any other girl who would have reacted as well as you did under the circumstances."

Maleaha was pleased at his praise of her. "I was just thinking how well you performed under danger, major."

"Coming from you, I consider that high praise indeed. Do you think the Arapahos will return to search for us?"

"I do not think so, but it would not do to let our guard

down. Most probably they think we do not stand a chance of surviving without our horses and water.''

Kane could feel the afternoon sun beating down on him. There was no breeze, no shade, nothing to shelter them from the heat. He looked down at the girl he carried in his arms. Her face was the lovliest he had ever seen, and she seemed almost childlike at the moment, depending on him because she could not walk.

Kane felt his body come to life and he tried to beat down the desire he was feeling for her at the moment. He doubted he would feel so drawn to her if they were not alone and dependent on each other for survival.

He smiled down at her and she gave him just the slightest smile in return. There was no sense fooling himself, he had wanted her ever since he first saw her at the fort. Although he had fought against his desire for her, he knew he had never been moved by any other woman as he was by her. Perhaps it was because she was so different from anyone he had known before. He tried to picture Lucinda under these same circumstances, or any of the other ladies he was acquainted with. He frowned. It was not really fair to compare Miss Deveraux with the gentle-bred ladies he knew. It would be just as difficult for her to function in an environment where women wore silk gowns and knew all the niceties of life as it would be for them to function in her uncivilized world.

''Major, if you will make for those pine trees you can see off to your left, you will find a stream where we can rest and refresh ourselves.''

Seeing the mountains in the distance, Kane shifted her weight and walked purposefully toward them.

"If I am too heavy, I believe I can walk now, if you put me down."

"Nonsense! You hardly weigh anything."

Maleaha observed his face through half-veiled eyes. She could see the black stubble that indicated that he needed a shave. His chin was firm and stubborn, hinting that he would always want his own way in everything. His lips were full, and Maleaha turned her face against his shoulder as she wondered what it would be like to be kissed by him.

When she looked up at him, she saw mockery in his silvery eyes, as if he had read her thoughts and was amused by them, and she drew in her breath as his eyes moved to her lips.

"Please put me down. I can walk now," she said through stiff lips.

"Why do you have to be so damn beautiful? I have been having some unconventional thoughts where you are concerned," he ground out.

Maleaha was incapable of answering as she felt herself drawn under his spell, and in her innocence she did not really understand the full extent of his meaning.

Was he going to kiss her, she wondered, as his lips drew closer to hers, and against her will, her lips parted in silent invitation.

"Oh no, you little enchantress, I will not fall under your spell. Are you not satisfied with all the hearts you must have extracted from others? Must you have mine to add to that number? Kane asked her mockingly.

"I was not aware that you had a heart," she snapped, angered by his statement.

"You are right. I do not have a heart. But I am a man, and I can feel the pull of your charms. Mangas must have enjoyed you last night. I am surprised he would let you go so easily."

By now they had reached the shelter of the tall pine trees, and Maleaha tried to squirm out of his arms, not understanding the harshness of his tone nor the meaning of his words. "I am very fond of Mangas, you know that."

"Obviously," he drawled, setting her on her feet to end her struggling.

When Maleaha's injured foot touched the ground, she bit her lip to keep from crying out in pain. She hobbled down to the stream, went down on her knees, and buried her face in the cool water. She then cupped her hands and drank deeply of the refreshing water, aware that the major was doing likewise.

Maleaha lay back on the cool grass, allowing the soft breeze to cool her overheated body.

Kane was lying beside her, and she turned her head to look at him. "Major, the Kincade ranch is no more than ten miles from here. I could give you directions, and you could be there before midnight if you were to leave right now."

"Are you suggesting that I leave you behind?"

"Yes, I would only slow you down. You could send someone back for me when you arrive. It is most important that you inform the colonel about the Arapahos as soon as possible."

"I have no intention of leaving you behind. We started out together; we will stay together until we reach our destination.''

"You do not need to concern yourself about me; I can take care of myself.''

"When I leave, Miss Deveraux, you will leave with me!'' he said in a tone of voice that showed he would not be swayed by her and that dared her to disagree with him.

"Let me have a look at your ankle,'' he said, sitting up and taking her injured foot in his hand. Before she could protest, he had shoved her doeskin dress up and was unlacing her moccasin.

Kane's eyes traveled over her long, shapely leg to her delicately arched foot. Seeing that her ankle was red and swollen, he frowned. "This is much worse than I thought. When did you injure it?''

"When we were climbing the hill trying to get away from the Arapaho.''

He lifted her in his arms, carried her to the stream, and plunged her foot into the water. "I am angry that you did not tell me how badly your ankle was hurt. Did you think to impress me by being a martyr? I can assure you that ploy will not work on me.''

"I do not have the slightest idea what you are talking about! I did not tell you about my ankle because it was none of your business,'' she told him haughtily. "I pity you, major. You always seem to look for the worst in people. Does it disappoint you that I had no motive in mind when I did not tell you about my injury? I simply did not think it concerned you.''

"If I look for the worst in people as you say, I have rarely been disappointed, especially where females are concerned.''

Maleaha was angered by his assessment, as well as by his degree of sarcasm. "Poor Major Benedict, have you been sorely used by the ladies?" she said through clenched teeth.

"You should not put any weight on that foot for a few days." Kane said, ignoring her outburst.

Maleaha leaned back on the grass and rested her head against her folded arms while her foot dangled in the water, bringing relief to the throbbing ankle. She sighed, wondering what there was about the major that both drew her to him and pushed her away at the same time. There had been sparks between them ever since they had met. She decided not to think about it, afraid to examine her feelings too closely, concentrating instead on what they could eat. She felt almost weak from hunger.

"Major, if you will notice the trees off to your left— they are called piñon trees. The nuts that grow on that tree are edible and very tasty. While they will not fill us up, it will take the edge off our hunger. We don't have the ammunition to hunt game, and even if we had meat we could not chance lighting a fire."

Kane stood up angrily. Once again she was taking charge, but he had to admit grudgingly that what she said was logical, and that did not help his temper any as he gathered the nuts from the piñon trees.

Kane and Maleaha ate the nuts, and to his surprise they were indeed quite good.

After they had eaten, Kane decided that they would rest by the stream for the night and get a fresh start in the morning. They were both lying on the grass, feeling relaxed.

"Major, the Jojobas have a saying about the piñon nut. They say if a man had to live on nothing but the piñon nut, he would continuously be shelling the nut, deriving only enough strength from eating it to continue shelling it, to continue eating it."

"I fail to see the point of your story," he said, propping his head on his hand and looking at her with a bemused expression on his face.

Maleaha laughed delightedly. "Perhaps one must be an Indian to understand the humor of it."

Kane watched as she stood up and waded into the stream. When she reached the deepest point she disappeared beneath the water. Holding his breath, he waited for her to surface, and when she did it was some twenty yards downstream. He watched as she swam gracefully through the water, and he had a sudden urge to dive into the water and swim over to her.

Kane removed his boots and walked slowly into the stream. With a few powerful strokes he reached her in no time.

Maleaha seemed unable to move as his arms went around her waist, pulling her to him. Her green eyes fused with his silver ones and she felt them both sink beneath the surface.

His lips found hers and they were locked in a stormy embrace. Maleaha's arms were around his neck, and as she pressed her body close to his a feeling of drowning washed over her, although she knew instinctively that he would not allow her to drown.

She was aware that they had surfaced, but he did not release her lips, and she clung to him as if he were her lifeline. All her young girl fantasies were realized in his hungry possession of her lips. Love that she had dreamed of finding with the right man had come upon her unaware, and from the most unlikely source.

"Oh God, I have wanted to do that for so long," he murmured in her ear.

Maleaha felt him swimming toward the shore, and she laid her head against his chest, too overcome with feelings to speak. She could hear his heart drumming beneath her ear, and she thought surely he must feel as she did.

When they reached the bank Kane lifted her into his arms and laid her down on the grassy slope. His silver eyes held her spellbound as his lips moved over her satiny skin. Maleaha had never been kissed before, and she thought how right it was that he should be the first to kiss her.

"Where did you learn to swim?" He asked against her lips. Not that he cared what she would answer at the moment, it was just something that had popped into his mind, because he had never known a girl who could swim.

"Mangas taught me," she whispered.

Kane's hand tightened on her shoulder and his eyes darkened. "I should have known. What else did he teach you?" he asked her as his lips came down roughly on hers. He felt himself burning with jealousy at the thought of her in Mangas's arms, or any other man's, for that matter.

Maleaha's lips parted beneath his hard, demanding mouth, and she was overcome by the beauty of his kiss, for it was indeed beautiful. This new feeling was love—

love that he had forced her to feel almost against her will.

"You are a desirable little savage," he said as he rained kisses over her face. Kane's body had never felt so alive. It was as if every fiber of his being was attuned to the soft body he held in his arms. Raising his head, he stared down at her. Her face held a glow, and her lips were soft from his kisses. her black hair was still wet and it clung to her head like ebony velvet. Her green eyes were drawing him to her, almost against his will.

Kane laid his rough face against her smooth skin, and he knew at that moment that possessing her body only once would be to glimpse heaven and then be cast back to earth. He was surprised to find that he wanted more from her than just this one night. But what?

He ran his hand over her body and felt the wet buckskin that clung to her beautiful, slim body. It flashed through his mind that she had not uttered a word, but the look in her eyes spoke volumes.

He looked at her in puzzlement for a moment. What was it he sensed about her—youthful innocence? He shook his head to clear it, She was weaving a spell around him, and it flashed through his mind that he was in deep danger. But why?

Maleaha felt the uncertainty in him and wondered at its cause. Surely he felt as she did.

The sun had set, and the wind in the pines was singing its age-old song as Kane reached to the far recesses of his mind, trying to find answers for his confusion. Against his will his arms went around Maleaha and he drew her tightly into his arms. At last he found the answer he had been searching for. He wanted to possess her, not just tonight, but for many nights. It did not matter if she had been with many men before him. She would belong to him, and he would not allow her to continue with her permissive ways. He wanted to make sure that in the future he would be the only man in her life.

Maleaha felt his rough cheek against her face, and tiny shivers of delight ran through her body.

"I find you fascinating, little Indian."

"I thought you did not like me very well."

His lips were blazing a trail down her throat. "I fear my problem is that I like you too well. You are so lovely," he whispered.

Maleaha felt the first stirrings of womanhood coming to life within her body. Her arms went around his neck as his warm breath teased her lips.

"I think I have wanted to kiss you almost from the first moment I saw you," he told her just before his lips covered hers in a soft kiss. Maleaha felt as if a thousand stars exploded within her body as his kiss deepened and became more demanding.

"You stir a man's blood to the boiling point, little Indian," he whispered against her soft lips. "I want to make love to you. It matters but little how many men have known you before me. I only know I have to have you or go slowly out of my mind," Kane said harshly.

Maleaha was confused. Why did he think that she had kissed other men before him? She wanted to tell him that he was the first man she had ever allowed to take such liberties, but she was unable to speak as his lips prevented it with a kiss so demanding that she moaned deep within her throat.

Maleaha felt love so beautiful, so tender, that she wanted to share it with the whole world. Did he feel it too, she wondered? Surely he must, she thought. How could he not? It did not matter that since she had met him he had goaded her into anger and had insulted her at every turn. Nothing mattered but that he loved her and she loved him.

"This is a perfect spot for making love," he said in a passionate voice.

Maleaha felt his hands glide caressingly over her stomach then move upward to rest lightly against her breasts. She gasped as his lips took possession of hers, rendering her his willing slave. It seemed she could feel the heat of his hands through her deerskin dress, and the ground she lay on seemed to rock beneath her.

Kane's hands trembled as they moved over her soft curves. No, it did not matter, he told himself, that he was not the first man to sample her beautiful body. Yet he could not stop the nagging thought that he did mind. She belonged to him, and he was being haunted by the thought that others had had her before him. He drew away from her and studied her upturned face, thinking that he must make a commitment to her, and extract one from her, as well.

"Darling, I want you to know that I want more from you than just this one night. I want you to be with me for a long time to come. Do you understand?"

Maleaha shook her head, not understanding him in the least. Was he asking her to become his wife? There was a lump forming in her throat at the thought, and she found she could not speak.

Kane's voice was deep and soft as he touched her face gently, "I will buy you a house in Santa Fe, and see that you want for nothing. I will dress you in silks and satins, and all the men will know that you belong to me, and will keep their distance."

Maleaha frowned. What men was he referring to? She was about to ask him, when he continued speaking. "I will spend all of my free time with you, and since I do not ever intend to marry, we will have many years in which to love and get to know one another."

Maleaha stiffened and her heart felt as if it had been ripped to shreds. He was not asking her to be his wife, he was asking her to live with him without benefit of marriage. She closed her eyes, hoping the tears that were in her heart did not reach her eyes. She was glad when she spoke that her voice did not reveal how badly he had hurt her, for it sounded calm, even to her ears. "You do not want to marry me, major?"

He smiled at her indulgently. "No. I would not marry you, but you need never worry, I would not seek out other women as long as you were waiting for me. I became bored with all the women who have paraded through my life lately, but nothing about you bores me."

Maleaha wanted to slap the smile from his face. Rarely, if ever, had she known such anger and humiliation. Inside she raged over the tender feelings she had felt for him only moments before. She swallowed her anger, thinking she would see just how far he would go in his bold request.

"How would I know I could trust you? Perhaps you would soon tire of me and want to replace me with another.''

He smiled. "How can I be sure you will keep all your kisses for me alone? We shall just have to trust each other, will we not? I intend to keep you so happy you will not need to seek elsewhere for pleasure.''

"Why do you wish never to marry?" Maleaha asked between clenched teeth.

He looked at her with a serious expression on his face. "I must be honest with you so you cannot say later that I did not make our relationship clear. I believe in total honesty.'' He paused, wondering how to answer her. "You and I come from two different worlds, darling. You would never fit into my world and I am sure you realize that I would not fit into yours. But there is no reason why we cannot be lovers.''

"You are saying because I am part Indian that you would never marry me?''

"Partly. I suppose if I am going to be completely honest with you, I must tell you I would never marry someone who has shared her favors with half the territory of New Mexico, if I am to believe what I have observed about you to be correct.''

Maleaha's anger sparked higher, but the Indian in her remained calm, knowing she would soon set him in his place. What did he mean? She had never shared her favors with other men! Why could he not realize that he was the first man she had ever kissed? She felt his hand move up her arm and wanted to push it away, but not yet, not yet.

"Suppose there should be a child from our . . . relationship?" she asked, knowing what his answer would be before he voiced it. With each passing moment she seemed to die a little more inside.

Kane's voice took on a hard tone, and he gripped her arm firmly. "I have not thought that far ahead, but obviously you have. Don't think you could ever trap me into marriage by having my child, for I assure you, I will never marry you."

Maleaha sat up slowly, "It surprises me that you would think I would want to be your mistress, major. As for the nice house and the silk gowns, I would much prefer my buckskin dress to all the white ladies' trappings. What would an Indian such as I want with such finery?"

"I will not share you with anyone else. You can dress as you please, but you will tell all other men that you are mine exclusively," he said, completely misunderstanding her meaning.

Maleaha stood up to her full height and looked down at him, "You will never have any part of me, major." She ran her hands through her tousled hair, thinking how close she had come to giving herself to this hateful man. The newfound love she had felt for him moments before began to die a slow death, replaced with loathing and contempt.

He jumped to his feet and stood over her with an ominous glint in his eyes. "You little tart. Damn you for the slut you are. You teased me until I am half out of my mind wanting you, and now you think you can just walk away."

"Hobble away would be more accurate, major," she told him as she turned away from him angrily.

Kane grabbed her by the shoulders and drew her into

his arms, Maleaha tried to pull away from him as his lips crushed hers with a punishing force. She moved her head from side to side, but his hand went up to hold her face immobile. She bit his lip, hoping to gain her freedom.

"Damn! You uncivilized little wildcat," he said, raising his head and wiping his own blood from his mouth with one hand, while he restrained her with the other. Maleaha saw the passion that blazed in his silver eyes and feared what he might do.

"Re . . . release me," she said in a trembling voice.

"And if I refuse?" he asked as his grip tightened on her, pulling her into his arms once more.

"Reconsider, major," she said as she slipped the knife from where she kept it about her waist and pressed the point of it against his back.

In one quick motion he spun her around, grabbing the hand that held the knife and taking it from her with very little effort.

"Never draw a knife on me again, Miss Deveraux, unless you are prepared to use it. In the future it might be well for you to consider that. A simple 'no' would have sufficed."

"You left me little choice," she said, rubbing her sore wrist and wishing for the moment that she had plunged the knife into him when she had the chance.

Kane shoved her away from him angrily. "Consider the offer retracted. I must have been too long in the sun to ever have thought I wanted you," he told her bitterly. "Get some sleep; you will need all of your strength tomorrow."

"You still insist on taking me with you?"

"Yes, I insist," he said, lying down and turning his back to her.

"Can I have my knife back?"

"Why, so you can stab me in the back while I sleep?"

"No, it was Salador's knife. I want to keep it."

Kane turned over to face her and watched as she sank down on the grass and buried her head in her hands, appearing very young and vulnerable.

Suddenly Kane felt protective toward her. He remembered how young she was, and all that she had been through that day. Perhaps he had been a bit hasty in offering to make her his mistress so soon after she had lost the old Indian she seemed to care so much about. Maybe if he had waited until some future time she would have been more receptive to his offer.

"Was the Indian—Salador—a relative of yours, Miss Deveraux?" he asked, hoping to bridge the gap he felt yawning between them.

Maleaha raised her head and looked at him, dumbfounded at how quickly he could switch from adoring lover to polite stranger. She would show him that she had also forgotten what had transpired between them, for the moment. Later she would have her revenge.

"No. Salador and Lamas were sent by my grandfather, who was chief of the Jojobas, to look after my mother when she married my father and moved to Deveraux Ranch. After my mother's death they both stayed on to look after me."

"You loved that old Indian, did you not?"

"Yes, the one thing that stands out most in my mind about Salador happened when I was five years old. My

109

grandfather had given me a new horse, not a pony but a pinto mare. I couldn't wait to ride her, so I pestered Salador until he took me out to the barn where we kept her. Salador lifted me into the saddle, and before I was seated properly, I was thrown to the ground." A long pause followed, as if she were remembering.

"What happened then?" He asked.

"I . . . I began to cry, and I told Salador I would never ride that horse again. He knelt down beside me, so he would be the same height as me, and wiped the dirt and tears from my face. I expected sympathy from him, but instead he frowned at me. 'Humans are different from animals,' he said. 'Man was put on earth to be the master over all the animal kingdom, yet today you have shamed me. You let the horse be the master of you.' I remember feeling very ashamed at the time. 'What shall I do, Salador?' I asked. He stood up, gathered up the reins and handed them to me. 'You must be the master of this animal,' he told me. I somehow managed to climb astride that horse without his help, and to my surprise and relief, I rode her. Since that day no horse has thrown me, though a few have tried."

"I think he was a little harsh with you. After all, you were a little girl," Kane said, thinking how differently he had been brought up. There had been no one to guide him; he had been forced to find his own way.

"Perhap, but it was a lesson I never forgot."

Kane looked at the star-studded night through the top of the tall pine trees and felt a loneliness that he could not define. He knew that tomorrow he would be back at the fort and would probably never see the Indian girl again.

Somehow that thought bothered him more than a little. Closing his eyes, he thought he would apologize to her tomorrow. Perhaps he had been too harsh with her tonight. She was little more than a child, and maybe she had never had any man offer to make her his mistress before. Maybe she did not want anything permanent, he thought as he drifted off to sleep. His last thoughts were troubled. Why would an Indian girl refuse the offer of a house of her own and all the beautiful gowns she could want?

Maleaha lay down and rested her head against her arms. Her heart felt battered and bruised. She would never see Salador again, and she had loved him so much. In the space of one day she had found love and lost it. It had not died on its own, it had been killed by harsh words and hateful accusations. What had she done that he would think he could make her his mistress? She knew the answer even as she asked the question. It was because she was an Indian, and he did not have any respect for Indians.

Maleaha raised her head and saw that the major was sleeping. She would have her revenge. His insults to her would not go unpunished, she vowed. She was so weary, but her ankle was hurting her, making it impossible to sleep. Her mind reached back to her childhood, to the time when Salador, along with Lamas, had been her constant companion. Tears of grief blinded her as she wept silently. A Jojoba maiden was not supposed to cry, but perhaps just this once she could be forgiven.

CHAPTER SEVEN

The next morning when Kane awoke, Maleaha was lacing up her moccasins. She did not seem inclined to speak to him, so he in turn decided to ignore her. He walked down to the stream and washed his face, then took a deep drink, thinking it would likely be the last water he would taste until they reached the Kincade ranch.

Maleaha stood, watching him silently. She wished that her ankle was not so painful and she would not have to rely on his support to walk. She considered refusing to go with him, but she knew he would only force her if she voiced her thoughts.

Kane walked back to her and offered her his arm for support. She would have liked nothing better than to refuse, but now was not the time to act childish, and she knew it would only serve to amuse him anyway.

She rested her hand on his arm and limped along beside him.

Kane smiled down at her, knowing what she was feeling, and he could not resist goading her further.

"If you would ask it of me, I could be persuaded to carry you, as I did yesterday."

"Not a chance, major. I will walk, thank you all the same."

He smiled inwardly, knowing she would not be able to walk the ten miles, but he would wait until she asked for his help.

He watched her out of the corner of his eye. She tried to walk without limping, but he saw the pain on her face, even though she tried to hide it from him. She stumbled and would have fallen, but he steadied her, and was rewarded with a haughty glance for his trouble.

As they walked along her footsteps grew slower, and he could tell she was in great pain as her grip tightened on his arm.

He swung her into his arms, and when she tried to protest he silenced her with a glance.

"You would kill yourself rather than ask me for help. What a proud little witch you are." The way he said it left no doubt; he had not meant it as a compliment.

At first Maleaha tried to hold herself rigid, but soon she began to relax against him. "You will not be able to carry me the whole way, major," she taunted.

"When I become tired I will merely sit down and rest. Any objections?"

"It will take all day to reach the Kincades' at this pace."

"So be it. Now, will you try to remain silent?" he demanded.

It was late afternoon when they first sighted the Kincade ranch house. Maleaha knew the major was exhausted from carrying her, and she was able to derive some pleasure from that thought. He climbed the steps and set her down on the front porch.

Mrs. Kincade had been looking out the kitchen window, and she came out on the porch with a frown on her face.

"My dear, what has happened to you?" she said with a worried look on her face.

"We were attacked by the Arapaho, Mrs. Kincade. They killed Salador, and took our horses. I am afraid I have injured my ankle."

The older woman put her arms around Maleaha. "Oh honey, I am so sorry. I know how much you loved that old Indian, as we all did." Her voice was full of pity as she tried to console Maleaha.

"Forgive my bad manners, Mrs. Kincade," Maleaha said, quickly changing the subject, afraid she would break down in front of the major. "This is Major Benedict. Major, Mrs. Kincade."

Mrs. Kincade's face was grim as she nodded to the major. "How do you do, Major Benedict. Come into the house and I will fix you something to eat. You must be starved."

Kane bowed politely to Mrs. Kincade. "It is a pleasure to meet you, ma'am, and I would surely appreciate something to eat."

The older woman helped Maleaha walk into the house and gave her a look that showed she knew the sorrow she was feeling.

"I do not want anything to eat," Maleaha said. "I will just say hello to Betsy and borrow her horse, if I may."

At that moment Betsy entered the room, and, seeing her best friend, flew across the room and threw her arms around her. "What has happened to you? You look awful!" Betsy said, looking from Maleaha to the handsome officer.

"I will tell you all about it later, but for now I would like to introduce you to Major Benedict. Major, Betsy Kincade."

Kane nodded at the pretty blue-eyed blonde and gave her his most charming smile. "It is an honor to meet you, Miss Kincade," he said politely.

Maleaha bristled, remembering how differently he had reacted when he was introduced to her at the fort.

Mr. Kincade entered the room, and while his wife presented him to the major, Maleaha turned to Betsy. "Help me to your room and I will tell you all that has occurred, Betsy."

When they reached Betsy's bedroom, Betsy helped Maleaha sit down in a chair and looked at her. "That is the most handsome man I have ever seen! If I were not in love with Bob I swear I would have swooned at his feet," Betsy exclaimed.

Maleaha put her foot on the floor and felt pain shoot through her ankle. "You are welcome to him, as far as I am concerned, Betsy."

Betsy looked at Maleaha, whom she loved as she would a sister. They had gone to finishing school together in Boston. In fact, Maleaha's father had paid for Betsy to go since her parents did not have the money to send her. Last summer Maleaha's father had taken both girls to Europe with him. Betsy's folks were not very well off and Jonas Deveraux was a very wealthy man, but it did not affect the two girls' friendship; they had been best friends since childhood.

Maleaha loved to visit the Kincade ranch, Betsy's father was always laughing and jolly, and her mother had taken Maleaha under her wing when Maleaha's own mother was killed. She was a tiny blonde-headed woman whose face showed the rough life she had led helping her husband make a home in the wild untamed land that was New Mexico. Mrs. Kincade always had a smile on her face, and she loved to mother the motherless Maleaha.

Betsy smiled at Maleaha. "Why do I get the feeling that you do not like Major Benedict?"

Maleaha frowned, "Because I do not like Major Benedict!"

"Why ever not?"

"Do you know what he asked me?" Maleaha said, knowing she could tell Betsy anything and it would not be repeated.

Betsy shook her head, "No, tell me."

Maleaha fixed her eyes on Betsy's face as she spoke angrily, "Major Benedict asked me to become his mistress!"

Betsy gasped, and her hand flew to her mouth. "You must be mistaken. No man would ever dare ask you such a thing."

"He thinks me a savage, an Indian, and not worthy to be his wife, but he offered to buy me a house in Santa Fe," Maleaha said. The hurt she had felt crept into her voice, and although Betsy had never seen her best friend cry, she thought she detected tears in her eyes now.

"What made him think he could make such an offer to you?" Betsy said, her blue eyes flashing angrily.

"I let him kiss me," Maleaha said, trying to understand herself why he had made such a degrading offer to her.

"That was no reason for him to insult you. I have a good mind to march right out there and give him a piece of my mind."

"Do not worry, Betsy, I will see the day when the arrogant, pompous, major will beg for my forgiveness."

"Doesn't he know who you are?"

"He knows I am Jonas Deveraux's daughter, but he thinks of me as a lowly Indian, unworthy of him."

Maleaha told Betsy all that had occurred since she had left the fort. Betsy cried for Salador, and when she could stem the flow of tears, she looked at Maleaha. "Do you think the major will be attending the Grand Ball in two weeks?"

"I don't know. Why do you ask?"

"Because, you silly goose, at the Grand Ball you will be sought after by every eligible gentleman who attends. What better way to show the major what a grave mistake he made."

Maleaha smiled, "You are right. How sweet will be my revenge when I show him up to be a fool."

"I will do everything in my power to help you. You can count on me," Betsy said loyally.

"Betsy, tell no one about this. I would be so humiliated if anyone found out."

"Wild horses could not drag it out of me," Betsy said with conviction, and Maleaha knew from long experience that her friend could be trusted to keep her word.

"I want to borrow your horse, Betsy, and let me out the back door. I want to be gone before the major realizes I have left."

Major Kanen Benedict rode to the fort on his borrowed horse. He was still angry at the way Miss Deveraux had ridden away without informing him. It seemed strange without her by his side. He supposed he had grown used to having her with him. They had shared much since they had started out to find Mangas. Kane realized that she was angry with him, but that did not give her the right to leave without telling him good-bye. It had been damned awkward when the Kincade girl had told him that Miss Deveraux had left without a word to him.

Strange, he thought, he did not even know her first name. He had either called her Miss Deveraux or thought of her as the Indian girl. They had been together for days, and faced danger together, and he had held her in his arms, yet he did not even know her name.

A deep loneliness descended upon Kane as he spurred his borrowed mount to a faster pace. He doubted that his path would ever cross Miss Deveraux's again. He frowned. The thought of never seeing her again left him feeling sadly empty. He pushed all thoughts of her aside and concentrated on what he had to tell the colonel.

It was late evening when Kane finally rode through the gates of the fort. He went directly to Colonel Johnson's office and presented him with the evidence, in the form of the armband, and told him all that had occurred, with the exception of what had transpired personally between him and the Indian girl.

The colonel nodded his approval. "I want to commend you, major, on a job well done. Now that we know for sure who is responsible for the raids, we can be on our guard."

"Colonel Johnson, did you send soldiers out to try and follow us to Mangas's camp?" Kane asked, although he already knew the answer.

The colonel grinned broadly. "Yes, although I knew that Jonas Deveraux's daughter would soon discover she was being followed. It was a long shot, and it failed, as I was sure it would. She is a shrewd little lady; it must be her Indian blood."

"Yes, she deserves all the credit, sir. Without her help I would never have found Mangas."

"I know, my boy. You do not need to tell me about her; all of Santa Fe knows about her."

Kane wanted to ask what all Santa Fe knew about Miss Deveraux, but he didn't ask, fearing to hear about her promiscuous nature.

A few days later, Jonas returned to Deveraux Ranch. When Maleaha told him all that had happened while he had been away, omitting only the personal things that had taken place between her and Major Benedict, he was very angry for the space of one whole day. Then he quickly forgave her, knowing he could never be angry with her for long. He even admitted, grudgingly, that she had been right about Mangas.

Maleaha's ankle healed under the tender care of Margaretta, but the sadness in her heart at the loss of Salador did not heal. Nor did her need to avenge herself against Major Kanen Benedict grow any less. She counted the days until she could show him she was not the nobody he thought her to be. She was Maleaha Deveraux, daughter of Jonas Deveraux, respected and liked by all of Santa Fe. He would soon learn what a mistake he had made. She smiled, thinking how sweet would be her revenge.

The Grand Ball was the social event of the season. Invitations were coveted, but only the most socially prominent were invited. Included in that number, were the officers from the fort and their ladies.

Maleaha had chosen her gown with great care. She wanted to look every bit the young society miss. Her gown was made of white silk, and was very plain. It came down in a vee in front and rested on the edge of her shoulders with tiny puffed sleeves. It fit snugly around her tiny waist and flowed into a soft bustle at the back. Her matching shoes were of white satin. The whiteness of her gown complimented her lovely golden-colored skin. Her hair was pulled away from her face with an emerald and diamond clip and fell down her back to her waist. The only other jewelry she wore was a huge diamond and emerald pendant on a long chain. Slipping on her white elbow-length gloves, she surveyed her image in the full-length mirror.

"What do you think, Betsy, do I look all right?"

"You are lovely, Maleaha. I would be jealous of you if I did not love you so much."

Maleaha smiled at her best friend, who was dressed in yards and yards of pink lace, looking blonde and beautiful.

"You have nothing to worry about. I wish I had your lovely complexion and beautiful face."

"La, you silly goose. No one would notice me with you in the room, except maybe Bob. Speaking of Bob, he will be downstairs pacing the floor. Shall we go on ahead, and I will lay the groundwork? Do not forget, make some excuse to your father so you can arrive late."

"Do you think he will be there?"

Betsy knew who Maleaha meant. "I made sure he received an invitation; now don't fret, just remember, after tonight revenge will be yours."

Maleaha had received many invitations to attend the ball from a number of young men, but she had turned them all down, wanting to go with her father. She did not want to be with any one man that night. She wanted to be free to dance with everyone.

Kane stood beside the punchbowl, surveying the many beautiful young ladies who danced by in the arms of their well-dressed gentlemen friends. He had danced with many of the young ladies himself, but he was feeling bored and restless. He wondered why he had bothered to come tonight. He was considering returning to the fort when he saw a familiar face. The girl had just entered the ballroom escorted by a redheaded man. Betsy took Bob's arm and led him across the room to where Kanen Benedict stood. After introducing the two men, she looked about her, waiting for some of the gentlemen present to approach her and ask her where Maleaha was, for she knew it was bound to happen, as it always had.

"Tell me, Miss Kincade, have you seen Miss Deveraux lately?" Kane asked.

"Yes, major, as a matter of fact I saw her only tonight."

"Is she faring well?"

Before Betsy could answer, she saw Vernon Cribbs approaching. She knew he would ask her about Maleaha, and she was not mistaken.

"Betsy, have you seen Maleaha? I was told she would be here tonight," the handsome sandy-haired man asked.

"Oh yes, she will be here. I have it on good authority."

"I have not seen her since you two returned from that fancy school in Boston. I have called at the ranch several times but she was never at home."

Just then Trace Blackwell approached Betsy. "Is Maleaha coming tonight? I have been watching the door, hoping to be the first one to see her."

"She is not here yet, Trace, but she will be, have patience," Betsy said, beginning to enjoy herself. "Why do you not dance with some of the other young ladies, Trace?" Betsy asked him.

"Not on your life, I want to dance with Maleaha. Lord, it has been a long time since I have seen her."

Just then they were approached by a third man. "Betsy, where is Maleaha? Isn't she coming?"

"She will be here, Bill, just have patience," she answered smiling delightedly.

Kane was curious. "Who is this Maleaha, Miss Kincade?"

"Oh, I am sure you know Maleaha, major. Everyone knows her." Betsy was hardly able to suppress the giggle she felt rising in her throat.

"No, I have never met her. What is so special about her?"

"Here comes Frank Taylor, let us ask him what is so special about Maleaha." Betsy said, smiling.

"Betsy, have you seen Maleaha?" Frank asked.

"She will be here, Frank. Would you answer something for the major here, Frank? He wants to know what's so special about Maleaha."

Betsy could have chosen no one better than Frank Taylor to ask. He had been half in love with Maleaha for years.

"What's so special about Maleaha? Good Lord, you could never have met her, or you would not have to ask. It's more than the fact that she is the most beautiful, most graceful, kindest, most sought-after young lady in the New Mexico territory. It does not matter that her father is the richest man in the state. Maleaha—is Maleaha."

"I would like to meet this paragon of beauty," Kane said, half serious, half amused.

"Now is your chance, major. I believe Maleaha has just arrived." Betsy was looking toward the entrance of the ballroom.

Kane's eyes switched to the entrance and rested on the lovely vision on the arm of Jonas Deveraux. It seemed the whole room became silent as Maleaha raised her head and smiled at Betsy, ever so slightly.

Kane's eyes widened as he recognized the lovely vision in white. Maleaha. Maleaha Deveraux!

Maleaha was instantly surrounded by half a dozen gentlemen, and Kane heard her laughter as she spoke to each of them in turn. Surely he was mistaken! His face lost its color as the full impact of the situation hit him. God, what a fool he was. His eyes followed her as she walked gracefully down the three steps that took her to the dance floor. Apparently she had turned down the other gentlemen in favor of first dancing with her father. His eyes followed her around the room. Kane wondered how long he had been staring at Maleaha, and he turned to Miss Kincade.

"I don't understand."

"What is it that you do not understand, major?"

"Maleaha is Miss Deveraux!"

"Perhaps I can enlighten you, major. Maleaha is my best friend, and as you know, she is the daughter of Jonas Deveraux. She is the most sought-after young lady in the New Mexico territory, as you heard. She went away to finishing school with me, to Boston, at the request of her father. She has also been to England and France. There is not a man here tonight, with the exception of my Bob, who isn't half in love with her. She has received so many proposals of marriage, I'm sure she lost count long ago, but then, she is only seventeen. I am sure there will be more, as she grows older. She can outride and outshoot most men, but I am sure you already know that. She teaches at the Indian mission twice a week, and there has never been the slightest bit of scandal attached to her good name. We all love Maleaha, major, and would no take kindly to anyone who hurt her.''

Kanen's eyes narrowed, ''She told you about me?'' he asked pointedly.

''Major, Maleaha and I have no secrets from one another. As I stated earlier, she is my best friend. You hurt her very badly, and there is not a gentleman here tonight who would not shoot you on sight if they knew how you had insulted Maleaha. The best thing you can do is stay away from her in the future.'' With that Betsy Kincad moved away from him on the arm of her future husband, Bob, who was looking puzzled.

''What was that all about, Bets?''

''Nothing, just settling a score for Maleaha,'' she said as Bob swung her onto the dance floor.

Kane's eyes followed Maleaha around the dance floor as she changed partners many times. She was so graceful and her white gown swirled about her as she danced across the room. Her laughter drifted back to him and he clenched and unclenched his fists. Lord, she must hate him, he thought. He had decided he would leave, rather than face her, when he felt a tap on his shoulder.

''Major Benedict, I believe,'' Jonas Deveraux said.

Kane turned to face the older man, thinking how out of place he looked in the black suit and tie. He waited for the man's anger to show itself at the way he had insulted his daughter, but the smile on his face startled him, until he realized Maleaha must not have told her father all that had transpired between them.

''I want to thank you for saving my daughter's life, major. I was angry when I first heard about her going to

126

Mangas's camp, but knowing Maleaha as I do, no one could have talked her out of going. You will find I do not forget a debt, especially one such as I owe you.''

Kane could not have felt worse had the older man accused him of insulting his daughter. He did not want Jonas Deveraux's gratitude when he knew he deserved his contempt.

''Please do not think of it, sir. I did nothing.''

''You are too modest, my boy. I can assure you I will always be in your debt.''

Maleaha's laughter floated to the two men and Kane saw the pride in the old man's eyes.

''I want you to come to dinner tomorrow night, major, and I won't take no for an answer.''

''It would be my pleasure, Mr. Deveraux,'' Kane replied in total confusion.

''None of that Mr. Deveraux stuff, I want you to call me Jonas.''

''All right, Jonas, what time would you like me to arrive?''

''Come early. About five o'clock, if you can arrange it.''

''Sir, I would ask one favor of you. I would like to talk to Miss Deveraux, but I can't seem to get close to her,'' Kane said daringly.

Jonas laughed. ''That's easy, my boy.'' Kane watched as Jonas walked across the dance floor and took Maleaha's arm, leaving her startled dancing partner alone on the dance floor. ''See how easy it is, major, when you are her father,'' Jonas said, shoving Maleaha forward.

Kane's mouth twitched as he tried not to smile. ''Miss

Deveraux, would you honor me with a dance?'' he said, bowing gracefully before her.

''I shouldn't,'' she said.

''Maleaha, how can you refuse to dance with the man who saved your life? Go on, dance with him,'' her father urged.

Maleaha looked as if she might refuse, then as if she'd thought better of it. Her father would not understand her attitude toward Major Benedict. Kane smiled at her, knowing what was going on in her mind.

Kane took her hand and swung her onto the dance floor. Maleaha was stiff and unyielding in his arms, and she refused to look at him.

''I see your ankle has mended, Miss Deveraux.''

Maleaha gave him an icy glare, but said nothing.

''You are really enjoying yourself at my expense, aren't you?''

Her eyes half closed, and she felt his hand tighten about her waist. ''I'm sure I don't know what you are talking about, major.''

''Do you not?''

''I'm sure if you are feeling guilty about anything, it is of your own doing.'' She could feel the pressure of his hand, and it spread a warm glow throughout her body. All evening she had danced with many different partners, but none of them made her feel all funny inside, as Major Kanen Benedict did.

''I feel like hell, Miss Deveraux. I think you could safely say you got tit-for-tat. I wonder if you could find it in your heart to forgive me for my ungentlemanlike manners?''

128

"What do you mean?" she asked gazing across the dance floor. Her heart was beating so fast she could hardly breathe.

"Do you want me to state, word for word, all I said to offend you? I feel like a perfect fool." His voice came out in a deep raspy sound, and it sent tiny shivers down Maleaha's spine.

"Oh you are not perfect, major, but a fool nonetheless."

"You won't accept my appology, then?"

"Why should I? I am the same girl now that I was when you insulted me . . . no, perhaps I am a little older, and a little wiser now."

"Is there nothing I can say?"

Green eyes collided with silver ones. "You can say good-bye, major," she said softly.

The music had stopped, and he led her back to her father. He then bowed to her and turned to Jonas. "I will see you tomorrow at five, Jonas," he said. With one last glance at Maleaha, he turned and walked away.

Maleaha stared after him. Somehow her triumph had become a shallow one. She noticed how straight he held his head and how proudly he carried himself. She knew she should feel elated; she had humbled him. Why then, did she feel no satisfaction? Hadn't he got what he deserved tonight? Why didn't she feel happy?

"Maleaha," her father said, frowning down at her, "What's wrong with you? I can't believe how rude you were to Major Benedict, after he saved your life. I have asked him to dinner tomorrow night, and by damn, you will make amends. What's gotten into you?"

"He is coming to our house for dinner?" she asked in an unsteady voice.

"Yes, I invited him. You may make light about his saving your life, but I am grateful to him. It's plain to me that he likes you, so be nice to him."

Maleaha had no reply. What could she say? Somehow the fun had gone out of the evening. Frank came forward and claimed her for the next dance, and Maleaha did not hear one word he said to her as he whirled her around the dance floor. She dreaded the next evening when she would have to welcome Major Benedict to Deveraux Ranch.

CHAPTER EIGHT

Kane dismounted in front of the huge, Spanish-style ranch house, and a man rushed from the barn to take his horse, and lead it away. Dusting an imaginary speck from the front of his blue dress uniform, he climbed the steps. Before he could lift the knocker, the door swung open, and he was greeted by a cheerful Mexican lady who was obviously the housekeeper.

"Señor Major, come in. Señor Jonas is expecting you," she said, in smiling welcome.

There was no entry hall, he noticed, as he entered the sitting room, which seemed cool and elegant. The room was huge, with stairs that led to the second floor. Kane looked about him. It was a comfortable room, a room that blended the Indian's and the white man's styles, and here they coexisted in perfect harmony, complementing each other.

"Señor Jonas will be down shortly. Please to be at home," the woman said as she left Kane to attend to her duties.

Kane walked casually about the room, examining the

different objects. His eyes moved to the massive fireplace and the portrait that hung above it. Moving closer so he could have a better view, he stared up at the portrait in open admiration of the lovely Indian woman. She was sitting on a white bearskin rug, dressed in soft buckskins, her black hair hanging down her back like an ebony rivulet. Her face was breathtaking, her eyes a soft brown. Kane could see that the girl, for she could not have been much more than a young girl when the portrait had been painted, looked so much like Maleaha that there could be no doubt it was her mother. His eyes rested on the child who was sitting beside the lovely Cimeron, and he recognized the child as Maleaha. Her green eyes seemed to sparkle with mischief as she smiled up at her mother. The looks the artist had captured on the faces of Maleaha and her mother were of deep love. He was drawn to the portrait and found himself moved by the love between mother and daughter. Kane thought that if the portrait had a title it should be Mother and Child or Love Eternal. He was so obsorbed in thought that he did not hear Jonas when he entered the room.

''I see you are admiring my wife and daughter.''

Kane slid a sideways glance at Jonas. ''Yes, your wife was lovely, Jonas.''

Jonas's eyes moved lovingly over his wife's face. ''Yes, and she was as lovely on the inside as she was on the outside. In all the time I knew her, I never saw her become angry, and no matter how badly she was treated by some people, I never heard her speak ill of anyone. Cimaron was gentle, patient, and loving.''

Kane's eyes rested on the young Maleaha. At that early

age her beauty had already been apparent. As he looked into the green eyes that had been haunting him, he spoke without thinking. "The same cannot be said for your daughter; she has the devil's own temper."

Jonas's laughter echoed around the huge room. "It seems you know my daughter very well. She may be like her mother in looks, but her temper she gets from me," he said with pride. "Would you like a drink, major?"

"I will have whatever you are having, and please, call me Kane."

"All right, Kane. How about a brandy?"

Kane nodded and watched as Jonas poured brandy into two crystal glasses. "I have been admiring your home, Jonas. It is lovely and there is a feeling about it that I cannot describe. It is a—home," he finished, for want of a better word, comparing it with the elegant house that he had been brought up in, where only the most expensive furnishings had been displayed. It had never been a home, with its cold, impersonal atmosphere.

"Maleaha is responsible for the decorating. She wanted to utilize her Indian heritage. I remember when the house was completed, she told me it was a house where the white and the Indian world lived in perfect harmony."

"Yes, I got that feeling when I first saw it, Jonas."

Jonas motioned for Kane to be seated, then he handed him a brandy and sat down himself. "You know, Kane," he said, changing the subject, "I was as surprised as hell to find out it was the Arapaho, and not Mangas, who were responsible for the raids on the outlying ranches."

"Why?" Kane said in a surprised voice, "Your daughter was sure it was not Mangas."

"Don't misunderstand me. I like and respect Mangas, but he is full of hate for the white race, and with good reason, I might add. It was two white men who killed his father and his only brother. His mother died of smallpox, a disease unknown to the Indian until the white man brought it among them."

"I can see where he might not feel too friendly toward me, now. It's a wonder he did not shoot me on sight."

"Make no mistake about it, Kane. If Maleaha had not been with you, you would be dead at this moment."

"I noticed that Mangas seemed to be overly fond of your daughter. Do you think she returns his feelings?"

"Maleaha remembers Mangas from her girlhood; she does not know him as a man." Jonas was quiet for a moment as he studied the tip of his boot. "Maleaha does not know it, but Mangas came calling last week. He asked me to give him my daughter for his wife."

Kane took a drink of his brandy and waited for Jonas to continue, wondering why he felt jealousy burn within his heart.

"Mangas was mad as hell when I told him he could not have Maleaha. He is a fearless devil, and I would not put anything past him. I have asked Lamas to keep an eye on Maleaha when she is away from the ranch."

Kane frowned. "Would Mangas take her against her wishes?"

Jonas set his glass down on the long low table beside his chair. "You can bet he would take her without a by-your-leave, if he caught her alone. You see, if the chief of the Jojoba tribe sees a woman he wants, and if she does not belong to another, he can take her, with or without her consent. I have suspected for a long time that Mangas has not taken a wife because he has been waiting for Maleaha to grow up.'' Jonas paused, "Mangas considers Maleaha to be a member of his tribe."

Kane considered Jonas's words. "You do not think that Maleaha would want to marry Mangas? You said she was fond of him."

Jonas smiled, "Maleaha is fond of many people, but she would not want to marry any of them. No man has ever touched my daughter's heart as of yet, and besides, for all her loyalty to the Jojobas she has been raised as any other young white girl you might meet. You have seen both sides of her, the Indian as well as the white. You tell me if the young lady you saw at the ball last night would fare well in an Indian teepee."

"It is as if she were two different people, Jonas. I have never met anyone like her before. She has me completely baffled."

Jonas laughed. "Never judge her by the same yard-stick you would use on any other young lady. Maleaha is a rule unto herself. Throw out everything you ever knew about other women and start from scratch with her."

Kane grinned, "I believe you are right there. But tell me, do you think Mangas would come here and take her by force?" Kane was beginning to feel a prickle of uneasiness where Maleaha's safety was concerned.

"I don't think he will attempt that. It's not because he fears me, but I was married to a Jojoba princess, and there is an unstated, unwritten law that affords me some respect where Mangas is concerned. You have to understand though, the Jojobas are a rule apart from all other Indians. The chief is absolute ruler, and his word is law. In Maleaha's grandfather's time that was not a bad thing. He was a wise and compassionate man, where Mangas is full of pride and bitterness. It scares the hell out of me that he wants Maleaha. So much so, that I am tempted to send her back East for a while. I'll have to tell her about Mangas's offer so she will be on guard.''

Kane took a deep breath, ''I noticed last night your daughter had more than her share of admirers.''

''Damn right, but she cares nothing for any of them. They are all a bunch of puppy dogs sniffing around for a handout from her. Maleaha has yet to meet the man who can handle her, I know she is young yet, but if she ever met a man who could keep her in line, I would give him my full support—and sympathy. Lord only knows, she will be a handful. You saw how she rode off to the Jojoba village, with no thought of the consequences.''

Kane realized that he had drawn the wrong conclusion about Maleaha and Mangas that morning he had seen her coming out of Mangas's teepee. In fact he had drawn one wrong conclusion after another since he had first met her. Maleaha was a priceless jewel, and he had treated her like someone unworthy of him.

Kane's eyes were drawn to the top of the stairs, where Maleaha stood looking down at him. Her green eyes sparkled, as if she were preparing to go into battle.

Maleaha had been standing at the top of the landing that overlooked the sitting room. She resented the fact that her father had invited the major to dine with them, forcing her to be nice to him. She wondered why Major Benedict had accepted the invitation. Surely he could tell that she wanted nothing more to do with him. Her father and the major had not seen her, so she stood very still, observing them. They were in deep conversation, and her father's laughter drifted up to her. Her eyes moved to the major, and she could not help but notice how well his blue uniform fit his tall frame. Everything about him bespoke masculinity. Although she could not see his eyes, Maleaha knew they would be the color of liquid silver.

As he looked at her, Maleaha raised her head, gave him her haughtiest expression, and descended the stairs. Her yellow gown swirled about her, and as she walked across the room both her father and Kane watched her.

"That, Kane, is my real treasure," Jonas said, nodding toward his daughter and speaking in a low voice that only Kane could hear.

"Are you never sorry you did not have a son?"

"At one time I wished for a son, but I know if anything were to happen to me, Maleaha would be able to run Deveraux as well as any man."

Kane thought of how different Jonas was from his own father. Jonas loved his daughter and was not ashamed to show it. He wondered how different he might be today if his father had been more like Jonas Deveraux. But Kane realized in that moment that he could no longer blame his father for his own faults: The things he had said to Maleaha were his own doing, not his father's. Kane saw himself as Maleaha must see him and felt sick inside.

As Maleaha approached Kane she noticed he had the same arrogant tilt to his head, and his silver-gray eyes narrowed as she returned his wooden expression.

The smile on her lips was forced as she nodded slightly, "Major Benedict, welcome to Deveraux. It was nice of you to accept my *father's* invitation," she told him, letting him know that it was at her father's invitation that he was there, and not hers.

"Good evening, Miss Deveraux. It was kind of your father to have me to dinner," he told her, letting her know he had gotten her message.

Maleaha seethed inside. How differently he treated her now that he realized she was not a nobody and was respected by everyone. She had not missed the way he had risen politely to his feet when she entered the room, extending her the courtesy he had denied her on their first meeting. She turned to her father. "Dinner will not be for another hour and a half, Father."

Jonas sat back down and pulled Maleaha down beside him while Kane reseated himself on the sofa.

"Tell me, Kane, where is your home? I believe I detect a Northern accent."

"I was raised in Boston. My father still lives there."

Jonas leaned forward, "I know an Eli Benedict from Boston, but I don't suppose you would be related to him. Boston is a big place."

Kane looked at Jonas. "As it happens, my father's name is Eli. I wonder if he is the same man you are acquainted with?"

"The Eli Benedict I know has a large shipping firm.

He would be about the right age to be your father." Jonas studied Kane's face. "He told me he had a son, but I do not recall what he said his name was."

Kane smiled, "It must be a small world, Jonas, because I believe you are speaking of my father."

"Good Lord, Kane, imagine that. I know your father quite well. I have used his shipping company many times to transport livestock that I have purchased from all over the world. I have talked to your father on numerous occasions. Maleaha, you know the trip where I took you and Betsy to Europe? Remember how impressed you were with the ship we sailed on? That was Kane's father's ship."

"I am surprised major, that you are in the cavalry, and not in your father's business."

"I have never liked the shipping business, Miss Deveraux. I much prefer what I am doing now," Kane told her and then turned his attention to Jonas.

"May I ask you, Jonas, why you buy cattle from all over the world? It seems to me it could prove very expensive."

"It would be Kane, if I were not successful at it. Breeding cattle is a passion of mine, and I have had some damned good results. Deveraux cattle are shipped all over the world—allowing me to indulge in my favorite pastime and make a substantial profit while I am doing it."

Maleaha remained silent while Kane and her father discussed cattle ranching and then moved on to horse breeding, which, it seemed, was of interest to Kane. Maleaha watched Kane's eyes as he talked to her father about how he would someday like to raise blooded horses. She was surprised by his unlimited knowledge of the subject.

"Jonas, it has always been a dream of mine to raise Thoroughbred horses. It has always been in the back of my mind, but I suppose I dismissed it as a pipedream."

Jonas frowned. "You know, Kane, if you are really serious, I just might know some property that is available. It doesn't have a house on it, but it is a good location." Jonas looked at Kane. "Of course, I do not know if you would consider staying in New Mexico."

Kane was thoughtful for a moment as his eyes rested on Maleaha. "I have not thought that far ahead, Jonas. I never even considered that I might one day realize my dream."

Jonas placed his brandy glass on the table and stood up. "I wonder if you would accompany me to my stables? I have a horse that I would like to show you."

Maleaha stood up and excused herself, saying she would check on dinner.

When Kane and Jonas reached the stables, Kane saw that his own horse had been unsaddled and given water and hay. As Jonas led him down the row of horse stalls, he explained to him about each horse and its ancestry. Kane was enjoying himself. Apparently he and Jonas had something in common, a love for fine horse flesh.

Jonas had saved the best for last. Leading the way to the last stall, he watched Kane's face as he showed him the black stallion.

Kane whistled through his teeth as he reached out to touch the magnificent animal.

"Diablo," Jonas told him. "Which means devil in Spanish—and he lives up to his name, I can assure you."

"He is magnificent," Kane said as he watched the stallion rear up on his hind legs and paw the air.

"It took six months to break him, and I am not yet convinced that he is tame. A horse like this comes along once in a lifetime. He can outrun anything on Deveraux, most probably anything in the territory, and perhaps in the whole world."

Kane ran his hand down the satiny mane. "I have never seen a horse to rival him, Jonas."

"There is not enough money in the territory to buy Diablo, though many have made an offer for him." Jonas looked at Kane through half-closed eyelids. "Diablo is yours, Kane. I give him to you for saving my daughter's life."

Kane opened his mouth to speak as he looked at Jonas with a bewildered expression on his face. "I could never accept Diablo from you."

Jonas leaned against the stall gate and crammed his hands in his pockets. "Hell, boy, if you think my daughter is stubborn, you have never come up against her father. I told you the other night, I don't take no for an answer. Diablo belongs to you."

"But, Jonas . . ."

"No buts. I place a high value on my daughter, and to my way of thinking, she would not be here if it were not for you."

"In the first place, Jonas, I have no place to keep Diablo, and in the second place, perhaps I would not be here if it were not for your daughter."

"You can keep Diablo here until you are ready for him, and I believe the subject is closed." Jonas grinned, "Unless you would like to say thank you."

Kane knew he could no longer let Jonas go on believing he owed him a debt, when in fact he had insulted and humiliated his daughter. He remembered Colonel Johnson's telling him he would rather have Jonas's friendship and high regard than anyone he knew, and Kane had come to feel the same way. He hated to lose Jonas's respect, but he knew he must tell him the truth. He took a deep breath and looked into Jonas's green eyes.

"Jonas, do you remember that day at the fort, you gave me a piece of advice."

The older man looked thoughtful for a moment. "I believe I told you if you had any prejudices to put them aside."

Kane wished he did not have to tell Jonas how badly he had treated Maleaha, knowing how he felt about the people who had shunned his wife.

"Jonas, I did not heed your advice. When I first met your daughter, I was rude to her, thinking she was the most obstinate, pig-headed girl I had ever met. And then as the days began to pass I found myself being drawn to her against my will. But thinking she was an Indian I did not think it would be an insult if I . . ."

Jonas's eyes narrowed, "If you what, Kane?"

Kane focused his eyes on the black stallion, no longer able to look into Jonas's piercing eyes.

"I offered to make your daughter my . . . mistress."

The inside of the stable had become silent. It seemed

even the horses were waiting as Jonas Deveraux shifted his weight and looked at Kane with a piercing glare. Kane met Jonas's eyes and held his breath, waiting for him to speak. He was stunned when he saw Jonas's mouth twitch and then heard the deep laughter that echoed around the stable.

"I wondered what had happened between you and Maleaha to make her so angry with you. I assume we can safely say she refused your offer?"

Kane began to relax, still bemused by Jonas's reaction to his confession. "I have rarely, if ever, received such a tongue lashing. I am still suffering the effects of it."

"I can well imagine. I doubt that Maleaha has ever had a gentleman make her such an offer." His laughter boomed out once more and Kane smiled.

"If there is any satisfaction in your knowing, your daughter sought and got her revenge. You might like to know she had me eating a large slice of humble pie. I have felt like hell since last night at the ball when she came in on your arm and I realized what a complete fool I had made of myself."

"I would like to ask you one question, Kane. If Maleaha had turned out to be just what you thought her to be at first, would you be feeling bad at this moment?"

"I have asked myself that same question, and to be honest with you, I believe I would want her even if she were what I originally thought. Your daughter has a way of creeping into a man's thoughts, and there is no way to exorcise her. I cannot tell you how many times the last two weeks I have wanted to ride out here and drag her away with me. Then last night I realized how futile it

143

would be, and what a fool I had been."

Jonas smiled to himself. This man was different from all the others who vied for Maleaha's affection, and he had made her angry, but there was more to her feelings for Kane than she would admit. Jonas decided his daughter had finally met a man she could not wrap around her dainty little finger.

"Don't expect any help from me, Kane. You win or lose on your own, and I will just be an interested observer."

"You would not object if I were to try to gain your daughter's forgiveness?"

"I will be interested to see if you accomplish your objective. I have to warn you that you will not have an easy time of it."

"Your daughter is only being nice to me because of you, am I right?"

"Right on target."

"Jonas, I warn you I am going to try to win your daughter."

Jonas laughed, "I know you will try. I suppose as her father I should ask you what your intentions are?"

"Strictly honorable, Jonas. I would like to ask your daughter to be my wife." Kane frowned at his own words—it had come as a complete surprise to him that he wanted to marry Maleaha; he had not realized it until he had voiced his thoughts to Jonas.

Jonas nodded, "Let's go in. It would not do to make Maleaha angry because we were late for dinner."

As Kane walked beside Jonas he felt good inside. It was as if a weight had been lifted from his shoulders now that he had told Jonas about the trouble between him and Maleaha. He found himself liking this man more and more. He wished his own father was more like Jonas Deveraux. Here was a man to look up to and pattern one's life after.

CHAPTER NINE

Dinner was superb. The roast had been basted in wine sauce and was tender and delicious. They dined off delicate china and drank from crystal wine glasses.

Kane would have enjoyed the meal more if it had not been for the cold glances he received from Maleaha. It had been a long time since he had eaten a meal so well prepared.

Coffee was served at the table after the remains of the meal had been removed. Kane folded his napkin and placed it on the lace tablecloth.

"The roast was excellent, Miss Deveraux," Kane complimented her.

She gave him a slight smile. "I believe, if my memory serves me correctly, the first meal you had with me was roast beef. Do you recall asking me what it was?"

He returned her smile. "I have not forgotten."

Maleaha stood up and excused herself, glad to withdraw to the sitting room where she could be alone for a few moments.

Kane stood up politely and watched her as she left the

room, while Jonas watched them both. Kanen Benedict was everything he could wish for in a husband for his daughter, and he knew Maleaha had some deep feelings for him, but it would not be an easy victory for Kane to win her. There would be many battles before the end of the undeclared war between the two of them, he thought.

He offered Kane a cigar and then lit it for him. He then lit one for himself and watched as the smoke circled above his head, smiling to himself. Kane would learn a good lesson in humility before Maleaha was finished with him, Jonas thought.

When Kane and Jonas joined Maleaha, she put the book she was reading aside, and Kane picked it up and looked at the title. His dark eyebrows went up as he read out loud: *"The Pitfalls of Becoming a State*, by William Sully. Quite a deep subject for a mere girl is it not, Miss Deveraux?"

"What you mean is it is too advanced for an Indian, major."

He sat down beside her and thumbed through the pages. "No, I meant just what I said. Not many women would be interested in statehood, much less read a book on the subject."

Jonas sat down opposite them and propped his scuffed brown boots on the long low table in front of him.

"You know, the thought of New Mexico's becoming a state scares the hell out of me."

"Why is that, Jonas? There are many advantages to being a state."

"Too many disadvantages, as well. Should we become a state the government will come in and set up schools to educate the Indians, thinking they are doing it for their own good. Then they will decide to move the Indians to make more room for white settlers. Then they will finally be moved to a reservation. Of course the government will say it is for their own good, but in the end the Indian, who is the real owner of all this land, will be the loser."

Kane was listening to Jonas but his eyes were on Maleaha. "What are your views on statehood, Miss Deveraux?"

"I agree with my father in part, but unlike him, I believe the Indians should have an education."

"I have heard that you teach English to the Indian children twice a week."

"Yes, I do."

"Do you feel statehood would be a bad thing for the Indian?"

"Not entirely. Perhaps if we became a state the government would deal harshly with the crooked land speculators who are wreaking havoc across the territory."

Kane looked at her in surprise. He had not thought she would know about the crooked land speculators who had been hounding the army lately. So far they were operating inside the law, and there was nothing the army could do about them, with the exception of giving them a warning.

"I am surprised that you would be interested in such matters, Miss Deveraux."

"Why is that, major?"

"I suppose I have yet to meet the woman who thinks past what gown goes well with which hat," he told her, leaning his dark head back against the sofa.

"How sad for you," Maleaha said in a too sweet tone.

Jonas watched as his daughter's eyes blazed with anger. She was holding her own against Kane and she was not bored. She might be angry, and she might be indignant, but she was not bored!

"I would like to see the time, major, when the white man and the Indian could live together in harmony, a world where a man is respected for what he is like inside instead of what color his skin is, but I doubt that will come about in your time or mine."

Kane was silent for a long while, pondering her words. This Deveraux family was causing him to challenge many of his beliefs. His father would measure a man by the color of his money or his accomplishments, and perhaps by his social standing.

"Major, my mother's people have a saying: The eyes see the beauty of one's face, and the heart sees the beauty of the soul. The beauty of the face fades but the beauty inside never grows old. The eyes can go blind, thus one can no longer see the outer beauty, but inward beauty can be felt without the benefit of one's sight."

Kane stared into Maleaha's green eyes, and at that moment he felt he could see the beauty of her soul. Her eyes mirrored so many things: love, pride, uncertainty, and sadness. He wanted to learn from her, as well as to teach her, and most of all he wanted to see the beauty of life through her eyes. She was as wild and untamed as this beautiful land she came from.

Despite herself, Maleaha was held spellbound by Kane's silver eyes. He was mentally drawing her to him, and she was fighting the weakness in her that reached out to him. No, please! she thought, if I love him, he will destroy me.

Jonas watched the two young people, thinking how they were worlds apart. But their love would span the differences, and even though Maleaha would give Kane a valiant fight, he would win in the end.

At that moment the front door opened, and Kane looked up to see a giant of a man enter. He was obviously a rancher by his manner of dress. His sandy-colored hair was curly, and his eyes were blue and sparkling as he looked at Maleaha.

"What does a man have to do to get fed around here?" he drawled.

Maleaha stood up, and Kane watched as her face lit up.

"Aren't you going to welcome a weary traveler, Maleaha?"

Maleaha raced across the room and threw herself into his open arms, and as he hugged her tightly, she smiled up into his ruggedly handsome face.

"Clay, when did you return?"

"About two minutes ago. As soon as I washed and shaved I rushed over here to see you," he said, smiling down at her affectionately.

She leaned her head over on his broad shoulder. "You are teasing me, Clay."

"All right, it was three hours ago, and I ate before I came over. Did you miss me?"

"You know I did, Clay. Did you miss me?"

"Hell, yeah. Didn't I go all the way to Boston to see you last year?"

"Clay, you should not talk that way. You are begin-

151

ning to sound like Father," she scolded him mildly.

"You can't reform your father, and you might as well give up on me, too."

Maleaha gave him a bright smile. "That would be to admit defeat."

Clay placed a kiss on her pert little nose. "You would never admit defeat, would you, little Indian princess?"

"Come, Clay," she said, tugging on his hand. "I want to introduce you to my father's guest."

Kane stood up politely, thinking he did not like this man who seemed to be much too familiar with Maleaha.

"Major Benedict, I would like you to meet Clay Madason, a friend and neighbor."

The two men looked each other over as they shook hands, sizing each other up.

"Had I known you had a guest, I wouldn't have come," Clay said by way of an apology.

"Nonsense! Major Benedict is my father's guest, and you know you are always welcome," she said pointedly.

Score one for Maleaha, thought Jonas. "Clay here would like to add Deveraux Ranch to his spread, so he courts my daughter, Kane," Jonas said lazily.

Kane looked quickly at the giant sandy-haired man to see if he took exception to Jonas's words, but Clay only laughed.

"Jonas, you old cuss, the major is not blind. He can easily see why I am interested in your daughter, and it ain't Deveraux that attracts me. Anyone can see she is the prettiest little filly in the whole territory. Besides, I got more land now than I know what to do with."

Maleaha placed her hands on her hips and tapped her

foot in mock anger. "You had better think twice before you make an offer for me, Clay. Perhaps I have my eye on the Circle M ranch, hoping to add it to Deveraux."

"Honey, if I thought that would get you to marry me, I would wrap a big red ribbon around the Circle M, and hand it to you as a wedding present." In two strides he reached Maleaha and lifted her above his head. "You can fight all you want to little princess, but in the end you will marry me. I'm a good catch."

"I am not going fishing, Clay, and put me down this very minute," she demanded.

"I will have you one day, Maleaha, and it won't be because I want to join two ranches together."

Maleaha laughed as he set her on her feet and placed his arm around her shoulder. Clay was the brother she had never had, and she felt a deep affection for him. He always teased her, but she never took anything he said seriously.

"What makes you think I would have you, Clay?"

"It scares the hell out of me to think you won't."

"I never knew you to be a coward, Clay."

"See, you learn something new every day, Princess."

"Pretty words will never win my daughter, Clay," Jonas grinned.

Kane frowned as Maleaha linked her arm through Clay's and led him to the settee. Jealousy burned deep inside him. Another new emotion for him to deal with.

Clay sat down beside Maleaha and held her hand in his. It seemed to Kane that he was declaring his ownership of her.

"Tell me about your trip to Texas, Clay. I was disappointed when I returned from Boston and you were not here."

Clay crossed his long legs and smiled at her. "I can sum the trip up in one sentence: The wind never let up, the dirt blew, and it was hot as hell! What else would you like to know?"

"Oh, you enjoyed yourself, did you?" she mocked.

Clay glanced at her sideways. "One day that sassy mouth will get you in trouble," he teased.

"Kane, have you ever been to Texas?" Jonas asked.

"No, I have not had that pleasure."

Clay snorted. "Believe me, it's no pleasure. We have a saying here in New Mexico; 'You can tell if a man is coming from, or going to, Texas' "

"How is that, Mr. Madason?"

"Well, if a man is going to Texas he is eating beans and jerky, and if he is returning from there he is eating jackrabbit. Now, if you never had a jackrabbit, you couldn't possibly know how skinny and stringy it is."

"I suppose a man could eat worse things," Jonas said. "I have."

"What's that, Jonas?" Kane asked, rising to the bait.

Jonas leaned his head back and looked at the ceiling, his expression thoughtful, as though he were remembering.

"One winter I took my wife, Cimeron, to visit her people, the Jojobas. It had been a bad winter. It started snowing in late September and did not let up through March. Cattle had frozen to death by the hundreds, and game was scarce. If the white man was having a hard time, the Indians were starving. Cimeron and myself

154

were snowed in at the Jojoba village and could not return home until the weather let up. One night I was surprised when my wife's mother served meat at the evening meal, since our diet had consisted of nothing but corncakes for the last few weeks. Well, being hungry, I did not ask any questions, and the meat was quite tasty. I did not think too much about it, until my wife came to me later, and whispered in my ear, 'Jonas, do not ask where Sam is, you ate him for dinner.' "

Jonas waited for Kane to speak, and he did not have long to wait.

"Who was Sam, Jonas?"

Maleaha looked at her father expectantly; she had never heard him tell this story before.

"Sam was the best damn hunting dog I ever had."

Maleaha gasped and Kane leaned forward with a serious look on his face.

"There are worse things to eat than dog meat, Jonas."

"What would that be, Kane?"

Kane crossed his long legs and rested his hand on his shiny black boot.

"Once during the war, after a battle outside Gettysburg, my men and I were also snowed in. We were starving, but unlike you, we didn't even have corncakes to eat. Our horses had run away, and I was becoming desperate, not knowing how I would feed my men and keep them alive. Well, as you can imagine, I was pondering how I was going to feed thirty-six hungry cavalry men. I knew if I did not come up with something fast we would all perish."

Kane waited, letting Jonas ponder his words.

"What did you come up with, Kane?" Jonas asked.

"I decided the only meat we had to eat was human flesh, Jonas."

Kane looked at Maleaha, who was absorbed in his tale and waiting eagerly for him to continue. Clay leaned forward, listening intently.

"I found the idea very distasteful, as you can imagine, but I had no choice. We would have to resort to cannibalism."

Maleaha gasped and covered her mouth with her hand, thinking she would be sick.

"Imagine if you will, my dilemma," he continued. "I did not want to force any of my men to give up their lives so the rest of us could live, so I devised a plan. Each man would write his name on a piece of paper and drop it into a hat, along with what he was willing to sacrifice. Some chose to part with an arm, while others favored giving up a leg, or an ear."

Kane could see the shock on Maleaha's lovely face, and Clay was looking at him with doubt and disbelief. Jonas was grim-faced as he exchanged looks with Kane.

"W . . . what happened?" Maleaha said in a soft voice, her eyes wide and apprehensive.

"Well," he continued," I, being the commanding officer, could do no less than put my limbs on the line the same as my men, but as you can see, all my limbs are intact, so you know I did not lose in the draw."

Jonas leaned forward, "Who lost, Kane?"

Kane took a deep breath and let it out slowly. "I called the doctor to perform the amputation and later on the cook limped around on his one good leg preparing the meal. And as he tasted his own leg, he declared it was quite tasty, but a little tough. He turned to me and in a loud voice declared: 'Never let it be said that I am not tough!' "

Maleaha looked astounded as Jonas and Clay laughed so hard there were tears running down their faces.

"All right, Kane," Jonas said, when he could catch his breath, "You have proved you are a bigger liar than I am."

Clay shook his head. "You both had me believing you. You are the best damn liars I have ever listened to."

Jonas laughed. "I think he means that as a compliment, Kane."

"How about you, Miss Deveraux, did you also believe your father and me?"

"I . . . I thought, yes, at first."

"Well, it has been a long day for me," Clay said as he stood up. "I will see you next week, Maleaha," he told her as he moved across the room in giant strides. "Nice meeting you, major," Clay said just as he disappeared out the front door with the same suddenness with which he had entered it earlier.

Kane stood up with the intention of taking his leave since the hour was late, but Jonas stalled him.

"Kane, why don't you stay the night? It is late, and there is no reason for you to return to the fort tonight, is there?"

"No, if it will not be an imposition," Kane replied, looking at Maleaha, who now stood by her father.

"We would like to have you stay, wouldn't we, Maleaha?" her father said, reminding her of her duty as

157

hostess, with a look that warned her to be polite.

"Yes, please stay, major," she said, wishing him at the other end of the earth at that moment. "I will show you to your room if you are ready to retire," she added politely.

"You go ahead and go up to bed if you are tired, honey," her father said. "I want to talk to Kane for a while. I will show him to his room later. Which room will you put him in?"

"The yellow room. I will just go and make sure it is ready. Good night, major."

"Good night, Miss Deveraux."

Maleaha walked over to her father and kissed his cheek. Seeing the doubt in her eyes, Jonas hugged her tightly. He wanted to assure her that everything would be all right, but he patted her shoulder instead and watched her walk across the room and disappear up the stairs.

After Maleaha turned down the covers and opened the window in the yellow bedroom, she summoned Margaretta to bring fresh water. When she was sure the room was in readiness she went to her own room next door. Maleaha found she was very tired. The evening had drained her. But as she dressed for bed, she doubted she would be able to sleep.

Slipping between the cool bed sheets, she tried to shut off her mind, but thoughts of Kane kept creeping into her subconscious, no matter how hard she tried to think of something else. She found herself remembering how it felt to be in his arms and to be kissed by him. Maleaha did not want to love Kanen Benedict, but she knew by now that she was hopelessly in love with him, and the tears from her eyes wet the pillow she rested her head on.

She threw the covers off and arose, slipping into her robe. She then went out onto her balcony and walked down the steps that led to the patio below.

Kane entered the bedroom and looked about him. This room, like the rest of the house, was tastefully decorated. He could smell the soft lingering perfume that Maleaha had worn tonight, giving evidence she had been in this room.

He removed his blue jacket and draped it over a chair, then he unbuttoned his white dress shirt to his waist. He looked at the bed, with its yellow satin covering, and thought how inviting it was. It had been a long time since he had slept in a comfortable bed. He and Jonas had talked for over an hour, and although Kane was tired, he knew he would not be able to sleep. Walking out onto the balcony he observed the garden below and the stairs leading to it. Kane leaned against the railing and closed his eyes. What was it about this house that made him want to remain here?

Tonight he had found himself telling Jonas things he had never told another living soul, things about his background and his resentment of his father. Jonas had been understanding, so Kane had confided many things to him. The older man had asked him questions but had offered him no advice.

Kane had felt Maleaha's resentment toward him tonight, and he had been troubled by it, even though he knew it was well deserved. He found himself wanting her to look at him with love and respect. He, Kanen Benedict, had lost his heart to an ebony-haired seventeen-year-old, who was bright, intelligent, and overly desirable. Kane was in the depths of hell and feeling tormented. He had no illusions about himself. In the past he had been a user; he had used women, and when he became bored with them he had tossed them aside without giving any thought to their feelings. He had never allowed anyone to get close to him, and he had never been able to talk about himself as he had with Jonas tonight.

Kane remembered hearing once, "He who sows the wind shall reap the whirlwind." Was he now in love, never to have that love returned? Could a man who had lived as he had change? Had loving Maleaha made him aware of his faults? Could he grow to be a man she could respect, and could he win her love?

Kane looked down on the garden below. It was bathed in soft moonlight, and the pleasant aroma of the many flowers in bloom drifted up to him. He saw a movement as a shadow detached itself. He caught his breath, knowing it was Maleaha. She seemed to be unaware of his presence, and he found himself descending the stairs, hoping to have a word with her.

She seemed to be unaware of him as he came up behind her, or so Kane thought, until she spoke to him.

"So, you could not sleep either, major?" she said without turning to face him.

He stared at her unbound black hair and remembered how it had felt soft and silky to the touch. "No, I seem to be restless tonight."

Maleaha turned to face him. With his white shirt open

160

to the waist she saw the curly black hair on his chest. She could feel a tightening in her throat as she felt him pulling at her, although he did not actually touch her.

"Perhaps you would like me to get you a glass of warm milk?"

He smiled. "Do people still try that old remedy?"

"Margaretta swears by it."

They were both making small talk, anything to keep from saying what they were really feeling. Maleaha's hands gripped the trellis that the roses grew on, to keep from reaching out to him. She wanted him to hold her in his arms and kiss her as he had before. How many women besides her had lost their hearts to this man with the silver eyes?

"No, I do not want milk, but you could help me if you would," he said, moving closer to her and staring down into her upturned face.

"How?" she whispered through trembling lips.

"Say you forgive me, Maleaha," he said, using her name for the first time. There was a note of pleading in his voice, but a voice in her head was saying danger, danger!

"I think it is best if we both forget all that has happened in the past. Most probably we will not see much of each other in the future."

Kane took the short step that brought him closer to her and reached out his hand to touch her face, then let it drift down to her throat where he could feel her pulse drumming wildly. His own pulse rate had accelerated.

"Last night I sought to shame you, but when I was successful I felt no pleasure in your shame," she said so

161

softly he could hardly hear her.

Kane was startled by her honesty, and he felt hope fan to life inside him. "I deserved what happened last night. I ask . . . no, I *beg* you to forgive me," he said, as his hand drifted up to entangle itself in her dark hair.

"Say that I am forgiven, Maleaha," he pleaded.

"You are forgiven, if it makes any difference to you, major," she told him, loving the sound of her name on his lips.

"It matters a great deal. Do you hate me?"

"No, but I do not like you very well." She could have added that she loved him, but she did not.

"I suppose I should be grateful that you do not hate me, but I find I am sad that you do not like me, even though there is no reason why you should."

Maleaha was unprepared for his next movement. Kane pulled her into his arms, and she closed her eyes, loving the feel of the soft downy hair on his bare chest that tickled her cheek. She was so overcome with weakness that she held on to his shirtfront for support.

"Oh, God help me," he murmured against her ear.

Maleaha tried to understand his meaning, then fearing she would reveal her true feelings for him, she struggled to get out of his arms.

Kane released her quickly. He did not want to frighten her with his need for her, and he did not want her to think he was treating her other than with the greatest respect.

"I will wish you a good night, Maleaha. Most probably I will be gone when you get up in the morning. I want to thank you for a lovely evening, and for your hospitality for the night." He turned and left her, and her heart cried out to him not to go. Maleaha wanted to feel his strong arms around her once more, but she knew the danger to herself and closed her eyes.

He had seemed sincere when he asked for her forgiveness. Maleaha was mixed up inside. Why had he accepted her father's dinner invitation? She doubted she would ever know the answers, and she had so many questions. Why did she love this man? Surely there were other men she could have chosen to love who would have loved her in return. But then, she had not chosen to love Kanen Benedict, she had not even known of his existence until four short weeks ago, and yet she felt she would love him forever.

Maleaha did not sleep well that night. She tossed and turned feverishly upon her bed. The next morning she dressed before dawn, went to the stable, and saddled her horse, thinking a ride would clear her mind. Perhaps when she returned to the house, Major Benedict would be gone.

CHAPTER TEN

July was settling over the land, and the heat burned the green grasses of spring to a brown straw color. Even the occasional rain did not bring any relief from the scorching heat.

The fort was in an uproar, for the Arapaho had struck again, only this time they were not satisfied to just cause mischief. They had raided a small dirt farm, and the farmer, his wife and two children were dead—burned alive by the Indians. The surrounding territory was up in arms, demanding that the soldiers at the fort perform their duty and protect the citizens.

Kane had been called to Colonel Johnson's office, and he knew what the colonel wanted to see him about. He had been out on patrol for two weeks in a row without ever sighting the Arapaho, who were making fools out of the cavalry, as well as the United States Government.

When Kane reached the office, Colonel Johnson motioned for him to take a chair. Kane was weary, having only returned from his latest patrol late the night before.

"We have got to find these renegades, major. I'm under tremendous pressure from everyone, and who can blame them? If the cavalry can't be called on to protect the citizens, who can they turn to, I asked myself?'' He leaned forward. ''Do you know the answer I came up with, major?''

Kane shook his head.

''Mangas, major. Mangas is our only help.''

Kane was on his feet in a flash. ''But how will we find Mangas? I happen to know Jonas Deveraux has gone to Spain on a cattle-buying trip.''

''I believe you already know the answer to your question, major. As before, Maleaha will be your guide.''

''No,'' Kane said, forgetting that he was speaking to his commanding officer. ''I will not allow her to be placed in danger as she was before. You cannot know what faces her at Mangas's hands should he get her in his camp.''

''Major, I do not fully understand your objections, but I have already sent word to Maleaha, asking her to help us find Mangas. She sent word back to me that she would be here before dawn tomorrow morning.''

Kane's mind rejected the idea of placing Maleaha in danger. He would fight the colonel on this.

''I request permission for time off to go and talk to Miss Deveraux, sir.''

''Permission denied, major. Maleaha has already said she will accompany you in the morning, and I will not have you trying to convince her otherwise.''

''You cannot know what you have asked of her, colonel. She will be in grave danger from Mangas if you permit her to go with me.''

166

"What kind of danger, major?"

"I am not at liberty to say, sir. You will just have to trust my word on this."

"And you will have to see my position, major. Maleaha is the only one who can help us in this. I would like to think you will be able to protect her through whatever danger you think she might face. I need her help, and I will not permit you to try and talk her out of going. Is that clear?"

Kane stood at attention, masking his anger. How dare Maleaha agree to go to Mangas's camp, knowing the danger she was placing herself in. He wished she was within his reach right now so he could shake some sense into her.

"I cannot obey that order, sir. I will do all within my power to talk her out of going."

"That is insubordination, major. I could have you court-martialed, you know?"

"Yes sir, I know, and I want to go on record as having told you there is a danger to Miss Deveraux. Her father will not be pleased when he learns what you have done," Kane said, grasping at straws.

Colonel Johnson looked uncertain for a moment. "I would risk Jonas's displeasure if it will bring an end to these raids and drive the Arapaho from this land and restore peace once more."

Kane was silent as he wondered how he would protect Maleaha. He already knew he would be unable to keep her from going.

"Would you prefer that I confine you to the fort and send Lieutenant Maxwell in your place, major?"

"No sir," Kane said quickly, knowing if Maleaha must go he had to be there to protect her.

"Very well then, I suggest you try and get some rest, since you will be riding out early in the morning."

Maleaha had not easily given her consent to go to Mangas's camp. She was fearful of the consequences, but she felt it was her duty to help in any way she could, and if Mangas could be persuaded to help the army, maybe together they would deal with the Arapaho.

Her father had left over two weeks before for Spain, and he had wanted her to accompany him, but she had not wanted to go on a long sea voyage at this time. Jonas had been prepared to cancel his trip until Maleaha told him she might meet him in Paris next spring. She knew she would miss her father terribly, but deep inside she knew she did not want to go because she hoped she might see Kane again.

The next morning she waited for Kane outside the fort gates. She felt nervous. She had not seen him since the night he had spent at the ranch.

Kane was grim-faced as he rode through the gates at the head of his troops. He saw Maleaha and Lamas waiting for him. Once again she was dressed in her buckskins. He saw her nudge her mount in the flanks and she joined him at the front of the column, while Lamas fell in behind her. Kane was still angry with her and offered no form of greeting, but stared straight ahead.

They rode for over an hour at a fast pace before Kane gave the word to slow down. It was only when they had slowed their horses to a walk that Kane spoke to her in a quiet voice that could not be overheard by the others.

"Why did you feel it was necessary for you to come along, Miss Deveraux?"

Maleaha looked at him quickly, not understanding the anger she heard in his voice.

"I can assure you, major, it was not for the pleasure of your company. I, like many others, would like to see an end to this upheaval."

"Let me make one thing clear, Miss Deveraux. I am in charge this time. You will do as you are told, with no questions asked. Is that clear?"

"I understand, major. I will not challenge your authority as long as it agrees with what is best for all concerned."

The muscle in his jaw twitched, a sure sign that he was angry with her. This was the major as Maleaha understood him. He had been different the last time she had seen him, asking her forgiveness. She could easily handle this man, but she was unsure of herself with the man he had been in her garden the other night.

"You will obey my orders, or else return home at once."

"I have told you before, I do not answer to you. I am not on the army payroll," she told him angrily. And then she went a step farther. "I can always go home like you suggested, and then how would you find Mangas?"

Kane gave her a scalding glance. "I wish to hell you *would* go home. I am not the least bit happy about your coming along this time, Miss Deveraux."

"How would you find Mangas without me to lead you

to him?''

"Lamas could lead me to Mangas. It is not necessary for you to come along, and if you were not so stubborn you would see that.''

Maleaha smiled smugly, "Lamas could lead you to Mangas, true, but he could not talk Mangas into helping you, and perhaps I can.''

Kane was about to object but he clamped his mouth shut, knowing she was right. At that moment he would have liked to shake her until her teeth rattled. He remembered Jonas telling him what could happen should Mangas get his hands on Maleaha, and he was determined that Mangas would not touch her as long as he was alive to prevent it.

"Major, is it understood that I will take only you to Mangas's camp, the same as before?''

"Yes. Is the village located in the same place as before?''

"No.''

The sun was just rising, painting the sky with its glorious golden hue. Kane looked about him, filled with the beauty of the land. He wondered just when he had begun to love this enchanted land. When had he stopped resenting New Mexico? It felt almost as if in accepting this land, it had adopted him, and accepted him as surely as if he had been a native-born son.

Kane glanced sideways at Maleaha, who was looking at the distant mountains. She was lovely in her soft buckskins. How right it felt to have her riding beside him. For the first time in his life he wanted someone to belong to him. He wanted to put down roots, to build a home. How good it would be to awaken every morning with her lying beside him. A lump came into his throat, thinking how good it would be to lie beside her and take her into his arms, making her truly his. He wanted to stamp her as his possession, so that all other men would know she belonged to him.

They rode until early afternoon, then Kane raised his hand and called out to his sergeant.

"Company halt, sergeant."

"Company halt," the sergeant called out in a loud blusterous voice.

"Company dismount, sergeant."

"Company dismount," the sergeant echoed.

The soldiers dismounted amid the crackling of leather and the jingling of spurs. Maleaha slid from the back of her horse, to walk along beside Kane. His footsteps could be heard as his spurs jingled with each step he took. Maleaha's moccasin-clad feet made no noise as she took faster steps to match his long strides.

"Do we take the long way around this time, Miss Deveraux?"

"I am afraid so, major."

Kane removed his gloves and tucked them into his belt. "There is every need for haste, you know?"

"I am aware of that, major, but I cannot take you the direct route to the Jojoba village."

Kane gave her a disdainful glance.

"Company remount, sergeant," he called over his shoulder.

"Company remount," came the reply.

It was almost sundown when Kane gave the order to

make camp. Maleaha unsaddled her horse and spread her blanket about thirty paces away from the rest of the camp. She was beginning to feel uneasy, being the only female among so many men. It was at best an awkward situation.

Lamas laid his blanket beside hers, and, reaching into his leather pouch, he removed the roast meat and homemade bread Margaretta had prepared for him and Maleaha.

Maleaha took the food Lamas handed her and took a bite.

"Someone comes," Lamas told her. His keen hearing could pick up every sound.

Maleaha was surprised when she recognized Lieutenant Maxwell. He smiled shyly and sat down on a huge rock.

"I have been wanting to speak to you, ma'am. I was wondering if you think Mangas can be persuaded to help us find the Arapaho?"

Maleaha noticed the way he looked at her. There was no mistaking the look of interest in his soft brown eyes. She had met him briefly at the ball and had even danced with him once.

"I don't know, Lieutenant Maxwell. That remains to be seen."

"Miss Deveraux, I have admired you for some time now. I think you are very lovely." Then he lowered his head in embarrassment. "I also think you are very brave. I know of no other woman who would ride unafraid into Mangas's camp."

Maleaha smiled at him. "How many women do you know with my qualifications, Lieutenant Maxwell?"

172

He grinned. "Not a one, ma'am, and no one I know is as pretty as you, either."

Maleaha could not keep from laughing. He seemed so sincere. Most probably he was older than her by some three or four years, and yet he appeared so young to her.

Kane stood in the shadows, feeling angry at the scene he was witnessing.

"Lieutenant Maxwell, who gave you permission to leave camp?" Kane said in a velvety-smooth voice.

The young lieutenant snapped to attention and looked shamefaced. "I am sorry, sir, I had not thought . . ."

"No, you did not think," Kane interrupted him. "You might want to pass the word that Miss Deveraux is off limits to all soldiers, and that is an order."

Maleaha watched as the lieutenant walked away quickly, feeling very foolish for being reprimanded in front of her. She felt pity for him, thinking the major could have been a little nicer to him.

"You were a little harsh with him. He was not doing anything wrong," she declared hotly.

His eyes flashed dangerously, "Miss Deveraux, I would appreciate it if in the future you would not hold private conversations with my men. It will be hard enough for them to keep their minds on their duties with you along to distract them, much less if you encourage them to seek you out privately."

Angry words tumbled to her lips, but she never got the chance to voice them because he turned his back and walked away from her.

Maleaha had a good mind to ride away and leave him to find Mangas on his own. She stood up and angrily kicked a stone. Her reward was the pain that shot through her foot. Sitting down on her blanket, she rubbed her aching foot.

Lamas had watched all the proceedings with his usual look of boredom, but he could not help the look of amusement that washed over his wrinkled old face.

"Lamas, that man makes me so angry I have half a mind to go home and let him try to find Mangas on his own."

Lamas shrugged his shoulders. "He is a good man."

"Good for what?"

"Good for you, I think. He returns," Lamas told her at the same time she detected Kane's footsteps.

Looking up, Maleaha saw that Kane carried his bedroll, which he tossed to the ground.

"I have decided it is not safe for you to sleep so far from camp with only the old Indian to protect you," he said, unrolling his bedroll.

"I am safe enough with Lamas. He detected your foorsteps long before you came into sight."

Kane watched as the old Indian stood up and walked away, soon to be swallowed up by the night shadows.

"I do not like to have to repeat myself, but I am in charge, and what I say goes. Do I make myself clear?"

"Oh, I understand what you are saying, major, and if it makes you feel more in charge to be asserting your authority over me, so be it," she said flippantly.

With a quick motion he grabbed her by the wrist and pulled her to her feet.

"My God, you try a man's patience. I have taken about all I intend to from you." He pulled her into his

174

arms.

Maleaha struggled as his hands moved down her back, drawing her tightly against his body. Looking into his face, she saw the anger leave him, to be replaced by a look she could not define. His silver eyes froze her into immobility.

She felt herself being pulled under his spell. It was as if she were being drawn to him, as a helpless moth seeks the flame knowing it will get its wings singed.

Maleaha waited expectantly as his lips moved to within a hairs-breadth of her waiting lips.

"Damn you," he ground out between clenched teeth as he shoved her roughly away from him.

Maleaha looked away from him, feeling heartsick and ashamed. She knew at that moment he had felt drawn to her, as she had to him, but she was wise enough to know that attraction was not the same as love. Did he resent the fact that he was drawn to her? Was he repelled by his attraction to her? Deep inside, did he still think of her as nothing more than an Indian?

Lamas had returned and lain down on his blanket, and Maleaha walked over to him on shaky legs, needing to put Kane out of her mind. She heard him lie down on his bedroll, and she sat down beside Lamas and folded her legs beneath her. The old man's eyes rested on her. How like her mother she looks, he thought. Lamas had secretly loved Cimeron, and her daughter was very dear to his heart.

"Do not be troubled, Maleaha. Look at every day as a gift. When one wastes time worrying, then the gift is wasted."

"Lamas, I have many worries on my mind, not the least of which is wondering what Mangas will do when he sees me again."

"I have heard it said that Mangas wants you for his woman. I told you it was not wise for you to go to his camp. I will try to prevent him from taking you, if I am able."

"I knew the danger when I agreed to come, but I felt I could help sway Mangas to aid the army in rounding up the Arapaho." She sighed. "I am frightened, Lamas. What shall I do?"

The old man was quiet for a moment, pondering her words. "You could tell Mangas you are this man's woman. It could work well for you if Mangas's spies are watching you, and they see this man lying beside you."

Maleaha looked over her shoulder to where Kane was lying on his bedroll. His arms were folded behind his head and he seemed oblivious to his surroundings. She eased herself to her feet and walked slowly over to her blanket. As she lay down she noticed Kane had turned his back to her. She supposed her reputation would be in shreds when it was learned she had slept beside the major, but that was the very least of her concerns at the moment.

"I suppose you will wreak havoc with my reputation, major," she said sadly, not really expecting him to understand.

"Go to sleep, Miss Deveraux," he said wearily.

The same pattern was repeated the next night. The major came to where Maleaha and Lamas were camped and unrolled his bedroll, then turned his back on her and drifted off to sleep.

In the daytime, as she rode beside him, he was silent. Word must have reached the rest of the soldiers that they were not to have any conversation with Maleaha, for not one of them had approached her. Every so often she would see Lieutenant Maxwell watching her, and she would smile at him, but she noticed he would look around for the major before he would return her smile.

Around noon on the fourth day they stopped to eat and rest the horses. Maleaha sought out Kane. He had been talking to his sergeant, and he watched her as she approached. He noticed the way her hips moved as she walked, and by the look on the sergeant's face, he knew he had noticed also.

"I'm an old man, major, but that is the prettiest little gal I have ever seen. Makes me feel good just to look at her, sir," The sergeant told Kane.

"I suggest, sergeant, that you tend to your duties and forget about Miss Deveraux."

The sergeant laughed. "I'll go about my duties, sir, but I doubt I will forget about Miss Deveraux."

By now Maleaha had reached Kane's side, and he turned angrily to face her.

"What do you want, Miss Deveraux?" he asked in an incensed voice.

She blinked at the anger in his voice. "I only wanted to tell you there is a stream about five miles from here. If you will have your men camp there, you, Lamas, and I will go on to the Jojoba village alone."

She watched as Kane angrily stalked away. Was that man always angry, she wondered. He surely spent most of his time being angry with her. She shrugged her shoulders and went in search of Lamas.

After Kane had instructed Lieutenant Maxwell on what he wanted him to do, he mounted his horse and rode away beside Maleaha, with Lamas riding just to the rear.

Maleaha looked at him and noticed that he was still angry, so she did not try to talk to him.

By nightfall they were deep within the mountains, and that night they set up camp in the dense forest. After they had eaten, Maleaha disappeared, and she had now been gone for over an hour. It was dark, and Kane paced back and forth, waiting for her to return.

"Why does she not return?" he asked Lamas, but the old Indian merely shrugged his shoulders and acted unconcerned.

Kane had just decided to go and search for her when he saw her emerge from the trees. Her hair was wet, so he suspected she had been bathing. She stopped beside the old man and spoke to him rapidly in the language of the Jojoba, and then Lamas stood up, and was soon lost among the dark shadows.

Maleaha walked casually toward Kane.

"Act natural, major; we are being observed."

Kane reached out and put a protective arm about her shoulder. "Did you discover you were being watched before or after you bathed?"

"It was during my bath that I realized I was being watched," she told him with a look of amusement.

"Do you think it is the Jojoba?"

"I cannot be sure, but I pray it is."

The two of them waited tensely for Lamas to return.

178

When he did reappear, he was so silent that Kane did not see him until he was beside them. Kane waited while the old man spoke to Maleaha.

"We have nothing to fear, major. It is the Jojoba."

Kane looked past her into the dark forest that surrounded them. How was it that she could see and hear things that no normal person could detect? It was irritating to him that she always seemed to have the upper hand where he was concerned.

He unrolled his bedroll and placed it under one of the trees. He was surprised when Maleaha walked over to him with her blanket and spread it beside him.

"Major, I am going to do something you may not understand, but please trust me and ask no questions." She removed her moccasins and lay down beside her blanket.

Kane looked from her to the old man, in total confusion. Apparently Lamas found nothing out of the ordinary about the sleeping arrangement. He merely yawned and rolled up in his blanket, turning his back to them.

Kane lay down on his bedroll, and was further confused when Maleaha moved over and placed her head on his shoulder.

"What the hell do you think you are doing?" he asked, as he grabbed a handful of wet, ebony-colored hair and forced her to look at him in the face.

"What game are you playing?" He looked into luminous green eyes and drew in his breath as her sensuous lips parted in silent invitation.

"Kiss me, Kane," she said, using his name for the first time.

The use of his name and the feel of her soft body

179

pressed close to him was his undoing. His lips came down on hers hungrily. But no sooner had his lips touched hers, than she shoved him away and laid her head down, looking at him with amusement.

Kane glanced at the old man, who appeared to be sleeping. "Did you wish to test me to see if you could make me want you, Miss Deveraux?" Kane said through stiff lips. The brief contact with her had stirred his body to life, with awareness of her. Every nerve end cried out to possess her.

"I am sorry, major. You must think my actions very strange, but please trust me, and ask no questions."

Her lips opened in a provocative smile. "Do not worry; your virtue is safe with me."

Kane had the impulse to turn her over his knee and give her the spanking her father had probably never given her.

"God, it must be some sort of punishment for me to endure. I think you are aware of what you are doing to me and are enjoying yourself at my expense. Just be warned that you have almost pushed me to my limit."

"And what will you do when you reach your limit?" She taunted, unaware of the dangerous ground she was treading on.

Kane's hand shot out and grabbed a handful of ebony hair and jerked her toward him. His face was a mask as he looked deep into her eyes, and Maleaha saw his nostrils flare as his silver eyes narrowed.

"Congratulations, you have just succeeded in pushing me to my limit," he whispered against her lips. "Now *you* can feel what it is like to be driven half out of your mind."

Kane's lips moved over her face, teasing and arousing, but never settling on her lips. Maleaha turned her head, trying to capture his lips with hers, but he always moved out of her range. She heard his deep laughter as he nuzzled her ear, and a gasp escaped her lips.

"It's hell, is it not?" he whispered in her ear. Maleaha knew she should be angry with him, but all she could think of at the moment was the feel of his lips, and his hands, which were gliding sensuously down her back.

"Beg me for a kiss, Maleaha, beg."

"No!"

"You know you want me to, Maleaha," he said, his warm breath caressing her face.

"Please."

"Please what, Maleaha?"

"Please, release me. We are being watched."

Kane had forgotten all about the Jojoba Indians who were watching them. He cursed under his breath as he untangled her arms from around his neck and shoved her away from him. Gritting his teeth, he turned his back on her.

"Consider yourself lucky that I do not perform well in front of an audience, Miss Deveraux."

Maleaha swallowed a sob as she tried to stop her body from trembling. Her love for Kane was second only to her need for him. He had awakened her body from that of a child to that of a woman, and it was a long time before she finally fell asleep. Her only consolation was that maybe the watching Jojobas warriors would report back to Mangas that she was now Kane's woman.

The next morning as they broke camp and rode away,

Kane was silent and brooding. Maleaha knew he was sti
angry about the night before, but she knew of no way
tell him about her fear of Mangas. Most probably h
would not understand. One thing was for sure. Kan
would not like it if he found out she had used him la
night to fool Mangas.

As they drew ever closer to the Jojoba village, Ma
leaha's mind shifted to thoughts of Mangas. She love
him in a way that was hard to explain. He was the chief c
her mother's people, and a man whom she respected, b
she did not want to be his wife. She was proud of her In
dian blood, but she was too much her father's daughte
ever to be able to live the nomadic life of the Jojoba. Sh
supposed if she loved Mangas she would gladly live wit
him as his wife, but her heart belonged to another, on
who was unaware of the love she had for him. Nor woul
he welcome her love, should he ever find out about it.

Maleaha looked at Kane's dark, handsome face, an
when he looked at her she quickly turned her head, fear
ing he would be able to read the love in her eyes.

When they stopped for lunch, Maleaha found Kan
watching her, and when he walked over to her she turne
away with the pretense of filling the coffee pot with wate
from the stream they had been following all morning.

"What do you think you are doing?" he asked her a
she placed the pot on the fire and added coffee to it.

"I am making coffee for Lamas. He has a passion fo
coffee," she said, not fully understanding his question.

"That is not what I was asking, and you know it."

"Lamas is more like a white man than you may sup
pose. He likes to sleep in a bed with a soft mattress, and

as I said before, he has a passion for coffee," she told him nervously.

"I was referring to last night, and you know it. I have had a lot of time to think about it, and I have finally put the pieces together. Last night was not for my benefit. You were hoping that Mangas's warriors would report back to him that you and I were on . . . for want of a better word, friendly terms."

Maleaha drew in her breath at his perception. She stood up, ready to face his anger. It was not anger she saw in his face, but more of a troubled look.

"You are not angry with me?"

"Yes, I am angry with you, but not for the reason you may suppose. I am angry that you would place yourself in a position to be used."

Maleaha was stunned by his statement. "I thought you would be displeased because I used you to try and fool Mangas."

"Maleaha, it seems this time you are caught between the Indian and the white worlds, and both would try to use you."

There was a softness in his eyes that she had never seen before, and it made her all the more confused.

"I knew what I was letting myself in for when I agreed to come along."

"What are your feelings for Mangas?"

"I respect him." She lowered her head, unable to meet his probing glance. "I also fear him."

"At last I have found something you are afraid of," he said grimly.

"I do not fear that Mangas will harm me," she said

quickly.

"What do you fear from him then?"

"I . . . Mangas wants me for his wife."

"And you do not fancy yourself as his wife?"

"I do . . . not love him in that way."

"I see. Is there another man who holds that place in your heart, say, Clay Madason?"

Maleaha raised her head and stared, not into his face but instead at the brass buttons on the front of his blue uniform.

"I love Clay, of course, as I would love a brother."

Kane placed his finger under her chin and raised her face up to his. "A very enviable position, no doubt." With his free hand he touched her cheek softly. "I wonder if I would also rate the love of a brother, as Clay Madason does?"

Maleaha shook her head. "If you were my brother, I would ask that you be adopted out."

Kane smiled, "It is just as well. I have no wish to be your brother." He studied her beautiful face. "No, I do not wish to be your brother."

Maleaha wished she could ask him what he did want from her, but at that moment the coffee pot she had placed on the fire chose to boil over, thus saving her question, and his answer.

Maleaha quickly reached for the pot but Kane forestalled her. "Silly girl, do you want to burn yourself?" He pushed her aside, and using a stick, moved the pot off the fire.

Maleaha wondered why she felt like crying. Surely it had nothing to do with the fact that Lamas's coffee was

184

not fit to drink now.

Once Kane had removed the pot from the fire he stood up and looked at her. "It is my guess that you enjoy being the belle of Santa Fe far too much to give it up and be tied to one man. Am I right?"

Maleaha bristled. "Perhaps I am not unlike you in that respect. I have heard it said that you break a new heart every week."

"I was not aware that my personal life was of any interest to you, Miss Deveraux," he drawled.

Maleaha turned her back to him. What had she said to make him angry again, she wondered? She was growing weary of this constant war that went on between the two of them.

"Miss Deveraux, it is not too late to change your mind," Kane said, turning her to face him once more. "You can get on your horse and ride away right now, and no one will fault you for it, least of all me."

"No. I knew the Robertson family who were killed by the Arapaho. I want to see their murderers punished."

"All right, but don't say that you didn't have the opportunity to withdraw."

Maleaha watched him as he turned his back on her and walked away. She remembered Salador's once telling her that it was not considered bad for one to tell a golden lie.

"What is a golden lie, Salador?" she had asked.

"A golden lie is silence. It is when you do not voice the truth, but keep it to yourself," he had told her.

That was what she must do now. She would tell the

golden lie. She would remain silent about her love for
Kane. He must never know that she loved him with all her
heart.

CHAPTER ELEVEN

Mangas walked toward Maleaha. His dark face had a foreboding look on it. "So, Little Flower, once more you come among your mother's people with the white man," he said, his eyes burning into hers.

Maleaha slid from her horse and stood before him. "Mangas, I have brought Major Benedict here for a good reason. I hope you will listen to him and consider what he asks of you."

He was silent for a moment. His dark eyes seemed to become even darker as he looked at Kane. "I will listen to this man, but only because you ask it of me, Maleaha."

Maleaha turned to Kane and told him to dismount.

When they were inside Mangas's teepee, Maleaha asked Kane to be seated. "Tell Mangas I am honored that he has consented to talk with me," Kane told her.

"Have you heard about the latest raids, Mangas?" Maleaha asked, not bothering to tell him what Kane had said, since he understood for himself.

"Why did your father refuse my offer of marriage to

187

you, Maleaha?'' Mangas said in a quiet voice that was laced with anger.

Maleaha found herself blushing, and lowered her head. ''I love another man, Mangas. My father would not wish me to marry without love.''

She avoided Mangas's eyes, but she heard the sadness in his voice. ''I would have you for my wife, Maleaha.''

Not knowing how to answer him, and feeling fear at his words, she turned to Kane. Kane sensed she was frightened and he spoke quickly, trying to draw Mangas's attention away from her.

''Tell Mangas about the latest raids and the death of the Robertson family, and also that we would be grateful if he would help us find these Arapahos.''

''Mangas, the Arapaho have taken the lives of a white family, and this saddens me. I think they are having fun eluding the army and mocking the Jojoba.''

''Why should you think they mock us?''

''They trespass on Jojoba land to do their mischief, and do not forget they tried to implicate you when these raids first started. If it were not for Major Benedict's intervention, you would still be suspect. I would hope that you would help the army drive the Arapaho back to the Colorados.''

''You are wise beyond your years, Maleaha. I would like to have a wife who is as wise as she is beautiful,'' Mangas said softly. ''I have waited a long time for you to grow up, Little Flower.''

''Mangas, I love this man, Kanen Benedict.''

''Have you lain with him, Maleaha? Does he also love you?''

Maleaha tried to look into Mangas's eyes, knowing she must convince him that she and Kane had been intimate. "Yes," she said lowering her head, knowing he would be able to see the lie in her eyes.

"I do not believe you, Maleaha. You still have the look of innocence. I would not like it if I find you have not spoken the truth to me."

Kane watched the exchange of words between Maleaha and Mangas, knowing they were not discussing the raid by the tone of Mangas's voice and the look in his dark eyes. Kane imagined what must be transpiring between them. He had been a fool to allow Maleaha to come with him. He should have insisted she remain at Deveraux Ranch where she would be safe. He decided to try once more to distract Mangas.

"Tell Mangas the army is prepared to pay him if he will help us drive the Arapaho from the New Mexico Territory."

"Would you consider helping the army for pay, Mangas?" Maleaha asked, glad to talk about anything that would take his mind off her.

"I have no use for the white man's money," he said in a voice that plainly showed his contempt.

She turned to Kane, "Mangas says he has no use for the money, major."

"Tell him we are prepared to pay him in horses and cattle. The amount can be worked out to his satisfaction."

"Mangas, would you consider this?"

"I love the color of your eyes, Maleaha. I believe I would never tire of looking into your eyes," Mangas said caressingly. "I would like to see your eyes reflected in

189

the eyes of my firstborn son.'' He reached out and touched her face softly.

Maleaha instinctively reached for Kane's hand and clasped it firmly. ''The major is a very jealous man, Mangas.''

''Dead men cannot feel jealousy, Maleaha,'' Mangas told her in a menacing voice.

''If you harmed the man I love, I would hate you,'' she warned him, her fear for the man she loved wiping out her caution. ''Do not threaten me with his life, Mangas.''

Mangas stood up and crossed his arms over his broad chest. ''I will speak to you no more today. You and this white man will remain here until I have had time to think.''

He walked purposefully out of the teepee, and Maleaha turned frightened eyes to Kane.

''What has occurred, Miss Deveraux?''

''I am not sure, but Mangas has ordered us to remain in camp while he decides what to do.''

Kane watched as Maleaha paced up and down the width of the teepee. Then she went over to the tent opening and looked out.

''Why are you upset? Tell me what Mangas said to you.''

''I do not want to speak of it, major.''

''I can see that you are frightened. I will not allow Mangas to harm you. You are under the protection of the United States Army.''

She laughed, ''If Mangas decides that I have lied to him, not you or the army could save me.''

He was about to ask her to explain when Lamas poked

his head through the teepee and spoke to Maleaha.

"Mangas is angry with you, Maleaha. I do not know what he will do, but he went to see your aunt. Then he rode out of camp. It would be better if you go to your aunt now, and I will keep the white man with me."

"What do you think he will do, Lamas?"

"I do not know, but I shall keep my ears and eyes open. If it were possible, I would take you away from here, but we are being watched. It is best to act as if nothing is wrong."

Maleaha turned to Kane. He had never seen her so frightened. Not even the day they had been attacked by the Arapaho. He watched as she clasped and unclasped her hands.

"Major, Mangas is very angry with me. I . . . told him that I am your woman. I am sorry. It seemed the best thing to do at the time. You see, he wants me for his wife, and I am frightened," she admitted.

"Did he believe you when you told him you were my woman?"

"I do not think so."

"Was that the reason you slept beside me last night?"

"Yes, and apparently Mangas's spies told him we slept together, but he is still not convinced."

"Miss Deveraux, as long as I live I will never let him take you. You can trust me in this."

She looked into his silver eyes, and saw what? He was a brave man, but she knew he would not stand a chance against Mangas while they were both his prisoners.

"I would never allow you to be harmed on my account, major. I only hope I have not damaged the mission by refusing Mangas.''

''Will Mangas leave you alone if he believes me to be your . . . lover?'' Kane said in a deep voice.

''Yes, but he is not easy to fool, major.''

Kane reached out and took her chin in his hand and studied her beautiful face. ''It would seem you have been exploited by both sides: by Mangas, because he wants you as his wife, and by the army, because they want your help to catch the Arapaho.''

''You are not angry with me because I told Mangas I am your woman?''

He raised a dark eyebrow, ''Perhaps I should ask if you are angry with me. If I had convinced you to . . . be my . . . lady friend, as I tried to, you could have been honest with Mangas when you told him you were my woman.'' His voice was deep and his silver eyes probed deeply into her green ones.

''I should be angry with you, major. At least Mangas offered me marriage.''

Kane laughed, ''but you turned us both down. I wonder if there is any man who could get you to agree to be his woman?''

Oh yes, she thought, I would be your woman if you asked me to be. ''That is not our problem at the moment. You must go with Lamas and stay with him.''

''Where will you be?''

''I am going to visit with my aunt and uncle. I will inform you immediately should something happen.'' If I am able to, she added to herself.

''Why is it I feel I have not been in charge since that day I met you?'' Kane said as he swept out of the teepee and found Lamas waiting for him.

Maleaha hugged her aunt, who seemed troubled as she led Maleaha into her teepee. After they had eaten, her aunt spoke quietly, as if she were afraid of being overheard.

"Mangas is very angry with you, Maleaha. When he returns he will have decided what to do about you."

"I do not want to be his woman, my aunt."

"Is it true that you belong to the white man who accompanied you here?"

"No, I spoke falsely when I told Mangas I was the major's woman."

"I love you, Maleaha, and it is because I love you that I tell you that Mangas intends to set spies on you and the white man tonight to see if you spoke the truth. If he discovers your deception, I do not know what he will do. I think he will force you to be his woman, if he thinks you have tricked him."

"What can I do? I am frightened."

Her aunt took her hand and looked sadly into her eyes. "You must go to the white man and lie with him tonight."

Maleaha felt hot tears behind her eyes. "I cannot, I would be so ashamed."

"Maleaha, you must. It is the only way. Will the white man help you?"

"I do not know. Will I have to allow him to . . ."

"Daughter of my dead sister, I wish I could help you, but in this I fear the white man is the only one who can help you." She kissed Maleaha's cheek. "You must ask him to take you as his woman tonight. I am sad to tell you

193

this, but it is the only way to stop Mangas.''

"I cannot bear it. The major will never understand why I would offer myself to him. He will think I have done this kind of thing before.''

"No, he will be able to tell that you have never been with a man before.''

Maleaha looked at her. "I do not know if I will be able to go through with it, but I suppose if it is the only way, I do not have any choice.''

Her aunt nodded in agreement. "It is the only way to keep Mangas from taking you.''

"Do you think the major will be in any danger if I go to him?''

"No. I believe Mangas loves you. I do not think he will harm the white man if he believes you want him.''

"I do not know why Mangas loves me, my aunt. I do not like the idea of deceiving him. I like him a great deal.''

"I have known for a long time that Mangas loves you. It is the reason he has never taken a wife. I think he always thought you would belong to him someday. I know in my heart you would never be happy living with the Jojoba. This is why you must not hesitate tonight when you go to the white man. He will know what to do.''

"Is it . . . will it be very painful?''

"Only at first.''

Maleaha could no longer stop the flow of tears. She would be pushed to her limit tonight. She would be forced to humble herself before the man she loved. Kane thought of her as nothing more than an irritant, and the fact that he had offered to make her his mistress before did not help.

Would she be able to convince him of her reasons for seeking him out?

"Tell me what I must do, my aunt."

"I shall arrange it so the white man has a teepee to himself, and when it is dark you must go to him. When Mangas returns he must find you with this man."

"What would happen should Mangas return, and I were not with the major?"

"He would make you his woman tonight, and no one could stop him."

Maleaha stood up. "I will do whatever I have to, my aunt."

Kane sat on the rough buffalo robe. He had been given food and water, but was not allowed to leave the teepee. When he had looked out a moment ago there had been a man standing guard just out front who had motioned for him to go back inside.

Very little light penetrated the teepee as night descended. He lay back on the buffalo robe. He had heard stories of the different Indian tribes having lice-infested living quarters, but this tribe seemed to be the exception. They seemed to be very clean. The buffalo robe on which he was lying was as clean as the teepee.

Sitting up, he unbuttoned his jacket and removed it. It was hot inside the teepee, and he wished he could sleep outside under the stars. He had no idea what was going on at this moment. A short while ago a woman had come into the tent and Lamas had left with her. Where was Maleaha? Could she be with Mangas? He cursed himself as a fool for allowing her to come with him. He had known Mangas wanted her. Jonas had told him about the Indian chief's asking for her. Kane knew he must try and find Maleaha no matter what the consequences might be. He reached for his jacket, with the intention of searching for her.

CHAPTER TWELVE

The tent flap was pushed aside, and Kane watched as Maleaha entered the teepee. She stood silently for a moment and seemed to be avoiding his eyes.

Maleaha wondered how she would ever be able to tell him what she wanted. Her instincts told her to run from this teepee and never look back. She raised her eyes slowly. They started at his black boots and traveled up his long blue-clad legs. When her eyes reached his chest she saw he had removed his jacket and shirt. Black curly hair covered his muscular chest and disappeared in a vee beneath his blue trousers. Maleaha found she could not meet his gaze, so she lowered her head and stared at his shiny black boots instead.

Kane frowned at her strange behavior, then he realized she must be embarrassed by his naked chest, so he reached for his jacket and slipped it on, not bothering to button it.

"Has Mangas returned?" he asked.

"No, not yet," she replied, wishing she could die rather than ask him what she must.

"There is something wrong. What is it?" He de
manded.

Maleaha shook her head, unable to speak, not knowing
how to ask him to help her.

Kane forced her head up and looked at her with a puz
zled look on his face.

"There is something wrong! What is it?"

"Major, I do not know how to ask you this . . ." Her
voice seemed to have failed her, and she tried to drop her
head, but Kane kept a firm grip on her chin, making it im
possible.

"What is it you wish to ask?" His silver eyes swept
over her face, noting the red tinge to her cheeks. What
ever it was that she wanted to ask him was causing her
great embarassment.

"Major, my Aunt Kosha has told me that Mangas does
not believe I am your woman. H . . . he plans to take me
as his wife tonight when he returns."

Kane frowned. "Explain what you mean."

"I mean that Mangas will force me to his bed, and af
terwards make me his wife." Her hands gripped Kane's
jacket front, and he could see the fear that was written on
her beautiful face and reflected in her green eyes.

"I see. What can I do to help you?" His voice was
soft, and his eyes looked deeply into hers.

"Will you help me?" she said in a voice that pleaded
for his help.

"You have only to tell me what to do, and I will do it. I
feel it is partly my fault that you are here now."

In spite of his restraining hand on her face, Maleaha
lowered her head.

"I am very ashamed, major. I will . . . would you . . ."

Kane smiled slightly as she buried her face on his shoulder, trying to overcome her embarrassment.

"I believe I know what you are asking me. What I don't know is how far you want me to go to convince Mangas that you are my woman."

"I do not really know what happens between a man and a woman, but if you would not mind . . . if you would . . ." Maleaha raised her head and looked at him, and Kane saw the unshed tears that sparkled in her emerald-green eyes.

"Do not make me say it. I cannot!" she pleaded.

His arms tightened protectively around her. He drew her head down to rest against his shoulder. Anger burned deep inside him at the thought that she must seek him out to save herself from Mangas. He thought he could never love her more than he did at that moment. Kane knew he would never let Mangas touch her as long as he lived. For perhaps the first time in his life, Kane considered a woman's feelings before his own. As much as he wanted Maleaha, he did not want her under these circumstances. Where he had once thought she was wild and promiscuous, he now knew her to be frightened and innocent.

"Oh darling, I know what it must have cost you to come here like this," he said in a loving voice. "I would never do anything to dishonor you, don't you know that?"

Maleaha closed her eyes, loving the way he had called her darling. She remembered the time he had asked her for just what she was now offering him. She felt she must make him understand that if he did not indeed take what she offered, Mangas would, when he returned.

"Major, my aunt says I must ask you to . . . I do not know the word for it," she said in a pain-filled voice.

She heard his sharp intake of breath. "Are you asking me to take your innocence from you?" His voice was soft, and Maleaha could feel his lips on her face.

"Yes," she whispered as she buried her face in the soft, curly black hair that covered his chest.

There was complete silence in the teepee as the full impact of her words hit him. He had thought she wanted him to pretend that he had made love to her. He had no idea she had been asking him to actually do it.

"I will not do what you ask of me, Maleaha. I think we can convince Mangas without . . . you will have to trust me."

Maleaha raised her tear bright eyes to his, "You do not want me?"

Kane closed his eyes and pushed her gently away from him. "Oh Lord, if you only knew how much I want you, you would run to Mangas to escape me. I never envisioned myself turning down such a tempting offer, but I am angry that you, who are only seventeen and still such an innocent child, should be placed in such a degrading situation."

Not fully understanding his rejection of her, Maleaha backed toward the tent opening. "If you will not help me, I must find someone who will." She turned on her heels, with the intention of fleeing into the night to hide her shame.

Perhaps she could sneak out of the village. But her aunt

had told her Mangas was having her watched to prevent just such an attempt, and she could not leave Kane to face Mangas's anger alone.

Kane grabbed her roughly by the shoulders and spun her around to face him.

"Damn you, are you so anxious to have your maidenhood taken from you that you would offer yourself to anyone?"

"It was a mistake for me to come here. Release me." Maleaha demanded.

He released her, and Maleaha watched as he removed his jacket and tossed it to the ground. Then his hands went to his belt and he began to unbuckle it.

"When will Mangas return?"

Maleaha shook her head, unable to answer.

"If you are modest, I suggest you go into the corner to disrobe," he told her angrily.

Maleaha was humiliated and trapped, trapped by a situation that was not entirely of her own making, And as frightened as she was, she knew she must not balk. She must go through with her plan, or else before the night was ended she would be the wife of Mangas, with no hope for escape.

She moved to the darkened corner, and with trembling hands began removing her moccasins. She closed her eyes, and her mind, as she removed all of her clothing, knowing she must call on all of her courage to see her through to the bitter end.

There was no joy in Maleaha's heart, only bitterness and shame, knowing what Kane must be thinking of her. In his way of thinking she must look a complete fool.

201

Her mind shied away from what would become of her after this night. She would be little better than what Kane once thought her to be.

When the last of her clothing was removed Maleaha hugged the dark shadows, not knowing what to do next.

"Come here, Maleaha," Kane said in a soft voice.

She felt trapped by her own daring, and wished she could make a dash for freedom. She stood on shaky legs, calling on all her courage, and stepped out of the darkened corner. Her eyes refused to move past Kane's bare chest as she swallowed a lump in her throat. When she looked into his face, she saw his silver eyes moving slowly over her body, and she blushed and lowered her head.

Kane drew in his breath as his eyes moved over her perfect body. She was slender, and her hips were softly rounded, her legs long and shapely. Her breasts were beautifully shaped, and in that moment, Kane knew that before him stood the most beautiful and perfect woman he had ever seen. Every woman he had known before her faded into insignificance. For the moment he did not look at her as a man who wanted to possess her beautiful body, but rather as a man who was in love. He no longer wondered if her skin was the golden color all over, for indeed it was.

She looked like some golden goddess, meant to be carved into a masterpiece and preserved for eternity.

He was silent for so long that Maleaha raised her head and looked into his eyes. Seeing the look of adoration in his eyes, she froze.

Kane walked slowly toward her, and when she stepped

back he reached out for her and drew her gently into his arms.

Maleaha's senses reeled as she felt his naked body press against hers. Kane reached up and pushed the curtain of ebony hair from her face, knowing what she was feeling.

"Do not be frightened, darling, I will not do anything to you, trust me," he whispered against her ear. "I believe we can make Mangas think we are lovers without actually completing the act."

Kane lifted her into his arms and laid her down on the rough buffalo robe. As he lay down beside her and pulled her into his arms, Maleaha began to tremble. But it had nothing to do with fear. Her love cried out to him through silent lips. Her virgin body became soft and yielding against his hard muscled body. He was her love, and it was only right that she should be in his arms, she thought.

Raising her face, she looked into the silver eyes that were so soft it took her breath away.

"Lord, give me strength," he murmured against her soft cheek.

"What should I do?" she asked innocently.

Kane's hand moved over her back, down to her waist. "Try to lie still, and for God's sake, don't look at me like that. I am trying to hold on to my sanity."

"I do not think I understand, major."

Kane closed his eyes. "Lord, what an innocent you are." Then he looked at her and grinned. "Under the circumstances, perhaps you should call me Kane."

"All right, Kane, then what?"

"Stop asking questions for one thing, while I try to

push the thought of you lying naked in my arms out of my mind.''

''Maj . . . Kane, I think I should tell you that Mangas understands English.''

''I have come to suspect that he understood what I was saying to him.''

Suddenly the camp seemed to come to life. They could hear the sound of many riders returning, and the sound of men talking, while the dogs barked in welcome.

Maleaha threw her arms around Kane's neck and moved closer to him.

''He has returned. Mangas is back!''

Kane pulled the edge of the buffalo robe over Maleaha, taking care to cover only part of her body, leaving her legs and shoulders bare.

''What shall I do?'' she said in a pleading voice.

''Trust me,'' he whispered, knowing that Mangas would be hard to fool. He knew he must make it appear that they had indeed made love, and to convince Mangas of that fact. He would have to make sure Maleaha appeared softened by lovemaking, and not frightened as she was now.

His lips moved over her face as his hands roamed over her body. He could feel her trembling.

''Don't be frightened, darling, I will not harm you. Relax. Don't think, just feel,'' he murmured.

His hands moved over her flat stomach and then lower. Maleaha gasped as his hands caressed the most intimate part of her body. Kane saw her eyes were fever bright as he aroused a need in her. That was the look he wanted Mangas to see when he came into the teepee.

"Relax darling," he breathed against her lips, just before his mouth covered hers in a passionate kiss.

Kane was in agony as he tried to beat down the passion Maleaha's silky body had aroused in him. Maleaha was writhing and groaning under the masterful manipulation of his hands.

They were both aware of when the flap was thrown angrily aside and Mangas entered the teepee.

Kane felt Maleaha stiffen in his arms. "Do not be afraid," he whispered in her ear.

Maleaha looked up into Mangas's face and saw anger, but there was grief as well in the dark eyes that looked back at her.

Mangas walked hesitatingly toward her and dropped down on one knee. He reached out his hand to her, and then reconsidered, clenching his hand into a fist.

"I had thought we would love each other, Little Flower. I never wanted anyone for my wife but you. I think it would have been good between us."

Mangas had spoken in English, and Maleaha felt pity for him. She had not known until that moment the full extent of his feelings for her.

Kane's arms tightened protectively about Maleaha, and he gave Mangas a look that said he would die for her if he had to.

"Maleaha is my woman, Mangas. She belongs to me."

Mangas shifted his piercing eyes to Kane. "Do you intend to make her your wife, white man?"

"That is not your concern, Mangas."

"It *is* my concern. Maleaha has the blood of chiefs in

her veins. She is a Jojoba princess.'' Mangas's eyes were dark and foreboding as he looked at Kane. ''You have lain with her, and unless you make her your wife, she will be shamed before the whole village. If you do not wish to take her as your wife, say so now, and I will make her my wife.''

''I do intend to marry her,'' Kane said, ''but I wanted to wait until her father returned.''

''That would be too late, white man. I will perform the ceremony myself. I will leave you for the moment, but when I return, have your clothing on, and I will join the two of you together.'' Then he arose and left abruptly.

Maleaha buried her face in her hands. ''I feel so awful, I did not mean to hurt him. Oh Kane, did you see his face?'' she said in a voice filled with misery.

Kane turned his back to her. ''I think you had better dress yourself. It seems you and I are about to be joined in marriage.''

Maleaha gathered the buffalo robe about her and stood up. ''Kane, you do not need to go through with this. I did not intend to involve you to this extent.''

''You heard what Mangas said. If I do not stand up as your bridegroom tonight, he will.''

Maleaha ducked her head. ''I do not know what to do. I did not expect Mangas to go this far. I just wanted him to think I was your woman.''

''It doesn't matter, but unless you want Mangas to return and find you still undressed, I suggest you put your clothing on.''

''Little it matters now. You and Mangas have both seen too much of me tonight.''

Kane smiled to himself, wondering what the Indian marriage rites would be like. He knew after tonight he wanted Maleaha for his wife, but he wanted her tied to him through a proper marriage, one that would bind her to him for the rest of their lives.

Maleaha had just finished lacing her moccasins when Mangas returned, and he was not alone. Maleaha quickly presented her aunt and uncle to Kane and explained that they did not speak or understand English. Lamas was the other member of the wedding party.

"Jonas Deveraux will not like this," Lamas said, startling Kane with his command of the English language.

"At the moment there does not seem to be much that I can do about it," Kane said, noticing that Mangas had taken Maleaha to a corner of the teepee and was talking quietly to her.

"If this is not what you want, say so now, Maleaha."

Maleaha met Mangas's dark eyes and was able to tell him truthfully that she loved Kane.

"I have loved you for a very long time, Little Flower, never knowing that I would be called on one day to give you to another."

Maleaha's eyes filled with tears. "I am so sorry, Mangas, I never meant to hurt you."

He touched her face softly. "It is a hurt that will heal, Maleaha. Feel no pity for me. It is your wedding night."

At that moment Maleaha wished with all her heart that it was the tall dark chief of the Jojoba whom she loved, because she knew that the man who had won her heart did not love her in return.

Mangas took Maleaha's hand and led her over to Kane.

Maleaha caught her aunt's eye and smiled at her. Her aunt nodded her head in understanding.

Mangas looked at Kane, and there was intense dislike in the dark eyes. "Tonight, white man, you will be tied to the fairest of maidens. She is lovely for the eye to look upon, but she is so much more, she is true and loyal. Treat her with love and kindness, as she deserves."

"I am aware of her good qualities, and I will give her all that she deserves," Kane told him.

Mangas took Maleaha's hand, and then he reached for Kane's hand as well. "As chief of the Jojoba tribe, I give to you, Kane, the Princess Maleaha as your wife. You are bound by your honor to keep her from all harm, and to love her above all else." Mangas said the words in English, and then repeated them in the language of the Jojoba, for the sake of Maleaha's aunt. "I say this because I am the chief, that from this night on, Maleaha is your wife."

Maleaha tried to stop the tears from falling down her face. It was with this ceremony that her own father and mother had been joined in marriage. Her heart swelled with love for the man who was now her husband.

Mangas released Kane and Maleaha's hands, and turned to the others who had witnessed the marriage. "Let us leave them alone," he told the others, and Maleaha watched as her aunt and uncle filed out. Mangas turned to her at the entranceway, and spoke to her in the language of the Jojobas, then he ducked out the flap opening. Last of all Lamas left, giving Kane a look that plainly told him he was displeased.

Kane turned to Maleaha as he thought what a strange

night this had turned out to be. He still could not believe half of what had occurred.

"What did Mangas say to you just before he left?"

Maleaha buried her face in her hands and was crying softly. "He . . . he said that he was in such pain," she sobbed. "I wish I had not hurt him so badly."

"He left you little choice," Kane said, pulling her into his arms.

Maleaha looked up into the face of her husband as she dried her tears on the back of her hand. "I want to apologize to you about tonight. I feel terrible." More than anything she wanted to be his wife, but not this way, never this way.

"Why should you feel badly? In the space of one night I have gained myself a beautiful wife and made one very powerful enemy . . ."

"Kane, do not jest. I am serious."

"So am I. I may come to enjoy having you for a wife," he told her half joking, half serious. "Kiss me, Mrs. Benedict."

Maleaha met his lips halfway, as she felt his arms tighten about her. She put all the love she felt for Kane into her kiss, and when he raised his head his silver eyes were glazed with passion.

"How will I ever forget that I held you naked in my arms?" he whispered.

"Why would you want to forget?" Maleaha asked him as she pulled his head down to her and kissed his lips softly. She felt no shame as she had before, because he was now her husband. Perhaps he did not want her for his wife, and most probably he did not, but in her heart she was his, and always would be. Tomorrow did not matter, tonight was all that counted, she told herself.

Kane's arms tightened around her as he crushed her to him. "Are you aware of what you are doing?" he murmured against her lips.

"Yes," she answered as she began unbuttoning the brass buttons on his uniform.

"Maleaha, I am warning you, I may not be able to stop as I did before."

She slid her arms around his neck and laid her cheek against his. Kane pushed her away and stepped back. "Have you lost your senses? There is no longer any reason to pretend. You are safe from Mangas now."

Maleaha turned her back to him, feeling miserable. Kane was angry with her. She remembered that day by the river, when he had told her he would never marry her. Did he think she had tricked him into marriage? She wanted him to make love to her, and he must think her brazen and forward. It was just that she loved him and wanted to bind him to her. Perhaps if she allowed him to make love to her, he would want to keep her. With that thought in mind, she turned back to face him.

"I know there is no longer any reason to pretend, Kane. I was not pretending."

A smile played on his lips, and his brilliant eyes glinted like liquid silver. "I don't think you have the slightest notion that you are playing with fire, Maleaha." His voice sounded amused.

"I'm not playing, Kane," she whispered, moving closer to him. The amusement on his face changed, and he lazily lowered his eyelashes. Reaching out his hand, he started to touch her cheek, then thought better of it.

Maleaha reached for his hand and laid it against her face. "I am not pretending, Kane," she said once more.

Kane watched spellbound as Maleaha bent over and removed her moccasins. She did not know what was causing her to act so boldly. Perhaps deep inside she knew this was the only night she and Kane would ever have together. Perhaps she was grateful to him for saving her from Mangas, or maybe it was because she wanted him to make love to her.

Her eyes locked with Kane's just before she lifted her gown over her head. He closed his eyes as she stood naked in front of him. When he opened his eyes, they roamed over her silky body, and against his will he stepped closer to her.

"What are you trying to do to me?" he said in a strangled voice.

She took the one step that brought them together. "I want you to make love to me, Kane," she whispered, surprised at her own daring.

She was trembling as he began to remove his clothing, all the while watching her. This time she did not turn her head away, but watched him boldly, thinking how magnificent his body looked. He was beautiful, she thought.

Kane must have read her thoughts, because he picked her up in his arms and laid her down on the buffalo robe and lay down beside her, then pulled her into his arms.

"You shouldn't look at a man like that, Maleaha," he murmured against her cheek.

"Why?"

He shook with mirthful laughter. Raising his head, he

saw the gleam in her green eyes and caught his breath. "Because, you beautiful, desirable little savage, you have tempted me beyond endurance. This time, Maleaha, there will be more than touching and a few kisses."

"I know," she told him innocently.

"Damn you, Maleaha, how many victims do you want tonight? Was it not enough for you that you ripped Mangas's heart to shreds?"

"What do you mean?" She whispered, not really caring, because his hands were moving over her, molding her to his hard body.

Maleaha felt his hands glide over her breasts, and she began to tremble violently. Her lips sought his, and he did not turn away, but took command of her lips and kissed her deeply.

Maleaha had never felt such deep feelings, such love, and she wondered if Kane felt the same as she did. He rolled her over on her back and stared down at her. Then his lips crushed hers in a soul-shattering kiss. She laced her fingers through his ebony-colored hair. Kane groaned and looked at her through veiled lashes.

"It's not too late to back out, Maleaha, but I warn you, in a matter of seconds I will be unable to stop myself."

Maleaha tried to speak but seemed unable to make a sound. She reached up and pulled his dark head down and parted her lips in silent invitation.

"Maleaha," he cried as he gave her the kiss she had silently begged for. Kane was mindless. Her silky skin was driving him to the edge of madness. He raised his head, breaking off the kiss.

"Darling, I will try to make it as painless as possible,"

212

he said in a voice that shook with emotion.

Kane parted her legs, and at that moment Maleaha tried to pull away from him.

"No, darling, don't pull away from me now."

His lips found hers and she moaned beneath the smooth manipulation of his hands. Kane shifted his weight, and Maleaha opened her eyes in shocked surprise as pain ripped through her body when he entered the most intimate core of her womanhood. The pain disappeared almost before it started as his body took command of hers, and Maleaha felt herself being transported to another world, a world where there was only touching, feeling, and loving, a world she had not known existed until now.

To Maleaha it seemed that her body no longer belonged to her, that it had become a possession of Kane's, to do with as he wished. She felt his lips on her breast and she groaned as still stronger, deeper feelings lifted her upward.

Kane closed his eyes, thinking that his possession of Maleaha was the single most beautiful thing that had ever happened in his whole life. He had been with too many women to even count, but they were nothing compared to Maleaha. This was love in its purest form, and his body told him he had found the other half of himself, the perfect woman for him. Never had he been lifted so high. Never had he felt such perfect fulfillment until now. Maleaha had touched his heart and changed him. His body seemed to be reborn. It was as if God had created him for this very moment. He had possessed many women, but none of them had ever possessed him, as Maleaha now did. His lips moved down her throat to find the sweetness of her breasts.

Maleaha gasped in pleasure. She was surprised and de
lighted that her body was giving Kane pleasure. After all
her body belonged to him as surely as her heart did
Mountains of feelings washed over her body as she
groaned and turned her head from side to side. So this
was what it felt like to be a woman, Kane's woman. The
two of them scaled heights, locked in a fiery embrace
Kane knew just how to get her to respond to him. With
softly spoken command, or the touch of his hand, he in
structed Maleaha in the art of lovemaking.

Their bodies had become wet from perspiration, and
Maleaha laced her fingers through Kane's wet hair.

''Maleaha, Maleaha,'' he murmured over and over in
her ear.

Words of love tumbled on Maleaha's tongue, but she
dared not voice them. ''Oh, Kane, I never knew that life
could be so beautiful,'' she whispered.

''Yes, beautiful, beautiful, Maleaha,'' he murmured
half out of his mind with desire and love.

Suddenly Maleaha experienced a new feeling. It was
pain and it was delight. Her hands tightened in Kane's
hair, and her body shuddered, answered by Kane's body
He rolled over to relieve Maleaha of his heavy weight.

Kissing her deeply, he pulled her into his arms. ''Dar
ling, you are so perfect,'' he said against her ear.

Maleaha wanted to tell Kane so many things, but she
suddenly felt shy, and buried her face against his shoul
der.

''Well, little Indian, you taught me a few things to
night.'' She could feel the smile on his face as he laid his

cheek next to hers. "It was good between us, Maleaha."

His lips covered hers in a kiss that seemed to burn her mouth with the heat that radiated from his. Maleaha gasped as he pulled her fully against him, and their bodies seemed to fuse together, one body, one soul, one heartbeat.

"I can never get enough of you," he said gruffly.

Once more Kane took her on the wings of love to a world high above the earth as he made love to her for the second time. But unlike the first time, Maleaha knew what to expect, and her body readily obeyed the silent commands Kane issued her. There was such beauty and love that she felt tears running down her cheeks. He had not once said that he loved her, but for the moment it did not matter, she had enough love for both of them. This was her husband, and she readily gave him all he asked of her.

Afterwards, Maleaha lay exhausted in Kane's arms, loving the way his hands moved caressingly over her body.

Kane felt he had indeed stamped his claim of ownership on Maleaha, and even though she had not said that she loved him, he knew he had held her as no man ever had before, and he was determined that after they returned to Santa Fe he would ask her to marry him in a proper ceremony. He smiled to himself. Maleaha had accomplished what many other women had failed to do. In a short time she had wound him around her little finger and made him think about such things as settling down, building a home, and starting a family.

Suddenly he needed to hear her say that she felt as he

did. Kane knew he would never want to seek pleasure from another woman. He had found perfection and total satisfaction, and he would never again settle for anything less. How strange that he, a man who had known many women, would fall under the spell of a girl hardly out of the schoolroom, he thought.

His hand settled on her smooth, flat stomach. "Did I hurt you, Maleaha?"

She looked into his eyes, unable to speak, and shook her head.

"Did you feel as I did, Maleaha?"

Maleaha closed her eyes as a tear escaped and ran down her cheek. How could she tell him that she felt she belonged to him, and after tonight she would always be his. But he must not know that. He must not know that she loved him.

"I feel very different inside. I am no longer a girl, but a woman now." It was not what she wanted to say, but she saw danger in revealing her innermost feelings to him.

Kane frowned. She had not told him what he wanted to hear. Did she feel none of the love that he felt for her? Had she merely used him to stop Mangas from taking her as his wife? The tender feelings he had for her were pushed aside by his anger. Good Lord, he thought, he had been on the verge of telling her that he was in love with her. His voice was harsh when he spoke to her. "How easy it is to arouse your body now that you have been awakened by a man's caresses, Maleaha," and to prove his words, his hand slid up her long silky leg to rest on her stomach, and Maleaha gasped.

Maleaha felt herself being crushed in his arms.

"God help me. If I die tomorrow, I have finally felt alive." He held her so tightly that she marveled in his strength. Time passed and he did no more than hold her in his arms, and soon they both fell asleep.

The next morning when Maleaha awoke, Kane was not beside her. Looking around the teepee, she saw he was sitting on the edge of the buffalo robe, fully dressed. His silver eyes moved over her beautiful body, and she felt no shame that he seemed to find her beautiful. After all, he was her husband. It was on the tip of her tongue to tell him that she loved him, when his eyes turned to silver ice.

"I suggest you get dressed, Miss Deveraux. The way people come and go around here you might find yourself in a most embarrassing situation," he said coldly.

Maleaha stiffened at his cold words. He had called her Miss Deveraux! Last night he had called her Mrs. Benedict. What had occurred to make him change his mind? She remembered the tender moments they had shared last night, and she searched his face to see if he remembered also, but his eyes were cold as he stared back at her. Oh no, she thought, as realization dawned on her. He did not feel married to her, and why should he? Last night he had been forced by Mangas to go through with the marriage, and it had been she who had sought him out. She had given herself to him without hesitation, and she felt real shame as she realized how it must have appeared to him.

Kane stood up and peered down at her as she pulled the buffalo robe over her nakedness. "I want to tell you now, that I do not feel bound by the marriage performed by Mangas last night," he told her.

Maleaha wrapped the robe around her and stood up.

"There is no reason that you should, major." She hoped her voice sounded calm, though she was anything but calm on the inside; she was feeling heartbreak and shame.

"I would like to thank you for helping me last night, and I think you will understand, after what happened between us last night, that I hope our paths will not cross in the future," she said, letting him go, freeing him of any obligation he might feel toward her, and praying he would not know about her golden lie.

Kane had been watching her sleep while he rehearsed how he would ask her to marry him. He had planned their future down to the the smallest details. As soon as the Arapaho could be dealt with, and he had returned to Santa Fe, they would have a proper wedding.

He would look into purchasing the land Jonas had told him about, then he would have a house built on it. Maleaha would have to move to the fort with him for a while. There were quarters to accommodate the officers and their wives, and while they were not exactly what she was accustomed to, they would not be too bad. The main thing was that they would be together.

Kane watched her walk across the room to where her clothes were. Had he heard her correctly? Had she said that she did not want to see him again? Was she out of her mind? Did she not know that what they had shared last night came to few people in a lifetime? Anger and frustration carried him across the space that divided them, and he grabbed her by the arm and turned her to face him.

"What do you mean you hope our paths never cross again?"

Maleaha raised her head and give him a look of indifference that she was far from feeling.

"I do not wish to repeat what happened last night," she told him, knowing she was being very dishonest, something she had very rarely been in her whole life.

His fingers tightened on her shoulder, and he forced her to look at him. "Why do I get the feeling that you used me last night?"

She raised her head and gave him her coldest stare. It was better that he should think her promiscuous than find out that she loved him. "I admit I used you last night, but you cannot say that you did not use me as well."

"Damn you," he said, shoving her away from him. His silver eyes narrowed to tiny slits and he clenched his fists, wanting to hit out at something or someone.

"It was my pleasure, Miss Deveraux. The next time you are in need of a toss on the robe, I hope you will consider me."

Maleaha raised her hand, and before he could react, she struck him hard across the face.

Kane grabbed her hand, and, pinning her arms behind her, pulled her tightly against his body. "I would not ever try that again," he said through clenched teeth.

"Release me. I hate you!"

"You did not hate me last night. You were not very experienced, and usually my taste runs more to the older, more experienced female. Perhaps when you are more experienced . . ." his voice trailed off.

Maleaha struggled with all her might, wishing she could strike him again for his insulting words. She wondered how she could ever have thought she loved him.

Her newfound love died a speedy death. Why was it with Kanen Benedict she could swing from love to hate so quickly?

Lamas chose that moment to enter the teepee, and in two strides he was across the space that divided them. "Does he hurt you?" he asked Maleaha in the language of the Jojobas.

"No, I am all right."

Lamas watched Kane carefully as he spoke to Maleaha. "Mangas wants to see you and the white man at once." His dark eyes were threatening as he looked at Kane.

"Tell Mangas we will be there as soon as I dress."

Lamas nodded and walked toward the opening, giving Kane one last warning glance as he disappeared.

Maleaha clutched the buffalo robe about her, and looked up at Kane, who still gripped her by the shoulder. "Mangas wants to see us right away."

Kane nodded and released his hold on her. Turning his back to her, he walked over to the opening and peered outside, allowing Maleaha time to dress. His anger had cooled but little as he watched a group of young Indian boys run around in circles playing some game that resembled tag. He turned to Maleaha, who was now sitting on the buffalo robe lacing her moccasins. Feeling his eyes on her, she looked up. After tying the leather strap of her moccasin she stood up.

"Major, I really am grateful to you for last night. I know at best it was an awkward situation. I had no right to become angry with you, as you only did what I asked of you."

220

The muscle in his jaw twitched. Grateful, damn! Again his anger ignited. He did not want her gratitude. Why couldn't she see that what had happened between them last night was special. He was afraid she would be able to read his expression, so his mask fell into place once more.

"As I told you before, it was my pleasure. If you are ready, let's see what Mangas wants."

He held the tent flap open for her to pass through in front of him. She avoided his eyes as she stepped outside. Her feelings were still too raw, and the tears were too near the surface. Today there was a deep ache inside her body, but, if she could just hold up until this ordeal was over, then later there would be time for tears.

At Mangas's teepee the flap was pushed aside by a fierce-looking warrior. "Mangas awaits within," he told Maleaha.

Mangas motioned for Kane and Maleaha to be seated on the buffalo robe across from him.

Maleaha's eyes were drawn by his dark glance. There was no recrimination in his eyes, only a deep sadness. He gave her just the slightest smile before he turned to Kane.

"White man, I have decided to help you find the Arapaho. I would not usually help a white man against my Indian brothers, but I like the Arapaho even less than I do the white race."

Mangas had taken Kane completely by surprise. After last night he expected anything but the offer of help Mangas had just given him.

"I am pleased that you offer your help, Mangas. You will not find the United States Army ungrateful."

221

Mangas's dark eyes rested on Maleaha, "I do not do it for the army. I do it because Maleaha asked it of me. She is a Jojoba princess, therefore I want to honor her wishes."

"I thought perhaps that was the reason," Kane told him.

Maleaha smiled brightly at Mangas. "I am so pleased that you will help drive the Arapaho from our land."

Mangas fastened his dark gaze on Kane once more. "You will deliver to me, at a designated spot, fifty horses and fifty head of beef, is that understood?"

Kane nodded. "It will be done."

"You do not haggle, white man. Perhaps I set my price too low."

"I would not insult your intelligence by haggling with you. It is a fair price."

Mangas looked at Kane suspiciously. "Can I trust your word? Maleaha seems to think so."

"Yes, I will see to it at once. If you like, Maleaha can go with me to see Colonel Johnson. I know you trust her."

"Yes, I trust Maleaha to do this, but you will not be going with her. If I am to help you with the Arapaho, there will be no time for you to return to the fort. Is this acceptable to you?"

"Yes, I will do whatever you think is best," Kane told him.

Mangas turned to Maleaha. "Go and say good-bye to your aunt, Little Flower, then I want you and Lamas to leave right away. Do not fear that you will encounter the Arapaho, for they are to the east of the direction you will be traveling.''

''I will write her a note to take to Colonel Johnson,'' Kane said standing up. ''Are you sure she will be in no danger?''

''I would not send her otherwise,'' Mangas told him.

''I will go to my aunt now, Kane. That will give you time to write to Colonel Johnson,'' Maleaha said, sweeping out of the teepee.

''You are a very fortunate man, major. Maleaha is what every man seeks in a wife,'' Mangas said, fixing Kane with a dark gaze.

''Yes,'' Kane admitted. ''There is no other like her.''

Each man sized the other up, and then Mangas turned away. ''Write your letter, major. It may be the last time you will see your wife. The Arapaho are a fierce enemy. Many will not return from the battle we go into. They are more than a hundred strong. I know you have only twenty-five men, and I will take forty warriors with me. We will be outnumbered. Does this bother you?''

''I will ride at your side, Mangas. I have no fear.''

Word had spread throughout the Jojoba village that Maleaha had married the white man, and she received many good wishes. Maleaha knew that many of the young Indian maidens were happy that she was married, because they could now hope that Mangas would choose among them for a bride.

After Maleaha bade her aunt farewell, she found Lamas had already saddled her horse and was mounted, waiting for her. She saw Kane standing beside her mount.

He handed her the note for Colonel Johnson. She took it and swung herself into the saddle.

Kane grabbed her horse's reins. "Maleaha, when this is all over we need to talk."

Her eyes gleamed brightly as she looked at him. "I have nothing to say to you, now or in the future. I would like it if you would not seek me out, nor will I ever trouble you again. Last night is better forgotten." She jerked the reins from his hand and whirled her mount around and raced out of the camp in a cloud of dust.

Had she looked back, she would have seen the look of pain on Kane's handsome face. But she did not look back. It was Lamas who witnessed the pain in the silver eyes that stared after Maleaha.

Maleaha let the tears flow freely. Kane was going into battle, and he could die. She wanted to ride back to him and beg him to be careful, but she didn't dare. She would pray for his safety, for she knew she could not stand it should anything happen to him.

CHAPTER THIRTEEN

After Maleaha had delivered the message from Kane to his men, she and Lamas rode hard across country, knowing if they hurried they could reach the fort in two days' time.

That night as Maleaha lay beneath the stars, she thought of the previous night when she had lain in Kane's arms. Her body felt feverish, and she tossed and turned. She would never be the same after last night. She was a woman now with a woman's desires. But those desires were for one man. In her heart she felt Kane was her husband, even if he did not share her feelings. Perhaps it was because her mother and father had been married by the laws of the Jojoba that she felt bound by their laws. How was it possible to love a man and feel contempt for him at the same time? Why could it not have been Mangas she loved, or any of the dozens of men who would have loved her in return? She tried to channel her thoughts in a different direction.

"Lamas, why do you suppose Mangas agreed to help the army fight the Arapaho?"

"He is crafty. The army will be helping him get rid of an old enemy, and pay him at the same time. I believe he will one day be a great chief."

"Do you think me foolish for not accepting Mangas as my husband?"

"You are more white than Indian. It is easy enough for you to go to the Jojoba village for short visits, but you would not be happy living there for very long."

"I would have done it, had I loved Mangas."

"You are the wife of the white man."

"He does not think of me as his wife. I don't even like him."

Lamas smiled to himself. "Have no fear. I am told that the Arapaho will outnumber the white men and the Jojoba. Perhaps your husband will not return."

Maleaha sat up and looked at Lamas with fear in her eyes. "How do you know this?"

"Mangas told me."

"Oh, Lamas, I could not stand it if anything happened to Kane. Why did you not tell me this before?"

"What does it matter, you said you did not like the white man."

Maleaha closed her eyes. "I don't like him, Lamas, but I love him."

"Go to sleep, Maleaha. I'm an old man, and I need my rest." Lamas smiled to himself. The white man would know many sleepless nights before he won Maleaha. He would ask the Great Spirit to keep him safe. Out of the corner of his eye, he saw Maleaha kneeling, her head bowed in prayer. She was asking the white God to look after her husband, he thought. He felt the hard ground beneath him and thought of his comfortable bed at Deveraux Ranch. He had grown too accustomed to the white man's comforts.

Two days later, just as Maleaha had predicted, they rode into the fort, where she delivered Kane's message to Colonel Johnson. Then she and Lamas rode for Deveraux Ranch.

Kane had stretched out on his bedroll, thankful not to feel a moving horse beneath him. Mangas and his Jojoba warriors rode at a killing pace. Each night they would not stop to camp until long after dark, and more often than not, they would be mounted long before daybreak. Kane's body was sore, and his need for sleep was great.

He had not heard Mangas come up beside him, and he almost jumped out of his skin when he heard him speak: "Kane," Mangas said, calling him by his name rather than his military title. "How would you like to pay a little visit to the Arapaho tonight?"

Kane sat up quickly, and the tiredness seemed to slip away from him.

"What do you mean, Mangas?"

Mangas tossed a pair of moccasins at him. "The Arapaho are camped less than an hour's ride from here. I thought you might enjoy a little night prowling."

"You bet I would," Kane said, not bothering to disguise the excitement in his voice.

"Put on the moccasins. Those boots you wear would alert every Arapaho within hearing distance of our coming, and for now we have the advantage of surprise."

Kane had come to respect the chief of the Jojoba over the last ten days as they had pursued the elusive enemy. Manga's fierce warriors obeyed his slightest command without question. Kane had come to know the man, and had been surprised to find that Mangas had a sense of humor. This was demonstrated one night, when, after riding hard all day, they had stopped to make camp. Kane had just dismounted when Mangas appeared at his side.

"Kane, I wonder if you would allow me to mount your horse? I have often seen the white man's saddle, and have wondered what it would feel like to ride as you do."

Kane handed him the reins, and Mangas looked the horse over, first walking to one side and then to the other. He tested the stirrup by standing up in it, and then he swung his leg over the horse's back. Blue-clad soldiers and fierce-looking Indians watched as the mighty chief urged the horse to a walk. Building up confidence, he nudged the horse forward at a lope, then he galloped at a full run. When he returned to the group, he said something to his warriors that the white men could not understand, but the warriors seemed to find whatever he said funny, and they laughed. He dismounted and handed the reins to Kane.

"I do not like your saddle, Kane. It is uncomfortable and I like to feel the horse under me."

"What did you say to your warriors that they found so funny just now, Mangas?" Kane asked curiously.

The Indian chief smiled. "I told them that riding a horse with a saddle was like making love to a woman with all your clothes on."

Kane had laughed, amused by Mangas's observation.

Kane removed his boots and slipped into the moccasins, lacing them up his legs. Then the two of them rode off into the night. They had not been riding long when Mangas held up his hand to halt. Kane secured his mount since Mangas had told him they would be going the rest of the way on foot.

"Try to walk like an Indian, Kane. The white man walks as if he uses the ground to push himself along. The Indian rests his foot on the ground as if he were caressing a beautiful woman."

"Lead on, Mangas. I will try to walk silently."

Kane followed Mangas up the steep incline, grateful he did not disgrace himself by starting a rock slide. When they reached the top, Mangas dropped to his knees, and Kane followed his lead.

Kane saw the Arapaho below them. They had apparently bedded down for the night. There were a few guards posted, but their campfire gave witness that they were not trying to keep their presence a secret.

Kane frowned and looked at Mangas. "Why do you think they have taken no precautions? They must be aware by now that we are following them."

"If they are so brazen, it can only mean one thing. They do not fear us, and if they do not fear us they must have something in mind, but I do not yet know what it is," Mangas said.

"I count somewhere around fifty men," Kane observed. "You said there were over a hundred. Where are the others?"

"I think the others hide from us. I wonder why?" Mangas said.

"What if we were intended to follow this group of warriors? Then the others could come up behind us and have us sandwiched between them?" Kane said thoughtfully. "What would happen, if instead of following this group, we swung around and took on the main body?"

Mangas looked at Kane with renewed respect. "Careful, Kane, you are beginning to think like an Indian," he said smiling.

"Have you any ideas where the main body is hiding, Mangas?" Kane asked.

"No, but I will before morning."

Kane and Mangas did not stay any longer. They had found out what they needed to know.

After they returned to camp Mangas sent out three groups of warriors in different directions, to try and locate the other Arapaho. Kane and Mangas sat beside the campfire, waiting for the men to return.

"You were right when you said we would be outnumbered, Mangas."

"Yes, but do not let the numbers mislead you. A Jojoba warrior is worth three Arapaho."

"I don't doubt that, Mangas. Perhaps the Arapaho did us a favor by splitting their forces." Kane studied Mangas's face. His English was very good, and Kane wondered how he had learned the language so well.

"Mangas, how is it that you speak English?"

Mangas took a deep breath and looked overhead at the branches of the tall pine trees they were resting beneath. "Maleaha's grandfather wanted me to learn the white man's tongue, so he sent me to one of the mission schools when I was very young. Each summer I would go to the

230

school, and I hated it," he smiled. "I believe I was a trial that the teachers had to endure. Then one summer when I came back to camp I lost my heart to a young Indian maiden, and I thought to please her I would study the white man's language until I could speak it well."

"You speak of Maleaha, do you not?" Kane said, realizing for the first time the extent of Mangas's love for Maleaha.

Mangas's eyes grew sad as he looked at Kane. "Yes, I have loved her since she was thirteen years old. I waited for her to grow up so I could tell her of my love. I would sometimes ride to Deveraux Ranch just on the slim chance that I would get a glimpse of her. Her father sent her away, and she was gone for two years." Mangas stood up and turned his back to Kane. "You know the rest. I would sooner see her happy with you, so deep is my love for her."

"Mangas, I am sorry, I never realized until this moment how you really felt about Maleaha." Kane felt new admiration for the powerful Indian chief. He doubted that he himself would have been willing to be so self-sacrificing.

"Let us never speak of this again, except I will tell you this: If you ever hurt Maleaha, I may one day have to kill you." The threat was uttered so softly Kane was not sure he had heard correctly.

"I think it will most probably be Maleaha who will hurt me, Mangas."

Mangas turned and looked at him. "Why do you say this?"

"I have never loved a woman before, and it is very

painful to me."

"Why should that be, Kane?"

Kane knew he could not tell Mangas that Maleaha did not love him but had used him to thwart Mangas's plans for her. "I am never sure where I stand with Maleaha."

"It is not important. Maleaha is your wife, she will do as you ask her to."

Kane could not tell Mangas that she never wanted to see him again. "I have made many mistakes with Maleaha, and she is angry with me much of the time."

"It is good when a man thinks about his mistakes, Kane, it means he is ready to change."

"Yes, I believe this is true."

They both lapsed into silence, each lost in his own thoughts. Suddenly Mangas sat down again beside Kane.

"Act normally, we are being observed by the Arapaho."

"How do you know this?"

"Naman just gave me a signal. Look slowly to your right, yes, behind the large tree with the broken branch."

"Will they attack tonight?"

"No, just as we observed them earlier, they now watch us."

At that moment, the scouts Mangas had sent out to find the main band of Arapaho rode into camp. They spoke quietly to their chief, and when they finished their report Mangas turned to Kane.

"My warriors have found the Arapaho. They are to the east of us. They do not light a campfire, and are trying to go undetected. I believe you were right about their intentions, Kane."

Kane picked up a stick and began drawing in the sand.

"I have a plan I think may work."

Mangas watched him and waited for him to continue.

"We could separate our forces into two groups sending some of our men after the first group, then you and I, along with the rest of our men, could hit the main party before first light in the morning, thus hopefully catching them off guard. What do you think, Mangas?"

Mangas smiled. "Once again you think like an Indian. It is a good plan. Once we overcome the main party we can ride to the aid of our other group."

"There is one flaw in the plan, Mangas. If our plan is discovered, we will have cut our forces in half and left ourselves open and hopelessly outnumbered."

"I think we should go with your plan and hope we are not found out."

The next morning Kane found that their plan worked even better than he had hoped. It was an unprepared and unaware band of Arapaho that the Jojobas and the United States Cavalry swooped down on, taking them completely by surprise.

Mangas and his warriors were the first to strike, knowing they could creep up on the Arapaho silently. Kane and his men followed shortly after the first assault, and in no time at all the Arapaho were either dead or fleeing for their lives. When Kane saw that Mangas had the situation in hand, he ordered his men to ride with all possible speed to the aid of the men they had sent after the smaller group of Arapaho, leaving Mangas to deal with the already defeated enemy.

Kane and his men rode hard, knowing that should the Arapaho turn and fight, his men would be hopelessly outnumbered and not stand much of a chance against the larger force.

One thing was on their side now, however. There was no fear of being attacked from the rear. The trail was not hard to follow, and it led Kane into a deep canyon. He could hear the sounds of battle and knew they had already engaged the enemy. It flashed through Kane's mind that the Arapaho must be wondering why their fellow warriors did not come to their aid.

The enemy had turned to engage his men in the middle of a long, narrow canyon, and if they had gotten the reinforcements they expected, victory would have been sure and swift, for they would have caught Kane's men and Mangas's warriors in the middle of the two forces. As it was, Kane was still outnumbered, but they now stood a chance, and if Mangas could come in time, they could turn the tide of battle.

Kane threw his empty rifle to the ground and drew out his pistol, as there was no time to reload. Soon the pistol was empty also, and he threw it down. He wrapped his hand around his saber and spurred his mount into action. With a powerful thrust he felt his saber enter the body of an advancing Arapaho.

The Arapaho were a brave and fierce adversary, and at the moment it seemed they were winning. Kane was relieved when he realized that Mangas and his warriors had joined him. It soon became apparent that the tide of battle was turning in their favor as the United States Cavalry and the Jojoba fought side by side.

They forced the enemy backwards until they had them trapped against a cliff. The enemy, seeing they were beaten, renewed their efforts.

Kane felt a stinging sensation on his temple as blood and sweat blinded him. He wiped it away with his sleeve, only to have it return. Out of the corner of his eye, Kane saw Mangas being dragged from his horse by two Arapaho. Kane jumped from his horse and grabbed one of the men around the neck and wrestled him to the ground. The two men rolled on amid flying horses' hooves and whizzing bullets. Kane could feel the Indian's strength slipping away as he wrestled a knife from his hand. With a powerful thrust Kane drove the knife into the now helpless enemy. Turning to Mangas, he saw that two more Arapaho had Mangas pinned to the ground, so he leaped across the space that divided them and grabbed one of the Indians in an arm lock. Applying pressure, he felt the man go limp.

Kane did not see the Indian who aimed a rifle at him, but at that moment he turned, and the bullet that had been aimed at his heart entered his chest. He didn't even feel the bullet that entered his leg. He felt a weakness wash over him, and he felt pain so intense that he cried out. He felt himself falling, and he called out for Maleaha. Then all went black and he knew nothing more.

Kane was not aware that they had won the battle against the Arapaho nor did he know that Mangas knelt over him, binding his wounds and trying to stop the flow of blood. Mangas examined his head wound and saw it was no more than a scratch, but the wound in his chest could be fatal. The wound to his leg was bleeding badly, and Mangas bound it tightly.

Seeing the danger to the man who had just saved his

life, Mangas mounted his horse with Kane in his arms
and urged his mount forward, racing against time, knowing that if Kane was going to survive he must get him to
the fort.

In the two days it took Mangas to reach the fort he
stopped only long enough to tend Kane's wounds and to
change horses at a ranch. It had been under the cover of
night when Mangas snuck into the barn and exchanged
his horse for one of the unsuspecting rancher's. On he
rode, not even stopping to rest, and when dark descended
on them, still he rode.

Kane regained consciousness only twice, and Mangas
could tell he did not know where he was or what had happened to him. Determined to save the life of the man who
had saved his and who Maleaha loved, he raced on
through the night and into the next day.

It was a startled sentry who opened the gate to the tall,
fierce-looking Indian who carried a wounded cavalry officer upon his horse.

As Mangas rode through the gates of the fort, he
was immediately surrounded by blue uniforms. Mangas
looked around the group of soldiers, but could see no one
who seemed to be in charge. Then he spotted Colonel
Johnson, who was rushing across the compound but-
toning the brass buttons to his blue uniform.

Mangas spoke directly to him. "I have brought Kane
to you. He is gravely wounded. Care for him, for he is a
very brave man. I owe him my life, and without him we
would not have won a victory against the Arapaho."

Colonel Johnson ordered two men to carry Kane to the
infirmary, then turned his attention to the Indian who

looked back at him with dark, unreadable eyes.

"You are Mangas," The colonel said, in awed voice, for there was no mistaking the tall Indian. He could be none other than the chief of the Jojoba tribe.

Mangas nodded and spun his horse around.

"You say you won against the Arapaho?"

"They will not trouble you again. Take care of Kane, I would not like for him to die." Mangas rode out of the gates of the fort and was soon lost in a cloud of dust, while the soldiers and their commander stared after him.

Colonel Johnson watched until the chief of the Jojoba disappeared behind a hill, then he turned to face his men and ordered them to carry on. There was a frown on his face as he made his way to the infirmary.

Word was spreading quickly about the victory against the Arapahos and how the mighty chief had himself delivered the gravely wounded Major Kanen Benedict to the fort.

During the next two days Kane slipped in and out of consciousness. The bullet had passed through his leg, saving the doctor the trouble of having to remove it. But the one in Kane's chest had gone deep. It had not struck any vital organs, but he had lost a great deal of blood, and there was always the fear of infection.

On the third day Kane awoke and looked about him. By now many others who had been wounded in the battle with the Arapho had been brought to the fort, and they occupied every available bed. Kane, seeing that he was back at the fort, could not remember how he had gotten there. He was in agonizing pain and would feel hot and then cold, and at the moment he did not care if he lived or died.

That night Kane became delirious from his fever and the doctor tried to make some sense out of his rambling speech.

"Maleaha, Maleaha, it was not a real marriage. I want you to . . . be mine forever . . . Maleaha, I love you. Maleaha. Maleaha." He called out to the woman many times, and the doctor shook his head sadly, thinking the woman Kane called for must live far away in Boston.

Late the next afternoon Kane's fever had subsided, and the doctor felt confident he would live. Kane tried to sit up, but the pain was so intense it ripped through his chest, and he fell back on the pillow gasping for breath.

"I would not try to sit up just yet, Major," the doctor scolded. "You have been very ill, and your body needs time to heal before you try to resume your usual activities."

"What happened? How did I get here?"

The doctor pulled up a chair and sat down beside Kane. "As to what happened, we are still receiving firsthand accounts of the battle. And as for how you got here, Mangas brought you here himself."

"I do not remember anything past the battle."

"You are a hero, Major." The doctor felt his forehead, and seeing it was cool, stood up. "If you feel up to it, the colonel wanted to talk to you as soon as you regained consciousness. I am sure he can tell you all you wish to know.''

Later, Colonel Johnson sat down beside Kane and inquired about how he was feeling.

"Sir, can you tell me about the outcome of the battle? Did we win?"

"The Arapaho were beaten. The few who survived turned tail and ran for Colorado. I do not think we will have any more trouble out of them."

"The doctor said that Mangas brought me here."

"That is correct, and he told me if it had not been for you the battle would have been lost. We all owe you a great debt, my boy."

"I keep trying to remember what happened, but it is all so unclear."

Colonel Johnson stood up. "You should not dwell on it. Just rest and try to recover your strength." The colonel smiled. "I have a surprise for you. You have a visitor."

Kane closed his eyes as the colonel departed. Maleaha had come to see him, he thought. He hated for her to see him like this, with bandages on his head, chest, and leg, but it did not really matter. All that really counted was that she had heard of his wounds and had come to see him. Now he could tell her that he loved her, and ask her to marry him.

CHAPTER FOURTEEN

Kane watched the door of the infirmary as he waited impatiently for Maleaha to enter. Today would be the day he would clear up all the misunderstandings between them.

He saw the tall man who entered and frowned. He felt no joy as he watched his father approach his bed.

"What are you doing here, Eli? Aren't you a long way from home?"

Eli inclined his head. "I expected a better welcome from you than that, Kane. I have been weeks on the road, riding in foul-smelling coaches. I have braved heat, rough roads, flies, and mosquitoes. The least you could do was act as though you were glad to see me."

Eli Benedict was still a very handsome man, and Kane looked very like his father. Kane felt resentment that his father had come to New Mexico. There was no sign of affection on his father's face. His eyes were gray, like Kane's, but they had a hardness about them. Eli seated himself in a chair and waited for his son to speak.

"I didn't ask you to come here, Eli," Kane told him

resentfully. He had no desire to see him, nor did he feel up to the accusations and arguments he knew would be forthcoming.

Eli leaned forward. "I might have known you would not have changed. You never cared about anyone but yourself, Kane. I do not know why I even bother with you."

"Why *do* you bother?"

"I had hoped by now you would see the folly of your ways and agree to return to Boston with me."

"Not hardly, Eli."

The older man leaned back and let his eyes skim the infirmary, where there were a dozen or more soldiers occupying the other beds in the long, narrow room. Casualties of their encounter with the Arapaho.

Eli had been pleased with the praise Colonel Johnson bestowed on his son. He was always impressed by what people thought, and he found a certain pride in having his son hailed as a hero.

"The doctor tells me you are recovering nicely, Kane."

"So it would seem," Kane answered him dully.

"I hoped after you had sufficiently mended, you would agree to return home with me."

Kane looked at the ceiling. "How do you propose that I do that? The cavalry takes a dim view of a soldier's deserting his post."

Eli smiled. "As you know, I am not without influence. I have friends in Washington. How do you suppose you ended up in this hellhole in the first place?"

Kane looked at his father, hoping he had misunderstood him. ''What are you saying?''

''Merely that I had you transferred to the New Mexico territory, hoping that if you got a taste of life in this uncivilized land you would gladly return home and take up your rightful place as head of Benedict Shipping.''

Kane laughed deeply, and the sound startled his father. He had thought his son might be angry, and he did not understand his reaction. ''I should have seen your fine hand in this, Eli, it just never occurred to me that you would go to such lengths to punish me. I am afraid you have outsmarted yourself this time, however.''

''What do you mean?''

''I find that I like it here, and I have decided to make it my permanent home.''

Eli stood up, ''What's to like? I have never seen such a desolate country in all my life. There is nothing to recommend this place when one has been raised to expect the finer things in life.''

''Do not judge me by your standards, Eli. I find the life you lead boring and useless. For the first time in my life I am my own man, doing what *I* want to do, and not what you expect from me.''

Eli's eyes narrowed. ''If you are talking about your military career, that is over. I have your discharge papers with me right this minute.'' To prove his point, he withdrew an envelope from his breast pocket and handed it to Kane.

Kane tried to sit up, but pain shot through his body, and he was forced to lie back weakly. ''You have no right to do this,'' he said between gritted teeth.

''I have every right! You are my son, and I want you to

come home.''

Kane felt too weak to argue with him at the moment. The pain he was experiencing overwhelmed even his anger. All he wanted to do was sleep and forget everything, but he had not reckoned with his father's ability to have the last word.

''You will be released from the cavalry the day you are dismissed from the hospital. What do you intend to do then, Kane? You will be forced to look elsewhere for a career, and I think you will come home with me.''

Kane was aware that his father had left, but he did not open his eyes. He wanted to sleep. Tomorrow would be soon enough to face his father and decide what to do about his future.

Maleaha sat down slowly on the settee. She had just returned from Albuquerque, where she and Betsy had been visiting Betsy's grandmother. When her friend had asked Maleaha to accompany her to Albuquerque, she had readily agreed, wanting to get away, and hoping she could forget about Kanen Benedict, at least for a while. There had been no good in trying to fool herself. Maleaha would never forget Kane. All day her mind was on the danger he would be in when he met and engaged the Arapaho in battle. At night she remembered lying in his arms while he made love to her.

Maleaha removed her bonnet. It had been five weeks since she had ridden away from the Jojoba village. Surely there would be some word of the battle by now, she thought as she stood up. She would find Lamas and ask him.

"Ah, Señorita Maleaha, you have come home at last,'
Margaretta said, placing a vase of brightly colored flowers on the side table.

"Yes, I decided to come home early, Margaretta.
Would you have Lamas come to the house?"

"He is not here. He has gone to the camp of the Jojoba."

"Has there been any word of battle? Did Mangas find
the Arapaho?" Maleaha asked tensely.

"*Sí.* There was a great battle, and that is all anyone
talks about. There were many dead and wounded. They
say the Arapaho will not soon return to New Mexico."

Maleaha held her breath. Her hand went to her heart,
trying to still its tremendous beating. "Were there many
soldiers slain?"

"*Sí.*"

"Have you heard any word about Major Benedict?"

"*Sí.* He was gravely wounded, but I believe he is recovered by now."

"How do you know this, Margaretta?" Maleaha
asked, feeling tremendous fear for the man she loved.

"He is a hero! All of Santa Fe talks about his bravery.
They also say his father is at the fort, and they say the
major will go home with him, to marry some woman who
is waiting for him. At least this is the story that is being
circulated."

Maleaha felt as if her heart had just shattered in a million pieces. "Margaretta, are you sure he is well and out
of danger?"

"That is what they say, señorita."

Maleaha retied the ribbon on her bonnet. "I will go to the fort and see for myself if he is recovered," she said trying to hold on to her composure. How was it possible to hurt so much and still be able to act as if nothing was amiss. On the ride to the fort she did not cry, after all, she was half-Indian, she told herself, and Indians did not give in to the weakness of tears. She supposed she had become more white than Indian lately, for she had cried many times in the last weeks.

Maleaha dismounted and tied her horse up at the hitching post. Seeing the guard on duty, she walked over to him and inquired where she could find Major Benedict.

The guard smiled at her. "The major is a fortunate man, Miss Deveraux. He has had his share of beautiful ladies inquiring about his health."

"Yes, I'm sure he has," she said, masking her displeasure at his observation. It didn't please her in the least that Kane had had other lady callers. "Could you just tell me where I can find him?" she asked impatiently.

Kane limped about the room. The pain in his leg seemed to trouble him more than the pain in his chest now, although the chest wound had been the more serious of the two. Each time he took a step, pain would shoot up his leg, and he gritted his teeth to keep from crying out. The doctor had warned him to stay off his leg until it had more time to heal, but Kane had no time to stay in a sick-bed. He had too many things to do.

His father had come to visit him each day, and Kane had suffered his presence with ill grace. Each day Eli would pressure Kane to return to Boston with him, and each day, Kane refused. At first he had been angry with Eli for procuring his release from the cavalry. But he had had a lot of time to think and plan while he had been recuperating. He knew exactly what he wanted to do with his life. He had a substantial fortune, which had been left to him by his mother and grandfather. He would buy the land Jonas had told him about, and build a house on it. In time he hoped he could convince Maleaha to marry him. They could build a life together in this wild land that Kane had come to love. For the first time in his life, Kane felt good about himself. He was excited at the thought of Maleaha's becoming his wife. He wanted children by her. He wanted to come home each day knowing she would be waiting for him. If only he could convince her to be his wife. It still bothered him that she hadn't come to see him. Perhaps she was embarrassed about what had happened between them at the Jojoba village. Kane's pride kept him from sending word to her that he wanted to see her. There would be time to talk once he got out of the hospital.

He limped slowly back to his bed, and sat down, cursing the weakness that kept him confined to this room. He was ready to get on with his life, now that he knew what he wanted, now that he had made his mind up about Maleaha and building a ranch. When a Benedict made up his mind to do something, nothing could stand in his way.

Kane saw his father approaching and lay back on the bed.

"I distinctly heard the doctor tell you to stay off your leg until it has healed, Kane. Don't you give a damn that you might cripple yourself for life?"

"Don't you ever tire of badgering me? Why don't you just go home," Kane said, closing his eyes. He did not feel up to another bout with his father. "Why are you still here, Eli?"

His father seated himself in the chair before he spoke. "I would have thought that was obvious. I have no intentions of leaving until you are well enough to travel with me."

Kane sat up slowly. "How many times do I have to tell you I will never go back to Boston. I don't give a damn about your shipping business."

Eli's face became livid. "You are a total waste as a man. If I had any sense, I would leave you to your own destruction. Have you no thought for Lucinda, who has waited patiently all these years for you to grow up? She told me to give you her love, and to say she is still waiting for you."

Kane sighed heavily. Lord, was there no reprieve? Would Eli never leave him in peace? He suddenly decided it was time to tell his father about Maleaha. Perhaps then he would quit trying to pair him with Lucinda.

"I'm sorry you didn't consult me before making this trip, Eli. If you had, I could have told you I already have a wife," Kane said with a self-satisfied look on his face as he saw the color drain from Eli's face. Eli looked as if he were about to suffer an attack of apoplexy "I am no fool, Kane," his father said raising his voice. "If you have a wife, where is she, hiding under the bed?"

Maleaha opened the door to the infirmary hesitantly, observing the many wounded men who occupied the room. Finally she saw Kane, but he hadn't yet seen her,

e was talking to someone. Maleaha immediately saw the
nan's resemblance to Kane and she knew he must be
Kane's father. She was undecided about whether to dis-
urb them or not, when Kane's voice carried to her.

"Her name is Maleaha, and she is a half-breed. I was
narried to her by an Indian chief. Of course the marriage
s not a real one. I would like for you to meet her. I doubt
hat you would approve of her, however. She is nothing
ike the fair Lucinda, who waits patiently for me in Bos-
on. No, she is nothing like the wife you have chosen for
ne, but she does have something that draws me to her."

"Another one of your trollops, Kane? God only knows
ow many women you have bedded, but I thought even
ou would have drawn the line at an Indian!" his father
houted.

Maleaha didn't stay to hear any more. Tears blinded
er as she ran to where she had left her horse. What a fool
he had been to come here today. Her vision was blurred
s she rode out the gates of the fort and headed for Deve-
aux Ranch.

What was she to do? In her heart she felt as if she was
Kane's true wife. She hated him for the way he had ma-
igned her to his father. What kind of a man was he? "I
ever want to see you again, Kanen Benedict!" she
elled. "I will hate you forever!" she cried.

Four more weeks passed before Kane was released
rom the hospital. That same day he was discharged from
he cavalry.

He said good-bye to Colonel Johnson and his men with

249

little regret.

The first thing he did was to buy the land Jonas had told him about. It was one hundred and seventy-five thousand acres of prime ranch land. The Pecos River ran right through the heart of the property. There were tall pine trees on the eastern part of the land, and that was where Kane made plans to build a house. He wanted the house to be under construction before he approached Maleaha and asked her to be his wife. If she saw he was serious about settling down, perhaps he could win her.

He hired a crew of twenty laborers to begin the construction of the house and barn. It was difficult for him not to ride over to Deveraux Ranch and confront Maleaha. He was still hurting because she had not come to see him while he was recuperating from his wounds. He had heard that Jonas had gone to Spain, but he knew of course that Maleaha had not accompanied him. He found he wanted to see her, to hold her in his arms and pour out his love to her, but wounded pride and caution caused him to wait until just the right moment.

Kane was irritated that his father had not yet returned to Boston. It seemed that he had taken up residence in one of the local hotels, and nothing Kane could say would convince him to leave.

Three weeks later, Kane looked with satisfaction at the foundation of his new house. He had planned it with Maleaha in mind. It would be built in the traditional Spanish style, like the house at Deveraux Ranch. The barn had already been completed, and Kane had moved his belongings into it for the time being.

There was a fiesta being held at one of the hotels in

anta Fe, and Kane knew that Maleaha would be there.
e whistled a happy tune as he dressed for the occasion.

"Tonight you will belong to me, Maleaha," he said
ut loud as he tied his black silk tie. It felt strange to be
ut of uniform. He had not worn a black formal suit in a
ery long time. Did Maleaha ever think about the night
ey had made love in the Jojoba village? His hand was
nsteady as he ran it through his ebony hair. He would
nd out tonight.

Maleaha accepted Clay Madason's invitation to go to
e fiesta. She didn't really want to go, but Clay always
ade her laugh. And she needed to laugh. It had been a
ng time since she had felt like doing anything. Perhaps
st for this one night she could forget about Kane and
el young and carefree again.

Kane scanned the sea of faces, looking for Maleaha,
ut she was not at the fiesta. He was receiving many in-
iting glances from some of the young ladies, but he
erely smiled at them. He walked with a pronounced
mp, and he doubted that he would be able to dance with
nyone, since his leg still troubled him.

Kane stood in a corner watching the door. She would
ome tonight, he was almost sure of it. Once more his
lance traveled about the room, and he saw Betsy Kin-
ade.

Betsy smiled as she watched Kane approach. She had
eard about his bravery against the Arapaho, and, like
veryone else, she was impressed.

"Mr. Benedict, how nice to see you," she said

brightly. "You remember my fiancé, Bob Morehead."

"Of course. It's a pleasure to see you again, M
Morehead," Kane said, shaking hands with Betsy
fiancé.

"I am pleased to see you looking so well, Mr. Bene
dict. I heard about your feat with the Arapahos. It mu
have been a hair-raising experience."

Kane smiled. "I can tell you in all honesty, it is noth
ing I would care to repeat."

"You are quite the hero, Mr. Benedict. I have hear
that you are no longer in the cavalry."

"Yes, you heard correctly," Kane said, returning he
smile. "Tell me, Miss Kincade, will Maleaha be here to
night?"

Betsy frowned in consideration. "I'm not sure.
haven't seen her in over a month. She went with me t
visit my grandmother in Albuquerque a few weeks ago
Maleaha has not been to see me since we returned."

Suddenly the air seemed charged with excitement, an
Kane turned around to face the door. He watched as Ma
leaha advanced into the room on the arm of Clay Mada
son.

CHAPTER FIFTEEN

Maleaha's eyes scanned the crowd of faces. Seeing Betsy and Bob, she smiled brightly and waved to them, but the smile left her face and she gripped Clay's arm tightly when she recognized Kane. How different he looked dressed in formal attire. Even among a room of well-dressed gentlemen, Kane stood out. Her heart skipped a beat as his silver-gray eyes seemed to reach across the room to hold her spellbound. The look he gave her reminded her of the intimacy they had shared. Maleaha felt a light pressure about her waist as Clay led her down the stairs that took them onto the dance floor.

While Clay led Maleaha into the dance steps of a lively polka, she tried to forget about Kanen Benedict, but over Clay's shoulder she could see that Kane was watching her. She became so flustered that she missed a step, causing Clay to smile down at her.

"Easy there, Princess. Do you want me to think you are just learning to dance?"

Maleaha found she could not look into Clay's face. What if Clay should suspect that she was disturbed by

Kane's presence, she thought. "I'm sorry, Clay. I . . . I . . ." she lowered her head.

Clay released her hand and tilted her chin up, studying her face. "What's the matter, honey? You have been acting as fidgety as an old maid at a bachelor party," he said, looking at her with concern written all over his face.

"It's nothing, Clay. I guess I'm just a little tired. I haven't been sleeping very well at night."

"I bet you miss Jonas. Are you still planning to join him in Paris this spring?"

Again Maleaha lowered her head. How could she tell Clay, or anyone for that matter, that she would not be joining her father. She would be unable to face anyone once they found out her guilty secret. What if Kane should find out she was carrying his baby, she thought in horror.

Clay didn't seem to notice that she had not answered him. The dance had stopped and he led her over to the punchbowl. Pouring Maleaha a glass of punch, he handed it to her and gave her an inquiring look. "I never did understand why Jonas went rushing off to Spain."

Maleaha took a sip of her punch. "His old friend Señor Gomez is selling off his prize Brahman, and he gave Father first chance at purchasing them."

"I never can understand why Jonas goes off so far to build up his herd."

"He can afford it, Clay, and he is interested in breeding a better beef cattle."

"When are you leaving, Maleaha?"

"I'm not sure. Perhaps in a few weeks."

"I thought you weren't going to join him until

254

spring.''

"I have changed my mind."

Soon it was impossible to talk, for as usual Maleaha was surrounded by several gentlemen admirers. She willed herself not to search the room for Kane, but she could not stop thinking about him. Why was he here? She had thought he would have returned to Boston with his father. She had noticed he walked with a limp, and it tore at her heart to think he was suffering from his wounds. Glancing over Clay's shoulder Maleaha saw Kane talking to a pretty golden-haired girl, and he seemed to be enjoying himself.

Suddenly the walls seemed to be closing in on her and she knew if she didn't get some fresh air she was going to be sick. Excusing herself, she edged her way along the wall, hoping no one would try to follow her. Mr. Kincade was talking to Clay, so perhaps he would not see her leave.

There was a little garden room that she and Betsy had once played in, and she made her way toward it, thinking she would find solitude. It had been a mistake for her to come to the dance tonight. Had she known Kane would be here, she would have stayed at home. When she reached the back wall of the garden, she discovered that the garden house had been torn down. What a shame, she thought, remembering what a lovely place it had once been. When she and Betsy were children, the garden house had been their favorite place to play when her father brought them into town. Then it had been all glassed in with padded windowseats, and the owner, Mrs. Pucket, would allow her and Betsy to have tea parties in it.

Nothing ever stayed the same. Sometimes Maleaha wished she was still a child. How uncomplicated life had been then. But now she herself was carrying a child. Kane had denied that she was his wife, where then would that leave her baby? She had been born after her parents had been married in the Jojoba ceremony and no one had ever denied her legitimacy.

Maleaha leaned back against the trunk of a tree. How was this all going to end? It was fall now, and soon winter would be here. What could she do? Where could she go? She looked up at the full moon that bathed the garden in soft light. Surely Kane would soon be returning to Boston. Perhaps he hadn't gone yet because of his leg. She closed her eyes, praying she wouldn't ever have to face him again.

"Are you waiting for a rendezvous, or did you flee from your many amorous admirers?" the deep voice she knew so well spoke up from the shadows.

Maleaha caught her breath as Kane stepped out of the shadows. "Hello, major, or Mr. Benedict, I suppose I should call you now." Her voice sounded breathless.

"I see you heard about my discharge from the army? Can I also assume you heard that I was wounded?" he asked in a biting tone.

"Yes, I had heard something to that effect," she told Kane, hoping he would not move any closer to her. "I noticed you walk with a limp. I hope your leg was not injured permanently."

Kane seemed to loom over her as he leaned his hand against the tree trunk over her head. She could clearly see the sneer on his face. "Not that you really give a damn, but I will tell you anyway. I am told that given time my leg will be as good as new."

"Does it pain you very much?" she asked, hating the thought of his being in pain.

"It's nothing I can't live with."

"You may not believe me, K . . . Mr. Benedict, but I am grateful that your wounds were not fatal."

His eyes narrowed. "Did it never occur to you to come and see me while I was recovering from my wounds? I would have thought you would come, if for no other reason than to gloat over my incapacitation." Kane leaned closer to her and she could smell the brandy on his breath.

"You do not know me at all, if you think I would take pleasure in another's pain," she said, feeling very uneasy at the anger in his voice.

He placed his other hand on the tree trunk, trapping her between him and the tree. For a moment he said nothing, but continued to stare at her with his disturbing silver gaze.

"I have been away," she said, unable to think of anything else to say.

"When did you return?" he asked, staring at her lips with such intensity that Maleaha had a hard time gathering her thoughts.

"Why?"

"I was just wondering. Surely you could have found time to come and see me. I know you said you never wanted to see me again, but I didn't take you seriously at the time."

Maleaha remembered the day she had ridden to the fort to see him, and had overheard Kane and his father discussing her. It still hurt to think about the things Kane had said about her that day. "I didn't think you wanted to see me any more than I wanted to see you," Maleaha said, wishing he would leave her alone. She didn't know how much more she could take before she broke down and cried in front of Kane. All she really wanted was for him to admit he was her true husband so she could tell him about the child she carried. She wanted to feel his arms about her. She needed him to tell her everything would be all right. She knew he didn't love her as she did him, but perhaps he would care about his child.

Maleaha stiffened, as Kane's hand drifted down to touch her face. She did not voice any objections, however, when he drew her into his arms. She closed her eyes, loving him with all her heart. If she had loved him before, it was nothing compared to how she felt about him now that she was carrying his child. Maleaha rested her head against his shoulder as he buried his face in her midnight-black hair. He raised her head and rested his cheek against hers.

"Say you want me, Maleaha. Say you have thought about me. Even if it isn't true, say it anyway," he said in a passionate voice.

"I have thought about you," she allowed herself to admit to him. She was afraid to say any more. His hand moved down her back and over her hips, and Maleaha was intoxicated by the feel of his hands and the sound of his voice. He made her want to reach inside herself and reveal too much of what she was feeling. Kane's lips moved over her upturned face, and Maleaha thought her heart would burst with the love she felt for him.

"Let's go someplace where we can be alone, Maleaha. I have a room at the hotel, we could go there."

"I don't think I—"

"You know you want to as much as I do," he interrupted her. "Your lips may deny it, but your body doesn't."

Maleaha stiffened, realizing what he wanted from her. He did not speak of love, he thought only of desire. There was no happiness in her heart, knowing he only wanted to make love to her. She thought any one of the women who had hung on to him tonight would have served him just as well.

"You are fickle. Have you no thought of the woman they say is waiting for you in Boston?" she said, pushing against him.

Kane released her. "Is that what this is all about? Have you heard the rumors started by my father?"

"I like that, Mr. Benedict. Answer a question with a question, that way you don't have to commit yourself. It's an old Indian custom.

He smiled. "Are you jealous?"

Yes, she wanted to scream. She was so jealous she could easily scratch out the woman's eyes he was going home to marry, had she been standing there at this moment. She wanted to tell Kane that he was her husband, that he had no right to marry any one else. She tried to hide her anger behind still another golden lie.

"What right would I have to be jealous of you? You are free to do as you please, as am I."

Kane grabbed her and held her so tightly she could scarcely breathe. "Like hell you are free. You are the most obstinate, opinionated woman I have ever come up against. One day I will either break you, or you will break me." His words were harsh, but his tone of voice was almost pleading.

"I must go in now, Clay will be wondering what has happened to me."

"To hell with Clay Madason," Kane said as his lips sought and found Maleaha's. All of Maleaha's objections went for naught as she became soft in his arms. His mouth moved across her face to nibble at the lobe of her delicate ear, and Maleaha could not suppress the feeling of delight that spread throughout her body.

"I want you, Maleaha, and I will have you one way or another," he murmured softly in her ear. "Name your terms and I will abide by them."

Maleaha tried to think straight, but she could think of little but the man who held her in his arms. "Have you forgotten, I already turned down your offer to make me your mistress," she whispered.

"Yet I still had you," he reminded her, as his hand slid over her breast, causing her to catch her breath.

Maleaha fought with her wayward heart. If she didn't find a way to save herself, Kane would destroy her. "I don't want this. Please let me go."

"You want it," he said capturing her head and looking down into her face. "I know your body has been awakened, and you want me as much as I want you."

"Any man would do as well as you," she told him, feeling as if the heart within her body was crying at her lie.

Kane's hand tightened on her chin, and he felt something akin to pain at her cruel words. He was glad now he had not rushed headlong into asking her to be his wife.

"If any man will do, why not me," he said, returning cruelty for cruelty. "You need a man to satisfy you, and we both know I can fulfill that role." He did not wait for her answer as his lips came down on hers brutally, bruising her mouth with his anger. There was no love in the kiss, only anger and an unleashed passion. Maleaha felt as if her head were swimming, and her heart was drumming so loudly she was sure Kane could hear it. It was as if her body would not obey the command her mind tried to send it. Her arms went around Kane's shoulders, and she could feel the rough bark of the tree against her back as Kane pinned her between him and the tree.

"Kane, please," she pleaded as he released her lips and blazed a fiery path down her delicate throat. Her hands moved up his neck to tangle in his dark hair. She could not suppress the tattletale moan that escaped her lips as his mouth teased the upper portion of her breasts, which were revealed by her low-cut gown.

"I want you, Maleaha. You are in my blood. I can't seem to think of anything but you. I think about you all day, and then at night my dreams are also of you," he said in a passionate voice.

"No, no," she moaned, moving her head from side to side, knowing that if he pushed her to the ground where they stood, she would willingly give herself to him.

"So this is where you disappeared to." Kane recognized his father's voice. Raising his head he quickly tried

261

to shield Maleaha protectively with his body. He knew his father well enough to know he would try to belittle her.

"Well, Kane. I see you are up to your old habits. I had hoped by now you would have learned to have these little trysts in a not so public place," Eli said insultingly.

"I warn you, Eli, I will not stand idly by while you insult Maleaha," Kane shouted angrily.

"Maleaha, isn't that the little half-breed you were telling me about?" Eli said craning his neck trying to see what a half-breed looked like. "It's fortunate that Lucinda did not come with me as she wanted to. She would never stand for your meeting your trollop in such a public place."

Maleaha had never felt so degraded before. She tried to jerk free of Kane. All she wanted to do was run and hide in her shame.

"Maleaha, don't listen to my father," Kane said, tightening his grip on her wrist.

"Who should she listen to, Kane? You? Have you told her about all the women who have preceded her? How about the time you tried to juggle three mistresses at one time, until they found out about each other?"

Maleaha finally worked her hands free of Kane's grip and placed her hands over her ears, trying to shut out his father's hateful words. A loud sob escaped her lips and she was trembling violently. Tears of grief and humiliation blinded her eyes. Turning away she fled down the darkened path, hoping to escape before she broke down completely.

Maleaha could hear Kane running after her, calling her

name, so she ducked behind a clump of bushes and watched as he passed within inches of her hiding place. After he had disappeared from sight she made her way out of the garden by a side gate. She saw Betsy and Bob standing beside Bob's carriage, so she ran toward them. When she reached Betsy, Maleaha grabbed her by the hand.

"Take me home," she sobbed. "Oh, please take me home!"

Betsy's arms went around her friend. "What has occurred, Maleaha?"

"I can't talk about it right now. Just get me out of here," she cried.

Bob and Betsy exchanged glances, then Bob helped both girls into his buggy.

"Wait!" Maleaha said when Bob started to climb into the buggy. "Clay will be concerned about me. Will you tell him that you are taking me home, Bob? Tell him I have a headache and I didn't want to spoil his evening."

Bob nodded and made his way back to the dance, saying he would not be very long.

Betsy looked at Maleaha with a troubled expression on her face. "Tell me what happened, Maleaha. Did something happen between you and Mr. Benedict?"

"Yes, but I cannot speak of it now. Perhaps later," Maleaha said covering her face with her hands. It would be good to confide in Betsy. Maleaha had kept everything all bottled up inside of her for so long. Betsy could help her decide what to do.

"You are coming home with me tonight, and I will not

take no for an answer. We will drive by Deveraux and pick up your things,'' Betsy told her.

''Yes, I would like that, Betsy.'' Maleaha knew she didn't want to be alone. Kane might come by to see her. He was the last person she wanted to see. She never wanted to see him again.

Maleaha sank down in the feather mattress on Betsy's bed, while Betsy sat at her vanity brushing her hair. Leaning back on the bed, Maleaha closed her eyes. She didn't want to think about what had happened with Kane and his father tonight, but she had to. If only her father were home, he would know what to do. Maleaha felt Betsy sit down beside her and opened her eyes.

''Do you want to talk about what's bothering you now?'' Betsy asked her. ''I have known for some time something was bothering you, but until now you haven't wanted to talk about it.''

Maleaha sat up and reached for Betsy's hand. ''I have been living in a nightmare, Betsy. I don't know what to do anymore.''

''Papa always said two heads are better than one, Maleaha. Let me help you. That's what best friends are for.''

Maleaha cried as she told Betsy about Mangas and Kane. When she finished by telling her about what had happened with Kane and his father that night, Betsy was crying as well.

''You have to understand, Betsy. I felt married to Kane, but he made it clear that he was not married to me.''

"Oh, he is such a beast. If I were a man I would beat him with my bare fists,'' Betsy said loyally.

"To be fair, Betsy, I am the one who forced myself on him.''

"Yes, but he could have recognized the Jojoba wedding, or better still insisted on marrying you in a church.''

"You are forgetting the woman Lucinda who waits for him in Boston. I suppose he loves her,'' Maleaha said, feeling fresh tears in her eyes.

"Well, I say you are lucky that he will soon be leaving, and good riddance.''

"Betsy, there is more to it. I am going to have his baby.'' The room became silent and horror spread over Betsy's face.

"Oh, Maleaha, my dearest friend,'' Betsy cried. "Whatever shall we do?''

"I am not sure, Betsy. I don't know where to turn. I dreaded telling you, I was afraid what your reaction would be. You don't hate me, do you?''

"Hate you? What kind of a friend would I be if I turned my back on you just when you needed me most? I know what you will do. You can stay right here until your baby comes. You know Papa and Mama would want you to.''

"That is so like you Betsy, but I could never do that. I have been thinking and I have decided what I must do. Every one thinks I am going to join my father. I will let them think I left early to join him, while in truth I will go to my Aunt Kosha until after the baby is born.''

"But, Maleaha, have you forgotten about Mangas?"

"Mangas will not bother me now, you see, he believes me married to Kane."

"You can't go to the Jojoba village. You will need a doctor when your time comes."

Maleaha wiped the tears from her eyes and smiled. "The Jojoba have been having babies without a white doctor for many hundreds of years. I myself was born in the Jojoba village."

"If I were in your place, I would be terrified."

"I would be less than honest with you, Betsy, if I didn't admit that I also am frightened. I have no choice. I must go to my aunt."

"Do you suppose that Mr. Benedict would marry you if he knew you were going to have his baby?"

"I don't want him to ever find out. I hope by the time my baby is born he will have gone back to Boston. You are forgetting, he *was* married to me."

"Surely there is something I can do to help you, Maleaha. I feel so helpless."

"You can do me a favor of telling no one about this, not even your parents. Let everyone think that I have gone to join my father."

"I'll worry about you, Maleaha. How will I know if you are well?"

"I will have Lamas keep in touch with you. Do not worry, the Indian in me is a survivor, and the white in me no longer cares."

"Maleaha, do you hate Mr. Benedict?"

Maleaha was quiet for a moment, then she spoke. "No, I wish I did, it would make leaving so much easier.

After all that has happened between us, I find I still love him.''

It was a week later before Kane could gather up enough courage to ride to Deveraux Ranch to see Maleaha. After the night in the garden, he had told his father he never wanted to see him again, and Eli had finally returned to Boston.

As Kane rapped on the door he looked about him waiting for someone to answer. He noticed the leaves on the big cottonwood trees had turned a golden color. Fall was moving over the land, painting a colorful picture with nature's paintbrush. The past few days he had rehearsed over and over what he would say to Maleaha today: ''Maleaha, I love you and I want you to be my wife.'' He hoped he wouldn't lose his nerve when he faced her.

The door opened and Margaretta smiled at him brightly. ''Señor Benedict, I have been expecting you.''

''Is Maleaha at home, Margaretta?''

''No, she has gone to be with her father. I think they will not return until the summer.''

Kane felt his heart plummet. It was a long time until summer.

''Did Maleaha leave any message for me, Margaretta?'' he asked hopefully.

''*Si*, she said that you were to take Diablo if you came by.''

Kane had forgotten all about the horse Jonas had given him. He thought about refusing, but then thought better of it. He would take the horse and keep it for Maleaha.

As Kane rode back to his ranch leading Diablo behind him, his head was full of plans. Perhaps it was best that Maleaha had gone to join her father. Now he would have more time to make the ranch ready for her.

As he rounded a bend in the road he noticed a buggy coming toward him. Pulling up his mount at the side of the road, he waited for it to pass. As it drew near he recognized Betsy Kincade.

Bringing her buggy to a stop, she frowned at him. "Mr. Benedict, I would have thought you had gone by now."

Kane heard her biting tone and smiled at her. "No, as you can see, I'm still here."

"I'm surprised you have the nerve to hang around, Mr. Benedict."

He laughed. "I see Maleaha has told you about me."

"I'm in a bit of a hurry, good day, Mr. Benedict."

"Wait, I want to ask you about Maleaha."

"I have nothing to say to you about Maleaha." Betsy paused. She had never told an untruth in all her life. "Maleaha has gone to Europe to join her father," she said at last. She found she did not feel the least bit sinful for lying to him, in fact she had never known a lie could sound so convincing.

"Do you have an address where I can write her?"

"No, and if I did, I wouldn't give it to you."

"You don't like me very much do you, Miss Kincade?"

"I don't like you at all, Mr. Benedict," she said looking into his disturbing silver eyes. He was so handsome she could easily understand why Maleaha had fallen in love with such a man. "Please, just leave her in peace. If you have any human decency you will leave her alone." Betsy laid her whip to her horse, and the buggy jerked forward. She did not look back to see if Mr. Benedict was watching her. Her heart seemed to be thundering inside her. Even if Mr. Benedict was a cad, he had affected her in the most peculiar way. She thought of Bob and was glad she did not react to him in that way.

Kane stared at the buggy until it was out of sight. Hell and damnation, if he had any sense he would leave this land and never look back. How strange that he who had never let any woman get too close to him had fallen so hard for a half-wild little girl who would probably end up breaking his heart.

Kane spurred his horse forward. Diablo balked and reared on his hind legs and Kane yanked on the lead rope. "You are just like her, but I will tame you both before I am finished," he vowed.

CHAPTER SIXTEEN

A cold wind was blowing from the east as Maleaha wrapped the heavy blanket about her shoulders. She walked down to the river and stooped over, filling a jug with water. She had been at the Jojoba camp for over three months now, and she was still finding the Indian ways very hard to adapt to. Her aunt and the other Indian women worked very hard, while more often than not the Indian men would be off hunting to provide food for the tribe.

Maleaha and her aunt were growing closer as they got to know each other. Aunt Kosha had not hesitated to take her dead sister's daughter into her teepee, and she had been as loving and as kind as any mother would have been. Kosha understood better than anyone else why Maleaha had come to her, for she remembered what her own sister had suffered at the hands of the white race.

Maleaha was finding that all the Jojoba tribe were willing to take her in as one of their own. Her Uncle Ninah was a quiet man and hardly ever spoke to her directly, but he would often smile at her kindly, and he and her aunt would always offer Maleaha the biggest portion of meat, or the choicest tidbit.

As Maleaha grew bigger with Kane's child, she found it harder and harder to put him out of her mind. She knew he would have returned to Boston by now, but that did not stop her from loving him. With his child she would always have a small part of him with her.

She had written to her father telling him she would not be joining him, but she did not state why. Knowing him as she did, she knew that if he knew about the baby he would rush home to be with her. The one thing she dreaded the most was her father's finding out about Kane and herself. It had always been so important to him what people thought of her. How would he feel when he found out she was going to have a baby whose father would not recognize her as his wife, she wondered.

Mangas had been very kind to her, but for the most part had kept his distance. One day, however, as Maleaha lifted a heavy water jug to her shoulder as she had seen her aunt do and headed back to the village, she encountered Mangas and was surprised when he took the water jug from her.

"You should not be carrying anything so heavy, Little Flower. You are not accustomed to it."

She smiled at the tall, handsome chief. "It would not be wise for the people to see their chief doing woman's work."

He returned her smile. "I believe they might think it strange but I do not think they will say so to me."

"The weather is turning colder. I think it will snow

soon.''

"Yes, it will snow before the new moon." He stopped beside a huge rock and sat down. "Stay with me for a moment, Little Flower. I would like to talk to you."

Maleaha pulled the blanket tighter about her and sat down on the edge of the rock. "I have wondered why you had not asked to speak to me before now. I know you have wondered why I chose to come to my mother's people to have my baby."

"I have wondered, but it is not the Indian way to ask each other about personal things, and I will not do so now. I just want you to know I am your chief, and if you are troubled about anything you have the right to ask for council with me."

At that moment Maleaha knew a small part of her would always love this man who was chief of the Jojoba. He was the kind of man she could respect and look up to. She wished with all her heart she could love him as a man, and not only as a chief.

"I am grateful to you, Mangas, and if I ever feel the need, I will ask for your wise council."

He stood up and offered her his hand. Maleaha could plainly read the love in his eyes, and it tore at her heart to know she could never give him what he needed from her.

"Come, it grows colder and I do not want you to become ill."

After that day, Mangas did not seek Maleaha out again, and she knew he was waiting for her to come to him.

As winter advanced, Maleaha stayed pretty much in

her aunt's teepee. She tried to present a happy face to those around her, but sometimes it was a real effort, for with each passing day she felt worse.

It was almost sundown, and she and her aunt and uncle had just finished eating, when Maleaha felt as if every thing was closing in on her. Standing up, she walked out into the fresh air. It had snowed earlier in the day, but the clouds had moved on leaving a brilliant blue sky. Looking toward Mangas's teepee she noticed he was sitting in front of it working on a buffalo hide.

She had been so much in her aunt's company lately, and Kosha had a tendency to fuss too much over her health. Maleaha knew her aunt was giving her all the love she would have given her own daughter had she lived, but sometimes she just needed to be left alone.

Mangas looked up as she approached, and he nodded. "It is well that you are out in the fresh air, Maleaha. Do not allow your aunt to overprotect you," he said as he moved over and indicated that she should sit beside him on the buffalo robe.

"How did you know?" she asked.

"I know of the love your aunt has for you. I think she is afraid you will break."

Maleaha smiled. "I love her so much and I am grateful to her for allowing me to stay with her."

"There are many in the Jojoba tribe who love you, Little Flower. Do not forget that," he said without looking at her

"What are you doing?" she asked with interest, noicing he seemed to be working on a shield of some kind.

"I make the shield out of buffalo hide. Then it is coated with glue that is made from horses' hooves and hardened over a fire. When it dries it is very strong and nothing can penetrate it."

Maleaha watched as his hands expertly attached the buffalo hide to the frame made of bone. "What is it used for?"

"I will tell you, though it is a well-guarded secret. If I were facing an enemy I would hold the shield in front of me and gallop toward him. The enemy would fire at the shield, and before he could rearm I would dart in and strike with arrow and long spear."

"Why do you make the weapons of war? Are you expecting trouble?"

"As chief of the Jojoba, I must always be prepared for whatever comes. I find I have lost my taste for war, but should it come we will be ready."

"Wars are so useless, Mangas. Sometimes after they are over, no one knows what they were all about."

"Someday the Jojoba will either have to fight the white man or leave this land. If we do choose to fight we will know what it is about. It will be to remain free."

"I hope it never comes to a fight. I would hate to see you lose. You cannot win against them, Mangas, they are too many."

"I have heard what the white men do to the tribes they defeat. The men are asked to cut their hair, and plant corn like a woman. Then they want them to forsake their way of life and live like the white man. I do not want this for

275

my people."

"Nor do I, Mangas."

He stood up, and offering her his hand pulled her to her feet. "In the time of your grandfather life was good. Then came the white man, and with him he brought change and destruction. The buffalo have diminished in number, and the Indian goes hungry."

"I wish there was an easy answer, but I fear there is not. What do you think you will do?"

He smiled. "Would you like me to cut my hair and plant corn like a woman?"

"No, I would never want that, nor would I want to see the Jojoba be under the white man's thumb. I think my father will look after the Jojoba. He is a man of great influence in New Mexico. He would never stand idly by while the government pushed my mother's people aside."

"Your father cannot live forever, Little Flower."

"No, that is true, but when he is gone I will watch after my people, and then when I am gone, the child I carry will do the same."

Mangas pushed a dark strand of hair from Maleaha's face. "Perhaps in you, little princess, lies the salvation of the Jojoba people."

She touched his hand. "I pray it is so, Mangas."

"I think you have been too long in the cold, Maleaha. You should return to your aunt." He avoided looking into her eyes, and Maleaha knew he wanted her to leave.

"Don't love me, Mangas. I do not want to hurt you."

He looked at her for just a moment and she could read

276

the sadness in his eyes. ''Go now, the sun is setting, and with that come the cold winds.''

She turned away, knowing she had hurt him once more and wishing it didn't have to be so.

As winter advanced it brought with it the heavy snows and cold winds blowing out of the north. The countryside was covered with a blanket of white. There was smoke coming from the many teepees and Maleaha spent most of her time inside her aunt's teepee. The Jojoba had moved twice since she had come to stay with them, always following the game in their never-ending quest for food.

It was late March and the winter had been cold and the snowfall unusually heavy, because they were at such a high elevation. Mangas had chosen a site deep inside the forest that afforded them some protection from the wind. Most of the younger men had ridden off two days before to find fresh game, and Maleaha knew they would not return until they found sufficient meat.

Maleaha placed her moccasined foot lightly on the slick ice-covered ground, fearing she might fall in her advanced, clumsy state of pregnancy.

She heard the sound of riders and knew the hunting party was returning. She saw Mangas dismount and he led his horse over to her with a smile on his face. They had not spoken to each other since the day in front of his teepee.

''You should not be out in such weather, Maleaha. It would not be well should you fall and injure the child you carry.''

''You are beginning to sound like Aunt Kosha,'' she told him. He put his arm out for her to lean on, and she allowed him to lead her to her aunt's teepee.

''Are you feeling well?'' he inquired.

''Yes, my health is very good.''

Mangas seemed uneasy about something as he stopped in front of her aunt's abode, and Maleaha knew he had something on his mind. His dark eyes rested for a moment on the swell of her stomach, then he looked into her green eyes.

''Maleaha, I would not mind if you wanted to stay with us permanently.''

''I do not know what the future holds for me, Mangas. I suppose I am just waiting for my father to return.''

''Let us speak of Kane. Do you love him?''

''Yes,'' she whispered avoiding his eyes, knowing what it had cost him to ask about her love for Kane. ''I did not want to love him, but I could not help myself.''

''Maleaha, love is not a choice one gets to make. It is something that happens whether you welcome it or not.''

Maleaha nodded in agreement.

''I know it is not long until the child comes. If you will put your marriage to Kane aside, I would be a father to this child and a husband to you.''

Maleaha knew that Mangas loved her and if she accepted his offer he would love her child as if it were his own, for she had often seen him with the children in the village. He was always kind and understanding with them, and they seemed to adore him.

"Mangas, it would be easy to say yes to you, but you need a wife who can give you love, and you should have your own children. I believe the woman you choose will be very fortunate."

"I see you are not ready to consider me as your husband. I will wait, you may change your mind."

"No, I will never change, Mangas. I have no love inside me to give to any man at the moment, and I do not want to be a wife."

"You are already a wife, and you will soon be a mother. The child will need a father."

Maleaha was feeling the cold through her buckskin dress, and she shivered as Mangas pushed her inside the teepee. "We will talk after your baby is born."

Maleaha watched as he disappeared. She then removed the blanket from around her shoulders and sat down beside her aunt feeling very miserable.

"I heard what Mangas was saying to you," her aunt told her. "He would make a good father for your baby."

"I know, my aunt, but I do not love Mangas as he deserves to be loved."

"Sometimes the love is all on one side," her aunt summed up wisely, and Maleaha nodded in agreement, knowing it was the case between herself and Kane.

"Your baby will be born soon, you are already carrying it low."

"I will be glad when it is over, I feel so tired lately."

'It is because you do not sleep, have I not heard you tossing on your robe at night, and have I not heard you crying when you thought me and your uncle to be sleeping?''

"I cannot seem to help myself. I feel so miserable, so useless."

Her aunt put a comforting arm about her. "You feel this way now, but when your baby comes you will know you are useful and needed. Her aunt stood up and led her over to her robe. "You should sleep now, you will need all your strength for the labor that is ahead of you."

Maleaha did not argue but allowed her aunt to draw the robe over her, and she turned her face to the wall. Her hands went automatically to her swollen stomach, and she could feel her baby moving inside of her as tears of self-pity stung her eyes.

She wondered not for the first time if Kane had returned to Boston with his father to the woman he was to marry. Most probably he had left long ago, and perhaps he was even married by now.

She would always think of him as her husband, and she would have his baby to remind her of that fact. Had he already forgotten about her?

It was late that night that Maleaha's pains started. She was awakened by a sharp pain that started in her back and moved to her abdomen. She moved from side to side trying to find some relief from the pain. She tried to be as quiet as possible, not wanting to awaken her aunt and uncle, but she had not reckoned with her aunt's watchfulness.

"Awake, Ninah," Kosha told her husband. "My niece is having her baby. You must seek shelter in another place. I will send word as soon as the child is born.''

Ninah sat up quickly and stretched his arms over his head, then he stood up and pulled a blanket about his shoulders for warmth. ''Have a healthy baby, Maleaha,'' he told her as he walked toward the door.

''Send Hanna to me, my husband,'' Kosha told him. He nodded his head and disappeared into the cold night.

Maleaha had heard many stories of how women suffered in childbirth. She thought if the pain did not increase she would be not too uncomfortable. That hope did not stay with her for long, however, for before Hanna made her appearance her pains had become fierce, leaving Maleaha gasping for breath.

The sun had risen and set again, and still Maleaha labored to bring forth Kane's child. The whole village waited for the birth of her child, for Maleaha was very dear to them.

Sometimes the pain was so severe that Maleaha had to bite her lips to keep from screaming, for she knew a Jojoba woman must bear her child in silence.

Maleaha's body was wet with perspiration, and her aunt bathed her face with cool water and spoke soothingly to her. ''Your labor is hard, Maleaha, this happens sometimes, but you are not to worry, Hanna has brought many healthy babies into the world.''

Maleaha grasped her aunt's hand as pain ripped through her body.

''The baby comes,'' Hanna said as she reached for the tiny infant who had just made its appearance into the world.

"You have a daughter, Maleaha," her aunt told her as she wrapped the tiny girl in a warm blanket and handed her to Maleaha.

Maleaha had not once cried out with the pain of delivering her daughter, but there were tears of happiness in her eyes now, as she looked down upon the tiny girl. She rested her cheek against the soft black downy hair and then kissed her daughter's smooth cheek.

Kane shook the rain from his mackintosh and hung it by the open fireplace to dry. Looking about the empty sitting room he felt pride in his new home which had only been completed a week before. He hoped Maleaha would be pleased with it.

He now had a goal in life, and he found it felt good just waking up in the mornings. He even found satisfaction in coming home exhausted in the evenings, after a hard day's work. For the first time in Kane's life he felt good about himself. If only he could convince Maleaha to marry him, his life would be complete. He knew if he weren't so busy, time would lie heavy on his hands while he waited for Maleaha to return.

Kane had not wanted to furnish the house, hoping that as his wife, Maleaha would take on that job. The only room that he had bothered with was his study, aside from a table and cooking stove in the kitchen, and a cot in one of the upstairs bedrooms.

Kane felt a hunger pang and frowned. He had hired a Mexican woman to do the cooking for him, but so far he had not acquired a taste for the hot spicy food she always prepared. Perhaps he wasn't so hungry after all, he thought wearily.

Kane lay down on his cot and closed his eyes. Deep inside of him was always this dull ache that he knew only Maleaha could soothe. When he remembered making love to her his body trembled. Never before had the memory of a woman stayed with him for so long. Everything he did now was to please her. He found himself wondering if she would like the place he had chosen for a garden. Would she think the stables were too near the house? Would she like the dark red tiled roof on the house? Everything had to be just right for her.

He wondered if she ever thought of him, or was she too busy meeting admiring gentlemen in Europe. Remembering their last meeting, he knew if she did think of him at all it would be with loathing. His father had hurt her badly that night at the dance. Knowing all about Maleaha's pride, he cursed his father for his cruel words. If his father had not interfered that night, Maleaha might at this moment be lying beside him as his wife.

As Kane fell asleep he had no way of knowing that Maleaha was not in Europe as he thought, but only two days' journey from where he slept.

Kane was awakened not by a sound but more from a feeling of another's presence in the room. Opening his eyes he was startled when he saw Lamas standing beside his cot.

"Mangas wants to see you."

"Right now?" Kane asked, trying to shake his need for sleep.

"He said to bring you now," the old man said, handing Kane his mackintosh. "I have saddled your horse," Lamas said as he turned his back and walked away.

Maleaha's daughter was four months old, and Maleaha had named her Cimeron after her mother. Cimeron was a beautiful child and was a favorite with everyone. Her hair was soft and dark and her face was angelic and lovely. Her disposition was sweet and loving. She now had a smile for everyone. Cimeron's eyes were the same silver-gray color as Kane's, and she had the same dimples in her cheeks that Kane had.

It was June, and it had been raining for the past two weeks, but as Maleaha watched the sun rise over the mountains she could see that it would be a bright, cloudless day. As she made her way through the village, she could see it coming to life. Reaching the stream, she bathed her face in the cool water and then smiled at Hanna who was filling a water jug.

As Maleaha walked back to her aunt's teepee she remembered the strange conversation she had had with Mangas the day before. He had asked her if she knew where Kane was, and she had told him he had probably gone back to Boston with his father. She remembered how oddly Mangas had looked at her. He had asked her once more if she would put her marriage to Kane aside, and once again she had told him she wouldn't. He had then asked her again if she loved Kane, and when she told him she would always love him, Mangas had left her abruptly.

She reached her aunt's teepee. Cimeron was awake, so she began to nurse her daughter, forgetting about the conversation of the day before as she became absorbed in the baby.

Kane rode beside Lamas wondering what Mangas wanted to see him about. The last time he had seen the chief was the day they had clashed with the Arapaho and he had been wounded.

"How far is it to the Jojoba village, Lamas?" he asked when they dismounted to rest the horses.

"No more than two days."

"Do you take me the long way around this time?"

"No, Mangas trusts you."

"Why does Mangas want to see me?"

"He will tell you when the time is right."

Kane soon became weary of trying to get any answers out of the old Indian, and he lapsed into silence.

That night when they made camp, Kane tried to question Lamas again, but the old man shrugged his shoulders, saying nothing.

After two days of hard riding they finally reached the Jojoba village. As Kane dismounted Mangas greeted him with a smile, and the two men clasped arms in Jojoba fashion.

"I am glad to see you, my friend. It has been too long for good friends to be parted," Mangas told him.

"That's true," Kane agreed.

"Come with me and we will talk, my friend," Mangas said, leading the way to his teepee. When they both were seated Mangas handed Kane a bowl of meat. There had been a time when Kane would have refused the food, but he had come a long way from the man he had once been.

Mangas watched Kane silently as if trying to read his thoughts.

"I never did get the chance to thank you for saving my life, Mangas. I was told that had it not been for you I would have died."

Mangas waved his thanks aside. "First you saved my life, Kane, so I returned the favor. There need never be a reason for thanks between friends." Mangas picked up his bowl. "I am told that you have built a house, Kane. Does that mean you are planning to stay in this country?"

"Yes, I have grown to love this land. I do not ever want to leave here."

"That is good to hear, Kane. I wonder why you built such a large house. I am told it has many rooms. Surely it is too large for one man to live in." Kane had a feeling his answer was very important to Mangas.

"Yes, you are right, it is a big house, a house large enough for a wife and children," Kane told him.

"I myself have decided to take a wife, Kane. I want strong sons to fill my life."

"That is good, Mangas. Tell me all about the woman you have chosen to be your wife."

Mangas smiled. "I have not yet decided who the woman will be, but I keep my eyes open." Mangas's eyes scanned Kane's face. He would find out how Kane felt about Maleaha, and if he loved her, as Mangas suspected, all would be well, but if he did not, he would not let Kane find out that his wife and daughter were in the village.

"It has been hard for me to find someone to replace Maleaha in my heart, Kane."

"We both love Maleaha, Mangas. I hope when she returns from Europe with her father I can convince her to live with me in the house I had built for her."

Mangas frowned. "Did you say Maleaha is with Jonas?"

"Yes, didn't you know? I hope they will be back sometime this summer, but I cannot find anyone who will tell me when they are returning."

"Do you really love Maleaha, Kane?" Mangas saw the answer to his question in the depth of Kane's silver eyes. They were eyes that were tormented and full of uncertainty.

"I love her, Mangas, but I fear she does not love me."

Mangas smiled. "One can never be sure with a woman. Sometimes I think women are very hard to understand."

The two of them finished eating and then Mangas stood up. "You have had a long journey, my friend, and you should rest. We will talk more later."

Kane stood up, puzzled. He still had no idea why Mangas had sent for him. Mangas walked outside with him and motioned for Lamas to come to him.

"Take Kane to Kosha's teepee," he said in the language of the Jojoba.

Maleaha dropped vegetables in the stewing meat and placed a lid on it so it would simmer. Her aunt had taken Cimeron for a walk, and Maleaha expected them back at any moment. Hearing the heavy footsteps outside the teepee, Maleaha frowned. Whoever it was wore boots, not moccasins. She turned around just as the tent flap was thrown open, and she blinked her eyes, thinking they were deceiving her.

It took Kane's eyes a moment to adjust to the dim light inside the teepee, and when he could see well enough he stood as though turned to stone.

CHAPTER SEVENTEEN

Kane and Maleaha stared at each other in disbelief. It was as if the whole world had paused to draw breath. Kane's eyes roved hungrily over the woman he loved. He noticed everything about her, from the wide leather band that circled her dark hair to the buckskin dress she wore.

Maleaha's heart was drumming loudly as she looked at Kane. He was wearing brown trousers, a brown shirt, and brown leather boots. She had not realized until that moment how much she had wanted to see him. She had the urge to fly into his arms.

They had both been silent, and now they both spoke at once. "I thought you had returned to Boston," she said. "I thought you were with Jonas," Kane told her.

Maleaha lapsed into silence once more. She was having a hard time believing he was there, and she saw confusion on his face.

"I was told you went to Europe to join Jonas."

"No, I have been here all the time. Why did you not return to Boston?"

Kane frowned. "It would seem we both have many unanswered questions, Maleaha."

Suddenly Maleaha remembered Cimeron. Kane must not find out about his daughter, she thought, beginning to panic. "Why are you here, Kane?" She needed to know.

"I'm not sure. Mangas sent for me, but he has not yet told me why."

Maleaha pondered his words. Why would Mangas send for Kane and not tell her? Her eyes widened in horror as she realized he had sent for Kane because of Cimeron. She had to make Kane leave before her aunt returned with her baby. One look at Cimeron and Kane would know she was his daughter.

"I do not know why you are here, Kane, but I wish you would just go away," she said, turning her back on him.

"Like hell I will. You and I are going to sit down and hash this whole thing out," he said, turning her around to face him.

She moved away from him and looked at him haughtily. "Remembering our last little tête à tête, I am not interested in anything you might have to say."

"I can see that time and distance have not sweetened your disposition any," he ground out between clenched teeth. "Lord, you are an obstinate woman."

Maleaha's keen hearing picked up the sound of her aunt's footsteps and she began to panic. It was too late to send Kane away. Maybe if she distracted him he would not pay too much attention to Cimeron.

"Go away, Kane. Can't you see that you and I have nothing to talk about? I hate you. Why can't you just leave it at that?" Her words seemed to hang in the air, and

Kane stared at her, feeling as if she had just delivered him a mortal blow. He did not notice that Maleaha's eyes were sparkling with unshed tears at the lie she had just told him.

"I suppose you are right. There is nothing more for us to say to one another," he said harshly. Maleaha caught her breath as her aunt came into the teepee carrying Cimeron. When Kane turned to leave he almost bumped into them. Stepping aside, he waited for Maleaha's aunt to move out of the way so he could leave. Kosha looked at her niece in confusion, and Maleaha silently pleaded with her to hide Cimeron from Kane.

"Please leave, Kane," Maleaha cried in a panic.

Kane's frown deepened. He could hardly leave until the Indian woman moved aside. His eyes moved carelessly over the child while Maleaha held her breath.

Kane might have left without ever knowing he had a daughter had Cimeron not taken matters into her own hands. Seeing the tall stranger and being of such a loving nature, she reached out and grabbed Kane's shirt-sleeve in her chubby little hand.

Kane gazed down at the child thinking she belonged to the Indian woman. She was a pretty child he thought, with her dark straight hair that just covered her ears. Something clicked in his brain as he noticed how white her skin was. This was no Indian baby. Holding his breath, he waited for her to lift her eyelashes so he could see her eyes, and when she did, silver eyes stared into silver eyes. His hands were trembling as he reached for the child and lifted her into his arms. His heart contracted when she smiled and he saw the dimples in her cheeks.

291

My God! This was his daughter. He swiveled around to face Maleaha in confusion. When he read the guilt in her eyes his confusion turned to anger. The little girl in his arms patted his cheek and jabbered in baby talk. Kane tried to speak, but his throat seemed to be closed off. This lovely child, this little girl, was his daughter. Her skin was light in color, and there was little trace of Indian blood in her.

Maleaha looked from Kane to her aunt in bewilderment. Kosha edged her way toward the exit, thinking it was time to leave Maleaha and her husband alone. She knew what her niece was feeling, but she could be no help to her. After all, she now had her husband to take care of her. She felt sad at the thought of Maleaha's going away and taking little Cimeron with her, but it was right that a wife should go with her husband. The sadness showed in Kosha's face as she darted out the opening of the teepee.

Kane paid little heed to the departing Indian woman. His attention was now divided between the child he held and Maleaha who was looking increasingly uncomfortable under his accusing glare.

Maleaha wanted to run to Cimeron and grab her out of Kane's arms, but the look in his silver eyes seemed to pin her to the spot.

"How could you keep this from me?" Kane said in a voice strangled with anger. When he saw the fear in Maleaha's eyes his anger abated somewhat. "I never thought the night we spent together would result in the birth of a child. Lord, you must hate me to keep this from me."

Suddenly Maleaha was spun into action. She flew across the room and tried to pull Cimeron from Kane's arms. "You can't have her, she is my baby! Give her to me. Go away, we don't want you here."

Kane shoved her roughly away. "Like hell I will. I will go away all right, but when I do my daughter goes with me." He looked down at the child who was now sleeping peacefully in his arms, and with a trembling hand he brushed a dark strand of hair from her lovely face. Her mouth was like a tiny rosebud, and her dark, silky lashes rested against her pale skin. She was so lovely that Kane felt his throat contract. He had never paid the slightest attention to babies, in fact he could never remember having held one in his arms. This child was of his flesh and blood and she belonged to him, and he pitied anyone who would try to keep her from him. Until a few moments ago he had not known of her existence, and Kane could not define the feelings that were washing over him like a tidal wave.

Maleaha caught her breath as Kane lowered his dark head and kissed the tiny rosebud mouth. She had thought that if he found out about Cimeron he would deny she was his daughter. She had not expected him to want her, and that frightened Maleaha even more than if he had denied her.

"What is her name?" Kane asked, looking at his daughter and not at Maleaha.

"Cimeron," Maleaha told him in a voice that was choked with emotion.

"You named her for your mother?"

"Yes."

"Cimeron," he said, testing the name out loud. "Cimeron what? Damn you, Maleaha, she has no last name.

The world will class my daughter as a bastard, and it's all your fault," he said, suddenly feeling protective toward the tiny girl who was his daughter. He knew what he must do.

"Gather your belongings together. You and Cimeron are coming with me."

Maleaha raised her chin and stared back at him bravely. "You must be mad if you think we are going away with you. Get out of here, Kane. Mangas would kill you before he let you take me away against my will." Her chest was rising and falling with the tremendous effort she was making to breathe.

Kane's eyes narrowed to translucent depths and his face became hard. Maleaha backed up as she watched him place Cimeron down on the buffalo robe and advance toward her. Suddenly her back was to the wall of the tee-pee, and Kane stood between her and the exit. She was frightened by the unbound anger she saw in Kane's face, but she would not allow him to see it. Raising her head defiantly, she faced him.

"You would not dare touch me," she challenged.

His eyes dropped to her fully rounded breasts and then slid up to her face. "Oh, I would dare, Maleaha, I would dare," he said in a husky voice.

She stumbled backwards and tears blurred her vision. She feared if he were to touch her, she would fall apart. She struggled within herself for something to say that would save her. This was a Kane she had never seen. He was hard, and she knew what he wanted he would take.

"Don't do this, Kane. Think of the woman you are going to marry," she whispered, trying to bring him to his senses.

His eyes drew her glance. "All I ever think about is the woman I want to marry," he said, reaching out and pulling her into his arms.

Oh, God, don't let him speak of the woman he loves, she pleaded silently.

"I think about her day and night. I crave her in my bed. I need her in my life," he whispered in her ear.

Maleaha wondered if a broken heart ever bled, as she felt heart break at his loving words about another woman. She pushed herself out of his arms, willing herself to hide the hurt she felt. "I hate you, Kanen Benedict!" she cried.

His face became a mask of fury. "So you have said on a number of occasions. I grow weary of hearing it." Turning away from her he scooped up his sleeping daughter. "You can come or stay if you like, but my daughter goes with me."

Maleaha took a step forward. "No, Kane, do not take her away from me."

He looked about the teepee grim-faced. "Is this the kind of life you want for our daughter? Why did you run off to have my child here? God only knows under what kind of conditions she was brought into the world. Didn't you know that had you told me about her I would have married you to give her a name?"

Maleaha wanted to shout at him that he had already married her, and that Cimeron was legally his daughter, but she knew he didn't feel bound by the Jojoba wedding as she did.

"I want no sacrifice on my account, Kane. Go home to Boston and marry your Lucinda. Cimeron and I will do very nicely without your name, thank you.''

''Don't go too far, Maleaha. I have taken just about all I intend to from you.'' His voice was hard and rough, and even though she saw the danger signal she did not heed it.

''If your father is to be believed, you must go about populating the whole country. You may have many children, for all I know. Surely you cannot offer to marry every woman you take to your bed.''

His eyes focused on hers and Maleaha saw the smoldering anger in the silver depths. ''I know of no other child I have fathered. Although I cannot be positive, I would hope that Cimeron is the only child entitled to my name.''

''What makes you so sure that Cimeron is yours?''

The smile he gave her was devoid of humor. ''Do you deny she is mine?''

Maleaha shook her head, unable to lie about anything so important.

''Whatever your faults are, Maleaha, I know I am the only man who has ever touched you. Do you deny that?''

Again she shook her head.

''You are coming with me whether you want to or not. You will stand before a man of the cloth and profess to love and honor me. Afterwards you will live with me if you want to be near your daughter, for I can assure you, I am taking her with me.''

She walked slowly toward him and he reached out and placed his arm lightly about her shoulder.

''How can you be so heartless?'' she asked, feeling defeated.

He released her and looked down at his sleeping

daughter. "You may think me heartless, Maleaha, but believe me I have a heart, although it has come as a surprise to me."

"I will not go with you, Kane."

He shrugged his shoulders. "Please yourself. It's a pity Cimeron is not awake so she could see her mother for the last time," he said, sweeping out the teepee opening.

Maleaha stood speechless for a moment, and then fear gave wings to her feet as she flew outside. She had not thought he would do it, but she saw Lamas had saddled Kane's horse as well as her own, and Kane strolled toward his horse purposefully. Seeing her aunt Maleaha grabbed her hand.

"Aunt Kosha, Kane is taking my daughter!"

Her aunt's eyes were sad. "I will gather your things together, Maleaha. It is only right that you should go with your husband." Maleaha opened her mouth to protest, but her aunt disappeared into the teepee. Maleaha looked about her frantically. Seeing Mangas standing in front of his teepee she ran to him, knowing he would help her.

"Mangas, stop Kane. He is taking my baby!"

Mangas looked deeply into her eyes, and she saw sadness written there. "It is right that a man should have his child, Maleaha. Go with him, you are his woman."

Maleaha felt as if she were being betrayed by everyone she loved. She watched helplessly as Kane mounted his horse with Cimeron in his arms. Her aunt came out of the teepee and handed Lamas Maleaha's belongings, which had been hurriedly crammed into a leather satchel.

Maleaha had never felt so alone. Would no one help her? Slowly she walked to her horse. Lamas offered to give her a boost into the saddle, but she brushed him aside and leaped onto her horse. "You too, Lamas?" she asked in a dull voice.

"You are not alone. I will go with you," he told her, turning away to mount his own horse. Maleaha whirled her horse about and rode out of the village without a backward glance. Kane had won, but only because she had been betrayed. She heard Lamas pull even with her but she refused to look in his direction. For the first time in her life, Maleaha was angry with Lamas.

She would go with Kane for the moment because she had no choice, but the first chance she got she would take her baby and hide where he would never find them, she vowed.

Kane rode up beside her, and seeing the stubborn set to her chin, knew what she was thinking. He smiled at the irony of the situation. He who had always scoffed at love and marriage had to force the woman he loved to marry him, using his child as bait.

Maleaha, seeing the smile on his face, thought he was feeling pleased with himself. For the moment he had her at his mercy, and he knew it, but it would not always be so, she thought.

They had to stop twice so Maleaha could tend to Cimeron. They camped that night before dark. Kane led the horses down to the stream to water them, and Lamas went off into the woods to hunt game for their evening meal. Maleaha spread out a blanket and sat down to nurse her daughter. Cimeron cooed and gurgled happily, and Maleaha's heart swelled with love for her. Hearing Kane return, she stared at him angrily. Kane did not notice her anger. He was staring at the beautiful sight of Maleaha nursing his daughter. Her breasts were larger, since they were filled with milk, and they appeared creamy and satiny.

Maleaha was embarrassed by his expression and laid Cimeron down and refastened her gown. Kane smiled at her and gathered up the canteens and walked once more to the stream.

Now was her chance to escape, she thought. Picking Cimeron up in her arms and casting a fugitive glance toward the stream, she crept silently in the direction of where her horse was grazing.

"Don't try it, Maleaha. I would only come after you." Maleaha jumped guiltily. She had not heard Kane come up behind her, and wondered why she had not detected his footsteps. Kane seemed to read her face and smiled.

"I learned many things from Mangas. One of them was how to walk silently like an Indian."

"You have no right to do this, Kane."

Cimeron held her arms up, wanting Kane to take her. He smiled tenderly at the tiny girl and lifted her into his arms. "I have the right, Maleaha. You gave me the right when you gave life to my daughter."

"Do you have no small doubt that she is your daughter?"

His shoulders shook with silent laughter. "Oh, Maleaha, Maleaha, would you have me think that anyone other than myself had enjoyed the joys of your beautiful body? Besides, Cimeron looks like me."

"How can I rid myself of you?"

"Surely not by claiming Cimeron is not of my seed. I

knew the moment I saw her she was mine.''

''There is more to being a father then just begetting a child, Kane.''

Kane looked down at Cimeron. ''Don't you think I know that? Today has been very unsettling for me. I find I like the thought of having a daughter. I want her to have all the love I never had from my father. Heed my words, Maleaha, I will do all within my power to see that she has both a mother and a father.''

Maleaha looked at Kane disbelieving. ''Why are you doing this? I never thought of you as a man who would want to settle down with a wife and child. I remember a time when you made your views very clear on that matter.''

''Yes, I recall saying that to you. Let us just say for the sake of argument that I have changed my mind.''

''I do not want to be your wife.''

He studied her face through half-veiled lashes, and Maleaha could feel the pull of his charm. ''Why, Maleaha?''

Trying not to think how handsome and magnetic he was, she raised her chin proudly. ''If I were your wife, I could never be sure when you were not with me that you wouldn't be with another woman. It would be humiliating to have a husband who had three mistresses on the side,'' she told him, throwing his father's words in his face.

Kane could have told her that he had no desire for another woman. Since the night he had made love to her it had become distasteful to him just to think about making love to anyone else. He was feverish in his desire to possess her again. He wanted to reach out and crush her in his arms and remove all her doubts about him, but he did not.

"If my fidelity is the only thing that is standing in the way of our marriage, put your fears to rest. I shall have no mistresses." He stared into her eyes, and she could not seem to look away. "Maleaha, if you will have me for your husband, I shall honor our wedding vows."

His words seemed to be spoken sincerely and she wanted to believe him. She had no idea why he wanted to make her his wife. She knew he didn't love her. Maleaha shied away from thinking about the woman who was waiting for him in Boston.

"What are your plans, Kane?"

"I know of a little mission in the mountains. I will take you there and we can be married quietly. Then I would like to have Cimeron christened, if you have no objections."

Maleaha nodded. "Then what?"

Cimeron had fallen asleep and Kane carried her to Maleaha's blanket and laid her down. Kane then took Maleaha's hand and led her down to the stream where they could still keep a watchful eye on Cimeron, but she would not be disturbed by their voices.

Maleaha pulled her hand away from Kane and sat down beside the stream, trailing her hand in the cool rushing water.

Kane sat down and rested his back against a tree and watched her.

"Maleaha, do you remember that property that your father told me about the night I dined at Deveraux?"

She nodded.

"I bought the land and had a house built." He paused, letting her digest what he had told her. "I would like it if you would live with me there. The house is not furnished, but you could decorate it any way you pleased."

Maleaha shook her head. This was not the Kanen Benedict she had come to know. How long would it take him to decide he did not like the life he seemed to have mapped out for them?

"You are confusing me, Kane. I do not understand why you want me and Cimeron."

Kane sighed in exasperation. "I have already told you I want Cimeron to have a mother and a father. I believe if you love her you will not deny her that right."

"If I did live with you, Kane, what would you expect from me?"

Everything, his heart cried out. "I would ask no more of you than you are willing to give," he told her.

"Do you believe you could live the life of a monk?"

His piercing eyes looked deeply into hers. "Can you?"

Maleaha felt herself being pulled under his spell once more, and she feared he would sense she was weak.

"I will marry you, and I will go with you to your home, but if it does not work out I will leave, Kane. I swear it."

Joy leaped into Kane's heart, but he did not let it show on his face. Instead he decided to change the subject, fearing Maleaha would sense how he felt about her.

"I believe Cimeron likes me," he said softly.

"Apparently all females like you, why should she be any different?"

"Surely not all. You, for instance?"

"I am only one among many. Surely you will not suffer knowing I do not care for you?"

"You can like me or not, that is your choice. As you say, it makes but little difference."

"I was already married to you once, Kane. Why do you insist on another wedding?"

"As I told you at the time, I did not feel that marriage was binding."

"Oh yes, I remember only too well. You made your views very clear that next morning."

Kane's head jerked up, for he had heard the hurt in her voice. It had never occurred to him that Maleaha might feel bound by the marriage Mangas had performed that night. He closed his eyes, thinking what a blind fool he had been. Of course she had felt bound by the marriage, because afterwards she had given herself to him willingly. He needed to hear her admit it.

"Maleaha, did you feel the wedding performed by Mangas was binding?"

Maleaha wished with all her heart that she could deny the truth, but he had asked her a direct question, and she could not speak falsely. "Yes, my mother and father were married in the same way. To deny that I am your wife would be to deny that my mother and father were married."

"Oh, God. I had heard that. I suppose I just forgot."

"There is no reason for you to feel bound by the marriage. You are not an Indian. As I recall you were forced into it by Mangas."

"Your father was not an Indian, yet he felt bound by

the marriage.''

"You are not like my father. He respects the ways of the Jojoba, and he knows that before God he was my mother's husband.''

"I am beginning to see more clearly. You do not feel then that Cimeron is illegitimate, do you?''

"If I believed Cimeron was illegitimate, then I must also be, for I was born from the same kind of union that she was. Had you known my mother, you would know she would never have lived with my father unless they were married. Do you consider me a bastard, Kane?''

"No, of course not.''

"Then neither is Cimeron.''

He was thoughtful for a moment. "I have hurt you many times in the past, haven't I?''

She looked past him to where Cimeron lay sleeping. "One must love before they can be hurt,'' she said, spinning another golden lie.

Once again Kane was stung by her cold words. "I cannot find it in me to regret that night we spent together, Maleaha. Although I only met my daughter today, I find I love her deeply.'' Maleaha watched as he stood up and walked off into the darkness.

Two days later Kane and Maleaha stood before a kindly old priest as he spoke the words that once again made them man and wife. Kane was very solemn when he repeated the vows, and Maleaha could not imagine what was going on in his head. Was he feeling trapped? Her vows were spoken hardly above a whisper. When they were pronounced man and wife, Maleaha felt no more married than she had the night Mangas had joined her and Kane together.

As they rode away from the mission, Maleaha saw the tired lines in Kane's face. She had noticed when he was weary that he would walk with a slight limp, and she wondered if his leg still pained him. She was sure it did when she saw him grimace in agony and run his hand along his thigh. Her heart went out to him wishing she could comfort him, but she knew he would not welcome her concern. She could see years of heartache ahead for them both. He was tied to a woman he did not love. She would be a good wife to him. She would tend his house and prepare his meals, giving him no cause to find fault with her. She would stay with him until he no longer wanted her.

Maleaha raised her head to the heavens and saw the clouds that had gathered in the direction in which she knew Kane's ranch was located. She felt his eyes on her and looked at him.

''Don't look so woebegone, Maleaha. You could have had a worse husband. At least I will never beat you.'' He smiled and added, ''Unless you provoke me.''

CHAPTER EIGHTEEN

It was early afternoon when they reached Kane's ranch. Maleaha drew her mount up as they topped a small hill and gazed down below at the huge ranch house. It was built in the Spanish style, and since it was new it had an unlived-in look.

Kane pulled his horse alongside Maleaha's and watched her face to see if she liked the home he had built for her.

"It's lovely, Kane, and not unlike Deveraux."

"I hope you will feel at home in it. As I told you, it is sparsely furnished, but I hope you will not find it uncomfortable."

They rode down the hill, followed by Lamas. When they stopped in front of the house Kane helped Maleaha dismount, since she was encumbered by the sleeping Cimeron. The house seemed to welcome Maleaha with its white limestone and red-tiled roof that gleamed brightly in the sunlight.

"I am sure with just the right touches it will be a very lovely home, Kane."

"Will you decorate the house, Maleaha? Money is no object. You will have a free hand to do as you like." She sensed an eagerness about him, as if he wanted her approval.

"Is that what you want me to do, Kane?"

"Yes, very much." He took Cimeron from her and led the way to the front door.

"Wait," Maleaha said. "Where would you like Lamas to stay?"

Kane paused on the doorstep. "Will he be staying here?"

"Yes, he will not leave me."

"He could have a room in the house."

"No, Lamas would not like that. He likes his solitude."

"Very well, he can stay in the bunkhouse for now. Later we will build him a small house of his own." For the first time since Kane had known the old Indian, he saw Lamas grin. Lamas spoke to Maleaha in the language of the Jojoba, then led the horses toward the barn.

Maleaha smiled as she climbed the steps behind Kane. "What did he say to you?" Kane inquired.

"He asked if he could have a front porch on his new house, along with a new rocking chair."

Kane laughed. "We will buy that old man the best rocker that money can buy. I have grown accustomed to having him around."

"You won't be sorry if you let him stay, Kane. Lamas knows more about cattle ranching than anyone I know, with the exception of my father. You will find he is a tireless worker."

"He is getting old. Don't you think he should take it easy?" Kane asked as he watched Lamas disappear into the barn.

"I hope you will never say that to him. He is a proud man and finds great joy in working with cattle."

"As you wish. Let's go in now. You must be tired."

Maleaha followed Kane into the house. A round, pleasant-faced Mexican woman came into the room wiping her hands on a white apron. Kane spoke to her in slow English.

"This is my wife, Mrs. Benedict," he told her.

"Pardon, señor?"

Kane looked at Maleaha in exasperation. "This is Rosita. She speaks no English, and I speak no Spanish. I have had a hell of a time trying to tell her I do not like beans and tortillas for every meal."

Maleaha turned to the woman and spoke to her in fluent Spanish. "I am Mrs. Benedict. Show me to a room where I can make my daughter comfortable, Rosita."

Rosita beamed. "Ah, *si,* señora. The señor is a very handsome man."

"Thank you, Rosita," Maleaha said taking Cimeron from Kane and following the Mexican woman up the stairs.

Maleaha opened all the doors to the upstairs bedrooms until she found the one that would be just right for Cimeron. Instructing Rosita to bring some quilts, the two of them made the baby a nice bed.

"Rosita, you stay with Cimeron while I go below. When she awakes you can bring her downstairs."

When Maleaha made her way downstairs, she found

Kane waiting for her. "Will you accompany me to the study, Maleaha? It is the only room besides the kitchen which is furnished."

She followed him down the hallway and he opened a door, standing aside for her to enter. The wooden floor was brightly polished, and the bookshelves were partially filled with leather-bound books. There was a huge mahogany desk and a leather couch. The draperies that hung at the windows were a deep wine color. Two leather wingback chairs stood in front of the window. It was definitely a man's room, Maleaha thought.

"I like this room, Kane," she said sitting down on the couch and folding her hands in her lap. "Did you decorate it yourself?"

Kane was not really listening to her. He was thinking what a charming picture she made sitting in her buckskin dress with her dark hair falling over her shoulders. Many times he had tried to imagine her in this house, and now she was actually here. Not only was she his wife, but he also had a daughter. His happiness would be complete he thought, if only Maleaha loved him.

"Kane, is something the matter?" Maleaha asked. He was looking at her so strangely.

"No, what were you saying?"

"It's not important."

"Thank God you were able to speak Spanish. I have been going out of my mind trying to make her understand me."

Maleaha laughed. "I can imagine."

Kane sat down beside her and his expression became serious. "Maleaha, do you think you can be happy here?''

"I don't know, Kane. I will try and make a home for you and our daughter. I have been doing a lot of thinking today. I love my father. He means a great deal to me. I do not want Cimeron to be deprived of her father. I will try to remember that.''

"I hope to God I can be the kind of father to our daughter that Jonas has been to you.''

"I am glad you wanted Cimeron. I didn't think you would.''

"Maleaha, I think if anyone asks we should tell them that we were married last summer, for Cimeron's sake.''

"We *were* married last summer, Kane.''

"We were twice married then, Maleaha.'' He smiled. "That should tie you to me forever.''

"Why would you want to be tied to a woman you do not love, Kane?''

"For one thing, I want Cimeron to have a mother and father, but I told you this already. What I did not tell you is that my father and I have never had a close relationship like you and Jonas do.''

"Did you have an unhappy childhood?''

He was thoughtful for a moment. "When I was growing up, neither of my parents paid very much attention to me. As I grew older they would both use me against each other. No matter what our feelings are for one another, Maleaha, I do not want it to affect Cimeron.''

Maleaha wanted to reach out and ease the pain she saw in his face. This was a side of him she had never seen before. She had grown up with a loving father, and it was hard for her to imagine what Kane's life had been like.

She could envision him as a lonely little boy living without love, and now he was married to a woman he didn't love. Even though he would never turn to her in love, she would show her love for him by trying to make him a good home.

"What role do you want me to play in your life, Kane?"

His eyes blazed for a moment, and he stared at her parted lips. Then he looked away to stare at the bookshelf. "I would like for you to assume the role of my wife, at least when others are around. I would like you to make this house into a home. One that you will feel comfortable in."

Maleaha bit her trembling lip. "Is that all?"

"Yes, that will be all I will expect from you, with the exception of common courtesies that two people show each other when they live together."

"Such as?"

"Letting me know when you will be leaving the ranch, and what time you expect to return. I would like to be informed ahead of time if we are having guests, that sort of thing."

"I will do as you ask. What can I expect from you in return?"

"I shall play the devoted husband. All I have I will gladly share with you. I will try to be considerate of your feelings. Is there anything I left out that you would like to add?"

Maleaha could think of many things he had omitted, but she did not voice them. She just shook her head.

"Do I have your word that the moment my back is turned you will not take Cimeron and disappear?"

"I don't know if you trust my word, but I give it anyway."

"I would trust your word before I would that of anyone I know," he said with feeling.

Suddenly Maleaha wanted to know about Lucinda, but she could not bring herself to speak her name. "Kane, did you never want to marry the woman you love and have children by her?"

His silver eyes darkened to a deep gray as he looked past her. "I have come to know that one can live without love, Maleaha—a lesson I have learned over the years."

"Kane, has this woman you love hurt you so badly?"

He looked into her eyes as if seeking some truths of his own. "She has torn my heart to shreds, Maleaha, and still I love her," he said in a raspy voice.

Maleaha had to look away for she couldn't bear to see the pain in his eyes. "How about you, Maleaha, has no man ever touched your heart?"

"Oh dozens," she said flippantly.

He smiled unexpectedly. "It seems I have run off with the belle of Santa Fe. Many young gentlemen will want to call me out for taking you out of circulation."

Maleaha warmed to his lighter mood.

"Perhaps they can heal the hearts of the women who will be brokenhearted because you are now married."

Kane laughed deeply. "Yes, perhaps they can console one another."

"Where the hell is everyone!" a beloved voice called from the sitting room.

Maleaha jumped up and ran from the room. Laughing and crying at the same time, she threw herself into the

313

arms of her father.

"Father, when did you get home?"

Jonas hugged his daughter tightly, then beamed down at her. "I got home just a few days ago. I rode to the Jojoba village only to find I had missed the two of you by hours."

"I'm so glad you are home, Father," she said, kissing his cheek.

"I have missed you, honey. I brought you presents from all over Europe." He looked about the empty room. "Looks like you could use a few sticks of furniture."

Kane was leaning against the doorjamb, watching father and daughter being reunited. "Welcome home, Jonas," he said, smiling.

Jonas rushed across the room and startled Kane with a rough bearhug. "Hell, I'm glad to see you, boy. From what Mangas tells me, you are my son now." For a moment Kane felt as if he were a part of the family. Kane felt good to be considered Jonas's son.

"I looked the spread over as I rode in, Kane. I am damned pleased with what I have seen so far. You have done a lot of hard work."

"As you can see, I took your advice and bought the property you told me about. I have a long way to go though before it will be a producing ranch."

"Hell, son, the main thing is the land. Now all you have to do is surround yourself with men who know what to do, and the first thing you know, you will succeed."

"My problem has been in finding the good men."

Jonas clapped Kane on the back. "Don't worry about that. That's why you have me for a father-in-law. I don't want to interfere, but if you want my help, I'll be more than proud to lend a hand."

Kane's face brightened, and Maleaha could see his excitement. "I would welcome any advice you could give me, Jonas."

The two men were so engrossed in their conversation that they did not see Maleaha climb the stairs to check on Cimeron. Just as Maleaha reached the landing she heard a blood-curdling scream, and Rosita came running down the hallway, crying that she had been attacked by a wild Indian.

Maleaha rushed into Cimeron's room to find Lamas sitting on the floor holding Cimeron on his lap.

"What has happened?" Maleaha asked, dropping down on her knees beside them.

"I caught that foolish woman trying to feed Cimeron beans," Lamas said angrily. "I told her to get out."

Maleaha could not control the smile on her face. "You gave her an awful fright. I can only imagine what she thought."

Rosita was in the sitting room waving her arms about talking rapidly in Spanish.

Kane looked helplessly at Jonas. "Can you understand what she is talking about, Jonas?"

"She says that there is a wild Indian in the bedroom and he took the baby from her."

"What wild Ind . . . oh, I bet it is Lamas," Kane said, smiling.

"All right, the Indian is Lamas but who is the baby?" Jonas asked.

Before Kane could answer Rosita began ranting wildly, while Jonas tried to calm her down. "She says she will not stay another night in this house, and she demands to be driven into town."

Kane shrugged his shoulders. "Tell her if she will stay until morning, I will have someone drive her into town."

Jonas finally calmed the woman down, and he winked at Kane as she sailed out of the room. "She says she will prepare dinner now. I explained to her about Lamas, but she says that either he leaves or she will."

"Lord, what a day this has been. I suppose she will leave in the morning, because it's for sure I won't ask Lamas to go."

Jonas grinned. "I'm afraid you are stuck with him for life. He stays wherever Maleaha is. He's not too bad once you get to know him."

"I don't think he likes me very well. Sometimes I think he tolerates me because of Maleaha."

"There's only one thing you can be sure of where that old Indian is concerned, and that is that he is devoted to Maleaha. He watches over her like a hawk. In the past years I took comfort in that. You should too."

"Come upstairs, Jonas. I have something to show you," Kane said, thinking Jonas could not know about his granddaughter or he would have demanded to see her.

When the two men entered the bedroom, Maleaha and Lamas were sitting on the floor with Cimeron. Jonas was silent as he knelt down and looked into the face of the child.

"What is this?" he asked, noting the child's resemblance to Kane.

"This is your granddaughter, Jonas," Kane told him.

Jonas tenderly lifted the tiny girl into his arms, and

Maleaha and Kane exchanged glances as they saw tears sparkle in his green eyes.

"What's her name," he said gruffly.

"Cimeron," Maleaha told him.

Jonas bent his head and kissed the soft cheek. "My God, she is beautiful. Maleaha, your mother would have been so proud of this baby." He wiped his face with the back of his hand. "Thank you for naming her after your mother, honey," he said, holding Cimeron tightly against him. He smiled up at Kane. "You are right. This has been one hell of a day. I got me a son and a granddaughter all at once."

Maleaha bent down and placed a kiss on her father's face. "Come, you must be starved. Lamas will sit with Cimeron while we eat."

"Welcome home, Jonas Deveraux," Lamas said, taking the baby from him.

"How have you been, Lamas?"

"I am good, Jonas. Kane is going to build me a new house and buy me a rocking chair."

Jonas winked at Kane. "How will you like riding for a new brand, Lamas?"

"I like Kane Benedict. He is a good man. He will make Maleaha happy."

Jonas laughed as he walked out the door. "Does that answer your question, Kane?"

They ate dinner that night in the kitchen since the dining room had not yet been furnished. Maleaha wrinkled her nose in distaste at the highly spiced greasy food Rosita had prepared. She vowed the first thing she would change would be the menu. She smiled as she watched Kane hang on to every word her father spoke. It was clear that he was a great admirer of her father. The two men hardly spoke to her. They were too busy discussing cattle and ranching. There were many questions she wanted to ask her father about his trip, but she knew they would keep.

When Rosita served a dessert that Maleaha could not put a name to she wrinkled her nose. "Is this the diet you have been forced to eat, Kane?"

"Only three meals a day, and then only if I wanted to eat."

Jonas frowned. Why were Maleaha and Kane talking like two polite strangers, he wondered? For the remainder of the meal he watched them closely, and he knew something was wrong. He had never been one to interfere, but he could tell that they both loved each other. The signs were all there. Maleaha looked at Kane with eyes of love, and Kane looked as if he could devour Maleaha. He would just watch, he thought. Maybe he would find out what was wrong between them.

Maleaha excused herself and went upstairs to make a pallet in one of the rooms for her father and to check on Cimeron. When she left, Kane and Jonas went into Kane's study.

They talked more about Kane's plans, and then lapsed into silence. Finally Kane took a deep breath and looked at Jonas.

"I'm sure you have noticed that things aren't right between me and Maleaha, Jonas."

"It's obvious to me only because I know my daughter so well. You want to talk about it?"

Kane told Jonas about the night at the Jojoba village when Maleaha had come to him to save herself from Mangas. He explained to him about the marriage Mangas had performed, and then about him finding Maleaha and Cimeron a few days ago.

Jonas did not interrupt, but silently watched Kane as he spoke.

"It appears to me that neither one of you is happy about your marriage."

"Jonas, I love your daughter. I would give her anything within my power to make her happy. I will admit that I used Cimeron to force her to marry me, and I would do it again if it was the only way I could get her."

Jonas leaned forward and knitted his brow. He knew Maleaha loved Kane, he had seen it in her eyes. Kane admitted he loved Maleaha. What then was the problem, he wondered?

"Well, the way I see it, you have a lovely daughter and that ain't a bad start. Give it some time, son. Sometimes a woman just needs time, especially when she has been through what Maleaha has."

"I'll give her all the time in the world. I will try to be patient."

Maleaha entered the room and sat on the arm of her father's chair. "I have made your bed. The next time you come you won't have to sleep on the floor."

"If the two of you don't have any objections I want to stay with you a few days. I want to give Kane a few pointers."

Maleaha hugged him tightly. "We would be delighted if you would stay."

"That's right, Jonas. I have so may questions to ask you it will take days just to ask them."

"I'll send for some of my top hands tomorrow, and they will get you rolling. As a wedding present I am giving you a thousand head of prime cattle."

Maleaha gasped. "Father, you are much too generous."

"Hell, it isn't generosity. All of Deveraux will one day belong to you. I'm just giving you a portion of it early, that way I can be alive to watch you enjoy it."

Kane stood up. "Call it whatever you please, Jonas. I could never accept such a large number of cattle from you."

Jonas arched his eyebrow. "Kane, have you forgotten about Diablo? I told you then I was a stubborn man. Do I have to remind you again?"

Kane laughed deeply. "No, don't remind me. You and your daughter are the two most stubborn people it has ever been my pleasure to run into."

Jonas squeezed Maleaha's hand. "I think we have just been handed a left-handed compliment."

Maleaha kissed her father's cheek and stood up. She folded her hands nervously in front of her as she faced Kane. "I will bid you both good night. I will be sleeping with Cimeron." The room became silent as both men watched her departure. Jonas noticed Kane's eyes and could not mistake the pain he felt.

"Well, it's been a long day for me, think I'll turn in. See you bright and early. We got a lot of work to do."

Maleaha lay beside Cimeron, thinking how awkward it had been when she had kissed her father goodnight and not Kane. She knew her father would know by now that things were not right between her and Kane. She tried to push Kane out of her mind but was not entirely successful. She could imagine him lying on his cot at that moment, and she wanted more than anything to be lying in his arms. She tried to think about all she had to do to the house. The first thing she must do was to go into town and find some suitable help. She needed a cook and a housekeeper. Rosita could help with the housework if Maleaha could convince her to stay

Kane had said money was no object, and she would take him at his word. Finally she fell asleep with all sorts of plans swirling around in her mind.

The next morning Kane awoke early. After he had bathed and shaved he went upstairs to check on Cimeron. Knocking lightly on the door, he opened it to find that Maleaha wasn't there, and Lamas was watching over Cimeron, who was still asleep.

Kane went back downstairs. To his surprise, when he passed the dining room he saw that the small table had been moved from the kitchen and Jonas was having breakfast.

''You must have an ironclad stomach if you are eating Rosita's breakfast, Jonas,'' he said, sitting down across from his father-in-law.

Jonas smiled. ''I can assure you I ate a hearty breakfast and even asked for seconds.''

Maleaha entered the room carrying Kane's breakfast on a tray. "You see, my daughter is an excellent cook."

Maleaha placed a plate of yellow fluffy scrambled eggs, ham, and homemade biscuits in front of Kane. His mouth watered as she poured a cup of coffee and handed it to him.

Maleaha poured herself a second cup of coffee and then refilled her father's cup.

"Now, this is what I would call a breakfast," Kane said, reaching for a biscuit and buttering it.

Maleaha beamed at his compliment. "I like to see a man well fed," she said, poising her coffee cup in her hand.

"If you feed like this all the time, I will have to let out my belt notches before too long."

"I said I like to see a man well fed, not fat. You had better eat hearty. Father has told me the two of you have a busy day ahead of you."

Kane took a sip of coffee to wash the egg down. "How do you intend to spend your day?"

"I thought I would have Lamas drive me into town. I need to hire some help. I thought I would also look for furniture and shop for fabrics. It would help if I knew your preference in colors and furniture, Kane."

"I like what you did with the house at Deveraux. As for colors, I will leave that up to you. Buy whatever you want and charge it to me."

Jonas stood up abruptly. "If the two of you are through decorating the house, there is a lot of work to do, and just so many hours in the day to do it in."

Maleaha watched as her father and Kane departed. She

could tell that they liked each other, and that made her very happy. Her father did not give his friendship easily, and she was glad he liked Kane.

Maleaha spent a busy day shopping. She found material for drapes and bought rugs. Some of the furniture she found locally, but other pieces she had to order from St. Louis.

After a quick lunch at the hotel, Maleaha found two young Mexican girls to help with the housework, but could not find a suitable cook. When she went back to the general store to buy linens Mr. Garson, the owner, told her of a widow lady who was looking for work. After Maleaha interviewed the woman she hired her on the spot. Mrs. Higgens was in her early forties and had been a widow for over two years. She had lived at the boarding house and had made a living cleaning other people's houses. Maleaha was delighted with her, for she seemed sweet and loved children. She would be the ideal person to help her look after Cimeron.

Word spread quickly throughout Santa Fe that Maleaha was now Mrs. Benedict, and Maleaha was besieged with well wishes from her friends. Many of them were curious as to why she hadn't had a large wedding. When she told them she had been married secretly last summer and had a daughter, they were even more curious.

The sun was just going down when the wagon laden with all the things Maleaha had purchased pulled up to the house. Maleaha was tired from her shopping, but she was happy. She could now start decorating the house for

Kane. She wanted everything to be perfect so he would be proud of her.

Kane. She would be making a home for the man she loved.

CHAPTER NINETEEN

The days seemed to pass quickly. Maleaha saw Kane and her father only at mealtimes. While she was busy with the house, Kane and her father were busy on the range. Most of the days they didn't come home for lunch and Maleaha would send Lamas to take them something to eat.

There were now drapes at most of the windows and rugs on the floor. There were only a few good pieces of furniture in some of the rooms. Most of the furniture had been ordered and had not yet arrived. The dining room table and chairs had been delivered that morning, and Maleaha looked about the room with satisfaction. It was a lovely room, and Maleaha was anxious for Kane to see it now that it was completed.

Mrs. Higgens was turning out to be a real blessing. Not only was she good with Cimeron, but she was a very good cook, as well. Mrs. Higgens seemed to be happy at the ranch, and she had told Maleaha she felt as if she now had a home.

Maleaha tried to devote as much time to Cimeron as

she could. Even with her busy schedule, she was determined not to neglect her daughter. She looked forward to the evenings when Kane would tell her all about his day, and he would listen with interest while she described her day to him. There were awkward moments when they would run out of things to say. Maleaha knew if it weren't for her father's presence it might have been unbearable at times.

All the bedrooms were now furnished, and Kane had moved upstairs to the master suite, while Maleaha continued to sleep in Cimeron's room. She wondered what it would be like when her father returned to Deveraux, for he had been a steadying influence on both her and Kane.

Maleaha placed a white linen table napkin beside each dinner plate and stood back to study the overall effect.

The rug was a deep red color, with matching drapes at the windows. The table and twelve chairs were of heavy dark pecan. The white-washed walls gleamed brightly beneath the crystal chandelier. The blue and white wedgewood china that Jonas had brought Maleaha from England graced the table. The table was further enhanced by the crystal goblets and heavy silverware.

Maleaha moved the flower arrangement for at least the sixth time, trying to center it just right.

Hearing Kane's voice, Maleaha began to feel nervous. What if Kane didn't like the room? She knew that Kane and her father would bathe and dress before coming down to dinner, so she went into the kitchen to make sure everything was just right.

Mrs. Higgens was spooning plum pudding into small bowls. Maleaha saw the trout they were having for dinner was just about done. She tasted the lemon sauce to make sure it was seasoned just right.

"Everything looks delicious, Mrs. Higgens."

The older woman beamed. "The mister will be pleased as punch when he sees the new dining room, ma'am."

"Let us hope so," Maleaha said as she untied the apron that had served to protect the green satin gown she wore.

When Maleaha entered the sitting room where she would wait for Kane and her father, she surveyed the room. A bright yellow and gray Indian rug covered the floor. The two couches were a bright lemon yellow, and the three chairs were gray. Dark gray draperies hung at the big double window that looked out on the front of the house. Walking over to the mahogany table, Maleaha gently picked up the Jojoba vase her grandfather had given her. It was painted with black and gray, and it was one of Maleaha's most prized possessions. When her grandfather had given it to her he had told her that it was more than two hundred years old. Placing the vase back on the table, Maleaha turned around in a circle. What fun she had had decorating this house. The downstairs rooms were almost completed, and next week she would start on the upstairs.

Her keen hearing picked up Kane's footsteps on the stairs, and when he entered the room, she turned to face him.

Kane gave her a smile and nodded his dark head. "This room is lovely, Maleaha. I like what you are doing to this house. It is beginning to feel like a home."

"Do you really think so, Kane? You wouldn't just say

327

so to spare my feelings, would you?''

Kane sat down on the sofa and motioned for Maleaha to sit beside him. ''I assure you I would never pay you a false compliment. If I didn't like the room, I would merely keep my mouth shut,'' he said, warming her with a smile.

''For fear of hurting my feelings, Kane?''

''Uh huh.''

''Promise me that you will tell me if something is not to your taste. Have no fear of hurting me. I want you to like this house.''

He picked up a strand of her hair and curled it about his finger. ''This house is you, Maleaha. How could I not like it?''

Maleaha stared into his silver eyes, and her heart seem to stop beating. She became keenly aware of the passion that flamed to life between them. His hand tangled itself in her hair, and his eyes moved to her tempting lips.

''Oh, beautiful, Maleaha. I ache for you,'' he whispered, pulling her head toward him. Maleaha did not want to respond to her need, but a strong force existed between the two of them. If she gave in to that force, tonight she would sleep in his bed, and tomorrow she would be sorry. Her mind cried out to resist him. Once he had possessed her she would be even more vulnerable.

''I want to make love to you, Maleaha. Don't you think you have punished me long enough? You are my wife, and I want you.''

His mouth dipped down to explore the sweet length of her lovely throat. A weakness washed over Maleaha. In an unconscious move, Maleaha's hands moved around

Kane's shoulders. She felt a tide of pleasure ricochet through her body. This was what she had been created for, to love and be loved by this man, she thought. Kane pulled her soft body against his hard muscled one. He could not get close enough. Maleaha heard his deep raspy voice, and it came out in an animal growl.

"I could take you now, Maleaha. You have pushed me to my limit."

"No, Kane, please. I don't want this," she pleaded as she looked into his face, seeing the pulse beat that was hammering in his temple. His eyes suddenly became as cold as hard steel. She watched as he stood up abruptly and turned his back on her.

"Am I never to touch you, Maleaha?" he asked in an agonized voice.

Her hands were trembling so badly she could not control their movements, and her breath was coming out in short gasps. "You gave me your word, Kane. You laid down the guidelines to our marriage, and this was not part of it."

He turned and looked at her through lowered lashes and she caught her breath.

"Is it your wish to keep me dangling, Maleaha? Are you so heartless that you cannot see what you are doing to me?" His voice was no more than a painful whisper.

"I . . . I don't want to be like that, Kane. Can't we just be friends?"

Kane looked at the ceiling and let out his breath slowly.

"No. I can never be just a friend to you, Maleaha. Friendship is not enough."

Maleaha stood up and ran a nervous hand down her

gown. "I should go and check on Cimeron," she said, making an excuse to flee the room.

Kane crossed the room to her and caught her by the hand. Maleaha was surprised to see the smile on his face. How quickly he could change from playing the lover, she thought. It was not so easy for her. Inside she felt like she was all jumbled together.

"I looked in on Cimeron before I came down. She is sleeping peacefully."

"Kane, I . . ."

"Look, Maleaha," he interrupted. "Forget what just happened between us. In the future I will try to exercise more control. Does that put your mind at rest?"

No, she thought. It did not put her mind to rest at all. He might be in control of his feelings, but she had never learned to master her own feelings. She loved him more than ever, and it would be hard to hide that love from him.

"All right," she said sitting down on the edge of the sofa and folding her hands demurely in her lap.

He sat down beside her, but took great care not to touch her. "Kane," she said, reaching for something to talk about, "have you hired all the men you will need for the roundup?"

He smiled, showing off his dimples and his flashing white teeth. "Yes, Maleaha." He reached out and covered her hand with his. He arched his eye brow inquiringly when he felt her hand tremble. "I have everything a man could ever want . . . almost."

Jonas entered the room at that moment. His hair was wet and slicked down, indicating he had just come from his bath. He watched Kane and Maleaha move apart quickly. It was the first time he had seen them touching each other. He had already shown Kane enough to keep him busy for a long time. There was not much left that he could teach him. Kane had taken to ranching as naturally as if he had been born to it. Jonas thought it was time to leave the two of them alone.

He sat down on a chair and stretched his legs out in front of him. "I have decided to go home tomorrow morning. I have done all I can for you, Kane. You will be able to run this ranch as well as I could."

"I wish you wouldn't go just yet, Father. I like having you here," Maleaha said, suddenly panicked.

Jonas saw the apprehension in his daughter's face, and he knew it was past time for him to leave. Perhaps with him gone, Maleaha and Kane would work out their problems.

"I gotta get home, honey. I have been away from Deveraux for over a year now."

"We will miss you, Jonas," Kane told him. "I can never even begin to thank you for all you have done for me."

"Hell, Kane. You are my son now. There isn't anything I wouldn't do for you."

"You have given me far too much, not the least of which is your help and advice. And how can I ever thank you for a horse like Diablo?"

Jonas's eyes twinkled. "I knew when I gave you that horse that I would be keeping him in the family."

Maleaha stared open-mouthed at her father, and she was further surprised when Kane's laughter filled the room. "You are the damnedest mind reader I ever met."

"It didn't take mind reading, son. It just took common sense and a good eye."

Words stuck in Kane's throat. He had never met a man like Jonas. He had been very forbearing, never losing patience with him if he didn't understand something, just firmly showing him the correct way of doing it. Jonas had showed Kane what to look for when buying cattle, and he had helped him hire only top hands to handle the cattle. Jonas now smiled at Kane as if he could read what he was thinking.

"Words are not necessary, son. I know how you feel."

Kane was glad that Mrs. Higgens chose that moment to announce that dinner was served, because he didn't know how to answer Jonas. Kane extended his arm to Maleaha, and she placed her hand on it. Maleaha had been so upset that her father was leaving that she had forgotten about the newly decorated dining room.

As they entered the room Kane looked about in surprise, then he smiled down at Maleaha. "You are a marvel, Maleaha. Is there no end to your talents?"

"Are you sure you like it, Kane?" she asked apprehensively.

He glanced at the red rug and drapes. He knew most women would never use such bright colors in decorating, but Maleaha's flair had made the bright colors appear elegant and charming. It was a room like no other he had ever seen. "I can assure you, Maleaha, I have never seen a more beautiful room. Somehow it speaks of you. It . . ." he searched for the words he wanted. "It feels like a home."

Maleaha smiled brightly, cheered by his praise. Kane pulled out her chair and she sat down. She had all but forgotten the confrontation they had had in the sitting room earlier.

At dinner they all laughed easily and the conversation seemed to flow. As always Jonas and Kane began to talk about ranching.

"You need to have a name for the ranch, son. Then you will need to have Jim Hanes, the blacksmith, make you a branding iron."

"I have thought about a name, but nothing seems to fit."

"You could always just call it Benedict Ranch," Jonas volunteered.

"Yes I suppose so, then the brand could be a B with a circle around it."

"No, you can't have the circle B for a brand. Dave Benson already uses that for his brand."

"How about something Spanish?" Maleaha spoke up.

"That is an excellent idea!" Kane said, smiling at his wife. "Have you any suggestions?"

Maleaha was thoughtful for a moment. "I suppose you could name it for the Pecos River that runs through it. Rio Pecos—but that is not quite right, is it?" She knitted her brow. "I know. You could call it El Paraiso."

"What does that mean in English?" Kane asked.

"The paradise," Maleaha said smiling and only half serious.

"Hum, El Paraiso," Kane said, testing the name out loud.

"Damn me if I don't think she has something there.

You could have a branding iron made up in a B with two wings on either side of it. The flying B,'' Jonas injected.

Kane smiled at Maleaha. "All right, El Paraiso it shall be.'' His eyes became dark and he held her gaze. "It will be our paradise, Maleaha.''

Maleaha caught the deep undertone in his voice and looked quickly at her father to see if he had caught it also. Jonas, however, seemed to be concentrating more on his plate of trout. When Maleaha glanced down at her own plate, Jonas looked at Kane and winked.

"Trouble in paradise?'' he speculated.

Kane chuckled, "Perhaps, Jonas, but I am not a man without hope.''

Maleaha began to feel uneasy at the two men's light banter, and she chose to change the subject.

"Kane, I am ready to start on the master suite tomorrow. What color would you like the room to be done in; What is your favorite color?''

He paused with his fork halfway to his mouth and grinned. "When it comes to eyes, I like the color green.''

"Oh,'' Jonas said, tongue-in-cheek. "I never knew you liked my eyes.''

Kane grinned. "Yours might be the original, but I prefer the copy.''

"Ah, I see. You were speaking of my daughter's eyes. I suppose they are rather nice,'' Jonas said, reaching across the table and squeezing Maleaha's hand.

"Will the two of you be serious for a moment? I need to know what color to do Kane's room in,'' Maleaha said in exasperation.

"What are your favorite colors, Maleaha?'' Kane

asked.

"For a bedroom I like blue and cream colors."

He smiled slightly and gave her a leering glance. "I would like the master suite in blue and cream, perhaps then I could entice you to share it with me."

It was the first reference anyone had made to her and Kane's sleeping apart, and Maleaha blushed a bright red while her father roared with laughter.

Maleaha felt her temper rising and stood up abruptly. "I can see there is no sense trying to have an intelligent conversation with either one of you. I am going to bed." She paused in the doorway. "I will see you in the morning, Father. Good night to both of you." She swept out of the room and both men stared after her.

"Don't worry, Kane. Maleaha will come around in time. She is a high-spirited little filly like her mother was. Sometimes she needs a strong hand to lead the way."

Kane stood up and motioned for Jonas to follow him into his study. Kane poured brandy into two glasses and handed one to Jonas. Both men sat down and then Kane spoke.

"Lord, Jonas, my patience is about exhausted. For the first time in my life I have met a woman whom I don't know how to handle. She has made this house a beautiful home. She sees that I have the best meals to eat, my clothes are always laundered and folded neatly in a drawer. If there is a speck of dust in this house anywhere I challenge you to find it. She has given me a lovely daughter, but . . . I do not know how to win her heart."

"As I told you, Kane, Maleaha needs a strong hand. Hell, son, she will never come to you if you wait for her.

She has the pride of the Jojoba running in her veins. You will have to take matters into your own hands.''

''Is that your advice to me?''

''Yep, for what it's worth.''

Kane took a drink of his brandy, then swirled the dark liquid around in the glass. ''I don't know, Jonas. I would never have taken half off of any other woman that I have from Maleaha. I am as unsure as a young schoolboy where she is concerned. I fear very few things in life, but I have a fear of Maleaha's finding out how I really feel about her.''

''Why is that?'' Jonas asked thinking his daughter suffered from the same fear.

''That's hard to say. I suppose if one were to analyze my feelings, one would find that I feared Maleaha's finding out about my love for her because she might . . . tear my heart out.''

Jonas leaned forward and studied Kane's face. ''Maleaha is at heart a very kind person. She would never deliberately hurt anyone. She is proud of you, Kane. I have seen this in her eyes many times. She has great pride in how much you have accomplished after starting with nothing.''

''I want her to be proud of me, Jonas. Perhaps that is why I have worked so hard, but I want more than for her to be proud of me. I want her love.''

''Then go after it son. You can't just sit idly by thinking she will come to you. Look, you wanted to have this ranch, so you got out and worked for it. Can you do any less with my daughter

''How, Jonas? Tell me how.''

"I can't tell you that, Kane. I bet you don't need anyone to tell you how to lure a woman to your bed, least of all the woman's father."

Kane laughed out loud. "I see what you mean." The smile left Kane's face and he became serious. "Hell, Jonas, that daughter of yours has me all tied up in knots."

Jonas lit a cigar and then leaned his head back against the leather chair he was sitting on. "Just remember that the end justifies the means. One thing I know for sure. You cannot accomplish much by sleeping in separate bedrooms."

Kane looked into the green eyes that were so much like Maleaha's. "Whose side are you on?"

"I am on my granddaughter's side. I want to see her mother and father together as they should be," Jonas told him lazily.

Kane could hear the cold winds blowing outside the house, and he glanced at the warm fire that glowed in the fireplace. "You know, Jonas, the first time I came to your house I could feel something special about it. That was when I began to question many things in my life. I found myself wanting what you had. I know I am not explaining myself very clearly. I am not even sure I know what I mean myself."

Jonas blew out a smoke ring and turned to Kane. "Don't you know what you felt about my house, son? You felt Maleaha's presence. It's never the house but the people in it that make a house into a home."

"Yes, I have come to know that."

"You know, Kane, you could live in the grandest house in the world, but if you don't have love you don't

337

have a damned thing.''

''I know. I grew up in such a house. How sad it is when one can live all one's life chasing the wrong rainbow. My father always had all that money could buy, and yet I doubt that he has ever been really happy.''

''Pity him then, son, because he has existed without having lived. From what you have told me about your mother and father, I gather you blame your father for everything that went wrong between them. I do not mean to speak ill of your mother, but it takes two to make a happy marrage and it takes two to destroy one.''

Kane closed his eyes. He had never considered that his mother was at fault in any way. It was a new idea, and he was bothered by it.

The next day was a busy one for Maleaha. After seeing her father off she had played with Cimeron and given all the servants their orders for the day. It was midmorning before she made her way up the stairs to begin work on Kane's room. She had just finished measuring the windows when Rosita came upstairs to tell her that Betsy was below. It had been a long time since she had seen Betsy, and she decided that the work on Kane's room could wait one more day.

Entering the sitting room, she was greeted by a brightly smiling Betsy. ''I am so glad to see you, Betsy. I hope you can spend the entire day.''

''I have been dying to see you, and I couldn't wait another day. Mother isn't expecting me home until late.''

After lunch Maleaha took Betsy upstairs to see little

Cimeron. Betsy was enchanted by Maleaha's daughter and played with her until Cimeron fell asleep. Maleaha showed her friend through the house and afterwards they sat in the sitting room talking.

"Maleaha, I love this house. It will be years if ever before Bob and I will have anything to compare with it."

"When do you and Bob intend to be married, Betsy?"

"That's what I want to tell you," Betsy said smiling brightly. "We have set the date. We bought the old Wilson place. The house has fallen into disrepair and will take a lot of fixing up, but I am so happy."

Maleaha squeezed her best friend's hand. "I am happy for you, Betsy. You and Bob have been in love since childhood, and you have always known you would one day marry." In truth, Maleaha envied her best friend. She would be marrying the man she loved and she was loved in return. "What is the date you have decided on?"

"The twenty-second of November. Will you stand up with me?"

"It would be my honor, Betsy. I would not have wanted you to ask anyone other than me."

Betsy gripped Maleaha's hand tightly. "Maleaha, are you happy?" she blurted out.

"I am not unhappy. I am married to the man I love, and I have his daughter."

"I can tell that you are not as happy as you pretend to be, Maleaha. Is Mr. Benedict good to you?"

"He is not unkind, but he does not love me. He married me again—did you know that? He wanted to give Cimeron his name. As you know, he did not honor the Jojoba ceremony."

339

Betsy's eyes became angry. "Surely he loves you. Why else would he stay in New Mexico, build this house, and make you his wife?"

"I know he married me only because of Cimeron. Sometimes I love him so much it hurts. I never thought I would feel this way about a man. I don't know what to do about it."

"Do not despair, Maleaha. I think he loves you or he would never have married you," Betsy said kindly.

"Let's talk about something else. It's much too nice a day to have long faces," Maleaha said brightly.

"I want to tell you before I forget," Betsy said softly. "I hate to tell you this, but I feel you have a right to know."

"What is it?"

"I ran into Mrs. Phelps last week in town and she asked me all about you. You know what a gossip she is?"

"Yes, and I can well imagine what she must be saying about me. What *did* she say?"

"She implied that you and Mr. Benedict were not married before the baby was born," Betsy said, hating to repeat gossip, but wanting Maleaha to know what Mrs. Phelps had been saying about her and Kane.

Maleaha sighed heavily. "I know there must be a great deal of speculation about Kane and myself and I shouldn't care, but I do."

"Don't worry too much about it, Maleaha," Betsy said, looking like the cat who swallowed the canary. "I do not believe Mrs. Phelps will ever try to malign you again. In fact, it would not surprise me the least little bit if she became your strongest champion."

340

"Whatever do you mean?"

"Well, she made me mad, so I told her that she had better have a care about what she spread around town about you. I reminded her what a temper your father had and how unkindly he would view a person trying to spread untruths about his daughter."

"What did she say to that?"

"Not much, but then I reminded her about the seven soldiers who killed your mother and how they all mysteriously died. You should have seen her face when I asked if she would know Mangas should he sneak up on her from behind some day."

Maleaha laughed so hard tears washed down her face. "Betsy, surely you didn't say that to her?"

"I can assure you I did."

"What did she say after that?"

"Well, as you can imagine, she looked over her shoulder and grabbed me by the arm. 'I have always known Maleaha is a good and decent young lady,' she told me. 'If I should hear anything to the contrary I will defend her good name,' she declared before she rushed down the street, still glancing over her shoulder as if Mangas were waiting in the shadows to pounce on her."

"Betsy, you are incorrigible. You must have scared poor Mrs. Phelps half out of her mind," Maleaha said laughing.

"That may very well be true, but I bet should someone hint that you were not married a full nine months when Cimeron was born, she will declare that you were."

"Now I know why I chose you to be my best friend," Maleaha said softly. "You are the sister that I never

341

had."

"I did no more than you would have done for me in the same situation. Besides, I spoke no more than the truth." Betsy giggled. "Of course, no one needs to know that you were married first by Mangas, although I bet if poor old Mrs. Phelps knew Mangas joined you to your husband she would carry around a big sign saying you and Mr. Benedict were married a good *ten* months before Cimeron came along."

The afternoon passed pleasantly as the two friends talked about Betsy's upcoming wedding. They were both seated on the floor while Maleaha drew sketches of wedding gowns, when a deep voice came from the doorway.

"What a pretty picture to come home to," Kane drawled. He was dressed in a plaid shirt and leather chaps that fit snugly about his trim waist and hugged his long legs, and Maleaha thought he had never looked half so handsome.

Betsy scrambled to her feet, and Maleaha looked at the clock on the wall. "You are home early today, Kane."

He advanced into the room and reached out his hand to help Maleaha to her feet and then planted a kiss on her cheek, much to her surprise. "I wanted to rush home to my beautiful wife," he said as his eyes twinkled merriment. He turned to Betsy and bowed slightly. "It is a pleasure to see you again, Miss Kincade."

"Thank you Mr. Benedict," Betsy said nervously. He always seemed to upset her when he looked at her with his silver eyes, and she still secretly thought he was the handsomest man she had ever met. "I did not intend to stay so late. I really must be going," she said, picking up her bonnet and tying it beneath her chin.

"She must stay to dinner, musn't she, Maleaha?" Kane said politely.

"Yes, please stay, Betsy," Maleaha urged. Tonight would be the first evening she and Kane would be alone in the house, and she wanted Betsy to stay.

"I am sorry, I can't. Bob will be coming over later, and I don't want to keep him waiting," Betsy said, picking up her drawstring bag. She gave Maleaha a quick peck on the cheek and half smiled at Kane. "Maleaha, I will be in touch with you. Good day, Mr. Benedict."

"Don't you think you could call me Kane? After all I am the husband of your best friend."

"If it is your wish, I shall call you Kane. In return, I would like you to call me Betsy."

She caught her breath as he smiled at her. "Betsy, it will be my pleasure." She could easily see why Maleaha loved this man. He was charming and gallant and she was sure that, regardless of what Maleaha thought, Kane loved her very deeply. She could see it in his eyes every time he looked at her.

"Betsy I want to have Lamas ride home with you. He can stay the night and then come home in the morning," Maleaha said moving toward the door. "I will only be a moment," she said leaving the room to find Lamas.

Betsy felt uneasy left alone with Kane, and she was sure it showed.

"I won't bite you, Betsy. I doubt that I have ever bitten a woman."

Betsy twisted the drawstring of her handbag nervously

343

around her finger. "I know you don't bite, Mr. Ben . . . Kane."

"Betsy, we are going to often be in each other's company because of Maleaha. How about if we call a truce."

"I don't know what you mean."

"Oh, I think you do. I am still smarting from your carefully executed plan at the dance last summer."

"It was no more than you deserved," Betsy blurted out.

"You are a true and loyal friend to my wife, therefore I would like you to be a friend of mine as well."

"I will be a friend to you as long as you do not hurt Maleaha," she said with a look that dared him to hurt her best friend.

"What if your friend is the one who does the hurting?" Kane asked. At that moment Betsy saw the misery and uncertainty in Kane's eyes. No longer did she have any doubt that he loved Maleaha. Betsy was grateful that Maleaha entered the room with Lamas, saving her from answering Kane's question.

When Maleaha returned to the sitting room after seeing Betsy on her way, she found Kane waiting for her.

He was looking at the sketches she had drawn. "This appears to be a wedding gown," he said, handing her the drawings.

"Yes, Betsy and Bob are to be married next month."

"I see. I apologize for my untimely arrival. Had I known the two of you were planning a wedding I would not have come home so early."

"Do not apologize, this is your home. Besides, Betsy and I had already decided what style of dress she wanted.''

"*You* and Betsy decided?''

Maleaha walked over to the desk and slipped her sketches into the drawer. "Yes, Betsy and I have always consulted each other about important matters.''

"Pity you were cheated out of a big wedding, then you and Betsy could have decided on a gown for you to wear.''

Maleaha turned to face him, unsure if he meant what he was saying or was merely being sarcastic. As usual, his face told her nothing. "Do you wish to bathe before dinner?''

"Yes, but first I want to see my daughter,'' he threw over his shoulder as he left the room.

Dinner had been an uncomfortable affair, and Maleaha was glad when it was finally over. There had been long lulls in the conversation. Kane had been unusually quiet, as if he were deep in thought.

Maleaha had excused herself and gone into the sitting room, while Kane went to his study. She stood at the window and gazed at the distant mountains, feeling lonely and sad. She supposed her sadness came from the thought of Betsy's upcoming marriage. Betsy would be so happy with her Bob, while Maleaha would continue to live on the fringes of Kane's life. She would give much to be able to know what Kane thought about anything, especially where she was concerned.

Maleaha felt something brush her shoulder, and she turned to see Kane standing just behind her.

"You have learned to walk silently. I can no longer hear your footsteps, Kane," she said, feeling strange because he was standing so near to her.

"I have been watching you for a long time, trying to figure out what you were so thoughtful about just now." His hand went to her tiny waist, and he pulled her toward him. Maleaha did not try to pull away as he rested his face against hers. "Dare I hope you were thinking about me?" he whispered in her ear.

"I was thinking about you," she admitted.

"Good thoughts, I hope," he murmured in her ear. He did not wait for her answer, but bent his head so that his lips were very near hers.

"I rushed home today knowing you would be here. I can't tell you how it feels to know when I come home each day that you and Cimeron will be waiting." His lips covered hers, and Maleaha closed her eyes, giving herself over to the beautiful sensation he had awakened in her.

CHAPTER TWENTY

Maleaha held on tightly to the front of Kane's shirt. She felt as if her legs had turned to jelly. Had she heard him correctly? Had he said he liked to come home to her and Cimeron? She knew that she had to put some distance between them or she would be under his spell once more.

"I . . . I want to go out for a breath of fresh air," she said, voicing the first thought that came to her mind.

"Fine. I wouldn't mind a breath of fresh air myself," he told her, taking her arm and leading her to the door.

Outside, he rested his arm casually about her shoulder. "I have come to love this land, Maleaha. Look at that sky. It looks as if one could reach up and pluck the stars right out of it."

Maleaha turned to Kane and studied his profile. "Is that the reason you decided to stay in New Mexico, Kane?"

He lowered his head and looked at her. "Partly, Maleaha, my lovely little Indian princess, partly." He dipped his head and she knew he was going to kiss her.

"Kane, no, someone will see us," she told him, trying

to push him away.

"You are right," he replied, scooping her up into his arms and carrying her into the house.

Maleaha's arms went around Kane's neck as he carried her up the stairs. He had been behaving strangely all evening, she thought, wondering where he was taking her. She had no time to protest as he entered his bedroom and lowered her to his bed.

Maleaha froze as he lay down beside her and pulled her into his arms.

Kane's face was in a half-light that shadowed his features, so Maleaha could not see him clearly. Suddenly she felt real fear. Why had he brought her to his room, she wondered. If he was of a mind to, he could destroy her completely. Dare she gamble that if she gave herself to him freely he would not later tear her heart to shreds? She remembered the night she had given freely of herself, only to have it thrown in her face the next morning.

Kane's hand drifted along her shoulder, softly up her throat, then tenderly he outlined the shape of her lips. When he suddenly moved his head downward, he was no longer in the shadows, and Maleaha could see his liquid silver eyes. An involuntary gasp escaped Maleaha's lips as she saw the torment in his eyes.

"Kiss me, Maleaha. Kiss me," he murmured in an agonized voice.

Maleaha knew she could no longer resist him, and her lips parted in silent invitation. She gloried in the feeling that shot through her eager body as his lips settled on hers.

Her hand slipped up to trace the lean outline of his face

and her body began to tremble as Kane deepened the kiss. She felt as if she were sailing on a turbulent sea as Kane parted her lips with his tongue. A whimper escaped her throat when he drew her tightly against his body and she felt the swell of his manhood pressed against her thigh.

"You may not love me," he growled against her lips, "but you sure as hell want me."

Hearing his harshly spoken words, Maleaha tried to fight against her rising desire. She was grateful that he did not suspect her love for him. His hand drifted down to her breast to softly caress the swollen peaks, and Maleaha clamped her lips tightly together to keep from crying out her love for him. She grasped his hand when she felt him unfasten her gown front, exposing her breasts.

Kane saw the look of uncertainty on her lovely face as he gently traced a pattern around her rose-tipped breast.

"I love . . . the color of your skin, Maleaha. It is soft and golden. I never saw a woman with your color skin before. You look like a golden goddess placed on earth only to pleasure a man. For my pleasure." His voice was low and caressing.

Maleaha lay as if paralyzed as he slowly moved her gown up her legs, and, raising her shoulders up, lifted it over her head and tossed it on the floor. With the same smooth movements, he removed her petticoats and undergarments, and in a moment they too lay on a heap on the floor.

The room was painted in the warm rosy glow of the last glowing embers of the dying sun. Maleaha was silent as she watched Kane stand up and begin unbuttoning his shirt. She watched his every move, fascinated as he discarded each article of clothing. As her eyes moved over his naked body, she thought Kane could easily have posed for the picture she had once seen of Michelangelo's David. He was the perfect male specimen, with his long, lean, muscular legs, wide chest and trim waist. When she looked into his handsome face she found he was staring at her, then his eyes dipped lower to take in her beauty.

Her body seemed to take on the rosy glow of the sunset. Her soft, creamy flesh seemed to invite a man's caress. Her firm, rosy-tipped breasts were perfectly shaped. Her stomach was flat and her waist was tiny. Her legs were long for a woman's, he thought. Long and well-shaped. It passed through Kane's mind that never had there been a woman to rival Maleaha in beauty. She was his. She might not love him, but she belonged to him, and that was a triumph, if only a shallow one.

Maleaha could no longer stand his close scrutiny, and her body began to yearn for the touch of his. She felt tears in her eyes as she raised her arms in a silent plea.

Kane walked slowly toward her and the bed dipped under his weight as he knelt over her. He drew in his breath as he saw the passion that burned in the depth of her green eyes. With a trembling hand he reached out and took her hand and drew it up to his lips. Neither of them spoke, but their eyes sent a silent message to each other.

Maleaha reached up and brushed a dark strand of hair from his forehead.

Kane lay down and pulled her on top of him and Maleaha closed her eyes at the beautiful feelings as her body seemed to melt into his. She planted tiny kisses on his chest as his hands began to move sensuously up and down her back.

Kane was in no hurry to perform the final act of love. He had waited too long for this moment and he wanted to savor every second. Maleaha seemed to sense his mood as she buried her face against his neck and allowed him the freedom of exploring her body.

The room was silent, with the exception of an occasional sigh or a deep groan. Suddenly touching and feeling were not enough. Kane rolled Maleaha over and poised himself above her.

Maleaha raised her eyes to his. "You said you would not expect anything from me," she whispered in a painful voice, trying to make some sense out of what was happening to her.

His hand trembled as he reached out and touched her face. "I know. Would you send me away for a promise I made in a moment of weakness?" His voice came out in a raspy plea.

"No," she said moving her hips in a silent invitation. "I will not hold you to that promise."

Kane leaned forward, pinning Maleaha into the soft mattress. He was heavy, but she loved the feel of his body and her arms went about his shoulders, trying to draw him even closer.

"Hold me. Touch me, Maleaha," he whispered in her ear. He was kissing her almost frantically and she was tossing her head from side to side. "Love me, Kane. Love me," she cried.

Maleaha rubbed her body against Kane's and she heard him groan. "You are not human, but a witch who was sent to earth to torture me out of my mind," he murmured. Kane's body took command, and he entered her with a heavy forward thrust. Maleaha felt that she was a tiny boat being tossed about in a stormy sea. Wave after wave of feeling washed over her as she matched Kane's forward thrusts. It was agony and it was beautiful.

Neither of them was to remember later how long they were locked in the embrace of fiery lovemaking. Many times Kane felt Maleaha's body tremble in total satisfaction, while he kept his own desire under control. Finally he reached a point where he could no longer control his passion, and his body exploded in a hurricane of feelings.

They spent that whole night making love. Twice Maleaha fell asleep, only to have Kane shake her gently awake. Her body responded readily to his urgent touch. The whole world for the two of them existed only in this bedroom. It did not matter to either of them that they had not eaten the evening meal.

At last Kane's passion had been satisfied, and he held Maleaha in his arms while she fell into an exhausted sleep. He saw her lovely face was soft from his lovemaking, and he bent his head to kiss her silky cheek. He loved her so much, and his love cried out from inside of him to be voiced. He reminded himself that had Maleaha had any feelings for him, she would have come to see him when he had been injured. No woman who loved a man would stay from him if she thought he might be in danger of losing his life. He knew he had satisfied her body, but that was not enough. He had taken too many women over the years not to know that someone could satisfy your body without touching your heart. He wondered if she had any notion how good their lovemaking was. She could not

352

know as he did that what happened between the two of them was a rare and beautiful experience.

He had been surprised when she had given in to him so easily. He knew one thing for sure—now that he had taken her to his bed, he did not intend to allow her to sleep in a separate bedroom.

He rested his chin against her sweetly scented hair. Maleaha, Maleaha, he thought, you have me where you want me, if only you knew it. With you I am very vulnerable. I would rather die than give you up.

He felt the softness of her body curled up contentedly against him in sleep, and he closed his eyes. His last thought was to wonder how anything could ever be the same between them, after tonight.

Maleaha awoke the next morning and stared about her in a daze. It took her a moment to realize where she was. Lifting her head upward she saw that her head was resting on Kane's shoulder. Remembering the night before she blushed and lowered her head. She had abandoned her virtue and responded to Kane with animallike pleasure. She knew if he made the smallest reference to her behavior she would die of shame.

He tilted her head up and smiled ever so slightly. "It would seem I taught you well, Maleaha. You could cause a man to want to spend his life in your bed."

Maleaha was stung by his words, and she felt her shame melt away into anger. Anger not at him, but at herself, for allowing him to make her forget last night what their relationship was.

"I was glad to accommodate you, Kane. I suppose we could say I performed my wifely duty."

His eyes blazed and the hand that had been resting on her arm tightened. "Oh, you have more than done your duty, Maleaha. You tend my house, care for my daughter, and come willingly to my bed. What more could a man ask for?" he said in a biting tone.

Maleaha watched as he pushed the covers aside and sat up, leaning back against the mahogany headboard. He gazed at her with detached boredom written on his face. She tried to harden her heart against him, but her heart was a traitor to her. She knew all Kane would need to do to have her in his arms would be to reach out and touch her.

She was being foolish, she knew, but she had hoped that Kane would feel that last night had been special, just as she had. Why should he think that she was special, she thought bitterly. The woman he loved was not the woman he had married.

She slipped out of bed and picked up her discarded gown, very aware that Kane watched as she slipped it over her head. Her hands were trembling so badly she could not fasten the buttons. She drew back a pace as Kane slid out of bed and performed that task for her without a stitch of clothing on.

Kane smiled at Maleaha's discomfort. He knew she was trying to avoid looking at him. When the last button was securely fastened, he raised her chin and smiled down at her.

"It is useless to pretend maidenly shyness, Maleaha. You already know every inch of my body, as I do yours."

She flung his hand away and turned her back on him. "I will see to your breakfast."

"Maleaha, wait a moment, there is something I want to say to you."

She turned at the door to face him. "Yes," she said, knowing already what he would say.

"Maleaha, you will move your things into this bedroom today. There will be no question of our having separate bedrooms. Is that clear?"

She did not bother to answer him as she turned and left hurriedly. After she had gone, Kane closed his eyes. It was one thing to possess her body, but quite another to have her heart. All during their lovemaking Maleaha had not uttered one word of love. He had wanted to tell her of his love, but the indifference she showed toward him afterwards had served to seal his lips.

When Kane reached the dining room he found that Maleaha was not there. Mrs. Higgens was cheerful as she served Kane his second cup of coffee.

"Where is my wife, Mrs. Higgens?"

"She told me to tell you, should you ask, that she has gone riding with Lamas. Said to tell you she would be home before lunch."

That evening when Kane came home he was told again by Mrs. Higgens that Maleaha was not at home. It seemed she had ridden over to see her father and wouldn't be home until late. Kane ate a solitary meal and brooded silently. After he had eaten he went up the stairs to his room to see if Maleaha had moved her belongings to his room. He became angry when he discovered that she had not done as he had told her to. He lay down on his bed fully clothed, waiting for her to come home.

When Maleaha finally did come home she went quickly upstairs to check on Cimeron. Seeing that her daughter slept, she undressed and slipped under the covers of the bed she had been using. She was grateful that she had not run into Kane. She had no idea how he would react to her disobeying his orders.

Maleaha was just drifting off to sleep when she heard the door burst open. Sitting up quickly, she watched as Kane advanced toward her. She could see from the light coming from the hallway that his face was a mask of fury.

"Please don't wake Cimeron up," she said, as she pulled the covers up to her neck.

He tore the covers off her, and she could see from the pulse beat in his temple that he was indeed very angry.

"I thought I made it clear this morning that we would no longer occupy separate bedrooms. Apparently you did not heed my words."

"Why are you doing this, Kane?" she said as he scooped her into his arms and carried her toward the door. Maleaha barely had time to see if Cimeron had awakened before he closed the door.

Kane did not bother to answer her as he carried her down the hallway and into his bedroom, where he tossed her roughly onto the bed. Maleaha scrambled to her knees, ready to do battle. "I asked, why you are doing this?" she shouted.

His eyes seemed to shoot out sparks as he scowled at her. "You are my wife," he said between clenched teeth. "I have been very patient with you up to now, but my patience is all but exhausted."

"Why did you not do this before my father left?" she asked, placing her hands on her hips. "Were you afraid he would not allow you to bully me this way?"

"Think what you will," he said, ripping his shirt down the front and tossing it on the floor. He knew why he was reacting so strongly to finding her in the other bedroom, but he could not tell her. After last night he was afraid to let her sleep apart from him, although he didn't take time to analyze his feelings. Perhaps if he let her have her own way he would lose her for good. At least when he was making love to her he really held her, if only for a time.

"I do not feel like your wife, Kane, but rather more like your whore, waiting to service you whenever the urge hits you." He was advancing toward her and she watched him stop dead in his tracks.

Reaching out, he grabbed a handful of dark hair and jerked her head toward him. "Play my whore then, if it pleases you," he said falling forward and pinning her beneath him. His lips were hard and punishing as they ground Maleaha's lips against her teeth.

Raising his head, he glared at her. "When I want you, you will come to me. Is that understood?" he ground out between clenched teeth. As Maleaha began to struggle, he moved away from her.

"No I will not, and you can't make me," she declared.

"Oh, can I not, Maleaha." His eyes were laced with anger as he grabbed her nightgown by the neck and ripped it all the way to the hemline. Maleaha tried to scramble off the bed, but Kane was too quick for her. Grabbing her by the arm, he swung her around to face him.

"This fighting is all so futile, Maleaha. You know by now that I am stronger than you."

"You are hurting me," she said, trying to pry his hands away from her arm.

His grip slackened immediately. "You brought this on yourself, Maleaha. You made me so angry that I forgot myself. I do not want to quarrel with you, rather I would like to make love to you as I did last night. Don't pull away, you know I can make you want me," he said, smothering her lips with a passionate kiss.

Maleaha groaned as his body covered hers. He was right, he could master her so easily. "No, no," she pleaded more to herself than to him. Already her body was molding itself to his. Soft curves fit perfectly against taut muscles. She heard Kane calling her name over and over, but she did not answer. She was incapable of answering as her lips parted and her hands moved up to entwine themselves in his ebony hair.

Afterwards, Maleaha detested the tears that gathered in her eyes. She felt humiliated that he could so easily cause her to forget her anger.

Kane stared at her for a long moment and then turned his back to her. "It is not difficult to bend you to my will, Maleaha. From now on you will come to this room when you are ready to retire. That way you will save us both a lot of trouble."

Maleaha moved as far away from him as she could and cried silently. She bit her lip to keep Kane from hearing her cry. It was not too long until she heard Kane's steady breathing and she knew he was asleep.

The next morning when she awoke he had already left the room.

Days passed into weeks, and Maleaha had her decorating to keep her busy. She and Kane occupied the same bedroom, and at night he would reach for her and she would go readily into his arms. More and more she began to feel like his puppet, for she could never refuse him what he wanted. And Kane continued to believe that the only time she really belonged to him was when he held her in his arms and made love to her.

Their lovemaking was always intense, but Kane noticed that Maleaha had become silent, and their relationship was beginning to suffer. Kane himself had begun to brood, and he snapped at her whenever she tried to talk to him. Both of them felt as if they were living at the edge of a volcano that could erupt at any moment. Cimeron was their only relief. Kane was a devoted father. He lavished love and attention on little Cimeron, and she adored him. Maleaha spent as much time with her as she could.

The house was now completely furnished. When Maleaha walked through the lovely rooms, she felt a great sense of accomplishment. Betsy had asked Maleaha to help her prepare her house for herself and Bob to move into after they were married, so Maleaha begin to spend most of her free time with Betsy.

Betsy and Maleaha had enjoyed sewing the gingham curtains that now hung at the kitchen window. Maleaha had polished the heavy oak table and chairs until they shone with a high gloss, while Betsy had scrubbed and polished the old cook stove her mother had given her.

Betsy was ecstatic the day her wedding gift arrived from Maleaha and Kane. Her happiness showed in her face as she carefully unpacked the carton that contained the china that she had admired in Santa Fe one day while she and Maleaha had been shopping for pots and pans. Maleaha had watched her face that day in the dry goods store and had noted the way Betsy ran her hand lovingly over a delicate plate. She had decided that day that the china would be the perfect wedding gift for her friend.

Betsy threw her arms about Maleaha's neck and squeezed her tightly. "You spent too much money on me. I should make you take it back."

"All right, if you insist," Maleaha told her laughingly.

"Not on your life," Betsy said, delicately touching a fragile teacup.

"Anybody home?" a familiar voice called out from the front porch. Maleaha smiled as she recognized Clay Madason's voice. He entered the room and grabbed Maleaha, crushing her in a bear hug, while smiling at Betsy over Maleaha's head. "Why is it that the two prettiest girls in Santa Fe are already spoken for? One is already married and the other is about to take the big step."

"That is what happens, Clay, when you don't make a commitment," Betsy told him. "The ladies get weary of waiting around and find someone who is more willing to marry them."

Clay looked down at Maleaha and when he spoke it was as if he had chosen his words carefully. "I had my eye on one girl and when I looked away she was taken right under my nose.''

Maleaha frowned. Was it possible that all those years when she had thought Clay was teasing her about becoming his wife, he had been serious? No that was ridiculous. Clay thought of her as nothing more than a sister. But the way his eyes were resting on her face made her think he might be more serious than she had ever contemplated. She didn't want to think of Clay as anything other than a dear friend.

''Goodness, look at the time,'' Maleaha said, glancing at the grandfather clock that stood in the hallway. ''If I don't fly I will be late for dinner.''

''I'll ride along with you, that way you can bring me up to date on what you have been doing,'' Clay told her.

Maleaha nodded and then gathered up her sewing basket. Placing a hasty kiss on Betsy's cheek, she hurried out the door.

Clay took Maleaha's saddle from the hitching rail that was attached to the front porch and quickly saddled her horse.

Betsy waved to them from the front porch as they rode away at a full gallop. After they were out of sight of Betsy and Bob's house, Clay motioned for Maleaha to slow her pace so they could talk.

''How is married life, Maleaha?'' he asked, watching her face closely.

''Why don't you stay for dinner tonight, and you can judge for yourself.''

''Can't. I am having dinner with Jonas tonight. Afterwards we are going to have a hot poker game with a few of your father's hands.''

Maleaha laughed. "How can I ever hope to compete with one of my father's poker games?"

"I do want to come over one day and see that daughter of yours. I hear from your father that she is a real heartbreaker like her mother."

"I can't deny that Cimeron is a charmer."

Clay reached for Maleaha's bridle and halted both horses. Maleaha gave him an inquiring glance.

"As you know, I have been in Texas. When I returned, I learned that you were not only married but had a daughter as well. You can imagine what a shock it was for me. The last time I saw you was at the night of the fiesta. I am puzzled that you married that cavalry officer."

"I know my marriage must be mystifying to many people," Maleaha said, knowing that in the past she had never been able to hide anything from Clay. Somehow she didn't want him to know that Kane had married her just for the sake of their daughter. She had already anticipated his next question.

"Are you happy, Maleaha?"

Maleaha looked away from him as she patted the side of her mare's neck. "When are you going to settle down and take yourself a wife, Clay?" she said, answering a question with a question.

She heard the leather of his saddle creak as he shifted his weight. Clay was quiet for so long that she raised her head, only to find him staring at her. "I can't marry anyone, princess. Not until I get over loving you."

"I don't like it when you tease like that, Clay," she said hesitantly, hoping he was indeed teasing.

"I have never been more serious in my life. Betsy was

right when she said I waited too long to ask you to marry me."

Maleaha saw the truth in his rugged, handsome face and it came as a heartbreaking blow to her. She felt heavyhearted that the man she had loved as a brother did not love her as a sister.

"Clay, I am so sorry. I never suspected that you might . . . that you . . ." her eyes grew misty and she tried to look away, but Clay reached across and touched her face softly.

"I can tell by your eyes, Maleaha, that you are not happy. Could you have grown to love me?"

"Clay, if you are asking me if I love you, the answer is yes. But if you are asking if I am in love with you, the answer is no," she said, feeling sad that she had not only hurt Mangas, but now Clay, as well. It had never been her intention to make either man fall in love with her. Clay seem to sense her sadness, so he smiled brightly.

"I will always be your friend, Maleaha. If you ever need me for any reason, don't hesitate to call on me."

The best Maleaha could manage was a nod of her head as she nudged her horse forward. Maleaha and Clay rode hard until they reached the ranch, and she was glad that they were unable to talk farther. How was it possible that she had won the love of two fine men as Mangas and Clay, but was unable to have the love of her own husband, she wondered miserably.

When they stopped in front of the barn, Maleaha would have dismounted, but Clay caught her hand and forestalled her.

"I meant what I said, Maleaha. Should you ever need

me for any reason, you have only to ask," he said lifting her hand to his lips and kissing it softly.

"I will remember, Clay," she said, just before he whirled his mount and rode away in a cloud of dust.

Maleaha was so deep in thought she had not heard Kane come from the barn to stand beside her.

"That was a charming little scene I just witnessed," he said as he lifted her roughly from her saddle and placed her on the ground. He motioned for Lamas to take her horse, and then took her by the arm and led her toward the house.

"I had no idea you were in the barn or I would have asked Clay to say hello to you," she told him, not understanding his anger.

"It was obvious from the way you and Clay were eyeing one another that you were not aware I was looking on," he said, applying pressure to her arm.

When they reached the steps, Maleaha jerked her arm free of his grasp as her anger began to smolder. She had only reached the second step when Kane spun her around to face him. His face was a mask of fury and his eyes seemed to spit fire.

"I was a fool to trust you. I believed you when you told me you were helping Betsy. Why did you lie to me?" he ground out between clenched teeth.

Maleaha shook her head as her anger died. No one had ever accused her of speaking a lie. Did Kane really believe that she had been sneaking off to see Clay? She ran up the steps and into the house. Kane caught up with her as she started to climb the stairs. His hand slid around her neck and he tilted her face up to him.

"Do I not keep you satisfied, Maleaha? Does it take me and Clay Madason both to service you?"

Maleaha could not believe she had heard Kane correctly. How dare he accuse her of such a foul thing? Did he think so little of her that he would think she would ever allow another man to touch her? "Take your hands off of me!" she demanded looking into his silver eyes and tossing her head back proudly. Inside she was hurting at his cruel words, but he would never know.

His hand slid upward to catch in her dark tousled hair. "Has Clay Madason felt the delights of your beautiful body, Maleaha? Did you give him by rights what should only belong to me?"

Maleaha clamped her mouth tightly together and pushed Kane roughly away from her. "I have no intentions of answering such an insulting question. I am going to check on Cimeron," she said, rushing up the stairs before he could forestall her.

Kane watched her retreating back and then turned and slammed out of the house. He felt as if his heart had been wrenched from his body. He had always trusted Maleaha, but the tender scene he had witnessed between her and Clay Madason had definitely suggested more than just two friends saying good-bye. He had seen Clay's eyes when he had raised Maleaha's hand to his lips. He was no fool. He knew that Clay loved Maleaha. He remembered back to the night he had first seen Maleaha and Clay together. He had known then that Clay loved her.

Entering the barn, he found Lamas rubbing Maleaha's horse down. The old man looked up but did not speak as Kane approached him. Kane leaned against the stall door and watched Lamas in silence for a moment.

"Maleaha has ridden this horse hard," the old Indian said.

"How well do you know Clay Madason, Lamas?" Kane tried to keep his voice even.

"I have known him since he was but a boy."

"What do you think of him?"

"He is not bad for a white man," Lamas said, leading Maleaha's horse into the stall and closing the gate.

Kane breathed in the sweet scent of the freshly bundled hay that stood against the barn wall and avoided looking into Lamas's eyes. "How does Maleaha feel about Clay," he asked, feeling the dark gaze of the old Indian.

"It is not for me to say, no more than it would be right for me to tell you how Mangas feels about her. If I were you, I would ask this of Maleaha," Lamas said, turning his back and walking out the door of the barn. Kane cursed under his breath. Had Lamas been trying to tell him that Maleaha felt love for Clay the same as Mangas did for her?

He walked hurriedly toward the house. He would have the truth from Maleaha. By now he had convinced himself that all the times Maleaha had told him she was with Betsy she had really been with Clay Madason. Taking the steps two at a time, he was out of breath when he reached the landing. Seeing the nursery door open, he walked purposefully toward it. By now his jealousy had given way to anger. How dare his wife allow another man to touch her?

Maleaha was bending over the crib, tucking the blanket about Cimeron when Kane entered. She saw his face was livid with rage, and she felt a prickle of uncertainty, wondering why he was so angry about Clay's escorting her home. Why had he accused her of spending time with Clay, when in fact she had been with Betsy?

Kane's eyes were blazing dangerously as he grabbed her wrist and pulled her out into the hallway, leading her into their bedroom.

Maleaha watched in confusion as he hurled her into the room and closed the door with a loud bang. Her confusion grew as he began unbuttoning his shirt.

"You had better be undressed by the time I am, Maleaha," Kane whispered harshly. "That is, if you treasure that lovely gown you are wearing. I can assure you I will have no qualms about ripping it off of you." He unbuckled his belt and stripped his trousers off while giving her a look that told her he meant what he said.

Maleaha shook her head as she backed against the door, looking into angry eyes that were the color of smoked ice.

She clasped her hands tightly together, thinking her heart would burst from her body it was beating so wildly. "Kane, I do not understand why you are so angry with me. I have done nothing to cause your anger."

He advanced slowly toward her, his naked body rippling with muscled strength. Maleaha plastered herself against the door, knowing she could retreat no further. His hand reached for her and she cringed as she felt him rip her gown from the neck to the waist. "Kane, what are you doing?" she asked as a sob broke from her throat.

"You think I am a fool, Maleaha, but let me assure you nothing could be further from the truth," he said, staring at her now exposed creamy breast. "You were not with Betsy today or any of the other times you told me you were with her. You were sneaking around behind my back with Clay Madason."

Maleaha shook her head, unable to speak. How could he think her capable of such a deception. "No, you are wrong. I never . . ."

"How many other times have you been with Clay?" he interrupted her. "How many times!" Maleaha tried to avoid his hand as he grabbed her gown once more and ripped it to the hemline. His hands were rough as he performed the same deed with her undergarments.

"Kane, don't do this please," she begged as he lifted her into his arms and carried her to the bed. Knowing his intentions, she tried to scramble off the bed, but Kane grabbed her roughly by the shoulders and pulled her against him.

His anger was now boundless, because he felt that Maleaha had betrayed him.

"I will service you, Maleaha, so there will never be any reason for you to seek the arms of Clay or any other man."

Maleaha tossed her head from side to side trying to avoid his lips. Kane caught her hands and raised them over her head.

"Fight all you want to, Maleaha. In the end I will win," he told her with a grim expression on his face.

Maleaha felt his mouth close over hers and she thought she would smother from want of air. Turning her face away she tried once more to reach Kane.

"Don't do this to me, Kane! Please, let me explain."

Raising his head, he looked into green innocent-looking eyes and almost weakened. How could anyone who looked so young and lovely be deceiving? Was he wrong? Was Maleaha innocent of any wrongdoing? No —he had seen the look in Clay Madason's eyes. The man's eyes had made love to his wife. Surely he had not mistaken that look. Kane was almost out of his mind with jealousy.

"I will drive every thought of Clay Madason out of your mind, Maleaha," he said in a deep, passionate voice as he spread her trembling legs apart and entered her roughly.

Maleaha felt Kane fill her body with his pulsing manhood. She wanted to scream at him that he took from her what she would willingly have given him had he asked it of her. Her face was wet with tears as Kane used her body in anger and revenge. All the fight went out of her and she lay there passive, wishing she could crawl off somewhere to nurse her broken heart.

When Kane finished with her he rolled off the bed and began dressing. Maleaha felt like a wounded animal and held her hand tightly over her mouth to keep from crying out loud.

Kane couldn't possibly love her or he would never believe the things he had accused her of. She knew at that moment that deep inside she had hoped one day she would be able to win her husband's love. That hope was now dashed into thousands of tiny pieces.

When she glanced up at Kane he was tucking his shirt inside his trousers. His silver eyes looked hostile.

"I will never trust you now, Maleaha, nor will I ever

seek you out again. I don't want a wife who has been with another man.''

Maleaha did not bother to answer him. Her whole body trembled with the effort she was making trying not to cry hysterically.

Kane left the room, slamming the door behind him. His anger carried him down the stairs and out the front door. As he stood at the front of the house watching an approaching buggy, his anger gave way to a deep, painful ache. Maleaha had wounded him deeply. Not just his pride had been trampled on, but his heart as well. He loved her so much, and she had lied to him.

He waited impatiently for the buggy to pull up in front of the house and was taken by surprise when he recognized Betsy. He stood silently as she disembarked and flashed him a nervous smile.

''Is Maleaha in the house?'' she asked as she climbed the steps to stand beside Kane.

''Yes,'' he said, thinking Maleaha would be in no condition to speak to anyone at the moment.

''I am in a bit of a rush—I want to get home before dark. Would you mind seeing that she gets her scissors. She forgot them, and I thought she might be needing them.''

''She forgot them today?'' Kane said with a sinking feeling deep inside.

''Yes, she was in such a hurry to get home before dinner, and Clay had come by and offered to escort her home. I suppose in her rush she just overlooked her scissors.''

''I will see that she gets them,'' Kane said, taking the

scissors that Betsy held out to him.

Betsy smiled at Maleaha's tall, dark husband. "I won't be taking up any more of Maleaha's time. We put the finishing touches on the house today. I want to thank you for allowing me to monopolize her time lately. She has been such a help to me, and I value her good taste in decorating, don't you?"

"Yes, I do," Kane said quietly.

"Well, I must go now," Betsy told him, rushing down the steps and climbing into her buggy. Ordinarily Kane would have helped a lady into her buggy, but his mind was on other things. He was hardly aware that Betsy had gone, as he stared off into the twilight. Dear Lord, what had he done, he wondered wildly. His footsteps took him away from the house, knowing he could not face Maleaha at the moment. When he reached the rail fence where two young colts frolicked about playfully, he realized he still held Maleaha's scissors in his hand.

Leaning against the fence, he watched as one of the colts ventured close to him and nudged his hand, seeking a carrot. Had he killed any hope of ever winning Maleaha's love? How could he ever make up to her for the cruel things he had said and done to her? Kane walked aimlessly, not realizing that it was now completely dark. Sitting down beneath a pine tree that was swaying gently in the wind, he stared into the night. Would Maleaha ever look at him again? Would she be able to understand the torment he was living in? The only times he ever felt she really belonged to him was when he was making love to her, and now he had even destroyed that with his jealousy and accusations.

"Maleaha, my love, why can you not love?" he cried out into the night, and his voice was carried away by the night winds.

It was long after midnight when Kane returned to the house. When he opened the door to his bedroom he could see that Maleaha was lying just where he had left her hours before. Evidently she had cried herself to sleep. He undressed and slipped into bed beside her. Kane pulled her gently into his arms, but she was in such a deep sleep she didn't even stir.

Kissing her softly he murmured love words in her ear. "I love you, darling," he said softly.

Maleaha was in a deep sleep. From a long way off she thought she could hear Kane's voice declaring his love for her. She was dreaming, she thought, not wanting to awaken because in her dream Kane was speaking the words she so desperately wanted to hear.

CHAPTER TWENTY-ONE

The next morning when Maleaha awoke it was not yet light. She could tell by the impression left on his pillow that Kane had slept beside her last night. Her heart felt heavy as she got up and began to dress. She tried to push her troubled thoughts to the back of her mind, but was not very successful.

Entering Cimeron's bedroom, she saw her daughter still slept. Pushing a tumbled curl out of Cimeron's face, Maleaha tiptoed out of the room.

When she reached the kitchen, Mrs. Higgens told her that Kane had eaten over an hour ago and had mentioned that he was riding into town.

Maleaha was glad she didn't have to face her husband, because she had not had time to examine her feelings after the night before.

She poured herself a cup of coffee and took it into the dining room and sat down at the table. She had hardly had time to take a drink when she heard the front door open and the sound of soft moccasin feet in the hallway. Maleaha knew it was Lamas before he poked his head around the open doorway.

"Mangas has sent word that your aunt is ill and is asking for you," he said in his usual calm voice.

Fear gripped Maleaha as she tried to read Lama's face. "My aunt must be very bad if she sent for me. We must hurry, Lamas!"

It took no time at all for Maleaha to run up the stairs and change into her buckskins. She hurriedly gave Mrs. Higgens orders concerning Cimeron and kissed her daughter good-bye. She then scribbled a note for Kane and left it on his desk so he would find it.

When Maleaha went outside, she found that Lamas had already saddled her horse and was waiting for her.

"Mangas says that we must hurry," Lamas told her as they both started out at a gallop. They rode hard all day and on into the night, stopping only when the horses could go no further. Fear for her aunt was Maleaha's constant companion. She was unable to sleep that night, fearing that her aunt might die before she could reach her.

He had ridden away from the ranch before sunup, not wanting to face Maleaha. He was deeply ashamed of how he had treated her. He had no idea how he would find the words to tell her what a fool he had been. He was afraid to face her, afraid that he would allow too much of his feeling to show. He had never been a coward before, but he was now. A coward when it came to his beautiful, dark-haired wife.

It was long after dark when Kane rode home. Seth, the young boy he had hired to keep the barn clean and tend the horses, rushed forward to take his boss's horse.

Kane climbed the steps leading to the house slowly, rehearsing in his mind what he would say to Maleaha. He would at last tell her that he loved her and had for a long time. He would convince her that he had been insanely jealous the night before and beg her forgiveness. He would be handing her a weapon to use against him when he finally admitted that he loved her, but what the hell. He was weary of all this secrecy. The worst she could do would be to laugh in his face, he thought.

He thought of Mangas, and Clay, who both loved Maleaha. Then there were all the men who hung around her at the dances. They too loved Maheaha. Would she consider him just another foolish man who had lost his heart to her?

Mrs. Higgens had heard Kane enter the house and came out of the kitchen to greet him. "I have kept your dinner warm, Mr. Benedict. If you are ready I will serve it to you now," she said smiling brightly.

"I am not really hungry, Mrs. Higgens. Where is my wife?"

Mrs. Higgens shook her head. "I'm not quite sure—she hurried away early this morning. The only thing she said to me was to watch over little Cimeron. I believe she said she would leave you a note on your desk."

"You said she left my daughter here?"

"Yes, sir. Your daughter has been asleep these last two hours," Mrs. Higgens said, puzzled by his reaction.

Kane dismissed Mrs. Higgens with a nod and then went into his office where he found Maleaha's note propped up against the inkwell.

Kane,
I received word from Mangas that my aunt is ill and is asking for me, so Lamas and I are going to the Jojoba camp. I left instructions with Mrs. Higgens concerning Cimeron. I don't know how long I will be away since I do not know the nature of my aunt's illness.

Maleaha

Kane reread the note, wondering if her aunt was really ill or if she was using her aunt as an excuse to avoid him after last night. He knew she would eventually return, since she had not taken their daughter—but when?

He crumpled up the note and tossed it into the waste basket. Then he went upstairs to assure himself that Cimeron was indeed still in the house. Seeing that she slept peacefully, he touched her face softly. He had half feared he would find her crib empty.

How strange, he thought, that Maleaha's aunt should become ill at such an opportune time, just after their quarrel last night. He walked toward the stairs with the intentions of riding to Mangas's camp to bring Maleaha home. He paused halfway down. He had no idea where Mangas's camp was. He remembered Lamas's telling Maleaha a few days ago that the Jojoba had moved their camp.

He considered riding over to Deveraux to ask Jonas to take him to Maleaha, but he doubted that Jonas knew where the camp was either.

A feeling of helplessness descended upon Kane as he stood undecided about what to do. Soon he climbed up the stairs went into his room, and sat down on the bed. Hanging his head down, he spoke to the empty room. "Why did you leave me, Maleaha? Damnit—don't you know that I love you?"

That night as Kane lay in his big empty bed, he thought how quiet the house seemed without Maleaha in it. She was the one who had made this house into a home. Now she was gone, and again it was nothing more than a house.

During the next three weeks Kane all but convinced himself that Maleaha was never coming back. Then he began to feel anger—anger that Maleaha should leave him and their daughter to live with the Jojoba. If that was the way she wanted it, far be it from him to try and find her.

He threw himself into his work, leaving the house before sunup and returning before dark so he could spend some time with Cimeron before her bedtime.

Jonas had sent word to Kane that he was making his annual trip to Albuquerque, so Kane decided not to tell Maleaha's father that she had left him until Jonas returned.

Kane dismounted at the barn and made his way to the house. He had purposely come home early so he could be

377

there for Cimeron's suppertime. Each day she was becoming more dear to him. He loved the way her eyes lit up when he went into the nursery to see her. She giggled and cooed whenever he held her in his arms. Right now Cimeron was the only thing that kept him from losing his mind, he thought.

Kane walked around the unfamiliar buggy that was parked in front of the house, wondering who it belonged to and feeling in no mood to pass pleasantries with any of his neighbors at the moment.

He removed his leather gloves as he entered the house and stopped dead in his tracks when he saw his father and Lucinda Blake seated before the warm fire that blazed in the open fireplace.

Eli stood up and waited for his son to acknowledge him, but Kane only stared at him in disbelief.

Kane swung his eyes to rest on Lucinda, and she stood up hesitatingly. Finding her courage, Lucinda ran across the room and threw herself into Kane's arms.

"Oh, Kane, it has been so long since I have seen you. I thought if you would not come home to me, then I must come to you," she said, looking up into his handsome face.

Kane frowned and pushed her none too gently away from him as he faced his father.

"I received no word of your coming, Eli. What are you up to now?"

Eli took a deep breath. "Same old Kane. I guess you will never change. How about asking if I had a pleasant trip? How about inquiring if Lucinda is faring well after such a tedious journey?" his father said bitterly.

Lucinda was watching Kane's face as it became ashen in color. This was not the welcome she had hoped for. Eli had assured her that when Kane saw her he would sweep her into his arms and soon afterwards ask her to be his bride.

Kane had been almost cold to her, and she saw no welcoming in his steel-gray eyes. Lucinda had waited for many months for Kane to come home, but when it appeared he would not return to Boston after he was released from the army, she had used all her charm and persuasion on Eli, until he had agreed to bring her to this backward, primitive corner of the world. Her father had readily agreed to the trip when her Aunt Harriet had consented rather reluctantly to accompany her.

The trip had been a nightmare. She had been forced to ride in dusty, creaky coaches, sleep in horrible hovels, and eat the most unpalatable food. It would all have been worth it, had Kane shown even in the smallest degree that he was happy to see her.

Since they had arrived over an hour ago, they had been forced to remain in the sitting room, waiting for Kane to come home. They had been welcomed by some dark lady who didn't even speak a word of English.

"Kane," Lucinda said, moving closer to him and looking at him with a pretty pout on her face. "Your father and I have traveled so far to see you. Aren't you in the least bit happy to see us?"

Kane's eyes darkened as he looked down at the pale hand that rested on his shoulder. "As your host, good manners dictate that I welcome you into my home, Lucinda, although I have not got the foggiest idea why you are here.'' Kane had not spoken truthfully, for he knew only too well why his father had brought Lucinda to New Mexico. Eli had hoped that if he brought her here Kane would do the right thing according to his way of thinking and ask Lucinda to marry him.

A smile twitched at the corner of Kane's mouth as he reflected on how his father would react when he discovered his son already married. It was evident that Eli was not privy to that information as of yet. If Eli knew about Maleaha's being his wife, he would not appear so smug and calm at the moment.

Lucinda moved her hand over the rough fabric of Kane's shirt and blinked her bright blue eyes, which seemed to be full of tears at the moment. Lucinda always had had the ability to cry easily, he thought in distaste. He was not moved by her white delicate skin, nor her blonde loveliness, because his heart had been touched by a golden-skinned, green-eyed, half-breed Indian princess.

''Kane, are you glad to see me?'' Lucinda asked in a breathless voice.

Kane gazed down into her upturned face, wondering whether to speak the truth or to be tactful. He let his eyes wander to his father, who seemed to be waiting tensely for his son's reply.

''I welcome the both of you to Paraiso. I am sure if my wife were here at the moment she would extend her welcome as well.''

Kane heard Lucinda gasp. He watched as his father's face lost all of its color. Eli tried to speak, but the words seem to catch in his throat, and they came out as an angry

380

growl.

"It was remiss of me, Eli, not to inform you about my marriage," Kane said, feeling satisfied with the reaction Eli was having at the news. Kane became aware that Lucinda had moved away from him, and he heard a sob escape her lips. It had not been his intention to hurt her. It was just that she happened to be in the middle of something that did not really concern her at the moment; she was caught between the bitterness of father and son. He felt momentary pity for her, thinking that she had been used by his father in the same way Eli had always used people to gain his own ends.

At last Eli found his voice. "You could have written me that you were married, Kane. Had you done so I would not have made this trip for nothing."

"Oh? Would you not have come to meet your new daughter-in-law?" Kane asked sardonically.

"It's damned awkward for Lucinda. She traveled a long ways to see you, and this is the thanks she gets for her trouble. You are unfeeling, Kane. How could you treat a lady of gentle upbringing in such a shabby manner?"

Kane felt his anger spark into flame. How dare Eli try to shift the blame onto him for Lucinda's being hurt? He had made it clear to his father on several occasions that he had no intentions of ever marrying Lucinda. Angry words tumbled to his lips, but he bit them back, knowing that to speak them would only hurt Lucinda unduly.

"Let us just say for the moment that we are both in the wrong, Eli. You for not letting me know about your arrival ahead of time, and me for not letting you know I am married.''

"Where is your wife?" Lucinda spoke up.

"Maleaha is away visiting a sick relative. I am sure if she were here she would welcome you openly, Lucinda.''

"Maleaha! That is the Indian girl you told me about,'' Eli said, sinking down into a chair.

Kane smiled. "Yes, you met her briefly one night. Do you remember?''

Eli's eyes narrowed, and in that moment one could have seen the resemblance between him and his son. "I am surprised she would have you after the things I told her about you that night. It does not speak well of her that she would marry you in spite of what I told her.''

Both men forgot that Lucinda was present, as the sparks began to fly between them. "It would seem strange, would it not. What if I were to tell you that not only did Maleaha consent to marry me, but she has also provided me with a daughter, making you a grandfather.''

Lucinda backed away, wishing she could flee from the room. She could see her chances to have Kane for herself diminishing before her very eyes. Already she had begun to hate the half-breed whom she felt had stolen him away from her. How humiliating to have traveled all this way only to find Kane married to a nobody. She had waited and hoped for years that she would one day become his wife. Now he was saying that he had a daughter by the savage he was married to.

"My Lord, are you telling me that I . . . that you had a daughter by that creature?" Eli shouted.

Kane stood silently for a moment, trying to bring his temper under control. He thought of how elated Jonas had been when he learned he was a grandfather. He thought also of his beautiful little daughter sleeping innocently upstairs. He was determined that Eli would never hurt her in any way. He wanted to shout at his father to leave the house and take Lucinda with him, but he managed with a great deal of effort to bring his anger under control.

"It grows late, Eli. I am sure that dinner will be served shortly. If it were not so late in the day, I know you would want to return to Santa Fe and a hotel. As it is late, I will offer you the hospitality of my home for the night." Kane crossed the room and called out to Mrs. Higgens. When Rosita answered his summons he then remembered that Mrs. Higgens was spending the night in town. Kane somehow managed to get across to Rosita that he wanted her to show his father and Lucinda to two of the upstairs bedrooms.

Lucinda followed Rosita reluctantly, while Eli paced the floor, ever so often casting his son a searching glance.

Kane knew from long experience that Eli did not like to be thwarted. He also knew his father was already planning what his new strategy would be. He was not a man to accept defeat easily.

Finally Eli stopped in front of his son. "I have no intentions of leaving until I have seen with my own eyes, this . . . this . . ."

"This woman I have married?" Kane supplied for him.

"That's right. How long will she be away?"

Kane sighed visibly. How could he give his father the satisfaction of knowing Maleaha might not be coming back at all? "I cannot tell you when she will be home for sure. You might have a long wait."

"That's all right, I have plenty of time," his father told him.

Lucinda was shown into a room where her aunt had been taken earlier. Harriet Blake saw the frown on her niece's face and sat up on the bed she had been lying on.

"Have you a headache too, dear? It's a wonder we aren't all sick from all we have gone through to get here. I must confess that this is rather a grand house, though. One would not expect such luxury in such a primitive place."

Lucinda felt annoyed at her aunt. Her aunt had such a frivolous mind and could dwell for hours on unimportant matters.

"I declare, I thought we would never get it through that Mexican woman's head that I had a sick headache and needed to lie down for a spell."

"Do stop chattering, Aunt Harriet," Lucinda said, rubbing her temples. "I have to think. Things are in a muddle, and I don't yet know what to do about them."

"Did Kane come home?" her aunt asked.

"Oh, yes, he came home all right, but he was not in the least pleased to see me. It seems he already has a wife."

Harriet Blake's mouth gaped open and her head bobbed up and down. "What will you do? Oh my poor dear girl, you have been jilted. The shame of it!'' she carried on.

"I have rarely if ever been so angry. I have waited for years for Kanen Benedict to ask me to be his wife. It would now seem as if I wasted most of my life waiting for him."

"You have not sat at home idly waiting for him," her aunt reminded her.

"I will not give up easily. I cannot believe that Kane would prefer a half-breed Indian girl to someone of his own class. No, I have not given up yet."

"Lord, save us all," Harriet Blake declared as her hand went to her heart. "Did you say he married a savage? I cannot stay under the same roof with an Indian!"

The Jojoba camp was in mourning for Maleaha's Aunt Kosha. There were many outward signs of grief for the Jojoba princess who had been so well loved by all.

Maleaha sat on a buffalo robe in front of her aunt's teepee, receiving many flowers and wooden tributes as the only remaining living Jojoba princess. She sat proud and dry-eyed, knowing it was what was expected of her. With her aunt's death had gone Maleaha's only living link with her mother's people.

Maleaha had sat beside her aunt during her illness, rarely leaving her. Her aunt seemed to be comforted by her presence, and toward the end, when Kosha's fever had risen, she had held onto Maleaha's hand, calling her by her dead sister's name.

Maleaha had loved her aunt deeply, and there was an

emptiness inside her now that no one could fill. She felt sadness that Cimeron would grow up without ever knowing her mother's people.

Maleaha was weary as she dismounted in front of the house and allowed Seth to lead her horse to the barn. It had been over three weeks since she had left for the Jojoba village, and in that time she had had very little sleep, and no time to think about her marriage to Kane.

Her footsteps hastened when she thought of her daughter. She wanted only to hold her in her arms and never to leave her again.

Maleaha opened the door silently and stepped into the room, flanked by Lamas. She was surprised when she saw two strangers talking to Kane. They had not yet noticed her. She was able to watch them while they were unaware of her. Her heart seemed to skip a beat when she recognized Kane's father. Maleaha then allowed her eyes to travel to the lovely woman dressed in a frothy pink gown, golden hair pulled away from her face and falling down her back in curls.

Maleaha saw the hand the woman placed on Kane's arm, just before she heard her husband laugh at some remark the woman had made to him.

Maleaha could not help looking down at her doeskin dress and moccasins. She wished that she could somehow get past them and make her way upstairs undetected. She now knew without being told who the woman in pink was—the woman was Lucinda, the lady Kane was in love with!

Eli was the first one to see Maleaha. His eyes moved over her at first in shocked surprise, and then she saw recognition register on his face. Maleaha caught his disapproving glance and she raised her head proudly. She would not allow Kane's father to make her feel ashamed of who she was.

"I believe your wife has returned," Eli said to his son.

Kane's head snapped up and his gaze moved to the door where Maleaha and Lamas stood. He gave her such an icy stare that Maleaha could feel the chill even from the distance that divided them. Anger turned his gray eyes to silver pinpoints.

"Lord, save us all. Are we being attacked by wild Indians?" Lucinda cried. She gripped Kane about the neck, flattening her body against his.

Lucinda looked from Maleaha back to Lamas, and Maleaha could not tell if her fear was real or just a ploy to get Kane's attention.

"It would be better if you would go now, Lamas," she told him in the language of the Jojoba.

Lamas nodded slightly, and he disappeared silently out the front door, leaving Maleaha to face three pairs of disapproving eyes.

"Paraiso?" he inquired.

"Yes, Paraiso is the name of my husband's ranch. It means paradise in English," Maleaha said, for no other reason than to have something to say to Kane's father.

Eli snorted. "It would have been more aptly named had you called it Hell."

Maleaha glanced up at Kane, wondering if he had taken exception to his father's remark. The muscle that twitched in his jaw told her that he had. She felt Kane's hand settle on her waist as he turned her to face Lucinda.

"Maleaha, I would like you to meet Lucinda Blake . . . an old friend. Lucinda, my wife, Maleaha."

Maleaha looked into hostile blue eyes. She tried to smile, but all the events of the evening had put her at a disadvantage. She was dressed in doeskin, while Lucinda was wearing a lovely gown. Maleaha's dark hair was windblown, while the other woman's hair was beautifully coiffured. She knew that she was facing the woman her husband loved and was supposed to have married.

"Welcome to our home, Miss Blake. I apologize for my absence. I trust you have been made comfortable?"

Lucinda eyed the woman whom she believed had stolen Kane from her. She was surprised to find her command of the English language was so good. This was no wild savage as she had hoped, but the loveliest woman she had ever seen. Lucinda had always prided herself on her creamy white complexion, but she found herself envious of Maleaha's smooth golden skin. She was taken aback at the green color of Maleaha's eyes. Never had she seen anyone with that color eyes. The Indian girl had high cheekbones, and her face was unbelievably lovely.

Maleaha stood inches taller than Lucinda, forcing Lucinda to look up to her. Even dressed in the Indian garb as she was, Lucinda knew that she was the one who was at the disadvantage. Kane's wife was too lovely to be real, and that fact did not make Lucinda feel too kindly toward her.

"What a quaint little dress you have on," Lucinda said, smiling through tight lips. "Can I call you Maleaha?" she asked prettily, linking her arm through Kane's.

"Yes, please do," Maleaha told her, ignoring the intimate way she hung on to Kane.

"It is a very difficult name to pronounce. Is it foreign?"

"No, it is Jojoba."

"Does it mean anything special in English?"

"Yes, it means beautiful one," Maleaha said, smiling slightly.

"You are quite pretty," Lucinda said, as if assessing Maleaha. "However did you get such dark skin? My mother would faint dead away if I ever allowed my skin to get so brown."

"Perhaps, Miss Blake, it is because I am half-Jojoba Indian. If you will excuse me, I will go up to my room and change. I will not be long, so there is no reason to hold dinner," she said, turning to Kane.

Maleaha rushed from the room, glad for any excuse to escape the room where she felt she had been on trial.

She dashed up the stairs and into Cimeron's bedroom. Maleaha found her daughter asleep, but she picked her up anyway and cuddled her tightly in her arms. She had

391

missed Cimeron so badly, and she needed the comfort of holding her for the moment.

"I want to see you in our bedroom at once," Kane spoke up from behind her.

Maleaha placed Cimeron back in her crib and pulled a blanket over her before she turned to Kane.

"As you wish," she said, brushing past him and making her way into their bedroom. Kane was right behind her, and he gripped her arm, turning her to face him.

"I am not at all pleased with you, Maleaha."

"I am sorry if I embarrassed you in front of your father and Miss Blake. Had I known they were here, I would have chosen a different entrance to the house." Maleaha was so tired, all she really wanted to do was undress and fall into bed. She did not feel up to facing the ordeal she knew awaited her downstairs, nor did she want to face Kane's displeasure tonight.

"I was not referring to how you entered the house. I was talking about your leaving me and our daughter without sending us some word from you in over three weeks."

"I left you a note."

"To hell with the note. You could have waited until I came home before you rode off to God only knows where. I don't for a moment believe that story about your aunt's being ill. You left just so you could get back at me for what I did that night."

"You think I lied about my aunt?"

"I wouldn't put it past you. Didn't you care that I have been worried about your safety?"

So Kane thought she had lied to him. Did he think so

little of her that he now not only thought she was seeing Clay behind his back, but that she had not been honest to him about her reasons for leaving.

"Lamas was with me. I did not think you would worry."

His silver eyes bore into her. "I suggest you make yourself presentable and be downstairs as soon as possible."

She moved away from him and raised her chin stubbornly. "Is that a suggestion or an order, Kane?"

"It's an order. If you don't obey me, I will drag you downstairs. I don't want my father and Lucinda to guess there is trouble in our little paradise." Maleaha watched as he strolled across the room, opened the door, and left. She wished she dared disobey him. He had wounded her pride once more. She would have challenged him but for one reason: She did not want Lucinda to think that her marriage to Kane was a farce.

Going over to her wardrobe, Maleaha chose a stunning black velvet gown her father had brought her back from Paris. She quickly washed the dust of the road from her body, as well as she could from the pan of water that stood on the small table near the door. She then twisted her hair into a knot at the back of her head and slipped into the black gown. She fastened a strand of pearls about her neck.

It had taken hardly any time at all for her to get ready. Maleaha hesitated at the door. She felt anything but joy at the thought of facing the three people who waited below for her. Sighing deeply, she squared her shoulders and descended the stairs. Jonas Deveraux's daughter was not about to let anyone make her feel inferior. She remembered her grandfather's words as she walked proudly into the room. "Remember that you are a princess, Maleaha. Bow your head to no man." It gave her the courage she needed to face Kane's father and Lucinda Blake.

Kane's father was seated on the sofa, and Lucinda was standing beside Kane, her hand resting possessively on his arm. Maleaha faltered only a moment before she smiled brightly.

"Please forgive my tardiness. I am afraid it was unavoidable."

Lucinda's hand dropped away from Kane's arm and she stared open-mouthed at the beautiful woman who was his wife. She felt her own beauty fade into insignificance. This woman with the dark skin was no savage, but so lovely that Lucinda felt jealousy flame to life deep inside of her.

Eli rose to his feet drinking in his daughter-in-law's loveliness "Your Indian name is most appropriate, Maleaha. You are beautiful," he declared, surprising not only himself but the others as well.

Maleaha silently thanked him while she favored him with a dazzling smile. "I thank you for the pretty compliment, Mr. Benedict."

Lucinda had the feeling she was losing an ally, and she knew in that moment that she must do something to make Kane's wife appear less than favorable. But what? The black velvet gown clung to Maleaha's tall, slender figure and draped behind her in a soft bustle. Most people's skin would look sallow next to that black, but it made Maleaha's skin appear smooth and golden.

"What a lovely gown, Maleaha. Did Kane pick it out for you? He always did have extraordinary taste in women's apparel."

Maleaha heard the irony in Lucinda's voice, hinting that she herself would not know how to choose her own clothing. "No, my husband has far more important things to do than shop for ladies' clothing." Maleaha smiled to herself as she watched anger turn Lucinda's pink complexion red with anger.

"If you would all accompany me to the dining room, I believe Mrs. Higgens is ready to serve dinner," Maleaha said, changing the subject.

Kane was relieved that Mrs. Higgens had returned and they would not be forced to dine on Rosita's spicy concoctions. He was proud of the lovely picture Maleaha presented in her high-necked black gown. He could tell that his father was surprised that Maleaha spoke with such elegance and moved with such grace. He looked down as Lucinda grabbed his arm, forcing him to escort her into the dining room.

Eli presented his arm to Maleaha and she hesitated before placing her hand on it. She was aware that he would have preferred that his son marry Lucinda Blake, and she remembered how hateful he had been to her the night he had found her with his son in the garden.

The seating arrangement had been preordained by Mrs. Higgens. Eli sat beside Maleaha at one end of the table, while Lucinda was seated beside Kane. Mrs. Higgens had taken the leaf out of the table, making it much smaller.

As the meal progressed, Maleaha began to feel more

and more the outsider. Mr. Benedict and Lucinda talked of mutual friends in Boston, while Kane listened quietly. Every so often his eyes would stray to Maleaha, and she could tell by his eyes that he was still angry with her.

She wondered how long Kane's father and Lucinda had been at Paraiso, but saw no way to ask them. She also wondered what Mr. Benedict thought of his granddaughter. She couldn't see how anyone could help loving Cimeron. Maleaha became aware that she was not eating, but instead was drawing patterns on the tablecloth with her fork. Glancing at Kane, she saw the smoldering anger in his eyes once more.

"My father has asked you a question, Maleaha," he said bitingly.

"What . . . I am sorry, Mr. Benedict. What was it you said?" she asked, looking into the face that was so like her husband's.

"I merely asked where you acquired such a good cook. I have rarely if ever tasted a more tender and tasty roast."

"Mrs. Higgens is orginally from Virginia. She and her husband came to New Mexico after the war. She is now a widow, and I do not know what I would do without her."

Eli nodded and turned his attention to Lucinda. Maleaha knew he had only been making polite conversation, so she once more lapsed into silence, wishing the meal were over.

When at last they migrated into the parlor, Maleaha once more felt on the outside. Lucinda sat as close to Kane as she could manage without actually being in his lap, while Eli wandered about the room examining different objects.

Maleaha sat down in a chair nearest the huge fireplace and struggled to stay awake. She had ridden hard for three days and was bone weary. Staring into the fire, she felt her eyelids getting heavy. Her head fell back against the chair and she felt herself drifting off. She was awakened suddenly, when a log fell noisily from its perch, sending sparks into the room.

Maleaha sat up quickly, feeling guilty for having fallen asleep. To her relief no one seemed to have noticed that she had dozed off. She heard Kane's father speaking in a quiet voice.

"You should not have any trouble finding a buyer for this ranch. You don't belong here. Come home with me."

Maleaha bit her lip and stood up. "If the three of you will excuse me, I think I will retire. It has been rather a long day for me. It has been a pleasure meeting you," she said, doubting that any one of the three would mind if she were to go to bed.

Eli looked at her as if he were angry that she had interrupted his conversation, and Lucinda smiled slightly.

"We would not want to keep you from your bed. You must be bored to tears, listening to us reminisce about old times," Lucinda said sweetly. Only Maleaha seemed to be aware of the malicious glint in Lucinda's eyes. She knew at that moment that the battle lines had been drawn between them. How could she fight this woman whom Kane loved? And how could she win if she did fight her? The only thing she had to hold Kane with was their daughter. She was not even sure that Cimeron would hold

Kane.

Turning to face her husband, Maleaha could not see what he was thinking.

"I will join you shortly," he told her.

As Maleaha undressed for bed, she felt as if her whole world had come tumbling down around her. Would Kane do as his father asked and sell Paraiso? Would he want to return to Boston? Would he expect her to go with him if he did? Perhaps he would want his freedom. He had already married her, thus giving Cimeron his name. Would he now feel free to set their marriage aside so he would be free to marry the woman he loved?

Maleaha slipped under the covers, feeling very wretched. She did not want to think about Kane's selling Paraiso. It was her home. They had worked so hard making it into a place they could be proud of.

Maleaha had been snubbed and cut to the quick that night. She had been forced to stand by while Lucinda had pawed her husband, and Kane's father had treated her as if she was of little worth. Not once had Kane come to her defense. She would not fight to hold on to him, she thought, as she wiped the tears from her eyes. Should he ask it of her, she would give him his freedom.

She heard Kane enter the room and closed her eyes, pretending to be asleep. He did not light a lamp but proceeded to undress in the dark. She remembered the last night they had spent together and wondered if he would remember also. She felt the bed shift under his weight and then felt his hand on her shoulder.

"Maleaha."

She did not answer, hoping he would believe her

asleep. She heard him sigh as his hand slipped to her waist, pulling her against his body. Her body melted against him, and she bit her trembling lip. She wanted him to make love to her and yet she was afraid that he would. Tense moments passed. When it became apparent that he did not want to make love to her, Maleaha hid her disappointment. Most probably he didn't want to make love to her with the woman he loved sleeping in the same house.

Kane had been asleep a long time before Maleaha fell into a troubled sleep.

The next morning Maleaha awoke early to find Kane still asleep beside her. He still had his arm about her waist, and she moved it over softly, not wanting to awaken him. In her usual quiet manner, she dressed and went silently into the nursery.

Cimeron was awake and clapped her hands delightedly when she saw her mother. With loving tenderness, Maleaha washed and dressed her daughter, then took her downstairs, wanting to spend as much time with her as she could, to make up for having been away from her for so long.

Mrs. Higgens smiled brightly as she removed a pan of golden-brown biscuits from the oven. "It's good to have you back with us, Mrs. Benedict. We have missed you around here."

"Thank you, Mrs. Higgens," Maleaha answered, thinking it was nice to know someone welcomed her home. "How long have my husband's father and Miss

Blake been at Paraiso?''

''They arrived but yesterday. Rosita tells me that there is another woman with them. Were you aware of that?''

''No. Who is the other woman?''

''I am told that she is Miss Blake's aunt. She went directly to the bedroom after her arrival and has not shown her face since then. Rosita says she was ailing. I suppose some people have a hard time adapting to this climate.''

''Perhaps you should prepare her a tray so she can eat in her room. I will look in on her later in the day,'' Maleaha said, lifting Cimeron above her head and being rewarded by a happy giggle.

Maleaha took the soft-boiled egg Mrs. Higgens had prepared for Cimeron and mashed it up. Blowing on it to help it cool, she began to feed her daughter. Cimeron began to wriggle, wanting to get down on the floor, and when Maleaha let her down, she crawled over to the box at the end of the stove, where Mrs. Higgens kept her cat. Maleaha sat down on the floor beside Cimeron, making sure she did not hurt the cat, and that the cat did not scratch her daughter.

She laughed as the fat tabby jumped into Cimeron's arms, then curled up contentedly and fell asleep, while Cimeron patted the cat softly.

''How long has this friendship been going on, Mrs. Higgens?'' Maleaha wanted to know.

Mrs. Higgens was kneading dough for the loaves of bread she needed to bake, and she smiled down at Cimeron. ''The first morning after you had left, I brought Cimeron down here with me so she could play on the floor while I made breakfast for Mr. Benedict. She and Tabby have been friends ever since.''

"I am sorry about the extra work you had to do while I was away. I am grateful for the good care you took of my daughter. I did not worry about her, knowing that you were caring for her.''

"I did not mind the work and I loved having Cimeron with me. She is such a good little girl and so pleasant to be around. I love the way Mr. Benedict dotes on his daughter. He is such a devoted father.''

Maleaha removed the sleeping cat and replaced it in the box. She was determined to feed her daughter and take her for a walk before the others came downstairs. After Cimeron had eaten what Malaeha considered a substantial breakfast, she bundled her up in a warm coat and cap and walked outside with her.

Maleaha was halfway to the barn when she saw Kane's father walking toward her. Apparently he was an early riser, she thought, preparing herself for her encounter with him.

Eli Benedict stopped in front of Maleaha and looked not at her but at the child she held in her arms.

Eli frowned as he looked into the lovely face of the child. Her eyes were the same color as Kane's and she looked much as his son had looked as a baby.

Cimeron did the predictable thing and held her arms out for him to hold her. Maleaha held her breath, fearing Kane's father would reject his own granddaughter. She felt relief when he took Cimeron in his arms.

"She looks just as Kane did when he was an infant,''

Eli said in a voice filled with wonder. He touched her soft cheek and then her dark hair. "I suppose I haven't given her much thought since I arrived. What is her name?"

"Cimeron."

"Like the river?"

"No, it is a Jojoba name meaning beloved. It was my mother's name."

"The Jojoba tribe seems to have a flowery language," he said, looking at the face of the woman who had given him a granddaughter.

"Cimeron, this is your grandfather. Can you say grandfather?" Maleaha asked her daughter.

Cimeron made an attempt at the unfamiliar word, and Maleaha and Eli laughed as she patted Eli's face and planted a wet kiss on his cheek.

Maleaha could see the softening in Eli's gray eyes when he touched a strand of dark hair that was peeping out beneath the cap Cimeron wore.

"I believe this child is the most beautiful child I have ever seen."

"I think Cimeron would be pleased that she has met with her grandfather's approval."

"I'll be going in now," Eli said, handing Cimeron back to Maleaha.

"You will find Mrs. Higgens has your breakfast ready, should you wish to eat now."

He nodded stiffly and walked toward the house. Maleaha watched his retreating back and shrugged her shoulders. She then turned her back and continued her walk. She had no idea how Kane's father felt about his granddaughter, but she could feel his displeasure toward herself.

Kane found his father eating breakfast and sat down opposite him. "I trust you slept well, Eli?"

Eli bit into a flaky biscuit and swallowed it before he answered his son. "I slept well enough under the circumstances."

Kane took a sip of the coffee Mrs. Higgens had placed before him. "What circumstances, Eli?"

"I would like to talk some sense into your head. Why do you stay in this godforsaken place other than to thwart me?"

"You give yourself too much importance, Eli, if you think I built this ranch and work from sunup until sundown merely to get back at you," Kane said lazily.

Eli picked up his coffee cup and raised it to his lips, then placed it back on the table without taking a drink. "I saw your daughter this morning. She is a lovely child. Did you get her mother with child and then have to marry her?"

Kane's eyes narrowed. "If you will remember, I told you that I loved her. Didn't you believe me?"

"Lord yes, love her, she is a lovely creature. Lavish her with beautiful things. Take her to Boston with you and set her up in a house. Give her everything she desires, but dissolve this marriage, it is a farce. I can't tell you what went through my mind yesterday when she came in dressed like some wild Indian."

At that moment Maleaha paused outside the dining

room door. She could hear Kane's father speak in anger.

"Hell, son, if you married her just to get back at me, you succeeded better than you might have hoped. This Indian girl is not the sort you marry. She is the kind you ask to become your mistress. Lucinda is the kind you marry!"

Maleaha was aware that Mrs. Higgens had come up behind her and had heard Mr. Benedict's angry words also. She quickly handed Cimeron to the housekeeper and ran out the door, but not before she saw the sadness in the eyes of the older woman. She had to get away. She would find somewhere where she could be alone to cry.

Mrs. Higgens stood outside the door listening to Kane's words to his father. "I told you, I love Maleaha. I did not have to marry her, as you put it. I told you we were married in the Indian village. We were also married by a priest. As I listened to you speak just now, I realize how much I was like you in the past. I remember the time I offered Maleaha just what you proposed I offer her. God, you make me sick. I warn you, I will not stand by and allow you to hurt her. If you cannot treat her with respect, I suggest you leave this house today."

"But she is half-Indian. . . ."

"I don't think you have any idea how important Maleaha is."

"Important to whom, some obscure Indian tribe?"

"I believe you are acquainted with one Jonas Deveraux?" Kane said, laying a trap for his father.

"Of course I know Jonas. He is a wealthy rancher and as fine a gentleman as you will find anywhere. You cannot tell me that you have met him and he has approved of your marriage to the Indian girl,'' Eli said, walking into Kane's well-laid trap unawares.

Kane smiled. ''He not only approves, he has welcomed me into his family with open arms.''

''You aren't making any sense to me. What has Jonas Deveraux got to do with you and me?''

''He shares a common bond with you, Eli. Cimeron is not only your granddaughter, but his as well. Maleaha is Jonas's only child, born to him by a lovely Indian princess with the same name as my daughter,'' Kane told his father with satisfaction. He watched as his father's face lost its color. ''I have never known you to be at a loss for words, Eli. Have I perhaps taken you by surprise?''

Eli shook his head. ''I knew that Jonas had a daughter; he had talked to me about her on many occasions. I believe she was attending a finishing school in Boston.''

''Yes, Maleaha spent two years in Boston. Don't you think she benefited by her education?''

Lucinda and her aunt chose that moment to enter the room, Lucinda in a bright yellow gown. She bent over Kane and kissed his cheek, while her aunt looked nervous and not at all well.

Mrs. Higgens came in bearing a tray filled with eggs, biscuits and bacon. She gave Lucinda a haughty glance, thinking that this young woman who put on such airs would cause Mrs. Benedict a lot of grief before she was done. Her heart went out to the kind, gentle mistress of the house. Mrs. Higgens had seen the pain in her eyes this morning as she had overheard her husband and his father discuss her. What a pity that Mrs. Benedict had rushed away before she had heard her husband defend her and declare his love for her.

"Where is my wife, Mrs. Higgens?" Kane asked.

"I'm sure I don't know," the older woman said, thinking most probably she was somewhere crying at that very moment.

"Your wife seems to have the habit of disappearing, Kane. One would think you cannot keep track of her," Lucinda told him.

Lucinda looked into Kane's storm-filled eyes and laughed at the scowl on his face. "My, my, I seem to have struck a nerve. You look positively fierce."

"Lucinda, I am sure you should not be saying those things to Mr. Benedict," her aunt told her.

"Pooh, Kane does not mind that I speak so openly to him, do you, Kane?"

Kane threw his napkin down and stood up abruptly. "I have things to attend to," he said sourly as he walked purposefully out of the dining room. He was not in the best of moods. He had not yet gotten the chance to speak with Maleaha, and he was still seething because she had ridden away to the Jojoba camp without first consulting with him. He still did not believe that her aunt had been ill. No, she had left because the two of them had quarreled. Damnit, he just wanted his father, Lucinda, and her aunt to return to Boston.

He saddled his horse and rode away from the ranch house in a cloud of dust.

CHAPTER TWENTY-THREE

Maleaha had ridden miles from the ranch house. She let the cool wind whip through her hair and dry the tears on her cheeks. She had the strongest urge to ride over to Deveraux and tell her father how brokenhearted she felt. But no, she could not bring herself to speak of the trouble between herself and Kane, not even with her father.

Where did she belong? She no longer belonged with the Jojoba. She couldn't return to her father. She did not belong with her husband. He wanted to be with the woman he loved, not with her. Could she give Kane up without a fight? Cimeron needed a father as well as a mother. Kane himself had pointed that out to her before they had been married by the priest. She could either swallow her pride and beg him to keep her as his wife, or give him over to Lucinda without a fight. In Maleaha's troubled state of mind, she didn't know which was the right thing to do.

It was long past the lunch hour before Maleaha finally

returned to the ranch house. Going first into the kitchen, she was informed by Mrs. Higgens that Kane had left just after breakfast. His father and Lucinda were in the sitting room, and Lucinda's aunt, whom Maleaha had yet to meet, was lying down in her bedroom with another sick headache.

Maleaha saw the searching look Mrs. Higgens gave her and knew that the older woman was worried about her having run from the house in tears that morning. She gave her a reassuring smile. "I am quite all right, Mrs. Higgens. Don't worry about me."

Mrs. Higgens gave her a kind smile and turned back to the dirty dishes she was washing. "Do you want to approve the menu for tonight?"

"No, I know whatever it is, it will be delicious," Maleaha said, smoothing down her wind-tossed hair and wishing she did not have to do her duty as hostess. She dreaded facing Kane's father and Lucinda.

Entering the sitting room, she found Lucinda was alone. Maleaha noticed the lovely yellow gown, which seemed to enhance the creamy white complexion. For the first time in her life Maleaha wished her skin were not so dark.

"Oh, our elusive hostess returns," Lucinda said, picking up the piece of pottery that Maleaha's grandfather had given her and turning it over in her hand.

"I am sorry, Miss Blake. You must think me terribly rude," Maleaha said, wishing she could reach out and take the valuable piece of pottery from Lucinda's hand.

"It is no more than I expected from someone who comes from this backward land," Lucinda said, as the pottery almost slipped from her hands.

Maleaha caught her breath. "I would ask you to be careful with that, Miss Blake. It is very valuable and was given to me by my grandfather. He told me it was over two hundred years old."

"This old thing valuable? I wouldn't have it in my home." Lucinda set it halfway on the edge of the table and watched with satisfaction as it crashed to the floor, shattering into many small pieces.

Maleaha was speechless. She knew that Lucinda had deliberately destroyed the pottery, and she could not understand how anyone could set out to break something so lovely.

"Oh goodness, what a shame. I suppose it isn't so valuable any longer, is it?" Lucinda taunted.

Maleaha bent down and began picking up the fragments.

"Leave that for a moment, I want to speak to you," Lucinda said, eyeing Maleaha with a malignant glare.

"I am listening, Miss Blake," Maleaha told her, standing up and placing the broken pieces on the table.

"You can't hold on to him, you know."

Maleaha's keen hearing picked up the sound of someone outside the room in the hallway, obviously listening to her and Lucinda's conversation. She knew by the sound of the footsteps that it was Kane's father.

"Whom are you speaking of?" Maleaha asked, determined to make Lucinda spell out what was on her mind.

"You know I am speaking of Kane. He does not love you. He told his father he married you only to give his child a name."

Maleaha drew in her breath. Lucinda's face no longer appeared beautiful, but was distorted with hate and jealousy. "You heard wrong, Miss Blake. Kane and I were married nine months to the day before our daughter was born. I do not believe Kane told his father that." Whatever Kane was, he would never say anything to cast a shadow on Cimeron's birth. It might be that he did not love her, but no one could deny that Kane loved his daughter.

"You lie! I do not believe you. Kane would never have married you unless he was forced to!" Lucinda yelled.

"You may think what you will, Miss Blake. I have no more time to spend hashing this over with you."

Lucinda grabbed Maleaha by the wrist, and Maleaha could feel the woman's fingernails biting into her skin. "Kane cannot love you! He loves me!"

Maleaha pried Lucinda's fingers from her wrist. "You may be right, Miss Blake. Kane might love you, but he is married to me."

Lucinda's eyes narrowed. "Kane must be in torment wanting to be with me. Did he make love to you last night? I doubt that he did. He must remember how good it was between him and me when we made love. He must be sickened by the sight of you."

Maleaha gasped. Never had she seen such hatred in anyone's face, and never had she heard a woman speak so brazenly about a man's making love to her. She closed her eyes, not wanting to hear any more. She could almost envision Kane making love to Lucinda. She felt tears gathering in her eyes and fought to keep them from fall-

410

ing down her face. She must not appear weak before this woman. If she did, Lucinda Blake would destroy her completely.

"I can still feel the way Kane's hands moved over my body," Lucinda continued.

"I will not listen to any more!" Maleaha cried. "My God, what a monster you are!"

Lucinda threw back her head and laughed. "There is not much you can do to be rid of me, Maleaha. You see Kane's father wants his son to marry me. I think Kane can dispose of you easily enough."

"If Kane wishes to be rid of me, he will tell me so himself. I do not believe he would approve of this conversation."

"Believe what you will. I think you already know that Kane loves me. Make it easy on him. Take your daughter and go back to that Indian tribe you come from." Lucinda moved in front of Maleaha, blocking her exit.

"If Kane wants his freedom, he can come to me and ask for it himself." Before Maleaha could make a move to defend herself, Lucinda's hand came up quickly and slapped her hard across the face. Maleaha's first instinct was to slap her back, but she only shoved her away and moved quickly across the room.

Maleaha had moved so quietly that when she reached the hallway she took Eli completely by surprise.

"Is that really what you want for your son, Mr. Benedict?" Maleaha asked, nodding toward Lucinda.

Eli looked from one woman to the other. Lucinda's face turned red when she realized that Eli must have overheard at least part of their conversation.

"H . . . how long have you been standing there, Eli?" she asked hesitatingly.

Maleaha did not stay to hear any more but rushed up the stairs. Eli watched her, thinking she had proved to be more of a lady than Lucinda. Kane had been right about Lucinda. She was not worthy to be his son's wife.

Lucinda watched as Eli advanced into the room. She moved forward and linked her arm through his. "I think in no time at all we can be rid of that woman. She is such an uncivilized little creature."

Eli shoved her arm away and removed his handkerchief from his pocket, placed the broken bits of pottery in it, then tied it into a knot. "I think you broke this on purpose, Lucinda."

"What? Oh yes, she said it was given to her by her grandfather. I think it was dreadful looking."

Eli had always appreciated valuable antiques and was appalled by her wanton act.

"I cannot see what Kane finds to admire in that woman, she is so uncivilized. Look at the way she treats us, and we are guests in her home," Lucinda said thoughtfully.

"I am going to see if I can get someone to drive me into Santa Fe. Do you want to come along?" Eli asked.

"Why do you want to go into town? It will be dark before you could get back."

"I want to see if I can find someone who can repair this pottery."

"Whatever for? It is nothing more than an old Indian relic."

"Yes, apparently very old," he said, leaving Lucinda with a puzzled look on her face.

Maleaha spent the rest of the afternoon with Cimeron. When she finally turned her over to Rosita to bathe and feed, she went to her own room to bathe and dress for dinner. She dreaded the evening meal when she would be forced to face Kane and Lucinda.

She thought about what Lucinda had told her as she arranged her hair on the top of her head. She had been devastated when Lucinda had told her that she and Kane had made love. How dare he bring a woman into this house that he had been to bed with? If she had any pride she would leave and never come back, she told herself. She was glad that her hurt was gradually giving way to anger. She wanted to throw Lucinda's words in Kane's face.

Maleaha went into the kitchen to lend Mrs. Higgens a hand with setting the table. Tying a white apron about her waist, she carried the china into the dining room and proceeded to put it out. She heard Kane come up behind her, and she spoke to him without turning around.

"Dinner will be ready in about twenty minutes."

"Where were you this morning? I had half decided that you had ridden off again without telling me."

"No, Kane, I would not do that," she said as she folded a white dinner napkin and placed it beside a plate. "If I decide to leave, you will be the first one I'll tell."

"I still intend to talk to you about that little episode. I

413

will not have you running off to Mangas every time we have a misunderstanding.''

She turned to face him. Her eyes collided with his and she raised her chin. ''I did not go to Mangas. I told you that my aunt was ill and she was asking for me.''

''So you said, but I don't believe you,'' he said, walking out of the dining room.

Dinner was just what Maleaha had expected it would be, long and uncomfortable. Lucinda again monopolized Kane's attention. Maleaha was surprised when Eli began to talk to her. He asked her about her father, and what it had been like growing up in New Mexico. He asked her also if she had enjoyed going to school in Boston. She would have enjoyed their conversation had it not been for the fact that Kane and Lucinda were talking quietly at the other end of the table.

Lucinda's aunt had still not put in an appearance, but had again taken her dinner on a tray in her room.

Maleaha at one point had to remind herself not to trust Kane's father. After all, it had been only this morning that she had overheard him talking about her to his son.

After dinner Eli asked if Maleaha would take him upstairs to see Cimeron. She readily agreed, leaving Kane and Lucinda alone.

Eli smiled down at his sleeping granddaughter. ''It is so strange, Maleaha. Today I seem to be facing many truths about myself, and it's all due to you and this little granddaughter of mine.'' He touched Cimeron lightly on

414

the cheek. "I had forgotten how sweet a child can be."

"I am so glad that you like Cimeron, Mr. Benedict."

He looked at her long and hard. "I wonder if you would consider calling me Eli?"

"Yes, if you would like." She wondered what game he was playing. No one could change so quickly. That morning he had not wanted her to call him by his first name. She was startled when he reached for her hand. "I would like very much for you to call me Eli, Maleaha."

Lucinda patted the sofa for Kane to sit beside her, and he did so with reservations. When he was seated she began working on him.

"Kane, you have been neglecting me shamefully since I have been here. I would have thought you would at least have offered to show me about your old ranch," she said prettily.

"Maleaha will show you about the ranch if you are interested. I am much too busy."

"I don't think your wife likes me very well. She was perfectly horrid to me this afternoon," Lucinda said with a pout on her mouth.

"I find that hard to believe, Lucinda. Maleaha would never be rude to a guest in our home."

"You didn't see her today. She yelled at me, and all because I accidentally broke an old Indian vase." False tears sparkled in her blue eyes as she laid her head on Kane's shoulder.

"I am sure you misunderstood Maleaha, Lucinda."

She raised her head and looked deep into his silver

eyes. "I am telling you the truth, Kane. Your wife was horrid to me."

"I will speak to her. I am sure she will make it up to you."

"You will not tell her that I complained to you, will you?"

"No, of course not."

Lucinda laid her head back on Kane's shoulder, and that was the way Maleaha saw them when she and Eli entered the room.

Kane stood up abruptly, and Maleaha thought he looked guilty, while Lucinda smiled at her smugly.

"I wish to be excused," Maleaha said, barely able to conceal her anger.

"Don't you think that would be rude to our guests, Maleaha?" Kane said, looking very displeased.

Maleaha's anger intensified as Kane criticized her before Lucinda and his father. "I have had a long day, Kane, and I am going to my room," she said, sailing out of the room without a backward glance.

"See what I mean," Lucinda spoke up, giving Kane her most helpless little-girl look.

"You should not take it personally, Lucinda. I believe Maleaha is angry with me, and it does not concern you. If the two of you will excuse me, I will also wish you a good night."

Lucinda put a restraining hand on his arm. "Do not go. I wanted to talk to you."

"Let him alone," Eli spoke up. "He said he wanted to retire."

Lucinda looked at Eli and then back to Kane. Eli had

never spoken so harshly to her before. She hoped to gain Kane's sympathy, but he was already halfway across the room.

Maleaha stood looking out the bedroom window. Tears of anger and hurt flowed freely down her face. What was the matter with her lately? She seemed to cry so easily. Deep inside of her the Indian part of her was ashamed of this weakness.

She heard Kane enter the room and slam the door behind him. She quickly dried her eyes and stood ready to face him.

"I didn't expect you to be able to tear yourself away from Lucinda. To what do I owe this great honor?" she asked angrily.

"Maleaha, I have had about enough of your childishness. Just because you are angry with me doesn't give you any right to take it out on Lucinda."

"Did she tell you that I was taking my anger out on her?"

"She said something about your getting angry when she broke some silly Indian vase."

"Is that what she said?"

"I insist that you apologize to her. It would be only decent of you to treat her with a little kindness. She has been through a very difficult time. Coming all this way from Boston was not easy for one as delicate as Lucinda is."

Once more Maleaha felt the prickle of tears. Kane was concerned for Lucinda, thinking she had been through a difficult time. He didn't for one moment consider her feelings. He didn't even believe that she had gone to be with her aunt because she was ill. It had never occurred to him to ask how her aunt was, and she was not about to tell him that she had died. He probably wouldn't believe her anyway. Lucinda was very clever. She had made her appear a spiteful, jealous person.

"I will apologize to her tomorrow, if that is your wish," she said dully. Maleaha wondered when she had become such a coward. Perhaps she was not accustomed to anyone's not believing her. She was an honest person and didn't know how to defend herself against dishonesty.

"I am glad you are being sensible about this. Your apology should clear the air."

Maleaha bit her lip against her angry retort. She could almost see the smug look on Lucinda's face when she apologized.

She moved away from the window and removed her robe. Pulling the covers down she climbed into bed and turned her back to Kane. She felt him sit down on the bed and hoped he would leave her alone. At the moment she wasn't sure what she felt toward him. It was possible that he was killing her love for him, degree by degree. After Lucinda's telling her about Kane's making love to her, she didn't want him to touch her. Go to Lucinda, she wanted to shout at him. See if I care, she thought angrily.

She felt his hand gently brush her hair and she closed her eyes. She was not being honest with herself. If Kane were to go to Lucinda, it would break her heart.

"Maleaha, I don't want to quarrel with you." His

hand drifted down her silky hair and across her shoulder.

"I don't want to quarrel with you either, Kane. In fact, I don't want anything to do with you."

He turned her over to face him. She could easily see his handsome face in the moonlit room. "I can't stand it when you are angry with me."

"You think I should not be angry with you?" she questioned.

"If anything, I should be unhappy with you. You left me under the pretense of visiting your sick aunt."

"This is not the first time you have accused me of telling a lie, Kane."

His hand strayed to the ribbon at the front of her nightgown. "I do not think you set out to deceive me. I suppose a man should expect a woman to weave fabrications."

"I am surprised you married me, thinking so little of my honesty."

His hand brushed against her breast. "Let's not quarrel tonight. All I really want to do is hold you in my arms and make love to you," he whispered in her ear.

Maleaha resisted the urge to push his hand away as it slid down to her stomach. All she could think about was Lucinda lying in his arms, while he made love to her. She tried to deny her body the thrill of his touch, but as his lips covered hers, her body ached for total fulfillment.

"Perhaps you should seek out Lucinda," she said and wished she could recall the words as soon as they had been spoken.

"What is that supposed to mean?"

"I don't want to be with you, Kane," she said, trying

to push him away.

"It's been so long, Maleaha. Don't punish me any longer," he said, pulling her nightgown over her head.

"You are my husband, and you can take whatever you want from me. But you will find me unwilling to give myself freely to you," she told him, already willing to give him anything he wanted. His hands seemed to burn into her delicate skin as they moved across her stomach to rest against her leg.

"Your body denies what your lips say, Maleaha. I can tell you want me as much as I want you." And to prove his point he bend his dark head and nuzzled her creamy breast until the points became hard in his mouth. His hand slid up her throat and he looked deeply into her eyes.

"Have you judged me guilty without a trial, Maleaha?"

What was it she saw in his eyes? Pain? "It is you who have found me guilty, Kane."

Maleaha had no chance to say anything further. Kane's lips settled on hers and her body began to tremble. Don't think about anything tonight, she told herself. Let him have your body. Give him what he asks for and take what he gives you.

She felt his naked body pressed against hers, and she sighed as he pulled her on top of him. She could feel the hair on his chest tickle her bare breast. His lips were hungry and demanding, and her lips opened invitingly to his kiss. All of her instincts awakened.

Kane might love Lucinda, she thought, but at the moment it was she he wanted. She could feel his warm male hardness pressed against her, and she gasped as he entered her body.

Her hands laced through his hair as he turned her over onto her back. She had been apart from him for too long, she thought. Her body had too long been denied the pleasure that only Kane could give her.

Maleaha responded to his lovemaking wildly, and when they had both been satisfied she curled up in his arms, sighing contentedly. She knew that she should still be angry with him, but for the moment she was too sleepy, and his body felt so good beside her.

Some time later she heard Kane get out of bed and get dressed. He seemed to be gone for a long time, and when he did return, Maleaha pretended to be asleep. She could smell the brandy on his breath as he pulled her into his arms and rested his face against hers. She wondered where he had been, and she hoped he had not been with Lucinda.

CHAPTER TWENTY-FOUR

The next morning at breakfast Maleaha and Eli were talking, when Kane swept into the room. Maleaha could tell by the scowl on his handsome face that he was in a foul mood.

Eli raised his eyebrow, but said nothing when Kane sat down and reached for his coffee cup without wishing anyone good morning.

Mrs. Higgens served breakfast with her usual cheerfulness, but only Eli seemed to notice. Kane glared at Maleaha over his coffee cup. He noticed her eyes light up as she stood up quickly and raced out of the room, calling her father.

Her damned Indian hearing, he thought sourly. She always heard everything before any normal human being could have.

When she returned a short time later, Jonas was with her. He greeted Kane and then shook hands with Eli.

"It's a small world, isn't it, Eli? Who would have thought that you and I would one day share the same granddaughter?"

Eli laughed. "I would never have believed it had you told me a year or even a few days ago. I only found out yesterday that my lovely daughter-in-law was your daughter."

Kane looked at his father, watching for some hint of sarcasm, and he was surprised that his father seemed to be speaking sincerely.

After Jonas was seated beside Maleaha and she had poured him a cup of coffee, he took her hand and squeezed it.

"Honey, I was sorely grieved to hear about your aunt's death. I know how much you loved her, and I was sorry I wasn't with you when she died to help you in your grief. I came home as soon as I heard. Lamas rode to Albuquerque and brought me the news."

Kane felt as if a knife had been twisted inside his chest. Good Lord, what she must have suffered over losing her aunt! He had accused her of lying about her aunt's illness, and Maleaha had been telling the truth all the while. When would he ever learn to trust her? She had not even tried to defend herself to him, nor had she told him that her aunt had died. He saw tears sparkle in her beautiful green eyes as she laid her head on her father's shoulder.

"I was glad I could be with her at the end, Father. She seemed to need me."

"I know, honey." Jonas kissed her cheek. "She was your last living link with the Jojoba tribe."

"I don't think I will ever want to return to the camp again."

"You feel that way now, honey, but the day will come when you will want to take Cimeron to visit the Jojoba, so she will feel pride in your mother's people, just as you do."

"I suppose you are right. I do want her to get to know them, and to know their worth." Maleaha glanced at Kane to find he was watching her. She saw the muscle in his jaw twitch and wondered what he could be thinking. She felt no joy in the fact that he now knew she had told him the truth. She had wanted him to believe in her.

"Speaking of my granddaughter, Eli. Let's go up and invade the nursery," Jonas said, draining his coffee cup.

"I think she is still sleeping, Father."

Eli stood up and smiled warmly at Jonas. "If she is sleeping, we will just have to awaken her. We have that right as her grandfathers, don't you think, Jonas? Did you know her nose resembles Kane's when he was a baby?"

"No, her nose is like Maleaha's," Jonas said emphatically.

"You are mistaken. She has Kane's nose."

"No, *you* are the one who is mistaken, but I will concede that she has Kane's eyes."

Kane watched as the two men left the dining room. He could not believe his father was acting the doting grandfather. He was not even aware that his father had paid the slightest attention to Cimeron. He frowned as he turned to face his wife. He was quiet for a moment, wondering how to speak to Maleaha. There were so many things that he wanted to tell her, and so little he dared say.

"Maleaha, about your aunt. I am sorr . . ."

Maleaha stood up and began stacking dishes on a tray. "I don't want to hear anything you have to say, Kane. You said it all last night."

Kane stood up and took the tray out of her hand and placed it on the table. "You are going to make it hard for me, aren't you?"

Maleaha placed her hands on her hips. "Which time do you wish to apologize for?"

"Damned if I know. It seems that I am always saying or doing the wrong thing where you are concerned."

"Save it, Kane. If you are wanting to make pretty speeches, say them for Lucinda."

"Did I hear my name mentioned?" Lucinda said, advancing into the room in a flurry of aqua-colored silk.

Maleaha turned to her and smiled sweetly. "Miss Blake, I am glad I have this chance to speak to you. My husband seems to think I have wronged you in some way."

Lucinda pouted prettily. "Kane is so kind. Which offense are you referring to? There have been so many since I arrived."

"Take your choice. Perhaps you and my husband could make a list and I will apologize one by one." She turned to Kane. "There. I have apologized, are you satisfied?" She picked up the tray of dirty dishes and hurried from the room.

Kane could not help smiling. Was there ever a woman to rival his wife? She was as headstrong as she was beautiful.

"Lord, your life must be in constant upheaval living with a woman like that," Lucinda said.

"You cannot guess." Yes, his life had been in chaos since he had first met Maleaha. He had never known a dull day since she had become his wife. His love for her seemed to grow with each passing day. Kane wondered how much longer he would be able to keep his love for Maleaha hidden. He chuckled, feeling pride in his wife. She had in no way humbled herself when she had apologized a moment ago. She was miles above Lucinda in every way. From her he was learning patience, loyalty, and honesty. She had been raised to live with dignity and honor, and she expected everyone else to be the same. She was learning a cruel lesson. She was finding out that others did not always behave as she expected them to. Kane found himself wanting to be a man she would look up to and respect. He wanted that almost as much as he wanted her love.

"I was hoping you would show me about the ranch today, Kane." He had forgotten that Lucinda was in the room with him. He looked at her absentmindedly.

"Please say you will show me around. I have never seen how a ranch operates."

Kane saw the pout on her face and was repulsed by it. Maleaha never played games as she did. "I am very busy, Lucinda."

"Oh please, Kane. I want you to take me riding, if only for a few hours," she said with tears glinting in her blue eyes.

He looked at her irritated. "You will have to find something more appropriate to wear. This isn't Boston, you know."

"I have the perfect outfit to wear. It is a crimson riding habit. Wait until you see me in it."

Jonas and Eli had ridden into town. Maleaha was kept busy for most of the morning changing the linens in the upstairs bedrooms. She rapped lightly on the door of the room Lucinda's aunt occupied but received no answer. She thought the lady must be sleeping and decided not to disturb her. She had yet to meet the woman. Poor lady, she thought, she must be very ill. She thought she would ask Eli if they should have the doctor ride out to take a look at her.

She found time later in the morning to play with Cimeron. After she had fed her lunch she tucked her into bed for a nap.

Going into the kitchen, she made two apple pies and put them into the oven to bake. She knew that Kane had taken Lucinda for a ride and that they had packed a lunch. She tried not to think what they might be doing. Jealousy was a new emotion for Maleaha, and she found that she had a hard time dealing with it. She wondered how Kane could love any one as frivolous and false as Lucinda was. He was such a special man, so strong and loving. She envied the love he gave to Lucinda. At times Kane had been kind to her. She knew that he often desired her as a woman, but desire was not love. Can I give him up, she wondered. You never really had him, she told herself.

She passed through the sitting room, straightening the whatnots on the bookshelves. She needed to get out of the house. She couldn't just wait here for Kane and Lucinda to return, she thought.

When Maleaha rode away from the ranch house, she heard a rider coming up behind her. She slowed her mount, allowing Lamas to catch up with her.

"I have not seen much of you lately, my friend," she told him, looking at the wrinkled face that was so dear to her.

"I went to Albuquerque to tell your father about your aunt's death," he said, glancing over his head at the fleeting clouds that had passed over the sun.

"Cimeron misses you."

"I have stayed away from the big house." His face eased into a grin. "I seem to scare your guest."

"I would like to frighten one of them myself," Maleaha mumbled under her breath.

Maleaha's problems seem to lessen as she urged her horse into a full gallop. The wind was cold, and it brought a rosy tint to her cheeks. For the moment she wished she could ride forever and never return to the house, where so many troubles seemed to be piling up for her.

She thought about the apology she had given Lucinda that morning. Perhaps Kane would think twice before asking her to apologize again.

After riding for half an hour, Maleaha halted her horse at the edge of a deep mesa. She dismounted and drank in all the beauty of this land she loved so much. She seemed to draw her strength from this wild, untamed land. It was in her blood, and it was her birthright. She remembered her grandfather's telling her what a difficult life she would have with one foot in the Indian world and the other in the white world. He had been right. It was very difficult when one was born a half-breed.

Lamas stood beside her and glanced into her lovely face. She looked so much like her mother at the moment. Her long black hair was blowing freely in the wind, and her lovely face was creased into a worried frown. She wore the doeskin dress with the ease that any Indian maiden would have. She was troubled about something, something that he could not help her with.

Maleaha saw the dark clouds that were gathering in the east. "Winter comes early this year, Lamas."

He nodded. "It will snow before two days pass."

"Cimeron will be delighted with the snow."

Lamas spotted the two riders who came out of the pine forest. He recognized Kane and the white woman as they dismounted beside the stream. Looking at Maleaha, he saw that she had also seen them.

Maleaha stiffened as she saw Lucinda throw her arms around Kane's neck and then kiss him firmly on the mouth. She wanted to look away, but she couldn't. Her eyes were drawn to her husband and the woman he loved. She felt the prickle of tears in her eyes. Oh, she hurt so badly. Her heart was shattered into a thousand pieces. She watched as the two of them moved apart, and covered her face with her hands.

"What in the hell do you think you are up to, Lucinda? I don't have time for your little games," Kane said angrily.

"I love you, Kane. I have always loved you. Say that you care for me just a little," Lucinda said, tears sparkling in her eyes.

"Lucinda, I do not mean to be cruel, but I am married, and I love Maleaha."

"But you could not love her, Kane. She is so different from you and me."

Kane's thoughts had been on Maleaha all day. He had loved her for a long time, but he had not truly understood her worth until this morning. He had twice accused Maleaha of lying to him, and twice he had found out she had told the truth. Dear Lord, what kind of woman was she? What strength of character she possessed. When he had accused her of lying about Clay, and then again about her aunt, she had not even tried to defend herself to him. For so long Kane had looked for the worst in people, and more often than not, he had found it. That was before Maleaha had come into his life. She was teaching him that there were decent and honorable people in the world, and she, his wife, was one shining example of that fact.

"No, Lucinda, Maleaha is not like you and me, but if I am damned lucky, perhaps some of her goodness will rub off on me."

"I don't understand you, Kane. She is nothing but a half-breed!"

Kane grabbed her by the arm, and she cried out in pain. "You and I are not worthy to stay under the same roof with Maleaha. I know she doesn't love me, but I cannot give her up."

"But, Kane, I always thought you and I would be perfect for one another. Your father thinks so, too."

He smiled not unkindly at her. "You and I would never be right for each other, Lucinda. We are both too selfish, or at least I once was. Lately I believe I have changed a great deal. My wife has taught me many worthwhile things, not the least of which is humility."

"Are you saying that you don't love me at all?"

"Lucinda, I don't even like you. I never did."

Kane's eyes were drawn beyond the stream to the distant mesa. He saw two people, and he recognized Maleaha's horse. His heart contracted as he watched her mount and ride away with the ever faithful Lamas riding beside her.

Kane shoved Lucinda away from him, knowing how the scene that had taken place between them might be misinterpreted from a distance.

"Isn't the English translation of the name of your ranch paradise?" Lucinda asked with a spiteful gleam in her eyes.

"Yes," Kane said, watching as his wife disappeared over the rise.

"Well, Kane," Lucinda said, holding out her hand for him to help her mount, "I think there will be trouble in paradise tonight."

Maleaha dismounted and unsaddled her horse, while Lamas watched her, knowing what she was feeling inside.

"Everything is not always as it seems, Maleaha. Sometimes the eyes deceive."

Maleaha lifted her saddle onto a rail and turned to face him. "That's true, Lamas. It is also true that things can be much worse than they appear."

"I believe that Kane cares for you."

"You may believe that, Lamas, but let me assure you it is not so. He loves Lucinda Blake."

Lamas watched her walk toward the house and leaned against the stall door. Kane did love Maleaha. He did not know what the white woman meant to Kane, but he could not love her. Too many times Lamas had seen the love burning in Kane's eyes when he looked at Maleaha. He wondered why the white man played games with love. The Indian way was much better. If an Indian brave loved a maiden, he would tell her so.

Maleaha went directly to her room and threw herself down on the bed. She rolled over onto her back and stared dry-eyed at the ceiling. Today she had final proof that Kane loved Lucinda. Her Indian logic took over, pushing aside her white woman's heart. If Kane wanted Lucinda, then she would not stand in his way. But I love him, the white side of her cried. He does not love you, the Indian side of her answered.

Inside of Maleaha raged a war, logic against love. Love him, the Indian side prompted her, but set him free. Love that is not freely given is no love at all.

She sat up and checked the time. Cimeron would be demanding to be fed and Mrs. Higgens would be needing help in the kitchen. Maleaha rose wearily to her feet, knowing that life goes on even if one's heart was broken. She wished she could be alone to think things through. She had never been one to act on impulse. Jonas had taught her to think carefully and to weigh all the consequences before reaching a conclusion.

Dinner would have been a miserable affair, had it not been for Jonas and Eli. The two men had spent the day together, and they seemed to have become fast friends.

Kane didn't contribute much to the conversation, and Lucinda was unusually quiet. Maleaha refused to look at either of them, and it was hard at times, for she could feel Kane's eyes on her. He knows that I saw him and Lucinda, she thought. He knows, and perhaps he is glad that

433

it is finally out in the open. Kane had never struck her as the kind of man who would sneak around behind one's back. That was what was bothering her more than anything else. She had thought him to be a man of honor. It had not been a deed of honor today when he had kissed Lucinda beside the stream. She shied away from thinking what else could have transpired between them earlier, or after she had ridden away.

Against her will, Maleaha raised her head and stared into the silver eyes of her husband.

Kane saw disillusionment and pain in the green eyes of his wife. I did not betray you, he wanted to shout to her. Can't you see that I love you?

He wants to tell me that he loves Lucinda, Maleaha thought as she looked away from him. She would never heal from the pain she was feeling today. She would never stop loving the man who was her husband. How would she ever be able to give him his freedom without crying and begging him not to leave her. She tried to pull her mind away from Kane, and soon her father's words reached her.

"Eli, my daughter was always the champion of the weak. When she was a child," Jonas was saying, "I remember the day particularly because it was her tenth birthday. We were visiting one of the mission schools. I had donated the money to build the school, and I wanted to see how it was faring. While we were there a fight broke out on the playground. It seemed that three big lads had ganged up on one smaller one. Before I could stop Maleaha, she went flying across the playground and tackled one of the larger boys. She quickly wrestled him to the ground and then flew at another. I watched the third boy take flight just as a teacher came out of the door of the schoolhouse and approached Maleaha. The two remaining boys were crying and declared that Maleaha had attacked them, which indeed she had. The teacher asked Maleaha to accompany her into the schoolroom, where she threatened to spank her. I informed the woman that she was not to lay a hand on my daughter. Well, the teacher went away murmuring something about the over-indulgence of some parents. I never encouraged Maleaha to fight, and to my knowledge she never had a fight other than that day.''

Eli laughed. ''One would never know there was a wild streak in you, Maleaha. You look every bit the well brought-up young lady.''

''Oh, don't let her delicate looks deceive you, Eli. Underneath she is strong in will as well as deed,'' Jonas said proudly.

Eli stood up and towered over Maleaha. ''My dear, I have something for you. If you will excuse me, I will go and get it for you now.''

When he reappeared a few moments later he handed Maleaha a package tied up in brown paper.

''What is it?'' Maleaha asked. She glanced down the table to where Kane sat and noticed he had a puzzled expression on his face.

''Why don't you open it and see for yourself,'' Eli said, smiling at her.

Maleaha untied the string that was bound about the package and pushed the paper aside. She gasped when she saw what appeared to be the piece of pottery that her

435

grandfather had given her. Her hands ran over the smooth surface, tracing the dark pattern with her finger. When she raised her eyes to Eli, he saw tears sparkling in the green depths.

"How did you . . . when . . . I do not understand," she said in confusion.

"I took the broken pieces into Santa Fe yesterday and found a potter who assured me that he could mend the vase without anyone's being able to tell where it had been broken."

Maleaha handed the precious piece of pottery to her father and threw her arms about a startled Eli's neck. At first he stood stiffly as she kissed his cheek, then he laughed and hugged her tightly.

"I love you, Eli. You are the kindest man I have ever known," she told him, placing her smooth cheek against his rough one. Eli looked over her head at his son, and Kane was astonished to see just the hint of tears in his father's eyes.

Kane stood up and walked over to Jonas and took the vase, studying it for a moment. He could see nothing special about the vase. He could not understand what all the fuss was about.

"I assume this is the vase that Lucinda accidentally broke the other day?"

Eli nodded. "It was very valuable, son. Maleaha's grandfather had given it to her." Eli looked at Maleaha. You were misinformed by your grandfather, my dear. The man who repaired it said it would be close to four hundred years old, making it two hundred years older than you thought."

Lucinda stood up and walked around the table and stood beside Kane. "Lord, I never saw such a fuss made over an old vase. One would think I broke something of great value," she said spitefully.

"It was valuable, Lucinda. The man who repaired it told me it would easily have brought three or four thousand dollars, and any museum would have been delighted to add it to their collection." His eyes narrowed and Lucinda looked uncomfortable. "Because of you, Lucinda, the vase is only valuable to Maleaha because her grandfather gave it to her."

Lucinda's eyes widened. Why was Eli speaking to her in such an accusing tone? He had always been so kind to her. "I didn't break it purposely, Eli."

"Oh yes, you did, Lucinda. I overheard you talking to Maleaha and you most certainly did break it deliberately."

"It is of no great importance, Eli," Maleaha intervened. "What's done is done. Let us drop the matter."

Eli's face softened as he looked at Maleaha. "You are too kind, my dear. I listened to the hateful things Lucinda said to you yesterday. You even stood there while she struck you. How can you forgive her, and how can you forgive me for bringing her here?"

Maleaha was confused. She felt her father's arm go around her shoulder. She looked at Kane's face and saw him watching his father in bewilderment. She expected any moment to hear Kane defend the woman he loved. She would have run from the room, but she felt the pressure of her father's hand and knew he was urging her to face whatever came.

"Tomorrow morning I shall take Lucinda and her aunt into town," Eli stated. "There is a stage leaving for the East by the end of the week, and I intend that we will be on it. I can not expect you to forgive me, Maleaha. I hope in time you will come to like me half as much as I like you. I believe my son to be a very lucky man to have you for his wife. I have rarely if ever met such a shining example of womanhood."

"Oh, Eli," Maleaha cried, moving across the room to be enfolded in his arms. "I not only like you, I love you. I will hate to see you go."

Eli closed his eyes. Yes, she was one in a million. He had tried to push her from his son's life, and instead she had pulled him into her life.

Lucinda stormed out of the room and up the stairs, but no one seemed inclined to go after her.

Eli smiled down at Maleaha, and Jonas laughed deeply. "I told you my little girl was special, Eli."

"Damned right, she is special," Eli agreed.

Mrs. Higgens began clearing the table and Jonas suggested that they move into the sitting room. Maleaha sat down between her father and Eli, while Kane seemed to detach himself from them and sat silent and brooding beside the fireplace.

Maleaha could only guess what he was thinking. Did he wish to go to Lucinda and give her comfort?

"Maleaha, I bet you didn't like me very well when you first saw me, did you?" Eli asked. "I remember you were with Kane in the garden at the fiesta. I said some very harsh things to you that night."

"Actually that was not the first time I had seen you,

Eli. I saw you before that night but you did not see me.''

"When?''

"I was in Albuquerque with my best friend when I heard that Kane had been injured, so I rushed back to see him. I saw you and your son together, and I didn't want to disturb you.''

Kane's head snapped up as he caught her words. He had been haunted for months, thinking Maleaha had not thought enough of him to come to see him when he lay injured. Maleaha was admitting that she had come! The color drained from his face. Dear God! Could Maleaha have loved him? If she had ever loved him he had surely killed that love. What could she think about a man who accused her of lying? Could she love a man who had made her apologize to Lucinda, when in fact it should have been Lucinda who apologized to her? He had made one mistake after another where she was concerned. She had humbled him and brought him to his knees. The worst blow of all must have been today when Maleaha had seen the kiss Lucinda had given him. She had not approached him about Lucinda. Hell, she had hardly even looked at him tonight. Perhaps she just didn't give a damn, he thought.

Kane stood up and stalked out of the room, leaving the others to wonder at his action.

That night Kane didn't come to bed. Maleaha was troubled; what if he had gone to Lucinda? Slipping into her robe, she made her way quietly downstairs. She saw the light coming from beneath the crack underlying his study door. Opening the door softly, she saw Kane asleep on the leather couch. Closing the door quietly, she went back upstairs. He was not with Lucinda, but he was not with her either.

The next morning after breakfast, Maleaha stood on the doorstep beside Eli as Kane pulled the buggy up to the front of the house. He leaped to the ground and began placing the luggage in the back of the buggy. Maleaha noticed that Kane avoided looking at her. When he took Lucinda into Santa Fe, would he want to stay with her?

Lucinda had not joined them for breakfast, but had asked to have a tray sent to her room so she could eat with her aunt.

Lucinda swept past Maleaha, never giving her a second glance. Eli smiled understandingly at his daughter-in-law.

"You know I am going to miss that granddaughter of mine. I am wondering if you would allow me to visit again soon?"

She slid her arm around his waist, then looked up into his face. She gazed into eyes so like Kane's. "I hope you will take the first available stage back to Santa Fe. I have grown very fond of you, Eli, and besides Cimeron needs both of her grandfathers."

"Do you mean that, Maleaha?"

"I can assure you that I do."

Maleaha felt someone bump into her and turned to see a pale-looking woman making her way to the buggy. Eli chuckled and whispered in Maleaha's ear. "Mrs.

Blake would not come out of her room once she heard you were half-Indian. I think she feared she might forfeit her life.''

Maleaha laughed and kissed Eli on the cheek. "Have a safe trip." She raised her voice so it would carry to Lucinda's aunt. "Watch out for wild Indians."

Maleaha did not mind being snubbed by Lucinda and her aunt, but she did mind that Kane seemed to ignore her completely. She stood watching as the buggy pulled away from the house, feeling as if the space between her and Kane was growing. She entered the house, knowing that when Kane returned there would be a confrontation between them.

Maleaha kept busy so the day would pass quickly. She had lunch with Cimeron and then bundled her up and took her for a walk. Dinnertime came and went, and still Kane had not returned. Maleaha was restless as she wandered from room to room looking for something to do. She wished her father had not left early that day, perhaps if he had stayed she and Kane could postpone their talk. No, that would be cowardly. It was best to get it over with.

Entering the sitting room, Maleaha absentmindedly straightened the books in the bookshelves. Walking over to the window, she stood staring out into the twilight as the first snowflakes of winter began to fall. What if Kane had run into trouble? Suppose he was injured? Stop this, she chided herself. She pulled the draperies together and walked over to the sofa and sat down. She found herself watching the clock tick off the minutes. She heard the buggy returning just as the clock struck nine o'clock. She waited silently, knowing Kane would most probably unhitch the buggy himself. Time passed before she heard his heavy footfall and felt a blast of cold air when he opened the front door.

CHAPTER TWENTY-FIVE

Kane stood silently appraising Maleaha, and she could not tell what his thoughts were. He removed his heavy coat and draped it over the wooden coat tree. Maleaha stood transfixed as Kane's silvery eyes pierced through her. He removed his leather gloves and dropped them on the table.

"I apologize for being late. I drove to Deveraux to see your father."

"You do not owe me any explanation."

"Do I not?"

"No. Have you eaten?"

"No, I don't want anything." He sat down beside her and leaned his head back against the sofa. Maleaha noticed the dark shadows beneath his eyes and wanted to reach out and comfort him.

"You should have something to eat. I will bring it to you on a tray if you would like."

He turned his head to look at her. She looked so beautiful with the firelight glistening on her black hair. Her green eyes were filled with uncertainty and Kane could

not resist reaching out to touch her soft cheek. "I don'
want anything to eat. It just feels good to be home."

"Do you think of this as your home, Kane? Do you no
wish to return to Boston with your father and Lucinda?'

He ignored her question. "My father was full of praise
for you. I don't know how you managed it, but it seems
that you have bewitched him in some way."

Maleaha would have stood up, but Kane reached for
her hand and restrained her. "Don't go. I want to talk to
you."

"Could it not wait?" she asked, wishing with all her
heart that she could postpone the inevitable.

"I fear that I have postponed it too long already, Maleaha. I will not wait another day to say what must be
said."

"Kane, please," she pleaded in a soft voice. "I don't
know what you want of me. Have I not always done as
you asked me to?"

"Yes, all I ask of you and more. For the moment, I
would like you to accompany me upstairs to our bedroom."

Maleaha gave him a questioning look, and he smiled.
"I want no more than to talk to you where we will not be
disturbed. Mrs. Higgens could come into the room at any
time. What I have to say to you is for your ears alone."

Maleaha could think of nothing more to postpone their
discussion. She stood up and followed Kane upstairs.
When they reached the bedroom, Kane closed the door
and motioned for her to sit down on the bed.

Maleaha hesitated. Kane, seeing that she did not trust
him, picked up a chair and placed it beside the bed. He

then sat down on the bed and offered her the chair.

Maleaha sat with her hands folded demurely in her lap, knowing that what was yet to come would be very hard to endure. Her eyes wandered over her husband's handsome face. His dark hair fell carelessly across his forehead. She looked into his eyes and noted that they were pain-filled. She swallowed hard, knowing he was having a hard time telling her about his love for Lucinda. She loved him, but she was not about to make it any easier for him.

"Maleaha, I have to go back a long way in hopes of making you understand about myself. I have found you to be a very forgiving person. I hope you can find it within you to forgive me."

She started to speak, but Kane silenced her with a glance.

"Before I met you, Maleaha, I was a very selfish man. I took from everyone, but never gave of myself. I could make all kind of excuses for myself, but that would be trite. I have known many women, Maleaha, I will not deny that. I never loved any of them. I didn't know how to love."

"But Lucinda . . . ?"

Kane held up his hand for her to be silent. "One day, on a day that started out much as any other, I met this lovely Indian maiden. From the first I felt drawn to her. She . . . you turned out to be more than I had bargained for. You were highly intelligent. In most instances you made me look like a fool."

"No, Kane, I never . . ."

"Let me have my say before I lose my nerve, Maleaha. You have no idea how difficult this is for me."

She nodded.

"As you will remember, I wanted to make you my mistress. What a foolish bastard I was. I found out that night of the ball just how low I had sunk. You made me squirm that night, did you know that?"

Maleaha smiled. "Yes, I know."

He glanced at the ceiling, and Maleaha waited for him to continue. This was not what she had expected him to say. She could see no point to what he was telling her.

"The night when you came to me at the Jojoba village and asked me to save you from Mangas, I knew I would do anything to keep him from getting his hands on you. I wanted no one to have you save myself. I would have killed Mangas before I would have allowed him to touch you."

His voice became deep and husky and Maleaha could not meet his silver gaze.

"When I made love to you that night, I knew I had never felt that way with a woman before. . . ." He paused as if he was having a hard time speaking. When he did speak his voice came out in a painful whisper.

"I knew that I loved you more than my own life. When Mangas united us that night, I knew that I wanted to tie you to me forever."

Maleaha placed her hands over her face. He had said that he loved her. Oh, please don't let it be some cruel jest, she pleaded silently. Maleaha felt tears wash down her face, and she brushed them away hurriedly.

"I intended to ask you to marry me when I returned to Santa Fe, but you know what happened then. I was wounded and was unable to come to you, and I thought you had not come to me.'' He closed his eyes for a moment, before he could bring himself to continue.

''I was half out of my mind when I thought you did not care enough about me to come and see me.''

''I came, Kane, but I didn't stay to see you. I heard you and your father discussing me.''

''Is that what happened? Is that why you left without seeing me?''

Maleaha nodded.

''Tell me what you overheard.''

''You . . . I heard you say I was a . . . half-breed, and your father would not think I was good enough for you,'' she said in a voice that plainly showed how hurt she had been that day. ''I left not wanting to hear any more.''

''You should not have left, Maleaha, for had you stayed, you would have heard me telling my father that I loved you and wanted you for my wife.''

''Kane, I thought you wanted to marry Lucinda. I thought you loved her.''

''No, Maleaha, I never loved Lucinda. She is the last woman I would ever have wanted to marry.''

''But, Kane, why didn't you tell me all of this before?''

''I was going to. The night you came to the fiesta with Clay Madason, I was eaten up with jealousy. I was going to ask you to marry me that night, but, as you recall, it didn't quite work out that way. After you had run away I searched for you. When I heard you had gone away to join your father, I knew there was nothing I could do until you returned. I bought this land and had the house built, hoping when you returned I could convince you to marry me.''

''You had this house built for me?''

Kane could see the tears in her beautiful eyes, and wondered if they were tears of pity. ''Yes. I wanted it to be the kind of house you would feel comfortable in. I wanted you to fix it up as you had your father's home at Deveraux.''

Maleaha shook her head, unable to speak.

''Do you have any idea how I felt when I was summoned to the Jojoba village by Mangas, and found that you had run away to have my child?'' He didn't give her a chance to answer. ''At first I was angry and confused, then I began to see Cimeron as a means of forcing you to marry me. I admit I used our daughter to get you, Maleaha.'' He seemed to want to avoid her eyes. ''I love Cimeron, Maleaha. But I used her.''

''Kane, please . . . I . . .''

''Hush, darling, allow me to finish and then you can have your say.''

Maleaha wanted to reach out to him. He loved her! She could hardly believe that they both loved each other, and that they had kept that love hidden.

''When I forced you to accompany me to the mission, and the priest married us, I felt that with time and patience, I might earn your respect. It was too much for me to hope that I would ever have your love. I thought if I didn't make any demands on you, you wouldn't leave me. I hadn't reckoned with my desire for you, however. When I was near you, all I could think about was making love to you. I wanted to make love to you as I had that night in the Jojoba village."

His eyes were soft as he searched her face. "It was good between us, Maleaha, even you will have to admit that. I knew even if I didn't have your love, that I could satisfy your body. When I made love to you was the only time I felt you truly belonged to me. At times I would want to tell you about my love for you, but I was a coward. I feared you would scorn my love."

"Kane!"

"No, let me finish, darling. I want you to know the worst and the best of me." He reached for her hand and pulled her onto the bed beside him. Raising her hand to his face, he closed his eyes.

Maleaha felt a sob deep inside her throat. Kane was such a strong, proud man, she knew it was very difficult for him to humble himself like this.

Clasping her hand tightly, he continued. "Maleaha, each afternoon after working hard all day, I could not wait to come home to you and our daughter. I cannot tell you how good it was walking through that front door and knowing you would be waiting for me. You didn't love me, but you would be here all the same. You would have a nice meal waiting for me, and you would listen while I told you about my day. I don't know how long things might have gone on as they were had you not started helping Betsy. Let me say now that I was eaten up with jealousy when I thought you were not with Betsy but spending time with Clay Madason."

"Kane, I never . . ."

"I know that, Maleaha. I am so sorry, my love, for not trusting you then, and again when you went to the Jojoba village to be with your aunt." He touched her face and looked deeply into her eyes. "I am so sorry about your aunt's death, Maleaha."

A tear escaped her eyes, and Kane bent his head to kiss it away. "I promise you, darling that I will never doubt your word again. Believe me, I finally know what a wonderful person you are. I have never known anyone finer or braver. Stay with me, Maleaha. Allow me to love you and hopefully learn from you."

"Kane, when I returned from the Jojoba village and your father and Lucinda were here I thought you were ashamed of me."

He smiled. "Is that what you thought?"

"Yes."

"No, I have felt many things for you, but never shame. I have come to treasure your Indian heritage, and I want Cimeron to grow up feeling pride in her Indian blood the same as her mother does. That day I was angry because I had been half out of my mind worrying whether you would ever come back to me. I thought you had left me because of the way I had treated you the night before you left."

"Kane, none of this is important."

"Is it not? What about when I made you apologize to Lucinda, when in fact she should have been the one to beg your pardon."

"I didn't exactly apologize to her, did I?"

Kane laughed and hugged her tightly to him. "No, darling, you did not exactly apologize."

Maleaha's head was resting on his shoulder and she looked at him. "I thought you loved Lucinda and wanted to be rid of me.'' His eyes were so bright she had to lower her own eyes. ''You once told me you loved a woman who did not love you. I thought that woman was Lucinda.''

He tilted her chin up. ''You poor misguided darling. Did you not realize that I was speaking of you?''

''Me?''

''Yes, you, my beautiful love. Always you.''

''But I saw you and Lucinda. . . .''

''What you saw was Lucinda kissing me. I did not kiss her. I told her that I loved my wife. In fact I told her I didn't even like her.''

There were conflicting emotions written on Maleaha's face. ''Lucinda told me that you and she loved each other and that you had . . . been very close.''

''Maleaha, I will not lie to you. I have been intimate with Lucinda, but that happened years ago. I never loved her, nor have I ever told her that I loved her. When she stood beside you, Maleaha, she came off as a selfish, spoiled, dishonest woman. I admire nothing about her.''

''She is very beautiful.''

''Not to me, Maleaha.'' He swallowed hard. ''Nothing is so beautiful and rare as shining green eyes. No face can compare with your lovely face.'' He reached out and touched her long ebony hair. ''Did you know when the firelight reflects on your hair it appears to be soft satin, and when you are in the bright sunlight your hair looks blue-black? I have never known anyone kinder than you. I am proud of your honesty, and your valiant spirit. I love you, Maleaha!''

Maleaha was startled when he went down on his knees

and laid his dark head in her lap and he clasped his arms about her waist. There was silence in the room as she placed her hand on his head. She felt as if her heart would break when he raised his head and she saw tears sparkling in his silver eyes.

"I know you don't love me, Maleaha, but I will do anything you ask of me if you will stay with me." A tear rolled down his cheek and Maleaha knew she was also crying.

"Don't leave me, Maleaha," he pleaded.

She cupped his face in her hands. "Oh, Kane, my dearest love. How can you be so blind? Why do you not see that I have loved you for a very long time? I am not quite sure, but I think I loved you from the first. I believe I fell in love with you the first time you scowled at me with those silver eyes of yours."

Kane closed his eyes as he grabbed her and crushed her in his arms. "What did you say? Did you say that you loved me?" he asked in a choked voice.

"Yes, my dearest. I told you that I loved you."

Maleaha could feel his deep laughter as he pushed her over on the bed and lay down beside her. Gathering her tightly in his arms, he bent his head and kissed her so tenderly that it brought fresh tears to her eyes. When he raised his head, his silver eyes were soft.

"I don't know what I did right to make you love me. I pray I will never lose your love," he told her.

"Kane, I see in you a man of great worth. I feel I am the lucky one."

He crushed her tightly to him again, not daring to speak until the lump left his throat. "I am the man that loving you has created. I found in you all the things I admire, but never thought to find, especially in one small girl. Teach me to look at life through your eyes, Maleaha. Help me be the kind of man you can love.''

She laughed, and the sound of her laughter resounded around the room. ''Please don't change, Kane. Stay the man I fell in love with.''

His eyes moved over her face lovingly. ''I cannot deny you your slightest wish. If you want a stubborn, overbearing, robust, unyielding husband, then I will not change.''

Their laughter blended, as Kane sprinkled kisses over Maleaha's upturned face. Maleaha saw the laughter leave Kane's face to be replaced by the look of desire. They stared into each other's eyes, both knowing that they wanted the same thing.

Maleaha could feel the desire building up inside her body. In the newfound love she had just discovered, she wanted to give all of herself to her husband.

Kane's hands were caressing, but he soon became impatient with the clothes that were a barrier between them. Maleaha ran her fingers down the front of his shirt caressingly as she began to unbutton it. She ran her hand over his broad chest and smiled at the fire that had leaped into his eyes, turning them to smoldering silver. She arched her neck back as he began kissing her throat.

''Love me, Kane,'' she whispered, ''love me.''

His sensuous lips traveled up her throat to take command of her mouth. Maleaha groaned as he easily removed her clothing.

''Your wish is my command, my love,'' he murmured

against her parted lips.

Maleaha thought she would die from the ache that came from deep inside of her, as his lips playfully nibbled at her rosy-tipped breast.

Maleaha laced her fingers through his dark hair. In a haze of passion she was aware that Kane had removed his clothing.

Kane gazed at her through half-closed lashes. His hand trembled as it moved over her perfect body.

"Have I told you that I think you are the most beautiful woman I have ever seen?" he asked in a deep, husky voice.

"I want to be beautiful for you, Kane," she answered, holding her arms out to him.

Kane's body reacted by trembling, and he lowered his tall frame down on top of her.

Maleaha's legs opened to receive him, while her hands moved over his muscled back.

Time passed, but the two lovers had no knowledge of its passing. They made love leisurely, savoring their new awareness of each other. This time their lovemaking was different, for they both knew they were loved by the other. They murmured words of love and their love was also communicated by a gentle caress or a passionate kiss.

When at last both of their bodies had been satisfied, Maleaha lay curled up beside Kane. "I love you, Kane," she told him softly.

He favored her with a bright smile. "It's lucky for me that you do, otherwise I would be miserable at this moment, instead of the happiest man alive."

She rested her head on his shoulder and played with the soft mat of hair on his chest. "Kane, I have something to tell you."

"What is it?" he asked, nibbling on the lobe of her ear.

"I am . . . carrying your baby."

He turned her over on her back, and frowned. "How long have you known this?"

"I began to suspect before I went to the Jojoba camp."

His hand moved over her stomach. "Why didn't you tell me before now?"

She looked away from him, not wanting to spoil their newfound happiness. "I . . . when I thought you loved Lucinda, I decided not to tell you."

"Why?"

"I thought you wanted to be free of me, and I didn't want you to think I was trying to hold on to you through the baby."

"You now know you were wrong. Maleaha, never keep anything from me again. Let us always be honest with each other."

"Are you pleased about the baby?" she asked, fearing he would not welcome another baby.

He laid his rough cheek against her stomach, then spoke so softly that she almost didn't hear him. "I love the child already. It will be one more way to tie you to me forever."

As Maleaha lay sleeping in Kane's arms, he stared at her lovely face. He smiled, thinking about the baby she carried. He hoped it would be a boy, but it would not really matter if it turned out to be another girl. His hand rested softly on her stomach. He wished he could feel the baby. He would be glad when the child began to show. This time Maleaha would not have to give birth alone. It would be an experience they would share. He could not contain his happiness, and it made itself known by the laughter that rumbled deep in his throat. He was completely domesticated by his tiny raven-headed wife. Maleaha had given purpose to his life. He rested his face against hers, and he heard her sigh in her sleep. She had not only changed him, but with her loving nature she had changed his father as well.

Kane thought that after all the years of quarreling with Eli, perhaps now they could become friends.

Maleaha smiled in her sleep as if she had read his thoughts, and her smile melted his heart.

"Sleep darling, there will be other nights. Many other nights," he whispered.

EPILOGUE

It was Christmas Eve and snow covered the land. Kane looked out the window and smiled as he watched Jonas and Eli trudging toward the house, each carrying an armload of firewood.

He heard them stomping their feet on the front porch to get rid of the snow that clung to their boots. He turned and watched them enter the room, as a blast of icy air circulated the room from the open doorway.

"Jonas, I told you a hundred times, Cimeron has Kane's nose," Eli said as he dumped an armful of wood into the iron rack beside the fireplace. Then he raised his dark brow, daring Jonas to disagree.

Jonas piled his load of wood on the rack and then removed his gloves. "You must be half blinded with age, Eli. Anyone with half sense and one eye can see that Cimeron has Maleaha's nose."

Maleaha was sitting before the warm fire, holding Cimeron in her lap. Kane caught her eye, and they both smiled. It was very evident that she was expecting a child, from the gentle swell of her stomach.

"Eli, have you not noticed Cimeron's hands?" Maleaha asked. "Her fingers are long and well shaped. I believe they will be lovely when she is a young lady."

Eli knelt down and picked up Cimeron's hand and examined it carefully. "Yes, I can see what you mean. Her hands are very nicely shaped," Eli said.

"She has your hands, Eli. Did you never notice that?"

Eli turned Cimeron's tiny hand over and reexamined it. "Yes, I believe you are right," he said, looking pleased. "Look here, Jonas, Cimeron has my hands."

Jonas looked as if he might debate that fact, when Kane lifted his daughter in his arms and kissed her soft cheek. "Cimeron may have your hands, Eli, but her chin definitely resembles Jonas's. See how stubborn it looks. When she is displeased about something, I can see Jonas in her."

Jonas took his granddaughter from Kane and studied her face. His green eyes sparkled as he looked at Eli. "She might have your hands and my chin, but her nose is the same as Maleaha's," he held out stubbornly.

Kane and Maleaha looked into each other's eyes, and the message they sent to each other was one of love and contentment. They were a family, and their love had reached out to Eli and made him feel part of their closeness.

Eli had sold all his holdings in Boston and had moved all his belongings to New Mexico. He and Jonas had become good friends, so Jonas had invited Eli to live with him at Deveraux Ranch. The two men sometimes argued, but it was never over anything very serious. They had a mutual liking and trust for one another.

The only real problem was that Kane and Maleaha feared the two doting grandfathers would spoil their daughter. At one point Kane had to insist that neither his father nor Jonas buy Cimeron any more toys or clothing without first consulting Maleaha.

"I'm gonna take Cimeron upstairs and put her to bed. It's long past her bedtime," Jonas said.

"Wait, and I'll go with you," Eli said, following behind them. "Cimeron likes me to tell her a story before she falls asleep."

"You aren't to tell her any tales that will cause her to have nightmares." Jonas's voice drifted back to Kane and Maleaha.

Kane reached down and pulled Maleaha up into his arms and rested his chin on the top of her head. "Did you see all the presents they brought Cimeron? They both put them under the tree, fearing we would object, I suppose. I fear between the two of them they will spoil our daughter," Kane said.

"You cannot spoil someone with love, Kane. I am living testimony of that fact," Maleaha said, looking upward at the face of her tall husband.

"Are you referring to the love your father gave you when you were growing up?" Kane asked.

"No I was referring to the love given to me by my husband."

Kane chuckled. "I will always want to spoil you, Mrs. Benedict."

Maleaha touched Kane's face softly. "I love you, Kane." She had to close her eyes to the love she saw shining in his soft silver eyes. She knew she would keep the imprint of Kane's look of love in her heart forever.

The sound of laughter drifted down the stairs to them as the two grandfathers prepared to rejoin them.

"The new baby will be a boy," Jonas said.

"I bet you are right. Still, another girl like Cimeron wouldn't be bad at all," Eli said.

Kane winked at Maleaha and pulled her head to rest against his shoulder.

The snow drifted slowly past the window, turning the beautiful countryside into an enchanted land. The wind blew down the mountains, swaying the pine trees and causing the icicles that hung from their branches to make a soft, tinkling sound. It was cold outside, but warm and cozy inside the big ranch house.

Lamas was leaning against the barn, listening to the sounds of laughter that came from the house. He smiled as he pulled his warm coat about his neck. Blinking his eyes, he thought he felt something soft touch his cheek. He was not an overly superstitious man, so why then did he think he could feel Maleaha's mother Cimeron's presence?

He walked toward the house, knowing he would be welcomed beside the warm fireplace. He knew he would sit down at the table with the family tonight and dine on good food. It was Chirstmas Eve, and he hoped Kane would remember that he had promised him a rocking chair as a Christmas present.

Once again something soft touched his cheek, and he

was sure he heard Cimeron's laughter. Wherever she was, she was telling him she was happy, because her daughter, Maleaha, had found happiness.